Last Train From Berlin

A NOVEL

Irene Magers

Shady Tree Press, New York

iMg BOOKS
Published by SHADY TREE PRESS
136 East 64th Street, 7th Floor
New York, NY 10065
U.S.A.

PUBLISHER'S NOTE
A work of fiction, names, characters, and places stem from the author's imagination, except where historical or political names and incidents enter into the story.

ISBN-13: 978-0-9841211-0-6
ISBN-10: 0-9841211-0-2

Other Books by Irene Magers
COACH FROM WARSAW
NIGHT CROSSING TO ATHENS
DOWN AND OUT IN MANHATTAN

Cover design by Sonja Lohmeyer and Dennis Kreibich

www.ShadyTreePress.com
Printed in the United States of America

Last Train From Berlin

A Novel

BOOK III in a TRILOGY

For ZARA, KEIRA, and JORDAN
With All My Love

Chapter One

Berlin, 1938…

Spring was fooling around in Grunewald Park, the new greenery trembling with birds flittering from branch to branch, reclaiming their territory with cheerful chirps and titters. Making equally happy sounds, children ran among the trees, gathering fistfuls of the white anemones carpeting the forest floor.

Pedestrians out on their daily constitutionals nodded to fellow strollers, occasionally stopping to remark on the pleasant weather and the abundance of daffodils in the park's flowerbeds. Men tipped their hats to the widowed Baroness von Renz, silently wondering why time had not been equally kind to their own wives. Tall and lithe, at fifty-eight, Dorrit von Renz was still a beauty and when she turned her dazzling green eyes upon them, they were completely enchanted and found themselves enjoying altogether ungentlemanly thoughts.

That she had remained a widow for twelve long years puzzled everyone except those who'd known her late husband, the eminent Herr Baron Doctor Johann von Renz. Others puzzled over the fact that she was saddled with not one but *two* grandchildren; for the fact remained that her flamboyant oldest son Max and his Greek-born wife were more committed to their archaeological explorations in foreign lands than to the task of rearing their offspring. All agreed, however, that the baroness was doing a remarkable job, managing without any male influence in the house after her younger son Fritz, a syndicated newspaper columnist, had married that frivolous Danish dish and moved to an apartment in the center of Berlin.

Indeed, being a full-time caregiver had not taken its toll. Dorrit von Renz's posture was that of a much younger woman and although her hair was streaked with gray, it was invariably swept into a stylish chignon matching her fine taste in clothing. Today, walking in the park with her little granddaughter, she was wearing a fashionable wide-belted trench coat with a colorful silk scarf and a black felt beret perched at a jaunty angle on her head.

After the prescribed hour in the fresh air, which Dr. Tarnoff insisted was crucial for maintaining Sigrid's health, Dorrit left Grunewald, holding the child's hand securely as they crossed Lindenstrasse, which ran the length of the park and where the von Renz villa sat among a row of equally stately homes facing the woods. But instead of going directly home, they continued toward the semi-commercial Hohmann Strasse, prudently staying on the sunny side of the street to take advantage of its lining of warmth. It was Wednesday, Mademoiselle Morisot's day off, and since Nurse Heller - employed since the children were born - was suffering a migraine, it fell on Dorrit's shoulders to fetch Sigrid's brother at the Koenings Allee School. She glanced down at her frail six-year-old granddaughter to confirm that her blue poplin coat was buttoned against the wind. Delicate since birth, Sigrid had nearly died from scarlet fever three years ago, the sole reason Nurse Heller remained employed along with the French governess.

"Are you tired?" Dorrit asked the pretty little girl, who, at Ben Tarnoff's urging, would start school a year behind her peers to give her immune system a fighting chance.

"No, not a bit." As if to prove it, Sigrid let go of her *Oma's* hand and skipped ahead on the sidewalk. "Are we stopping at the bakery?" she wanted to know, turning and waiting at the curb.

"Yes, darling, as soon as we pick up Peter." Dorrit smiled adoringly at the child. In sharp contrast with her physical weakness, Sigrid's long curly hair - auburn like Dorrit's own tresses had once been - bounced with health and vitality.

"Um..." Sigrid licked her pale lips and again took hold of her grandmother's hand as they crossed the street to her brother's school.

It was not clear if Peter appreciated the escort because when the dismissal bell sounded, he bolted from the building, flying down the wide stone steps among a flurry of boys and with barely a glance toward his *Oma* and his sister standing at the gate. Running ahead on the sidewalk, it was a while before he acknowledged their presence, doing so only after the last of his friends had rounded their respective corners for home and were out of sight.

A few months shy of his eleventh birthday, Peter was tall for his age. He had Max's long legs, Cassandra's black hair and, bursting with the energy of youth, was not the least bit encumbered by the heavy leather book bag bouncing on his shoulders as he kicked a pebble around on the sidewalk like a soccer ball. At the corner of Hagen Strasse, figuring *Oma* would be buying bread and pastries, he stopped in front of Kaufman's Konditorei and watched as the proprietor climbed up on a ladder to scrub the windows. Running a hand through his dark hair in bewilderment, Peter was about to ask why there was red paint on the glass, when *Oma* walked up and saved him the trouble.

"Herr Kaufman!" she exclaimed. "My goodness, what happened to your windows?"

Squinting against the sun's glare, the proprietor turned briefly, acknowledging his regular customer and mumbling something about boyish pranks before he went back to work, rubbing the glass till it squeaked.

Shaking her head, Dorrit herded the children into the bakery and had them take some seats at a table near the windows where hanging pots of pink geraniums filtered the sunlight. There were plenty of seats to choose from, she noted, surprised to find the shop empty. Ordinarily, there'd be a queue for purchases, the lace-covered tables occupied by people enjoying their afternoon coffee and fruit tarts.

Frau Kaufman, as meticulous as her husband, was wiping fingerprints from the tops of the display cases. "Good afternoon, *mein* Baroness," she said, smiling, as her customer approached.

"*Guten Tag.*" Dorrit pretended not to notice the lack of activity in the shop.

"What would you like today?" Frau Kaufman put aside the polishing rag and wiped her hands on her apron.

"Hmm, well, let's see..." Dorrit perused the trays in the display cases. There was little to choose from. "I'll have coffee. The children will have hot chocolate and two of those." She pointed to the Napoleons next to some marzipan pastry and a lone wedge of *linzertorte*. There were no fruit tarts, and the bins usually full of *semmel* rolls were empty. The loaf baskets on top of the counter held nothing but a dusting of crumbs. "You must have been very busy today," she ventured. "You're practically sold out."

"Busy? *Ach,* I wish." Frau Kaufman sighed dramatically. "It's quite the opposite. We have little to sell because of sudden shortages. We've been told it's temporary but I don't believe it. Something is wrong with our distributors. With our workers as well. Our baker quit yesterday without giving notice and this morning two apprentices didn't show up." Frau Kaufman looked toward the soiled windows and pinched her lips together. She appeared to have forgotten her customer.

"I'm sorry to hear that." Assuming there was again trouble with the labor unions, Dorrit dug into her purse for her wallet. "Well, we'll take two of those Napoleons." She fished out some bills in an attempt to stir the proprietress into action. "Unless they are reserved for someone?"

"Reserved?" Frau Kaufman was once again attentive. "No, but they're a day old and the cream might be going bad." She pulled the tray from the glass case and pointed. "May I suggest the *Mandel Kuchen* instead?"

Dorrit turned to Peter and Sigrid. "How about marzipan cake?" Both children nodded enthusiastically. After paying for her purchases, Dorrit joined them at the table.

Placing everything on a tray, Frau Kaufman experienced a sudden brainstorm as she carried the refreshments over to her customers. It might, in fact, be an excellent idea to reserve the Napoleons. If left unrefrigerated, by tomorrow the cream would be spoiled and she could give them to those boys in the brown shirts who'd come into the shop earlier, harassing her customers till they left, and then loitering around looking for trouble until she offered them each a piece of cake, *gratis*. She suspected the fellows who'd thrown red paint at the storefront were from the same uniformed group. If they returned tomorrow, she could take her revenge by watching them eat the free Napoleons, where an extra dusting of powdered sugar would disguise the rancid ingredients until much later when their stomachs erupted.

Dorrit was sipping her coffee and the children were digging into their cakes, when the sound of breaking glass instinctively made them double over and turn away from the windows where shards of glass crashed to the floor, sending the flowerpots swinging on their chains.

After the initial shock, Dorrit quickly confirmed that neither Peter nor Sigrid were hurt, brushed some splinters from their clothes, and rushed from the bakery behind Frau Kaufman, both women believing that Herr Kaufman had slipped and fallen against the window.

He had not. Standing on the sidewalk, he was waving his fists angrily at several youths speeding away on bicycles. Once they were gone from view, he turned to examine the damage. Peering through the broken window, a string of Yiddish exclamations tumbled from his lips until among the shards of glass he spotted a brick scrawled with words that silenced him: *Death to Jews!*

The Kaufmans had their window replaced. A week later it was again broken. Shortly thereafter the store was sold and the Kaufmans were gone. When Dorrit inquired with the new proprietor, she was told that they had moved to Holland where they had relatives.

By mid summer, shops all around Berlin began displaying signs with the words: BUY GERMAN GOODS FROM GERMANS. Stores without signs were boycotted and on a night in November had their windows shattered during a terrible riot that also destroyed the Central Synagogue on Fasanenstrasse. Although uniformed police officers were spotted participating in the rampage, Berlin's Propaganda Chief, Herr Goebbels, was quick to go on the radio and call the riot the work of foreign revolutionaries. In his weekly newspaper, *Der Angriff*, he promised to find and arrest those responsible.

Weeks passed. No arrests were made, except that of a lone journalist who foolishly reported that he had witnessed a group of Herr Hitler's home defense echelon, the elite Schutz-Staffel, beat some Jewish shop owners along Tauentzienstrasse.

Chapter Two

It was a cold and dreary December morning. Fritz von Renz was pacing the floor in a waiting room at Wirchow Hospital, where his wife was giving birth for the third time. He couldn't sleep and had spent the night, harboring no optimism about his and Lisbet's chances of parenthood. Neither one of their two prior babies, both full term boys, had survived. One was stillborn and the other lived only a few days. After the second funeral Fritz resigned himself to having no heirs, consoled by the fact that his older brother, Max, had guaranteed the von Renz bloodline by producing two children.

Still, in spite of his philosophical acceptance, the day Lisbet had announced that she was again pregnant she'd announced it with such unflinching and happy expectations that Fritz couldn't help but share her optimism. It was only now, here in this artificially cheerful room plastered with pictures of babies whose pink cherubic faces mocked him, that his hope lost ground. He'd been here twice before. His vision of newborns was that of the pinched, blue faces of his own dead infants. And as dawn finally appeared with a ring of gray light around the edges of the window shades, he watched enviously as another prospective father was roused from sleep with news of the arrival of a healthy boy. The man left, smiling triumphantly, and depression again dug its claws into Fritz. He had waited in this room longer than that chap. What was taking so much time? He took a deep breath and tried to resurrect Lisbet's confident demeanor last night when she was admitted in the early stages of labor.

My wife, the optimist, Fritz sighed as he picked up a magazine and leafed through it. He was amazed with Lisbet's resilience as well as her personal sacrifice. With her attempts at motherhood, she had interrupted her studies at the music conservatory, jeopardizing (maybe for good) her place as lead soprano. No small thing because she loved the stage more than anything.

"Herr Frederick von Renz?" A nurse in a pristinely starched white uniform and cap opened the door. Fritz felt himself go numb.

"Yes." He put the magazine down and rose, feeling lightheaded with fear of what she might tell him.

"You have a daughter!" she announced, tipping her head up because this new father was exceptionally tall. *And* handsome, she noted, despite the fact that he was unshaven and his clothes were ruffled after spending the night in this room.

"Yes…and…?"

"Pardon?" She raised her eyebrows. "Were you expecting twins?"

"No. I mean..." Swallowing convulsively, Fritz raked long slender fingers nervously through his dark hair. "Uh, what's wrong with her?"

"Wrong?" Frowning, the nurse pursed her lips.

"Will she live?" Fritz heard himself ask, his gray eyes narrowing, already flinching from the blow he was expecting.

"Of course she'll live," the nurse said, puzzled with his reaction. She was new at Wirchow and did not know about the two previous tragic babies. "She's as robust as any newborn I've seen."

Fritz allowed a warm shiver to run through him. "And my wife?"

"She's fine and sleeping soundly. You may see her and the baby in the morning." The woman glanced at her watch. "Oh, my! It's already morning. Well, I suggest you go home and come back later this afternoon." She walked over to the window, raised the shades, turned on her heels and was gone.

Fritz straightened his tie and grabbed his jacket and overcoat from the garment rack. *This baby was expected to survive!* He hardly dared believe it. *A girl?* Yes, the nurse had definitely said a daughter. Suddenly Fritz was filled with wonder. His head swam with all the things he would teach her and tell her and give her. He hadn't seen her yet but loved her with an emotion that saw no boundaries. He thrust his arms into the sleeves of his jacket, tossed the coat over his shoulders and rushed out into the hall and down the long corridor to use the telephone cubicle by the stairs. He had to call Dorrit. No matter the early hour, his mother and Lisbet's parents - who had come to Grunewald from Denmark only days ago to await the birth - would be awake, sitting by the telephone. After he had made that call, he would go see Lisbet and his daughter. He'd sit quietly in their room and watch them sleep.

He dared anyone on the hospital's staff to try to stop him.

Chapter Three

Repeatedly refusing to join the Nazi party, Fritz eventually lost his syndicated political column at the Berlin Zeitung. However, he was not fired outright, simply reassigned to the Arts and Entertainment Desk and, although writing film and theater critiques were not his strong suit, he remained in this lesser journalistic capacity to keep a foothold at the paper. He needed access to Nazi policies regarding the press in order to compile information for a book he was writing about the birth of a tyrant and the demise of a democracy. It was a dangerous project. If anyone discovered his material he'd be a dead man. But to record this German disaster in the making was of immense importance because he suspected there would soon be little truth or information available. Everything from domestic farm reports to foreign press releases were spun and distorted. Hitler's invasion of Austria and his later intrusion into Czechoslovakia under the pretext of liberating Germans in Sudetenland, were blatant examples of Nazi gall and political hyperbole.

With his diminishing responsibilities at the newspaper, Fritz took a part time teaching position in the Humanities Department at Berlin University - his alma mater - where he had enough friends among the faculty to overcome the lack of a Nazi badge. Of course, he was soon forced to color his lectures to suit the increasingly autocratic environment, something he justified because he needed first hand knowledge of how the intellectual community was influenced by current events and how it dealt with the insidious day-to-day government directives.

As 1938 came to a close, Fritz was for all practical purposes entrenched as a sleuth spying on a Germany fast disappearing, a country held in bondage by a corrupt regime which operated under such secrecy that it fooled not only its own citizens but the rest of the world as well. Fritz was scrupulously discreet about his writing project. If he came under surveillance his entire family would be in danger. As a precaution he told no one about his manuscript. There was safety in ignorance. Not even Lisbet knew about the draft he worked on late at night in their apartment on Uhland Strasse after she and the baby were asleep; a draft he kept locked away in a hidden drawer in the desk in his study. Intrigued by the secret compartment, he had bought this pricey French antique several years ago, though no practical use for the drawer had occurred to him at the time. Now he was extremely grateful to an old cabinetmaker's ingenuity.

The only person Fritz confided in was Helmut Niemann, a friend since childhood. Helmut knew about the manuscript and as a trial lawyer assisted Fritz by passing along unbelievable tales of corruption in the court system. Helmut told of attorneys who were blackmailed and brow beaten. He related horrifying accounts of judges who, refusing to comply with Nazi doctrines, suffered sudden heart attacks within the privacy of their chambers where members of the Gestapo were conveniently present to witness a death by "natural causes."

"People reading the obituaries must think an epidemic is afoot," Helmut said on a cold day in January 1939 as he and Fritz were strolling in Tiergarten, the forested parkland in central Berlin, the only place they dared talk freely. Having left their respective midtown offices at noon, they had lunched at a café on the Kurfurstendamm, where only frivolous conversation was possible because Nazi spies were everywhere and came in disguises ranging from benign old men to attractive housewives. "Bad health is claiming Berlin's judicial community at an alarming rate."

"Like a year or two ago when bankers and businessmen were found floating in the canals?" Fritz said, rolling up his collar and pulling some gloves from his pockets. "All were labeled suicides."

Helmut nodded morosely. "I fear we're heading for open season on the entire population. Anyone who criticizes our Fuehrer or questions his agenda is increasingly picked up for interrogation. Remember Frau Baden's boy?"

"Your housekeeper's son?"

"Yes. He vanished after ridiculing Herr Hitler in a public café."

"That was a long time ago," Fritz said. "Are you still looking for him?"

"No." Helmut fished a handkerchief from an inside pocket of his tweed coat, removed his glasses and wiped the cold fog from the lenses. "Julianne and I both believe he's dead. Of course his mother is still clinging to the hope he'll be found in a labor camp. At one point she actually believed he'd run off to America. Some Nazi probably planted that idea in her head." Helmut held his glasses up against the steely winter sky and, satisfied they were clear, put them back on, smoothing down his sand-colored hair in one fluid motion. "The Nazis are getting bolder. Occasionally entire families vanish. Jewish families in particular."

"Without a trace? Like Frau Baden's boy?"

"Yes and without inquiries. Few people have the fortitude to ask about their disappearing neighbors. If they do, they get some convoluted stories of temporary incarceration, resettlements, or population redistribution. And if they press the issue, they're labeled troublemakers and *pouf!* disappear as well. The medieval ax has been resurrected for civilian agitators."

"People are being *beheaded?*" Fritz said, shocked.

"You bet. Without a hearing and without a trial. Actually, some do get a trial. A secret, quick, and totally absurd spectacle with a Gestapo jury unanimously passing a death sentence, which is immediately carried out. No appeals. When families inquire about an arrested relative, they are simply told that the accused is still in custody, waiting his day in court. There's a steady stream of people coming to the gates of Lehrtestrasse Prison, leaving fruit baskets for loved ones long past the need of nourishment."

Fritz digested what he'd just heard.

Helmut looked him straight in the eye and said, "If you're planning to write any of this down, be careful. Be *very* careful."

Chapter Four

Nurturing a friendship spanning thirty-five years, Dorrit and Lillian spent a lovely morning in April, shopping in the boutiques along the Kurfurstendamm. As the sonorous bells atop the Kaiser Wilhelm Memorial Cathedral pealed the noon hour, they left their purchases to be sent home and headed in the direction of the Hotel Adlon on Pariser Platz to meet up with Anna von Steigert, Isabel von Brandt, and Gertrude Tarnoff. This group of old and dear friends met twice a month for lunch in the hotel's elegant glass-enclosed dining verandah. Today, however, Gertrude would not be joining them. She had called Dorrit this morning to cancel because of bronchitis.

Linking arms, Dorrit and Lillian strolled along the Kurfurstendamm toward a taxi stand. Lillian, her short, blond hair freshly dyed, was wearing a stylish beige linen suit and a white hat with colorful silk flowers in the hatband. Dorrit's navy pinstriped suit and matching cloche were more conservative, but equally fashionable. As they made their way along the crowded sidewalk, their ears pricked with the grinding sounds of demolition north of the Kurfurstendamm. Since Herr Hitler's ascend to power, there had been an enormous amount of new construction in and around Berlin, activity that regularly disrupted traffic. Today was no exception. The ladies got into a taxi only to soon sit in a bottleneck.

"That," Lillian pointed to a cleared zone on the left as the taxi crawled along, "is the site of the new Adolf Hitler Platz. Kurt and I attended a reception at the Reich Chancellery last month to view the models. They are spectacular!" To Lillian's way of thinking, everything about Herr Hitler was spectacular, including her husband's new position in the Fuehrer's inner circle.

"Will it be as vulgar as that?" Dorrit nodded toward the Italian

Embassy on the right, a pink marble monstrosity with excessive Gothic columns.

"Oh, even more so!" Lillian bubbled, missing her friend's choice of adjective.

"Where's the money for all this construction coming from?" Dorrit wanted to know. "Not another tax increase, I hope."

"Good heavens, no! That would be much too unpopular. The money comes from stamps."

"*Postage* stamps?"

"Uh-huh. The ones with the Fuehrer's picture."

Dorrit thought a moment. "All stamps carry his picture," she said.

"And why not?" Lillian giggled like a besotted schoolgirl. "He's so photogenic."

"But what about the postal service? Their revenues are being siphoned off for something that has nothing to do with the mail. Is that legal?"

"Of course. If not, someone at the Reichskanzlei would intervene."

Dorrit frowned but decided not to press the point.

Lillian Eckart was a Nazi.

Chapter Five

Anna and Isabel were sampling a wonderful dry Riesling as Dorrit and Lillian arrived at the Adlon, where the maitre-d always made the best table available for them, a table with a splendid view of the Brandenburg Gate.

Dorrit enjoyed the lunch and the company of her friends. The diversion helped throw off the lingering sadness from yesterday's funeral for her butler. Employed long before she moved to Lindenstrasse as Johann's bride, Schmidt's passing was the same as losing a dear friend. And she lost a faithful housekeeper as well when, immediately after the burial, his widow left for Mainz where she planned to live out her remaining years with her sister. So although Dorrit had long suspected that the Schmidts were both Nazis, she would miss them. Truth be known, some of her best friends were Nazis and while she didn't endorse their politics, she loved them nonetheless. Long enduring relationships survived partisan lines, however extreme. Indeed, she had hired another Nazi, a new housekeeper, who chose not to live-in. Frau Mueller lived on Potsdamer Strasse in the Kathreiner-Hochhaus complex, a cluster of high-rise apartment buildings constructed for blue-collar workers during Chancellor Stresemann's administration. Herr Hitler was not the first politician to concern himself with the welfare of the working classes, a fact that had escaped Frau Mueller. During her interview, she sang the Fuehrer's praises, giving him credit for her comfortable flat and for her husband's secure job in a ball bearing factory, where her son was guaranteed work once he finished his schooling in June.

Following a leisurely lunch, the four friends split up, heading in opposite directions. Lillian and Isabel left together, the latter's driver would drop Lillian off at her townhouse on the way to Isabel's home in

Charlottenburg. Anna von Steigert had an appointment with her dressmaker on Leipziger Platz and shared a taxi with Dorrit who was going straight home to Grunewald.

The cab soon became hopelessly stuck in traffic. Paying the driver, the ladies decided to walk past the gridlock and were nearing the heavily guarded Reich Chancellery, when they saw the cause of the congestion. The police were halting busses, cars, and vans to allow a column of assorted armored vehicles and goose-stepping soldiers to parade past the Chancellery where a balcony had been installed on the second floor, making it convenient for Herr Hitler to inspect his military might. The public had grown accustomed to these spontaneous displays; all that was missing today was a marching band.

As the lead tank approached Wilhelm Strasse, Dorrit grabbed Anna's arm and along with scores of pedestrians similarly inspired, hurried into the subway station at the corner. People were quick to leave the streets, some ducking into cafés, others taking refuge in shops; all recalling recent parades which had drawn jeers from unwise spectators, jeers silenced by gunfire sprayed into the crowd. Time had proven that the Fuehrer was not the kindly father figure or the stern disciplinarian many believed Germany had needed back in 1933. Of course, whether or not one approved of the man was immaterial. It was too late to have second thoughts about his leadership. Elections were banned, leaving people with no means to recall him or dissolve his police state. Only a skillful assassin could liberate Germany.

Once the military parade had passed by, people emerged from their shelters. Anna and Dorrit continued on foot to Leipziger Platz, where Dorrit found a taxi to Grunewald. Sinking into the plush seats, she checked her watch and trusted that Nurse Heller had met Peter at his school. Mademoiselle Morisot had abruptly returned to France last week at the behest of her family who were growing uncomfortable with the political climate in Berlin. The children, especially Sigrid, missed her. Mademoiselle had been both governess and friend and had done a remarkable job teaching them French.

Chapter Six

Before reaching Lindenstrasse, Dorrit made a snap decision and had the driver drop her off in front of the medical clinic, a short walk from home. Sigrid had a bit of a cough, and it'd be prudent to pick up a prescription from Ben before it developed into something worse. Dorrit also wanted to look in on Gertrude. The Tarnoff's maid had recently given notice and might already have left, in which case Dorrit would bring over some hot soup tonight and otherwise try to help Gert until she was back on her feet. Ben had enough on his hands as director and chief surgeon at the clinic. He was well into his seventies but pushed himself like a young intern.

Stepping from the taxi and crossing the sidewalk, Dorrit stopped in mid stride, her lungs emptying of air like the rush of wind from a balloon. Lightheaded, she steadied herself with a couple of shallow breaths while staring, thunderstruck, at the words scrawled across the double doors to the clinic: *Death to Jews!* This ugly message was commonplace around Berlin, but constant repetition made it no less menacing. The red paint was freshly applied, Dorrit realized, because thin veins were running in uneven streaks down the polished wood. Her eyes flew to the side of the building and the brass plaque bearing Johann's name. It had not been defaced, thank God, and helped her recover enough to climb the broad stone steps. Being careful not to come in contact with the paint, she reached for the door knob and tottered into the reception lobby; tottered, but at her age no one would find that strange.

Half a dozen patients were seated in the comfortable green leather chairs, leafing through magazines, apparently unaware of the grisly message outside. Dorrit went straight to the receptionist's desk where, before asking to see Dr. Tarnoff, she requested that the maintenance man be summoned to clean the front door. The woman looked puzzled, but picked up the telephone to relay the order. She did not question it. She had worked here when the Baron Doctor von Renz had been in charge and was not about to probe his widow for her logic.

Ben was with a patient so Dorrit sat down to wait until he was free. She welcomed the wait because she needed to compose herself. Picking up a periodical and skimming its pages, she decided she must convince Gertrude and Ben to go out to Bernau for a while. Her country house was available to them. There was no vandalism in Bernau or she would have heard about it from Gerlinde and Karl-Heinz. The Tarnoffs ought to leave Berlin until these nasty threats blew over. *Blew over?* Actually, they were getting worse. And why didn't the police do something? Why weren't they more diligent in rounding up the culprits? How could they allow this heckling and defacing of private property to continue with impunity?

As Dorrit flipped through another glossy magazine, a prickling at the back of her neck made her shiver despite the warm environment in the reception area. Threats invariably escalate into violence, she realized, and was reminded of Gertrude's and Ben's stories of persecution inside czarist Russia and their narrow escape. Suddenly she felt a queasy twinge. I am also foreign born, she reflected, Russian and Jewish, undesirable ancestry according to the Nazis. Were her old immigration papers still on file? Was Nazi efficiency such that obsolete records might become activated? If so, she might also become a victim of the hate mongers. Could she expect ugly scrawling and broken windows on Lindenstrasse? Might it be necessary to take refuge in Bernau along with the Tarnoffs until civil order was restored in Berlin?

Ben was exiting his consulting room with a patient, the attending nurse handing the latter his coat before disappearing into an adjacent room to assist another doctor. As the receptionist gave Dr. Tarnoff the folder of his next appointment, she nodded to where Dorrit was seated, whispering, "The Baroness von Renz would like a few minutes of your time."

Ben turned. "Dorrit! To what do I owe this pleasure?" he said, smiling and strolling toward her.

"Actually, Ben, I'm on my way upstairs to see Gertrude." Dorrit got up from the chair. "But first I need some medicine for Sigrid. She woke up with a cough this morning." Dorrit stopped herself. A child's mild ailment was suddenly unimportant compared with the hideous message on the door. And filled with renewed urgency to warn Ben about the death threat, she glanced around. She was jumping ahead of other patients, but it couldn't be helped. If she didn't speak with Ben now she'd burst. "I need to see you in your office," she said, plucking at his white surgeon's coat. "It'll only take a minute," she added for the benefit of those around her who had waited longer than she.

"Of course, Dorrit. Come along." He took her elbow, perplexed with the agitated look in her face.

Chapter Seven

They were walking arm-in-arm past the receptionist's desk when the front door opened as if rammed by a truck, the blast of air causing the magazines on the tables to flutter like leaves in the wind. People looked up from their reading material and immediately registered fear at seeing four SS officers march into the room with German Shepherds on metal choke leashes. The first thing that went through Dorrit's mind was the absurd hope that these men had come to investigate the defacing of the door. Of course that naive notion died the instant she saw people put their magazines aside and quietly exit the building.

Although the brown uniforms, red Nazi armbands, black boots and gun belts, sent a rattling chill to every bone in Ben's body, he squared his shoulders and faced the intruders. "Please, no dogs in the clinic," he said in a deceptively calm voice. "They must remain outside. I'll have to insist."

Ignoring him, the officer holding a clipboard stepped forward. "Benjamin Tarnoff?" he asked, studying Ben from beneath the black visor of his hat.

"Yes, I'm Dr. Tarnoff."

"Your wife?" The officer's steely gaze fell on Dorrit whose arm Ben was still holding in an intimate way, not the professional manner of physician and patient.

"No." Ben immediately let go and stepped away, indicating she was no relation, thereby saving her from scrutiny. "My wife is upstairs. She is ill."

"Is there an inside access?"

"Yes." Ben pointed past the receptionist's station.

Without taking his eyes off Ben, the officer signaled his men with a nod. The one holding the dogs remained while the other two left.

"Please, my wife shouldn't be disturbed," Ben quickly said in an effort to avert an intrusion into the apartment. "I can answer your questions."

"We're not conducting an interview," the officer snapped as boots could be heard pounding the stairs up to the Tarnoffs' apartment. "You and your wife are to come along with us."

Ben's shoulders sank. For weeks he had expected a visit from the SS. Several friends and colleagues had already been detained for interrogation and most were still being held. "Are we under arrest?" he asked bluntly.

"No. Temporary custody." The officer looked inconvenienced with the question and gestured to the officer holding the dogs. The man went outside.

"What are the charges?" Ben pressed him.

"Suspicion of subversive activities against the Third Reich." The man recited the standard answer from page twelve in the SS manual, one he was obliged to repeat several times each day.

All of a sudden Ben looked tired, his age showed; these same charges had been leveled at countless others who had vanished. He lowered his eyes.

From a few feet away, Dorrit was staring at him. His stoic acceptance of the false accusation was unreal and why was he being so polite? In the next instant her hands flew to her throat. The blond, nice looking officer in charge of the dogs had apparently tied them up outside and was now returning with handcuffs. She bit her lips to stifle a cry. *Gott im Himmel,* how humiliating! If Johann were alive, this would never be permitted. He would never have allowed this injustice to take place. He would have thrown these officers out on their ears, damned be the consequences. He would have demanded to see subpoenas certified by three judges. He would have done…*what?* For all his physical strength and personal power, what could Johann have done against four armed men in a political climate where the old order of law no longer existed and where citizens had no rights? Dorrit felt a sudden and bitter helplessness. She saw Ben's face sag in submission as his captor snapped the metal around his wrists.

"Oh, Ben!" she moaned from behind her hands, her lips trembling with vituperative protests that remaining in her throat by the look he gave her, imploring her not to interfere. Ben knew she could do nothing. If she raised her voice she would only make matters worse for him and bring repercussions on herself. Members of the Schutz-Staffel were known to come down hard on anyone questioning their authority. Furthermore, according to Nazi law, her ancestry was tainted, and if not for the “good” German name she carried, she was as vulnerable as he and Gert. It would never do to have these uniformed hounds smell blood and start nosing around.

An uneasy stillness descended on the reception area. It was eerily quiet. Glancing around, Dorrit saw that the clinic was now completely empty, even the receptionist had abandoned her station. Somewhere in an interior office a telephone was ringing. It went unanswered. Where were the nurses? Where were the other doctors? Was she the only one witnessing this miscarriage of justice? She raged inwardly at the absent staff and clenched her fists. *Cowards one and all!* But she remained silent. She, too, was a coward.

Chapter Eight

Noise on the back stairs broke the awful silence. A moment later the officers reappeared, herding Gertrude in front of them. Rudely pulled from her bed, feverish and disoriented, she'd been forced to dress quickly, wearing a black wool dress far too warm for today's weather. Hatless, her gray hair hung in disarray with no indication she'd had the wherewithal to fasten it into the neat bun she always wore. Clutching a small suitcase, two overcoats were draped over her arm.

Seeing her dear friend in such a state, Dorrit's heart broke. Gertrude, who'd comforted the entire von Renz household through that mind bending ordeal of Sigrid's scarlet fever, was now dragged from her own sickbed by strangers and given no comfort at all. In a sudden spurt of defiance of the officers, Dorrit hurled herself forward, embracing the older woman.

"Gert, I'll get help!" she whispered. "They won't keep you long. Don't lose heart."

Gertrude made a small choking sound before finding her voice. "I can't imagine what they want with us. We..." She wasn't allowed to finish; one of the officers stepped in, pulling the two women apart. As Gertrude turned to Ben, she spotted the handcuffs. The fever drained from her face. Chalk white, she was now escorted through the front door and down the steps ahead of her husband.

The sidewalk in front of the clinic was deserted, but across the street a handful of people had gathered to watch; one look from the officers and everyone dispersed. When several cars and bicyclists slowed down, they, too, were immediately waved on.

Gertrude was being placed in the back of the brown van parked at the curb, when Ben turned his head, his eyes raking over the imposing facade of the clinic as if trying to memorize every brick. He spotted

Dorrit following the last officer from the building.

"I didn't have a chance to give you Sigrid's medicine," Ben said to her. "Go see Doctor Viermetz."

"Silence!" One of the officers pushed him forward. Hands tied, Ben struggled to keep his balance and tripped over the curb.

Dorrit's restraint broke. She rushed forward to help him to his feet, but the officer with the clipboard held her back. Powerless, she witnessed Ben being dragged into the windowless van. The door shut with a metallic thud.

"Please!" she begged the officer restraining her. "I need to know how long you expect to keep the Tarnoffs. Many patients depend on Dr. Tarnoff."

The officer let go of her arm, his eyes narrowing, his face as hard and unyielding as the pavement beneath his feet. "What's your name?"

"M...my name?"

"*Ja, bitte!*" His tone was like a slap in the face.

Dorrit jerked her head back as if he'd actually struck her. The sudden movement sent adrenaline roaring through her veins. She looked at the officer, pride now burning like green fire in her eyes, helped by the fact that she was wearing her best spring ensemble with *haute couture* written all over it. The navy pinstriped suit and vermilion hat were both costly Parisian imports, something even this SS official might recognize.

"I am the Baroness von Renz," she said in her haughtiest tone, her back ramrod straight. "Widow of Baron Johann Maximilian von Renz. The founder of this clinic."

Ill-concealed surprise softened the officer's demeanor somewhat. Raised from the lower classes, his uniform and newfound importance in the Schutz-Staffel had not completely expunged his awe of nobility.

"Well, *gnadige* Baroness," he said with an imperceptible bow of his head, "rest assured that the clinic will be assigned a new physician tomorrow. A *German* doctor." With that he pivoted on his shiny black heels and moved briskly away, slipping the clipboard under his arm.

Still riding a wave of indignant courage, Dorrit took a few steps toward the officer in charge of the dogs. He was blond like Max, had a nice face and was kind to the animals. While the man with the clipboard rounded the van and prepared to get in behind the wheel, and the other two officers walked toward their car parked in front of it, this young man was petting the dogs affectionately.

"Please," she begged before he could board with the canines, "tell me where you are taking the Tarnoffs. They'll need an attorney." She touched his elbow to make him listen.

"If you insist on having your curiosity satisfied," he turned toward her, one boot on the running board, his blue eyes impaling her like shards of ice, "I'll gladly oblige you." He nodded stiffly toward the back of the van. "You can come along with them."

The threat stunned and silenced her because she knew it was real. Any one of these men had the power to arrest her without cause, and if she were taken into custody she might languish under lock and key for weeks. In the meantime what would happen to Peter and Sigrid?

Oh, dear God, I forgot about the children!

Dorrit took a couple of clumsy steps backwards. She dropped her eyes and held her tongue. How could she have thought that this young man had a nice face? How could she have compared him to her wonderful son, Max?

Paralyzed, she remained standing on the sidewalk long after the van had sped away.

Chapter Nine

Returning home, Dorrit did not mention what had taken place at the clinic. She didn't tell Nurse Heller and most assuredly not Peter and Sigrid. If the Tarnoffs were freed quickly, it would serve no purpose to upset the children. Besides, how could she explain a miscarriage of justice that she, herself, didn't understand?

It was much later that night, after the children were both in bed and Nurse Heller had retired to her quarters, that Dorrit finally settled down in the library and searched the newspapers for reports of vandalism and arrests. But, as she'd come to expect, there was no mention of property damage and not a word could be found about citizens being detained. *It's as if nothing of the sort takes place*, she thought bitterly, discarding the papers in a heap on the floor; they contained nothing of substance. Even the Zeitung, Berlin's flagship newspaper, was becoming a scandal sheet, a tabloid and a voice for Nazi propaganda. At best it ran redundant film reviews and escapades of famous stars, plus the predictable photographs of the Fuehrer surrounded by women and children or greeting foreign dignitaries at his mountain retreat at Obersalzberg. The Zeitung was no longer the journalistic powerhouse where Fritz had begun his career. *Fritz?* Dorrit realized she hadn't read his critiques. He had lost his political column, but she always made a point of reading his articles, regardless of the subject matter.

Moments later, after rummaging through the pile of newsprint on the floor, she was surprised to discover Fritz was back on the editorial page. The Zeitung must have had empty space to fill for them to run what was surely controversial commentary. Kicking off her shoes and curling her feet up under her, she began to read and was immediately reminded of why he was unpopular with the editors. Barely into the second paragraph, her skin crawled with fear for him. His article contained anti-Nazi undertones and went so far as to question Herr Hitler's claim that, militarily, Germany had no equals. To dispute Herr Hitler was ill advised and Dorrit wondered how Fritz's column had made it past the censors. It was dangerous journalism to say the least. She trusted Fritz knew what he was doing. In her next breath, she thanked God that Max was out of the country. For the first time in her life, she was grateful that his archaeological expeditions took him to foreign lands. Although he had no political convictions, Max would manage to sound off and with far less finesse than Fritz.

Dorrit put the paper aside and got back to the pressing matter of this afternoon's arrest. She had to find a way to help Ben and Gert. They needed an attorney. But which firms were safe? Nazi party members were at the helm of most of them, and the firm she'd retained for many years dealt exclusively with tax and estate matters. Could she approach them for a referral? Or might she be opening a hornet's nest? Who could she trust?

Helmut Niemann's name popped into her head. He was Fritz's closest friend and could be trusted. But he was a prosecutor, not a defense attorney. Besides, the timing was bad. Helmut and Julianne had just become parents for the second time, and Fritz had mentioned that Helmut was up to his neck in work with little spare time for his growing family. Lisbet said the same thing. She and Julianne spent a great deal of time together, Julianne bemoaning the many nights when Helmut stayed late at the office.

"Woe be it for me to burden him," Dorrit said out loud and got up from the sofa in a state of restless agitation that comes from dwelling on a problem without reaching a solution. She began pacing the Persian rugs scattered about on the parquet. But though it felt good to move around, nothing came of the exercise. Her eyes perused the leather bound volumes in the glass-fronted bookcases as if they might hold the answer. Next, the paintings in the room drew her attention. Studying the Monet and Cezanne, she wondered what had become of the Seurat from San Sebastian until she remembered that it hung in the hall in Bernau.

I'm growing absentminded; she scolded herself and stopped in front of Johann's desk, looking pensively at a framed photograph standing on the expanse of mahogany. She reached out to touch it. It was taken on their wedding day. Johann looked suitably solemn befitting the occasion, his arm was around her, his dark hair was neatly combed, but that streak of devilment she remembered so well gleamed in his eyes. Her heart swelled with a flood of wonderful memories.

"Oh, Johann, what shall I do?" she said, speaking to the picture and forcing her mind back to the present although the past was a far more desirable place to be. "How can I help the Tarnoffs?" Johann and Ben had been friends and professional partners for years. Ben had delivered both Max and Fritz, and had attended Johann as he lay dying in Bernau.

Bernau? Karl-Heinz? Yes, Johann would surely tell her to consult with Karl-Heinz. He was like family and completely trustworthy.

"But I can't go to Karl-Heinz," she whispered after a moment. "Times have changed, Johann. Karl-Heinz can't be brought into this. He's too vociferously anti-Nazi. In the belief that he's helping the Tarnoffs, he'll come storming into Berlin, demand answers from the SS, and end up getting himself arrested."

How about Kurt Eckart? Johann seemed to be suggesting.

"He's a Nazi, for heaven's sake!"

He is a friend, first and foremost.

Dorrit nodded. Yes, he's a friend and friendships take precedence over political convictions.

She felt better at once. She'd telephone him tonight. Kurt was not an attorney but had influence in the Nazi party; the kind that counted for something nowadays. She walked back to the sofa, feeling confident that a solution was just a telephone call away, and prepared to enjoy the tea Frau Mueller was now bringing in on a tray before leaving for the night. She was new on the job and Dorrit was happy to note that everything was going smoothly. Still, it was not until she heard the front door click and knew there could be no eavesdropping that she dared pick up the receiver and place her call.

Chapter Ten

Please, no political meetings tonight. Dorrit's heart sank with each ring. It seemed an eternity before she heard the familiar, "Hello?"

"Kurt!" she blurted. "I'm so glad you're home!"

"Dorrit, how nice to hear your voice. Let me get Lillian. She's upstairs."

"No, don't bother her. You're the one I need to speak with. Do you have a minute?"

"For you, darling, I have all evening. What's on your mind?"

Dorrit took comfort in the warm sincerity of his voice; telephoning Kurt had been the right thing to do. "It's about Gertrude and Ben."

"Oh?"

"You won't believe it but they were taken into custody this afternoon." There was a sudden silence on the line; it was as if the telephone had gone dead. "Kurt? Are you there?"

"Yes," came a toneless reply.

"Did you hear me? The SS arrested Ben and Gert."

"I heard you."

"Well, as you can imagine, it was horrible! They were taken away like common criminals. Ben was handcuffed!"

"You saw it? You were there?"

"Yes. And I'm frightened for them. They're charged with subversive acts, which is utterly ridiculous. You and I both know there's no one in Berlin *less* subversive than the Tarnoffs. I thought you might know what to do. They'll need an attorney. Can you tell me which law firm to call?"

"Dorrit..." Kurt sounded as if he were bracing himself for bad news, "did you protest? Did you say anything to the arresting officers?"

"No."

"You said nothing? Absolutely nothing?"

"Well, I did say something."

"What?" Kurt tensed, his hand on the receiver tightened.

"Only that the clinic depended on Ben. And I asked where he and Gert were being taken."

"*And...?*"

"That's all."

"Are you sure?"

"Yes."

Kurt let out his breath in an audible relief. "What did the officers say?"

"They wouldn't tell me anything. Do you know where they bring detainees? Please don't tell me it's to that awful Lehrtestrasse compound in town. Or Spandau."

"No. Ben and Gertrude are probably at a center outside the city."

"Where?"

"Perhaps Oranienburg. Or Weimar. Both have large and pleasant centers that are well maintained. They'll be comfortable at either place."

"Could you find out which one? I have to retain an attorney."

"Dorrit, listen to me! Listen carefully! The Tarnoffs cannot, I stress *cannot,* have legal representation."

"Why not? Surely everyone is entitled..."

"No! There aren't enough attorneys to go around. The Tarnoff are not the only ones being brought in. A large number of non-Germans are being questioned to determine if they have allegiances elsewhere. Particularly in countries that are hostile to us. Disloyalty from a single individual can weaken the society our Fuehrer is building for the benefit of us all." As Kurt continued with the familiar Nazi drivel, Dorrit detected little of his normal fervor; his words were the same but his tone was flat. "Anyone foreign born is under suspicion and cannot be trusted to put Germany first. Their hearts might harbor conflicts and disaffection."

"Disaffection!" Dorrit snatched at the word. "For heaven's sake, Kurt! You and I both know there's no one *more* loyal than the Tarnoffs. Remember how often Ben expressed his gratitude that Berlin gave him a safe home, something he never had in Russia where both he and Gert lost relatives in the *pogroms.*" Dorrit pinched her lips together, a heartbeat later whispering, "It's happening here, isn't it? Threats.

Vandalism. Arrests. Exactly like the Tarnoffs described. Tell me, will bloodbaths follow like they did in Russia?"

"No! And for God's sake, *hush!*"

Realizing Kurt was fearful that an operator might have picked up the line, Dorrit fell silent. As if by mutual compliance, both she and Kurt held their breaths, listening for clicks or a hollow echo. Once they were sure their conversation was private, Dorrit continued, keeping her voice barely above a murmur.

"Kurt, as you know, I'm foreign born. My mother was Jewish. The man who raised me was Jewish. Will I be called in for questioning?"

"No, you have nothing to worry about. And don't concern yourself with the Tarnoffs. They'll be treated well and be released shortly."

Dorrit was only half listening. "Kurt, what's happening to law abiding citizens?"

"Nothing! Listen to me! We're living in an enlightened society. We are not barbarians. Detentions are unfortunate but necessary. If the Tarnoffs are cooperative they'll spend very little time in custody."

"But why are they being held at all? They've done nothing."

"I know. But in the interest of national security they have to be watched for a while. Something that can only be done at an appropriate center."

"Like the one you mentioned in Oranienburg. And where else?"

"Weimar. Of course, the Tarnoffs could be assigned to a camp in one of our newly acquired territories in Austria or Czechoslovakia."

"Camp? That sounds so military."

"Forget it. It was a poor choice of a word. But what's in a name? Wherever the Tarnoffs are, they'll be comfortable. If the state can't find any evidence against them, they'll return home. The International Red Cross has access to our facilities and inspects them regularly. There'd be plenty of protest if any were found lacking."

"I suppose so."

Afraid he hadn't convinced her, Kurt plunged ahead. "Look, I can't promise anything but perhaps I can find out where Ben and Gert are."

"Oh, that would be wonderful. If they are nearby I could visit."

"No!" Kurt said, aghast; it wouldn't be safe for Dorrit to go within a hundred kilometers of any camp. "Absolutely not! You can write letters but you can't visit. Never! Do I have your word on that?"

"Uh, yes, of course."

"Also, don't forget, keep in mind that your mail will be opened and read before it reaches them."

"Don't worry. I know about censors. Letters from Cassandra and Max are routinely opened. Sometimes entire paragraphs are blotted out. We've learned to be discreet. We no longer write anything of a political nature."

"Good. I will see what I can find out. Be patient. It might take a while."

Chapter Eleven

Kurt's promise appeased Dorrit, just as he intended, but it was an empty one. Ben and Gertrude were as good as dead and it would serve no purpose to investigate their whereabouts; something he couldn't tell Dorrit because she might decide to probe on her own and stir up trouble for herself. He couldn't divulge to anyone that the regime was getting away with inhuman treatment of selected citizens right under the noses of decent Germans. While rumors of torture and death persisted, a climate ranging from paralyzing fear to watchful inertia prevailed. No one who knew what was going on could afford to talk. The price for a loose tongue was death. Besides, if he told Dorrit, she wouldn't believe him anyway. Human nature was such that if a story was sufficiently monstrous, honorable people rejected it outright. Also, he could never tell her what he'd done on her behalf months ago, when - the minute he learned that death lists were being compiled - he paid a visit to the archives on Wilhelm Strasse where immigration records were stored.

Aware of the risk to himself, he went late at night when only a skeleton crew was on duty and the chance of meeting someone he knew was negligible. Dressed in his uniform displaying his high position in the Nazi Party, and carrying an official notebook, he walked down the basement steps, flashed his impressive medical credentials to the guards and claimed he was tracking a new and virulent strain of tuberculosis, carriers of which were believed to be foreigners who must be identified and isolated. Tuberculosis was highly contagious, the guards were happy to cooperate, unlocked the storage room and switched on the overhead lights in the underground cavern, giving the eminent Herr Doctor Kurt Eckart unfettered access to the countless rows of metal cabinets.

While pretending to study selected dossiers, Kurt placed some of the binders on top of the cabinets to deflect the guards' eyes and to shield the true nature of his mission once he reached the end of the alphabet, where he expected to find a file on Dorrit and her father who had entered Germany from Warsaw around 1901. As he worked, he scribbled randomly chosen names and addresses in his notebook, circling some in red ink - a nice touch - should the guards decide to check. It was an agonizing hour of pretense before he finally reached the drawer marked Y - Z. Flicking through the files, he quickly found the two he wanted and pulled them out; now for the difficult part.

"*Mein* Herr! May I assist you?"

"Huh?" Kurt spun around and found he was facing one of the guards.

"If you're done with those," the man nodded toward the binders littering the tops of the cabinets, "I'll be glad to help file them away."

"Oh?" Speechless with the man's close proximity, and the fact that he had approached without making a sound, Kurt began perspiring under his uniform trimmed with the regimentals of his officialdom, which wouldn't help him if he were caught pocketing documents. *So much for counting on those piles to conceal my activity*, he thought wryly; they had, in fact, served to draw the guard's attention. Regaining himself, Kurt put the two binders he was holding down on the cabinet and casually turned a page in his notebook. "Thank you," he said and prepared to make notations. "I'd appreciate that. It'll speed things up. None of us gets paid overtime for working nights." He chuckled to cover a nervous catch in his voice.

The guard grinned with the pleasant camaraderie from this esteemed doctor and reached for the files next to him.

"Not those. I'm not quite done with them." Kurt tapped his pen against the open page in his notebook. "I still need to cross check the names. Perhaps you could start at the beginning of the alphabet?" He pointed toward the stacks of binders at the front of the room. "I'll finish here and work my way backwards, putting the files away as I go. We'll meet half way."

"Very well!" The guard clicked his heels and left.

Shaken, telling himself that he was too old to play games of deception, Kurt kept a sharp eye on the solicitous guard as well as on the fellow seated outside the open door. And now working with jittery haste, he lifted every scrap of information on Dorrit and her father from their files, carefully folding each piece of paper into small squares that fit into various pockets on his uniform. Once the binders were empty, he peeled the names off the flaps, slipped them into the tops of his black boots, and stuffed the cardboard folders - too thick to conceal in his clothing - underneath others in the drawer. Devoid of marks, they could not be linked to anyone. Finally, he began filing the stacks of dossiers back into the cabinets, slowly making his way toward the guard assisting him. "Well, it looks like we're done," Kurt said, patting his notebook. "Thanks for your help."

"It was no trouble, Herr Doctor," the man said. "I hope you can track down and quarantine the disease carriers."

"I'm sure going to try." Kurt read the badges on the guards' uniforms and bid them a cordial goodbye, addressing both by name. Leaving the records room, he mounted the stairs slowly, swinging his arms, showing that he was leaving empty-handed except for the notebook he'd brought with him. It was dangerous to appear to be in a hurry, and to further throw off suspicion, he stopped upstairs to chat with the guards in the front hall, putting the notebook down on their desk, giving them ample opportunity to leaf through it while he retrieved his hat and overcoat from the rack. Although the sheets hidden on his person seemed to crackle noisily with every move he made, he buttoned his coat leisurely and even stayed to listen to a lewd joke. Laughing hardily, he complimented the men on their sense of humor.

Kurt's driver was not waiting at the curb. He could not chance him knowing about this nocturnal mission and had taken a bus here. As he now started out for home, this time on foot, he chose dark side streets with little or no traffic. As he walked along, he reached inside his coat, removed the folded sheets from his uniform one at a time and carefully tore them into indiscernible bits, disposing of them in various trash receptacles along the way. He threw the last scraps into the Landwehr Canal and lingered a moment to ensure that they disappeared under the surface of the black moonlit water.

He slept little that night and, in the weeks following, feared a summons to explain his unauthorized business with the immigration files. But he was never called. The guards had not reported his activity. Now, months later, he slept extremely well, knowing he had saved Dorrit from the death lists. Johann's ghost would not haunt him.

After Kurt's visit to the immigration archives, Dorrit Zache ceased to exist. But there was another crucial step that had to be completed before she was safe. She had to be reborn a pure German, and for that Kurt needed to get his hands on a birth certificate, someone long dead with no living relatives. Only then could she apply for the new identification papers now required by the regime. So far Kurt had come up with only one possibility, a couple from Schoneberg named Beyer. They had been his patients during his early years at Wirchow Hospital and had been childless except for a daughter named Doris, who died in infancy. If Kurt could lift her birth certificate from the Office of Vital Statistics, do a bit of surgery on the name and make a copy, Dorrit could use it as her own. But it was a two-pronged mission, more dangerous and more difficult than his foray into the immigration files. Of course, after her encounter with the SS at the clinic today, he realized that before securing her new identity, he must at least prepare her in case she was again confronted by anyone in an official capacity.

Thankfully, he did not need to trouble himself about Max and Fritz. The von Renz name and ancestry was Prussian and aristocratic, both were born and baptized in Berlin and, therefore, raised no red flags. In fact, the day Kurt confirmed this, he saw that "mother" was simply listed on both certificates as the Baroness Dorrit von Renz. Benjamin Tarnoff, attending physician, had signed the birth certificates and left blank the space where the mother's particulars should have been noted, simply scrawling "same as above," drawing attention to Johann's impeccable lineage.

It had turned out to be a fortuitous omission. Or foresight?

Chapter Twelve

Deep in troubled thought, Kurt decided that he had to call Dorrit back and he'd better do it tonight rather than wait till tomorrow when more wiretappers were on duty. Straightening in his chair, he reached for the telephone, gave the operator the number and carefully listened for more than one click indicating another line remained open. When he detected none, he came right to the point the instant Dorrit answered.

"Are you alone?" he said, foregoing formalities.

"Yes. Frau Muller has gone home and everyone else is asleep upstairs."

"Good. This is extremely important. You need to change your name."

"*What?*"

"Just your *maiden* name. Listen carefully. I can't repeat myself. You were born in Berlin. Your father was Konrad Beyer. A schoolmaster in Schoneberg. He died in 1915. Your mother, Irma Beyer, died in 1918. You have no siblings. No living relatives. Got that?"

"Yes." Dorrit made notes on a pad on the desk. "When was I born?"

"Your real date of birth is fine for the time being. Just remember everything else. If you are ever questioned, stick to it."

"Suppose they want proof?" Dorrit was aware of the regime's delight in requesting identification. She had seen the SS stop ordinary people strolling in midtown and demand to see their documents.

"If you don't draw attention to yourself, no one will bother you. Stay away from any situation involving officials, such as today at the clinic. You were lucky. Don't press it. And, whatever you do, don't plan any trips." Giving no hint to his nocturnal visit to the immigration files, Kurt added, "I know your passport expired in 1934 and that you haven't renewed it. For heaven's sake, *don't* do it now. Burn the old one. Claim you've lost it."

1934? Dorrit's mind rushed back to when Fritz and Lisbet were married. Sigrid had been ill with scarlet fever, which, along with an expired passport, prevented Dorrit from traveling to Denmark for the wedding.

"I'm trying to get corroborating documents for your new lineage," Kurt went on to say. "In the meantime be careful. Needless to say this is between us. Not a word to anyone. No one!"

Dorrit suspected what he had done. "I won't say a word," she whispered into the telephone, moved to tears by his loyalty as she thanked him and bid him goodnight.

Replacing the receiver, Kurt leaned back in his chair, exhausted with an emotional fatigue that had drained him same as a twenty-kilometer march. He thought of Ben Tarnoff, friend and colleague he had cast aside long ago and whose plight today he again dismissed.

What has made me so callous? Kurt wondered. What's happened to the Nazi party he joined in the early days when its goals for Germany seemed new and exciting, a breath of fresh air for a torn and ragged nation that had never recovered from The Great War. Until that night of Herr Hitler's purge of influential citizens - killings Kurt had long ago stopped justifying - a spirit of camaraderie had bound party members together. But in the aftermath of that vengeful bloodbath, the bond had begun to erode and been replaced by mistrust, a fear of one's own shadow and most assuredly of everyone else's. With each succeeding year Nazi leaders slipped further into the dregs of trite, banal commonness. The wiser and more decent members had slowly eased away or been arrested for disloyalty and hung, leaving the way clear for lesser talent. A lust for personal power was now at the helm of every department. People of no background or consequence had risen to the top; their only qualification being undying allegiance to Herr Hitler.

Kurt frequently thought of resigning, but he was in too deep. He knew too much. If he withdrew he would be arrested. He had access to highly classified information. He knew about the camps, grisly torture, and executions. He knew of lies and blackmail and, although it ranked among his lesser sins, he presided over a medical board that rejected qualified candidates while making the way easy for friends of party members. The low level of accomplishments of those now entering medicine was appalling. In all professions, Adolf Hitler's grand vision for Germany was built on a foundation of mediocrity. But although

Kurt had grown disillusioned, he had no choice but to maintain an infallible pretense at loyalty. One misstep and Lillian, along with their married daughter Elsie, her husband and children, would be damned. Only those tending toward the ghoulish could possibly imagine Kurt's punishment, and he occasionally found himself praying for ill health, which would enable him to retire without suspicion.

Chapter Thirteen

Two weeks passed before Kurt called Dorrit, telling her that Ben and Gertrude were in Oranienburg. He was happy to report that the detention center was cheerful and that they were both well. Of course, if he'd had the slightest inkling that she intended to visit, he would have given her the name of a camp impossibly far away.

Eager to see the Tarnoffs, Dorrit conveniently forgot her promise to only write letters and immediately took the *Ring-bahn* to Bernau, where she spent the night at her country home, starting out for Oranienburg the next morning in one of the cars she kept at the barony. It was a beautiful day in early May and she took the convertible, carefully placing a food basket for Ben and Gert in the front seat next to her. Rounding the fountain in the courtyard, she drove through the tall iron gates and down the tree-lined lane, congratulating herself for having learned to drive years ago. Of course she limited herself to short trips on country roads. She had no plans to test Berlin traffic.

At the bottom of the hill, she turned left onto the main road, grateful that Heinrich had filled the gas tank before he left her employ. He had given notice the day he heard that drivers, regardless of age, were needed by the military. His departure left the care of the house to a few maids whose numbers were dwindling as they, too, left for jobs in the armaments industry. When Dorrit attempted to fill the vacancies, the clerk at the local agency informed her that it was unpatriotic to seek household help. "All able-bodied men and women are needed for service to the Fatherland, not to any one individual," she'd announced tartly before raising her hand, dismissing Dorrit with the popular salutation, "Heil Hitler!" This left the care of the house, the stables, and the lands to a skeleton crew, and Dorrit worried how they'd manage come summer. Cassandra and Max would be home during the month of

August for their regular vacation with the children, and of course Lisbet, Fritz, and little Karoline would spend at least two months here, during which time Lisbet's parents would pay a visit from Denmark.

After driving for the better part of two hours, Dorrit approached what she assumed was the detention center. It had taken her longer than expected to find the place; it wasn't on any of the maps she kept in the glove box, and whenever she stopped to ask for directions, townspeople and country folk alike were unsure of its location, causing her to take a number of wrong turns. Finally, on the eastern outskirts of Oranienburg, a farmer steered her to a little used road where she came upon a stretch of electrified wire fencing enclosing what looked like a manufacturing concern. Spotting the main entrance up ahead, she kept going although she suspected the farmer was mistaken.

She glanced woefully at the basket sitting exposed in the sun next to her. It contained fresh fruit, cured meats, cheese, two bottles of rare wine, and a large box of chocolates. She prayed none of it had spoiled in the heat and realized it had been foolish to take the convertible. Feeling warm, she slowed the car, keeping one hand on the steering wheel while the other unbuttoned her jacket, exposing a pin-pleated white cotton blouse. She felt better at once and was glad for the straw fedora; it didn't match her green linen suit but kept the sun off her head. Grinding the gears, she was in the process of stopping at the gatehouse when several heavily armed guards ran out into the road in front of her.

She slammed on the brakes.

"Halt!" the men ordered redundantly, because the Mercedes was already stopped, its motor stalled and silent.

"Good morning," she said pleasantly. "Can you direct me to the Oranienburg Detention Center?" She held up a white-gloved hand to shield her eyes from the glare of the sun and, although she was staring at four pointed rifles, managed not to blink.

"Why?" one of the officers snapped.

Dorrit raised her eyebrows at his rudeness. "Why?" she repeated, dropping her hand and squinting at the ring of men surrounding her car.

"Why are you looking for it?" the same officer wanted to know.

"I'd like to visit some friends staying there."

"Who?"

"Herr Doctor Benjamin Tarnoff and his wife. I have a food basket for them." Dorrit eyed the entrance to what was a depressing compound of barracks and brick buildings. Snarling dogs ran loose among some trucks and cars parked inside the double fencing. "This obviously isn't it," she said lamely.

"Why not?"

"It doesn't look...uh, I don't know." Dorrit lost her voice. The very idea that this was a civilian center was preposterous.

"Perhaps you were expecting a spa?" The officer's lips twitched as he assured her that she had, indeed, come to the right place. With no detectable sign of irony, he added, "Welcome!"

"Thank you." Dorrit wished herself a hundred kilometers away. "I had a lot of trouble finding it," she said.

"And I'm afraid you wasted your time. You missed our visiting hours." He glanced at his wristwatch. The other officers elbowed each other. "By twenty minutes."

"Oh." Dorrit digested her bad timing in silence and was ashamed with the relief she felt. In spite of having come this far, any interest in visiting Ben and Gert inside these dismal gates had vanished. "Since I'm too late, could I trouble you to deliver this basket to the Tarnoffs?" The men exchanged looks. "It's merely some foodstuff," she said. "You're welcome to inspect it."

One of the guards stepped around to the passenger side of the convertible, reached into the hamper and poked through the contents. Dorrit saw his expression change the moment he recognized the pricey wine. "A delivery can be arranged," he said, lifting the basket from the seat.

"Thank you." Dorrit restarted the engine and the men stepped off the road, signaling she was free to go. She drove away slowly. If she had learned one thing about living in a police state, it was to never appear to be in a hurry around people in uniform. It made them suspicious.

As she put distance between herself and the gatehouse, she took heart in the pleasant vision of Gert and Ben enjoying the contents of the basket. Institutional food was bound to be tasteless. Likewise, she hoped they would enjoy reading the long letter she had enclosed among the contents. It was full of social tidbits from Berlin, her promise to tend Gert's garden, plus a description of the new doctor assigned to the clinic. Older than Abraham, he'd obviously been forced from retirement to serve the Third Reich.

Looking for an eventual cross street that would take her back on the road toward Bernau, Dorrit realized she should have made a U-turn at the gatehouse and gone back the way she came. It was too late now. She had already gone too far; besides, she had no desire to turn around and pass by those men again. She continued driving along the far side of the detention center, hoping she'd eventually come to a familiar intersection.

Chapter Fourteen

She was out of sight of the gatehouse when a reckless impulse made her pull over to the side the road. Shutting off the ignition, she got out of the car and walked across a span of neglected grass between the pavement and the camp's perimeter. There were no snarling dogs along this stretch, but coils of barbed wire made the space inside the fence just as daunting. She spotted a sign warning that trespassers would be shot but, consumed with curiosity, ignored it and kept walking in the small hope that Gert and Ben might catch a glimpse of her from somewhere inside the compound. If they saw her, perhaps they could come and meet her here at the fence. Of course, the closer she got the less she believed anyone lived in this bleak place. The men at the gatehouse had probably lied to her. Nonetheless, she continued trudging through the deep grass.

Narrowing her eyes, she stopped at the high wire fence, searching for signs of life among the barracks, when something caught her attention. At first glance, it appeared to be sacks of dry goods piled up against the wall of a building. However, when the sacks stirred, she realized it was a group of people huddling together, sharing a bench that got the full sun. She raised her hand to wave. The minute she did so, the people got to their feet and like sleepwalkers rounded a corner and disappeared from sight. Dorrit wondered why they hadn't acknowledged her and she also wondered why more people weren't out and about. Kurt had claimed the center housed hundreds of detainees. Where were they?

Deep in thought, she didn't know how long she'd been standing by the fence, but decided it was time to leave. Backing away, her hands suddenly flew out in front of her as if she'd gone blind, warding off obstacles she sensed but couldn't see. Inadvertently, she touched the fence. A jolt of electricity surged through her. The blood drained from her face and she felt herself go white, not from the shock of the current - it hadn't been sufficiently strong - something else had jarred her. For a split second, her ears had picked up the macabre cry of a hundred voices. She held her breath, still listening, but the sound was gone as abruptly as it had come, dispersed on the wind that had carried it. For endless minutes, Dorrit stood immobile, wondering if she had imagined it. Shaken, she turned and looked around.

A farmhouse opposite the road was abandoned, its windows boarded up, and no one was working in the surrounding fields. She was quite alone. Her imagination had clearly gotten the better of her. She had done a lot of driving today, taken many confusing turns; the guards back at the gatehouse further unnerving her. She was tired and she was trespassing, something the roar of an approaching vehicle underscored. A patrol car was coming along the road from the entrance to the camp. The guards? What did they want? Identification? They had not asked for any. Were they coming to remedy the lapse in security?

Dear God, I have no papers! Dorrit wrung her hands. *Why didn't I just drive straight home? I could have been far away by now.* She felt her legs go numb and much as she willed them to move, they refused. Caught in a nightmare, her feet were rooted to the ground. She tried to remember her fictional ancestry. Maiden name: *Beyer*. Place of birth: *Schoneberg*. Father's name: *Karl. No, Konrad.* Her mind struggled. Her head was spinning. *Mother's name?* Desperately trying to concentrate, she looked down at her useless limbs standing knee-deep in grass and flowers. *Flowers?* Strange that she hadn't noticed them before because they were everywhere. Daisies, wild phlox, and yellow buttercups proliferated among the tall grasses, their cheerful colors taunting the inauspicious surroundings, their sturdy stems mocking her spine gone soft.

She bent down to pull at a few, if only because she needed an activity to keep from panicking. Besides, people might be shot for trespassing but not, as far as she knew, for picking flowers. Adopting a slow gait while gathering flora as if she didn't have a care in the world, Dorrit headed back toward her car, which suddenly seemed so far away. She couldn't recall having walked this far, and never before had a patch of grass been so difficult to cross. Each blade was a sinewy tentacle clinging to her feet and each step required a Herculean effort. She prayed the patrol was on a routine mission and not out looking for her. Had they found and opened her letter to the Tarnoffs? Had she written anything that might be considered sensitive?

With as many flowers as her jittery hands could hold, Dorrit reached the Mercedes, got in behind the wheel, threw the bouquet across her purse lying on the passenger seat, and adjusted her hat in the rearview mirror. It would look suspicious to speed away. The best thing to do now was to remain calm, remember to smile and, in the event they stopped, greet them with a respectful, "Heil Hitler!"

Chapter Fifteen

A long black sedan with Nazi banners flying on each side of the shiny hood slowed down as it came alongside Dorrit.

Gestapo! Dear God! The guards at the gatehouse were boy scouts compared to the secret police and, frantic to escape, Dorrit turned the key in the ignition. The well-tuned engine started immediately, its vibration covering her trembling nicely. But before she could drive off, the black vehicle had made a U-turn and come to a stop diagonally across the roadway, blocking her. The sound of its motor being shut off screamed at her. Never before had she felt so alone, so helpless, and so stupid. Kurt's words: don't draw attention to yourself, reverberated in her brain while hot flashes engulfed her, turning her complexion bright red. Beads of perspiration popped out on her forehead but sheer terror kept her from reaching under the flowers for her purse and some face powder.

The driver remained in place while the two officers riding in the rear seats stepped from the car. Dorrit's throat closed, she might as well have swallowed a bone. Breathless, she watched the black uniforms - pistols holstered in shiny leather belts - walk towards her, now stationing themselves on opposite sides of the Mercedes. The one who came to the driver's side was a heavyset, dough-faced man, his bulk blocking the sun and casting a shadow over Dorrit, enabling her to look at him without squinting. She detected no hair under his hat emblazoned with the eagle emblem, a swastika in its claws.

"Heil Hitler!" she said, raising her white-gloved hand like a flag of surrender, her lips trembling with the spasms of a forced smile.

"Sieg Heil!" He gestured for her to turn off the engine.

Her hand fumbled with the key. The motor died.

"Pleasant weather," he said, stone faced and without taking his eyes off her.

Dorrit wondered how an amiable comment could sound so sinister, but was happy to agree with him. “Yes, it's a delightful day,” she said, doing her utmost to keep a beguiling expression on her face. “It's nice to drive with the top down.” She knew the weather was the last thing he wished to discuss; however, since he had introduced it and since it was such a safe topic she was glad to prolong it. “They say we can expect more of the same tomorrow.” She kept smiling, her cheeks hurting with the effort.

“Perfect for taking photographs.” He pulled at his black leather gloves, removing them, a signal that could only mean search and seizure.

Dorrit swallowed. “Photographs?” she said in a tight voice.

“You left a basket at the gatehouse. I’m sure you’d like to have a souvenir picture in return. Don’t you carry a camera?”

Dorrit shook her head. “I’m not very good with the mechanics.”

“Mind if we take a look?” This was not a question but a demand. The officer opened her door, motioning her out while his partner leaned into the car on the other side, feeling around the back seats.

Standing on the gravel, Dorrit watched the heavyset officer open the trunk while the other man, having finished with the back seats, was now going for the privacy of the glove box. Outrage curled her lips but she kept silent; indeed, she couldn’t speak because only inches away her pocketbook without the required documents lay under the flowers and was bound to be examined next. Discovering that she carried no government-issued identification, a strict violation of the law, these men would rake her over the coals until her “good citizen” status could be established to their satisfaction. *Or not!* Her fear escalating, she couldn’t remember Herr Beyer’s first name. Her mind frozen, she watched the officer sift through the glove box, crushing the flowers in the process, when a sudden inspiration struck her.

“Oh, my poor bouquet!” she cried.

The man shut the glove box and looked on the verge of apologizing for flattening the flora, but didn’t, and as he shifted his weight to exit the car, Dorrit quickly leaned in and reached across the driver’s seat to spread out the damaged blooms as if to revive them, when, in fact, she was only making sure that her purse remained covered, out of sight, out of mind.

“The daisies were so lovely and fresh,” she lamented, hoping to further distract the men with chatter. “I saw the flowers along the road and couldn't resist stopping to pick some. My neighbor is ill and I had hoped they’d cheer her. The poor soul has suffered with grippe all winter. Even now, despite the wonderful weather, she is no better. She hasn't been able to get out into her garden and she's such a horticulture enthusiast. I felt sure these lovely wildflowers would give her a lift. The buttercups are small and delicate and, once picked, won’t last long but they add a pretty splash of yellow. Don’t you agree?” The officers, now running their hands under the car’s fenders, ignored her. “Oh, dear,” Dorrit sighed dramatically. “The phlox are terribly bruised. I don't suppose they can be salvaged. But at least the daisies seem to be all right. Their petals are sturdy.”

Both men finally came to the same conclusion: there was no camera or other *verboten* paraphernalia in the car. This silly and irksome woman had gathered flowers, not pictures. Determined not to waste any more time, they executed a sharp "Heil Hitler!" turned and walked back to their car. Dorrit heard them tell their driver to back up and allow her access to the road.

Lightheaded with her escape, she climbed in behind the wheel and started the engine; her hand on the key shook, but the motor idled smoothly. She put the car in gear, pulled away slowly and remembered to wave in a friendly fashion as she passed the officers. After a few minutes of driving, she glanced into the rear view mirror and saw them head back in the direction from whence they’d come. Still going at a deliberately slow speed, Dorrit looked over her shoulder toward the detention center. Thick black smoke was spewing from one of the tall chimneys on a large brick structure. She concluded it was an industrial site. The people huddled on the bench were workers taking a break in the sun. This was probably one of those secret ammunition factories, which would explain the dogs and the Gestapo. Kurt had been wrong. People were not housed here. The guards at the gatehouse had taken her for a fool and divided the contents of the basket.

Still shaken by her encounter with the Gestapo, she reached for the crushed bouquet. Intimidation is a powerful tool, she ruminated bitterly, the dominance of anyone in that black uniform is terrifying. She pledged never again to bruise herself against the impenetrable Nazi armor. She must not attempt to visit the Tarnoffs. In that respect, Kurt was right. She must be patient and wait for them to be released.

She flung the flowers from the car. The wind caught them,

depositing the colorful blooms over a stretch of upturned brown soil, leaving Dorrit with a vague but haunting feeling that she had just tossed flowers across a grave.

Chapter Sixteen

Several weeks after her ill-fated trip to Oranienburg, Dorrit again asked Kurt about Ben and Gert. Without disclosing that she had tried to visit, she fabricated a small lie, telling him that her letters were being returned, making her believe the Tarnoffs were not at the place he'd mentioned. Kurt promised to check further but had sounded so tired that she didn't remind him about the documentation she also needed.

In order to close the subject and put an end to her queries, Kurt eventually told Dorrit some convoluted half-truths regarding Ben and Gert. However, he no longer dared use the telephone for anything other than mundane conversations. Their first opportunity to speak privately came during a dinner party at the von Steigerts' villa in Wannsee. As the meal concluded and everyone left the dining room for the salon, he pulled Dorrit aside.

"Oranienburg became too crowded," he whispered hurriedly once the room had emptied. "Ben and Gertrude were moved to a center in Treblinka in Poland where they succumbed to an influenza epidemic that devastated the camp shortly after they arrived."

"Are you telling me they…they are d...dead?"

"Yes. But please know that they spent their last days in a cheerful place."

Cheerful? Dorrit cried inwardly; why did Kurt persist in using that word? "How can living in a camp against one's will be cheerful?" she moaned behind her hands. "I wish I'd known. I could have done something."

"There was nothing you or anyone could do." A maid came in to clear the table. It was no longer safe to talk. Kurt took Dorrit's arm and left the room. "For God's sake," he whispered, noting her pallor as they crossed the hall to join the others in the salon. "The Tarnoffs were old.

They lived a long life. Much younger people die of influenza. You've got to pull yourself together. Come on, now! Smile! Don't give anyone reason to wonder about our conversation. We must never talk about Ben and Gert again. It's dangerous for both of us. Do I make myself clear?"

"Y...yes."

"Good. So, give me a smile."

Although her heart ached, Dorrit did her best to hide her anguish as she entered the glittering salon. She knew she had to be careful. Kurt was not the only Nazi official among the von Steigert's guests tonight. Anna's brother, Georg Schellenberg, was now a high-ranking officer of the Third Reich as well. He had pursued Dorrit in the years after she was widowed, but she had always kept him at arm's length. Lately, she often wondered if he might be carrying a grudge and be motivated to investigate her roots now that he had the power to do so? Knowing he would be at this dinner, it had bothered her, which was why she was relieved when she saw him arrive with a svelte and much younger woman on his arm. He appeared to be completely smitten with this platinum blonde in a tightly draped black satin dress adorned with four rows of fake pearls and the predictable Nazi pin fastened over her heart. The woman was friendly but extremely nosy and had cornered Dorrit during the first part of the evening with personal questions not warranted for an initial meeting. Wondering if her curiosity was due to her youth, ill manners, or the nefarious Nazi inquisitiveness, Dorrit struggled to be evasive until from across the room, Anna, bless her, sensed a problem and came to the rescue.

With her flair for frivolity and no fondness for Nazis, Anna interjected herself into the conversation, chatting about nothing in particular before telling her brother's new lady friend that she and Dorrit both planned to join the Nazi Women's League as soon as a chapter opened in their suburban neighborhood. "We hope Grunewald and Wannsee will incorporate so we can be in the same chapter," she said, putting her arm around Dorrit's waist. "Of course if the organization keeps dragging its feet, we will have to take matters into our own hands and start one by ourselves. We are impatient to be wearing one of those." Anna reached out to touch the younger woman's Nazi badge, pretending to admire it.

"We can ask Lillian about the requirements," Dorrit added for good measure. "She'll know. She organized the Charlottenburg Chapter."

Chapter Seventeen

Following Germany's swift and brazen occupation of Belgium, Luxembourg, Holland, Denmark, and Norway, the United States grew concerned about Herr Hitler's designs on Europe and asked him for a formal guarantee of peaceful intentions.

"I am a peace loving man," the German chancellor answered President Roosevelt. "Not a warmonger!"

However, by summer of 1941, seventy-five percent of Hitler's strength was massing along the eastern front. Already locked in battles with both France and Great Britain, the German Fuehrer was soon to declared war on the United States as well.

Daily life in Berlin continued as before. The last war had not been fought on home soil and expecting much of the same this time around, people went about their normal routines of work and pleasure. The occasional testing of an air-raid siren became an inconvenience, but everyone accepted the trips below ground with good humor and bomb shelter jokes became the standard fare in nightclubs. However, the jokes stopped when some British explosives fell on Potsdam, the garrison town outside Berlin. Nobody had expected the Allies to perfect a bomber capable of flying the round trip without refueling. Herr Goebbels' radio broadcasts claimed such flights were impossible. "Our proud capital is safe and will remain untouched by war," he promised regularly, doing so again after the damage in Potsdam.

In October Lisbet gave birth to another daughter. They named her Arina, a name that had come to Lisbet's attention on a late August day in Bernau when she and Dorrit sat alone on the terrace. Max and Cassandra had left on the train early that morning, returning to their archaeological dig in Turkey. Nurse Heller had taken Sigrid and Karoline to the river beach for a swim, and Fritz and Peter were riding.

In the lull of that quiet afternoon, Dorrit soon became talkative, delving into her past, revealing her mother's short and tragic life and that of the Romanov prince. She told Lisbet of Herman Tzacheroff's fears and his constant need to move. This account of star-crossed lovers and family secrets appealed to Lisbet's sense of drama. She immediately declared that if her next child was a girl, she would be named after Dorrit's mother. In October, when a baby girl arrived, Lisbet kept her word.

Arina had blue eyes and a head that was soon covered by blond hair. Everyone agreed that she favored Lisbet in appearance, whereas Karoline took after Fritz. She had his gray eyes and dark hair and it soon became apparent that she shared his quiet intellect as well.

Fritz loved his small daughters with a devotion that saw no bounds. Unlike other males of his class, he was not above strolling in Berlin's parks with the baby carriage or shopping with the four-year-old Karoline in the children's boutiques on Tauentzienstrasse, where he bought her outrageously expensive dresses and impractical satin shoes. Admittedly, he had time on his hands for, although he managed to retain his post at the university, in December he was severed from the Berlin Zeitung when, in one of his articles, he suggested that history demonstrated violent dictators rarely enjoy long careers. He had carefully woven this commentary into his film review of a foreign war drama, but apparently not carefully enough because the editorial watchdogs rejected the piece and handed him his walking papers. Inadvertently, they probably saved him from a worse fate. Had his commentary been published, it would have been noted by the regime.

Chapter Eighteen

Something else must have come to the their attention, however, because a month later on a January night in 1942, from his library off the center hall in the apartment on Uhland Strasse where he and Lisbet had lived since their marriage, Fritz suddenly heard heavy boots storming up the stairwell. This was an elegant three-story building in Charlottenburg within walking distance of the Kurfurstendamm, and its tenants were respectable people who valued peace and quiet. The unusual noise late in the evening signaled a warning and heeding it, Fritz quickly gathered together the manuscript he was working on, stuffing the pages into a secret compartment behind the middle drawer of his desk. He checked his watch. It was past midnight. That fit. Nazi patrols usually did their dirty work at night. When the sound of boots continued past the second floor, Fritz realized that unless Count Golovkin in the loft apartment above him had come under surveillance, the von Renz flat was about to be searched.

He jammed the hidden compartment shut, closed the drawer in front of it and left the key in place so it would appear accessible and therefore less suspicious. Turning off the desk lamp, he left the study, wondering where he had slipped up. Had a sales clerk at the stationery store reported his purchases? Paper was getting scarce and expensive. Anyone who bought more than a few sheets at a time might be a writer and, for that reason alone, be suspect.

Tying the belt of his black kimono, Fritz ran across the dark hall and down the corridor toward the bedrooms. The doors to the children's rooms and that of their nanny were closed. He hoped they would not be disturbed. Lisbet would no doubt be roused. He entered the bedroom, saw she was sleeping soundly, and quickly ruffled his side of the bed so it'd look as though he'd been sleeping as well. Placing himself in the doorway, he held his breath and listened.

When there was a hard rap on the door, Fritz remained in place, waiting for another knock so it would appear that they woke him. Once the hammering began anew, he slowly made his way along the corridor to the hall. Crossing the foyer, he tousled his hair and cursed at being disturbed in the middle of the night - a natural reaction, one the SS would expect.

"This is a hell of time for visitors," he groused, deliberately shuffling his feet as he approached the door.

"Open up!"

"Huh? What?" Fritz feigned surprise. "Who is it?"

"Police! Open up!"

Fritz switched on the hall chandelier and raised his eyebrows in a questioning arch as he opened the door. "What's the meaning of this?" he asked, squinting against the harsh light in the stairwell.

Without being invited to do so, four SS officers filed into the apartment, forcing him backwards. He closed the door behind them and spread his hands. "What's the problem, gentlemen?" He did a good imitation of stifling a yawn. "Trouble in the building? A burglary?"

Without answering, two of the men stationed themselves in the hall on either side of Fritz while the other two fanned out into the apartment, starting with the library. They switched on the ceiling lights and began pulling books from the bookcases; apparently believing something was hidden behind the stacks. *Amateurs*, Fritz reflected with a wry twist on his lips. *These fellows have read too many detective novels.* He continued watching as they emptied the shelves, throwing books onto the sofa, some missing their mark and falling to the floor in loud thuds.

"Please," he took several steps toward the study, "my wife and children are asleep and I'd like them to remain so. What are you looking for?"

There was no response from the officers, but one of the men in the hall drew his weapon, aimed it at Fritz, and motioned him back. Fritz retraced his steps, thinking that this was another low point for the regime: holding people at gunpoint while officers of the law ransacked their homes.

An instant later his heart stopped. Having finished with the bookcases, the men were now going through his desk, opening each drawer and emptying the contents onto the floor. Shivers ran up Fritz's spine, not from the gun pointed at him but because he feared that the old desk, a delicate French antique with a number of authentic worm holes, might choose this very moment to weaken at the joints and give up its secret. With a painful pounding near his temples, he tried to visualize every step he'd taken as he stuffed the manuscript away. He tried to remember if the slat across the hidden compartment had clicked as he stowed it. Was it flush with the sides? Was a sliver of paper showing through a crack? If the officers found his work he was a dead man. It was entirely possibly that they would use a silencer and shoot him right here on the spot, place the gun in his hand and call it a suicide; their favorite modus operandi. If Lisbet woke up, they would kill her as well and conveniently report a murder-suicide. Nadia, the children's teenaged nanny, a recently imported worker from the Ukraine, would be questioned. If she refused to support their theory, she'd be diagnosed with dementia or assigned to a labor camp. Because of their tender ages, the children would be spared and sent to a government-sanctioned foster family where they would be indoctrinated as good little Nazis. Not a pretty picture, but a factual one. Fritz knew the ways of a police state. He had made it his business to know, and all this condemning information was stored within inches of these SS officers.

Chapter Nineteen

Several minutes passed. The desk kept its secret. Without realizing that he had been holding his breath, Fritz exhaled. The air felt cold as it left his lungs, such was the intensity of his fear.

Finished in the library the men crossed the foyer, took a sweep of the living room and dining room before walking down the hall toward the bedrooms, where Lisbet could be heard shrieking as lights went on. A moment later, she came running into the hall, barefooted, with a silver-blue satin robe thrown over her shoulders.

"Fritz! What's going on?" she cried, seeing him flanked by two officers, one pointing a pistol. She ran her hands through her blond hair in a frantic gesture and as she did so her dressing gown dropped away, displaying a full view of her skimpy pink negligee. Quick as the wind, she bent down, picked up the robe, thrust her arms into the sleeves, and fastened the sash securely around her waist with a double knot.

Eyeing her, one of the officers in the hall licked his lips. This woman was a delicious morsel. Shapely, she was exceptionally pretty despite being awakened from sleep. Under the same circumstances his own wife would look about as attractive as a boiled potato.

"Mama! Mama!" Karoline could now be heard wailing.

Lisbet realized that the officers were in the nursery. *Of all the nerve!* Anger flushed her face as she flew down the hall, coming back a moment later with Arina in her arms. Nadia, in a flannel nightgown, trotted behind her, holding Karoline by the hand. Dressed in red pajamas and clutching her teddy bear, Karoline was rubbing her nose and looking around the hall, confused. The minute her eyes adjusted to the light and she saw the man pointing a gun at her papa, she screamed, pulled away from Nadia, dropped her teddy bear and ran to him, anchoring herself to his legs. Fritz bent down, pried her loose, and picked her up.

To his credit, the officer saw no reason to scare the child and put his weapon away.

Holding Karoline against his chest, Fritz whispered in her ear. “Don’t be afraid. These men won’t hurt you. They won’t bother us for long. They’ll be gone in a minute. Then we’ll all go back to bed.”

“What do they want, Papa?”

“I have no idea, sweetheart.” Fritz was immensely glad that no one in his family knew about the manuscript, no facial expression, no unguarded word, would doom anyone. Even so, he was deeply sorry for what he was putting them through. These men were obviously after something having to do with his profession as a writer. Journalists without Nazi party membership were suspect, even those who were no longer published. Had his last article, followed by his severance from the Zeitung, been analyzed anew?

After her initial outburst, Lisbet remained uncharacteristically quiet. She picked up the teddy bear from the floor, holding it and Arina while listening stoically as the children’s room was torn apart. When a lamp crashed to the floor, she bristled, communicating her anger to Arina. The baby set up a loud and persistent wail and when she became impossible to console, Lisbet told the officers in the foyer that she needed to go to the kitchen to warm up a bottle of milk. One of the men stepped forward to accompany her. Trying to ignore him, she headed for the kitchen, motioning Nadia to come along.

“Not the girl!” the officer said. “And not the child! Both will stay here.” When Lisbet hesitated, he pulled Arina from her arms, handing her to Nadia, who immediately shrank into a corner of the hall where she found solace with the baby in the shadow of the tall grandfather’s clock.

Lisbet gave the man an icy stare, put the teddy bear down on the hall table, tossed her mop of sleep-crushed curls, and marched toward the dark kitchen. The officer who had assigned himself as her escort, followed. He was a lanky, redheaded man with thin lips and rimless glasses riding low on his nose.

Switching on the kitchen light, Lisbet took the milk from the cold storage cabinet, lit the gas burner, and reached for a clean baby bottle on a shelf above the sink. She was pouring the milk into a pan, when the officer sidled closer than he ought and reached out to caress her elbow, moving his hand up her arm.

"You're a pretty little *hausfrau*," he said. "So blond and..."

"Get your hands off me!" she hissed, pushing him backwards with such force that his shoulder banged into a cabinet, rattling the dishes and setting his eyeglasses askew.

A second later, Fritz was in the doorway. "What's going on?" he barked, his eyes livid.

The man adjusted his glasses, rotated his bruised shoulder, scowled but didn't answer. He was not obligated to explain himself. Besides, his partner appeared, weapon drawn, and ordered everyone out of the kitchen. Still rotating his shoulder, the lanky officer took out his anger on Fritz, roughly shoving him ahead of the pack.

The one holding the gun followed behind Lisbet. "So much for trying to accommodate you," he sneered at her back. "I will have to report your unfortunate attack on a uniformed officer."

Lisbet turned around. "I trust your report will include his lecherous attack on me! His behavior is a disgrace to the uniform. And you dare call yourselves..."

The man raised his arm, poised to strike her. Fritz turned, dodged past the other officer and dove into the man, toppling him and sending the revolver sliding across the floor. However, his victory was short-lived. The lanky officer picked up the wayward weapon and, showing surprising strength for such a thin man, pulled Fritz off his partner, ramming the butt of the gun into his chest with such force it knocked the wind out of him. Gasping, Fritz leaned against the wall, willpower alone keeping him upright; he was not about to give these men the satisfaction of seeing him lie crumpled on the floor.

Having heard the scuffle, Karoline came running and clawed at her father's legs. Still fighting for breath, wondering if the officer had cracked some ribs, Fritz didn't have the strength to lift her. He simply took her hand as they all now made their way back to the foyer, where Lisbet told Karoline to go over to the corner where Nadia was still huddled against the grandfather's clock, humming melodies from her homeland, which she regularly did when upset. The Ukrainian folk songs consoled her and tonight had a calming influence on both children as well. Although Nadia's falsetto voice generally irritated Lisbet, at the moment she was grateful.

Chapter Twenty

With a temporary peace restored in the hall, Lisbet walked over to Fritz, his arm wrapping around her as she leaned her head into his shoulder. Neither one spoke. Fritz drew short, shallow breaths against the sharp pain around his ribcage.

A moment later Lisbet's nostrils flared as she detected the smell of burnt milk coming from the kitchen. During the melee, she had forgotten to turn off the burner and was about to say something to the officers before deciding against it. She didn't want to chance going down the hall again with that lecher. Besides, maybe the vile smell would encourage the men to leave.

Having completed their search of the bedrooms, the two senior officers came back into the front hall and gave their colleagues an unpleasant look. They had heard the fracas, considered it unprofessional, but said nothing - the SS never reprimanded each other in public. Fritz saw that one of them was holding three government identification documents, which meant they had gone into Lisbet's purse and into his wallet he'd left on top of the dresser. The third document was obviously Nadia's. He was not surprised. Their search had been thorough. Nothing was off limits to the Schutz-Staffel.

"Your papers appear to be in order," the officer said, handing back the cards. Lisbet and Fritz took theirs without a word. Nadia curtsied and thanked him. She was young. Her fear of these men made her obeisant.

Without a hint as to why this nighttime raid had taken place, the men left, filing quietly out the door and down the stairs as if suddenly aware of the hour and the fact that the building was home to other tenants.

Before closing the door behind them, Fritz detected several discreet clicks as doors on the floors below were secured; their neighbors had obviously tried to listen to the commotion. Except for Count Golovkin, a womanizer around Berlin, who, as it happened, was returning home after a night on the town. Making his way up the stairs to his garret apartment with a voluptuous woman on his arm, he tipped his hat to the departing officers and bid them a pleasant evening.

Lisbet sent Nadia to the kitchen to turn off the burner and soak the scorched pot while she put the children back to bed. Thumb in mouth, Arina settled down easily enough, but Karoline was full of questions.

"Why were the men so mean?" she wanted to know.

"I don't know," Lisbet said, tired, as she picked up the cracked lamp from the floor. "No more questions tonight, sweetheart. We'll talk about it in the morning. The men are gone now. There's nothing more to worry about." As she tucked in the blankets around Karoline, she mumbled a few more reassuring words and, leaving a small light burning, left the nursery. She, too, was puzzled as to why the apartment was searched and hoped Fritz had an explanation. Lisbet found him in the study where he was putting books back on the shelves.

"They sure made a mess," she said, stopping in the doorway, hands on hips, surveying the room. "Do you have any idea why? Could it have anything to do with your severance from the Zeitung? Your last article?"

"Maybe," Fritz said as his eyes flicked guiltily across his desk. "My guess is that the search was a mistake. The officers probably had the wrong address. I hear people are regularly inconvenienced like this. It's not at all uncommon."

"Well, it sure is a nuisance. Not to mention extremely scary for the children. Karoline in particular."

"Yes. I'm very sorry about that. I will talk with her in the morning. Hopefully she won't have nightmares."

"How about you? That thug hit you pretty hard." Lisbet walked over and slipped her hands into his robe. "Is it painful?" She ran her fingers across his chest.

"No," he lied, swallowing the sharp sting as her hands exerted pressure where the handle of the revolver had hit home. His arms closed about her and, kissing the top of her head, he dismissed all discomfort.

Lisbet lifted her face up to him, thinking how bravely he had tackled that officer, ignoring his firepower and the license to use it. "Are you coming back to bed?" she whispered against his lips. "We can straighten up tomorrow."

"I'll be there in a minute, darling. I just want to put a few things away. Don't wait up for me."

"All right." Lisbet left the study, shaking her head at the upended drawers. Going back to the kitchen, she told Nadia to go to bed and, despite the raw January night, opened a window to air-out the place.

Fritz stayed in the library until he knew that both Lisbet and Nadia were asleep. He also knew that he could no longer work on his manuscript. The officers had missed the hidden compartment, an outright miracle, and he was not naive enough to think that he would be granted another. He was under suspicion. They would be back.

He sat down at the desk, contemplating how he might smuggle his work out of the country. He thought about bringing his manuscript to Lisbet's family in Denmark. Of course, border guards were wise to people attempting to get *verboten* material out of Germany. Travelers were searched, so was mail. Therefore, sending his work to his friend, Robert Grantham, for safekeeping in America was equally impossible. Besides, Robert was in the Air Force, Germany was at war with the United States, and Fritz had no idea where he was stationed. Even if he mailed a few pages at a time to Linda, or to the senior Granthams in Chicago, the envelopes would be opened and read by postal inspectors. His arrest would follow.

With a heavy heart Fritz started a small blaze in the fireplace and carefully began to burn six hundred pages of critical material he had worked on for four years.

Chapter Twenty-one

"Hey, Max!" Ernst Horstmann shouted from the open car as he brought the battered Citroen to a halt in a plume of dust at the edge of the excavation site. "Telegram!"

Ernst was returning from Istanbul where he had gone early this morning to pick up the week's mail. Setting the hand brake securely, he swung his legs over the door, hoisting himself from the convertible; its door had gotten stuck weeks ago and no one was motivated to force it open because it might never close again. Holding the telegram aloft, he walked over to Max bending over an unearthed two thousand-year-old wine vessel. This dig, some thirty kilometers northeast of Istanbul, had yielded remnants of an ancient village with several well-preserved homesteads and was considered such a rare find that the activities of Herr Doctor Ernst Horstmann and Herr Baron Doctor Maximilian von Renz, were regularly chronicled in the international press. Not only because of their important discovery but because a team of international archaeologists remained committed to the project despite the fact that their countries were locked in bitter battles with the Third Reich, a detail everyone on the dig managed to ignore.

Surprised by Ernst's unusual *joie de vivre*, Max stepped out from under the canopy, wiping dust from his hands, his eyes squinting against the relentless sun. There had been no rain in this part of Turkey for months. The papers predicted the spring of '42 would go down as the driest on record. Local growers wrung their hands and kept their eyes on the sky.

"Since when is a telegram a *cause celebre?*" Max frowned at his colleague's odd behavior. A constant companion since their student days at Heidelberg, Ernst was known for calm and level headedness; he never shouted or waved his hands.

"When it's from Berlin."

"A telegram from Berlin?" Cassandra walked out from under an adjacent awning where she'd been categorizing artifacts. She twisted her black hair into a knot and reached for a safari hat hanging from a tent pole, stuffing her hair into the bowl of the hat.

"I see you wasted no time opening it." Max snatched the telegram from Ernst. The seal was broken.

"Who's it from?" For an instant, Cassandra shivered under the blistering sun, remembering the scarlet fever Dorrit had not told them about until after Sigrid recovered. "Is it from your mother?" she asked, her dark eyes wide with concern.

"No, darling. It's from..."

"The chancellor's office. The big *brown shirt* himself!" Ernst said before turning to holler across the excavation site. "Mail's here!" he announced loudly and reached into the car for a sack of letters as colleagues and staff began milling about.

Max pulled a handkerchief from his pocket and wiped at the perspiration around his neck as he read the telegram. The heat was unbearable. He stepped back under the canopy to avoid the sun. Cassandra and Ernst followed.

"So, what does it say?" Ernst wanted to know. He had not opened it. That honor went to an over-zealous postal examiner who felt that even a wire from the Reich Chancellery needed to be scrutinized. "You been drafted?"

"God, I hope not. Besides, wouldn't an induction notice come from the War Ministry?"

"Yes, I guess it would. So what does Berlin want if it's not war related?"

"It doesn't say. It only says that I'm to meet with the chancellor at ten-thirty on the morning of April 22nd. And that I'm to report in uniform."

"In *uniform?*" Cassandra frowned. "Why?"

"It's a new dress code Herr Hitler insists on for those serving in any capacity he considers important." Max stuffed the telegram into his pocket. "How about we both go to Berlin and spend a few days with the family."

While that suggestion pleased Cassandra, the idea of Max in uniform troubled her, and she hoped the sudden summons to Berlin wasn't the first step in some new induction process. It was common knowledge that the military was expanding the eligibility age. Max was thirty-nine. Perhaps he was no longer safe?

Ernst suddenly remembered a package and went back to the car, leaning into the back seat, reaching for a flat box he'd picked up at the post office along with the mail. "This must be your uniform," he said, handing it to Max. "I wonder how they got your size?"

Chapter Twenty-two

At precisely ten o'clock on April the twenty-second, Max walked into the Reichskanzlei on Wilhelm Strasse in Berlin and presented his credentials to the agents in the reception rotunda. His appointment with the Fuehrer was not until ten-thirty but he'd been told to arrive early. After the guards checked his papers, he was escorted to a waiting area on the second floor where he sat down among various individuals with official business at the Chancellery.

Shortly, a slim, uniformed woman approached him. "Our Fuehrer will see you now," she said with a pretty smile. Max's tall, blond good looks weren't lost on her and among the assortment of seated men, all similarly dressed, he looked particularly stunning in the loden green uniform.

Max got to his feet, put his hat in the crook of his arm and followed her down a corridor guarded at twenty-foot intervals by armed military personnel. After his identification was again checked, he was ushered into a cavernous hall. The door closed behind him. An aide-de-camp stepped forward, pointing him toward a desk at the far end where Herr Hitler, flanked by two Nazi banners, sat dwarfed in the vast chamber. Crossing the expanse of black marble, Max recognized Herr Albert Speer - Berlin's official architect - seated in one of the upholstered chairs grouped in a circle to the right of the Fuehrer. Herr Speer was dressed in a uniform similar to the one Max was wearing.

Narrowing his eyes, scrutinizing the archaeologist coming into view, Herr Hitler pushed at the limp brown hair falling across his forehead. He noted with satisfaction that this scientist was extremely Aryan in appearance. He had read the complete file on Maximilian Johannes von Renz, and the information pleased him. Still, some questions remained regarding the origins of the man's mother; nothing could be found on her, which was unusual. But, inasmuch as the Baroness was listed in the social register dating back to the days of Kaiser Wilhelm II, and in view of the fact that his own diary showed he had met her early in his administration, where she was presented by a member of his inner circle, Herr Doctor Kurt Eckart, her genealogy was considered pure until proven otherwise.

"It's a pleasure to see you," Herr Hitler said, reached across the desk to shake Max's hand and waved Albert Speer over. Once a round of courtesies was dispensed with, the Fuehrer indicated both men take the seats facing his desk. "You're probably wondering why you've been summoned," he said, directing himself to Max and again pushing at the flap of hair that fell across his forehead.

"Yes," Max acknowledged with a nod. The telegram had not been specific, something he ascribed to the regime's fondness for secrecy.

"Your work in Turkey, and the fact that you are personally funding the bulk of the operation, has come to my attention." Herr Hitler leaned forward, putting his elbows on the desk. "I congratulate you on your selfless dedication and your brilliant career. Both reflect well on the Fatherland."

"Thank you." Along with being told to arrive early, Max had been instructed to keep his comments brief.

Herr Hitler pursed his lips. "Of course, it has also come to my attention that foreigners are involved in your excavation. I'll have to ask you to limit yourself to German scientists. Clearly, only Germans should be working on a German project." Herr Hitler consulted a sheet on his desk. "You'll have to replace these foreigners." He brushed his hand dismissively across a list of Max's colleagues. "You can leave an Italian or two on your team. Italy is one of our allies. But get rid of the British and the French. Their scientists can't be trusted and could, in fact, be sabotaging your work."

Keeping his eyes on Herr Hitler, Max fashioned a congenial expression, hoping it'd pass for an acceptable response, not necessarily one of agreement. He had no intention of letting any colleague go.

"Only Germans, can be at the forefront of our scientific endeavors," Herr Hitler pressed on. "The world must bow to our superiority. We are the leaders. We set the standards by which others measure themselves. Our achievements will soon be the envy of the entire planet and must not be diluted by foreign blood. To showcase our mastery, I have commissioned Herr Speer to design a large exhibition hall. A new museum for our proud *Hauptstadt* where we will display our latest triumphs."

Max smiled respectfully at the architect. "I have studied your designs in the Berlin papers delivered to us in Istanbul. They are very impressive."

"Thank you." Albert Speer said.

"The new museum I speak of will house archaeological treasures," Herr Hitler went on. "It's a science that fascinates me. Our Pergamon Museum is devoted to the ancient altar from the Terrasse der Akropolis. This new museum will house artifacts from the Valley of the Kings. The entire collection from Tutankhamen's Tomb will have a permanent home in Berlin. I hear you have some excellent connections in Egypt."

"Yes. I worked closely with Howard Carter, the late British Egyptologist. I was able to bring several of Tutankhamen's effects to Berlin on loan in 1931 and…"

"I saw the exhibits," Herr Hitler interrupted and Max realized the warning about keeping one's comments brief was to be taken seriously. "The collection was incomplete. Archaeology fascinates me. Incomplete exhibitions do not. Germany does not want a little of this and a little of that." Growing agitated, Herr Hitler again pushed at his hair; it promptly fell back across his forehead like a gentle slap.

"Very well. I will petition for a larger display," Max offered in a bid to calm the Fuehrer.

"*Petition?* You will *insist!* You must demand a complete and permanent display." Herr Hitler brought his hand down hard on the desk. "As a German scientist you hold a club over your foreign colleagues. By nature they are your inferiors."

"I don't believe a permanent display is possible," Max said quietly. "The artifacts belong to the Egyptian government."

Herr Hitler looked at him with controlled irritation. "In 1918 our enemies wasted no time seizing German colonies and the riches contained within them. Long after the armistice they continued to rob us blind. When they laid claim to our Ruhr district, they denied us our very livelihood. Repercussions lasted for two decades. Surely, you are not too young to remember the hardships?"

Max remembered but failed to make the comparison. "I will ask Egypt to loan us the entire collection."

"*Loan?* I thought I made myself clear. We don't ask for loans." Herr

Hitler spoke sharply before shrugging wearily and lowering his voice. “Anyway it’s academic. Once Egypt is annexed to the Third Reich the artifacts will belong to us. In the meantime I will make certain that your work experiences no war-related interruptions. Let no one say that our intellectual community is stymied because of the international hostilities foisted upon us. Despite the aggression from our neighbors your work will continue. The talent of the German people will not be stopped. Therefore, I have selected a number of distinguished scientists for unrestricted travel and petrol purchasing privileges. I understand you have a car.” Max nodded. “Good. Our enemies have threatened to disrupt our rail network and I suppose they'll manage to irritate us now and again. But automobile travel will remain reliable. Our roads are indestructible and are being expanded to transverse the entire continent.”

The Fuehrer unfolded a document and, dipping a gold pen into the inkwell, signed it. After blotting and refolding it, he put it into an envelope along with gasoline vouchers. Pushing the packet across the desk toward Max, he said, “My signature on the document exempts you from military conscription. The uniform you are wearing proves you are serving the Fatherland.”

As Max was putting the documents into the breast pocket of his uniform, Herr Hitler rose from his chair and forgave him the naive remark about borrowing Tutankhamen’s treasures; after all, scientists were not military men familiar with the spoils of war. He walked over to a roll of blueprints on a table nearby. “Now, let's look at these new designs,” he said. “Herr Speer needs your input on the halls that will house the collection from Luxor.”

Chapter Twenty-three

There was no leisure in Bernau during the summer of '42. Age and arthritis forced Klausen into retirement, the last of the field hands left for military duty, and the remaining maids took employment in a new munitions factory near Ladeburg. This left Dorrit and Lisbet to shoulder the household chores alone because Nurse Heller announced that she was not hired as a cook or a chambermaid. Dorrit should have fired her on the spot but an employee with haughty airs was better than none. Sigrid no longer needed a nurse, of course, but Dorrit felt that Karoline and Arina could benefit from the added supervision. Their nanny, Nadia, was only sixteen, and though she was known to be moody and withdrawn in Berlin, summering in the country seemed to agree with her. Dorrit and Lisbet noticed the change immediately when Nadia happily took on more than her share of the chores.

Each morning she ran eagerly to the orchards to pick the ripe fruit before the birds pecked at it. Next, she got Karoline and Arina out of bed and dressed. By the time the rest of the household stirred, she had prepared breakfast - the wonderful aroma of coffee and freshly made cinnamon buns greeting everyone as they came downstairs. Lisbet suspected Nadia's newfound cheeriness stemmed from the fact that she had grown up in a crowded orphanage in a Ukrainian coal town. Now suddenly finding herself living in a barony among rose gardens, she felt like an enchanted princess, of course without the physical similarities in storybooks. Her hair was a nondescript brown that she insisted on keeping boyishly short. Her features were sharp; her dark eyes too small, her jaw too broad.

During the summer, Fritz often wondered how long before his number was called. The army was recruiting men in higher and higher age brackets, something he never mentioned because it upset Lisbet and turned his mother quite pale. Besides, he was much too busy to worry about something he had no control over. He and Peter labored in the fields and in the stables from dawn to dusk. Herr Goebbels' radio broadcasts promised more workers would be brought in from occupied countries in time to secure Germany's harvest. But as critical weeks passed, Fritz stopped listening. The Nazis had pledged to end unemployment and it was a promise they kept; there was not a worker to be found. Fritz realized the harvest would fail. Eventually he also realized he had no choice but to empty the stable of horses, all except Peter's pony and Satan's Son - the stallion being too old to fetch a respectable bid. Buttercup, a brood mare Lisbet liked to ride, was also spared. With only three horses needing care, Fritz found an old groom living at the Black Wolf in the village who was willing to come out of retirement.

At the age of fourteen, Peter was not too old to blink away tears the morning the horses went to auction. He and Uncle Fritz had gone to the stables at the crack of dawn to oversee the departure and now watched as the caravan of trailers slowly rolled away from the compound like a retreating army. Peter loved the horses, every one of them, and the exodus sent his mood into a tailspin.

"Hey! Chin up!" Fritz said, seeing the boy's struggle. "We'll restock after the war." But as the dust settled behind the last trailer, Fritz realized that he, too, was depressed. Moreover, he wondered at Max's reaction come August when he arrived to discover that his favorite hunter was gone. But before concerning himself with the future, Fritz had to deal with the present, which included mucking-out the stalls. He and Peter grabbed some shovels and got to work.

After an hour, Fritz stopped to rest, wiped his brow on his sleeves and leaned over the partition to the adjacent stall where Peter was raking. "How about quitting?" he said. "The groom from the Black Wolf will be here in the morning. We ought to leave him something to do." Fritz nodded toward the remaining three horses frupping their nostrils and pawing the floors of their stalls. "I bet they could use some exercise. You feel like riding?"

"Sure, but there are three of them and only two of us. What about Buttercup?"

"We'll turn her loose in the paddock. She's skittish around noise and I was thinking that you and I might ride into the woods and do some target practice."

Peter stopped raking. "Target practice? Really?"

"Yes."

"You're serious?" Peter could hardly believe it. For a long time he had wanted to learn to shoot except *Oma* wouldn't hear of it.

"Of course I'm serious." Fritz pitched his rake into the corner of the stall and walked out.

Peter gave a whoop and a holler and threw his rake aside, sending it clattering across the floor.

"Your father was about your age when he first learned to shoot," Fritz said, tousling the boy's dark hair as the two of them turned their backs on the stalls. "How about you taking Buttercup out to the paddock while I go up to the house to get the Mauser."

"Are you gonna tell *Oma?*"

"No. I don't think so." Fritz gave the boy a conspirator's wink, washed his hands at the pump in the yard, scooped some water into his mouth and left the compound.

"Bring lots of cartridges!" Peter hollered after him.

Without turning, Fritz gave a thumbs-up sign over his shoulder.

Chapter twenty-four

The two riders soon found the spot in the woods between the Konauer and the von Renz properties that had once served as a shooting range.

"I remember the first time your father and I came here as boys," Fritz told Peter as they jumped down and tethered their horses at the edge of the clearing. "We came without permission and had a fine time shooting branches off the trees and scaring every animal in the vicinity. A farmer, fearing for his livestock, informed on us. Max being the oldest got an earful, the guns were locked away and, henceforth, if either one of us wanted to shoot, our father accompanied us." Fritz pointed to some old weather-bleached targets at the far side of the clearing. "He hammered those wooden slats into the trees so we'd have something harmless to aim at."

"They're *huge,*" Peter grumbled as they walked toward the targets. "I can hit those blindfolded."

Ignoring the surly remarks, Fritz stopped at a sporting distance from the targets and demonstrated how to load the rifle. He braced the butt against his shoulder, aimed and pulled the trigger. His first shot went wide. The second barely nicked the objective. "It's not as easy as it looks," he grinned, turning to Peter and handing him the rifle. "Let's see you do it."

Peter was surprised at how quickly Uncle Fritz let him have a go at it. "You mean it's already my turn?"

"Sure. After a few practice shots, we'll test your skill on that badge you're wearing. Pinned to one of the targets, it ought to give you enough of a challenge."

"What!" Peter was shocked. "You want me to use my Hitler Youth badge for target practice?" He placed his hand protectively over the shiny brass emblem fastened to his shirt collar. He'd worn it since the end of the school term, when the headmaster gave them to selected students who'd earned high academic marks and excelled in sports. It was an honor to be a recipient and it came with an important responsibility, that of assisting the Fuehrer. Disloyal citizens were sabotaging Herr Hitler's good works, so the children of the Fatherland were enlisted to help root out the evil by reporting what they heard and observed at home and in their neighborhoods.

"Why not?" Fritz persisted. "It's small enough to be difficult to hit and worthless enough to waste in case you get lucky."

"Small? *Worthless!*" Peter cried, offended. "How can you talk like that? Only eight students in my class qualified for a badge. Everyone is determined to earn one next term and you want me to shoot holes in mine?"

"Yes."

"Well, I won't do it! No way!"

"All right." Fritz shrugged, but it was not a shrug of indifference. Peter's badge bothered him because he knew what was required of the wearer. So far he'd managed to keep silent, but since they were alone in the woods this might be a good opportunity to set the boy straight. Max and Cassandra were not due for several weeks and it was high time someone, a father figure other than Herr Hitler, exercised some influence. "Tell me..." he said, "does the badge mean you've been recruited as a detective for the Third Reich?"

"A detective? Yeah, I guess you could call it that."

"And your duties include reporting anyone, even a family member, if you suspect that he or she might be disloyal to Germany?"

"Yes."

"Did you know that the Tarnoffs were accused of being disloyal?"

"Really? The Tarnoffs were spies?"

"No. But they were charged as such and arrested."

"Arrested? *Oma* said they moved away."

"That's what she was led to believe. Besides, she didn't want to upset you and Sigrid. They *did* move but not by their own choice."

"Where did they go?" Peter asked with little interest. The Tarnoffs were *Oma's* friends. He hadn't seen them in a long time...several years, and his memory had dimmed.

"I don't know. I suspect they were sent to a relocation center. One of those camps where people go until the war is over. Supposedly for their own protection"

"My teachers say there are no camps."

"Your teachers are wrong."

"Huh?" Peter remembered his teachers had warned about critics and naysayers. "There are no camps," he said again. "Anyone who believes it is plain silly."

"Are your teachers wearing Nazi badges?"

"Of course."

"Then they're Nazis, Peter, and clever liars."

"My teachers lie?"

"I am afraid so."

"I don't believe it!"

"Well, let's just say some of them do. The ones who are Nazis."

"Isn't everybody a Nazi?"

"No. It only seems that way because they are so vocal and so visible. Some people wear the regimentals but not by choice. Your father, for instance. He's not a Nazi but he's been ordered to wear the uniform."

"Aren't you a Nazi, Uncle Fritz?" It suddenly occurred to Peter that maybe he had taken too much for granted.

"No, I'm not. And it cost me my job at the Zeitung."

"How about *Tante* Lisbet?"

"Of course not. No one in our family is. I don't know about the employees, the few that are left. All I know is that it's safer to think of them as Nazis. It helps one remember to be careful. Contrary opinions, an unguarded word, can result in arrest."

"Uncle Fritz, if you're not a Nazi, then you're disloyal to Herr Hitler and his good works. You might be a spy."

"Do you believe that?"

"You? A spy?" Peter thought a minute, grinned, then shook his head. "No, I guess not."

"Do you suspect anyone in our household? Your grandmother, for example?"

"*Oma?*" Peter laughed out loud. "No." Suddenly he looked sly. "Come to think of it, there might be a spy in our house."

"Who?"

"Nurse Heller. She's been a pain lately. Bring me this! Bring me that!" Peter managed a fine impersonation of her nasal twang. "Ever since we've had no maids, she's been treating me and Sigrid as if we were born to serve her. And she's mean to Nadia. She yells at her for not understanding enough German. She also yells if her room isn't the first to be tidied up each morning. You'd think she was a queen or something. I ought to report her as a spy. If she were arrested, we'd be rid of her."

Fritz frowned. "Sounds to me as if you've just learned something."

"Yeah, it's very convenient to be a Nazi. You can have things your own way."

"Exactly. The real challenge, Peter, is *not* being one."

Peter unfastened the shiny badge from his shirt collar. He turned it over in his hand and looked at it for a long moment before deciding he could tell his friends that he'd lost it. If no one in his family was a Nazi, he didn't want to be the only one.

"Let's see how many holes we can shoot in this thing," he said.

Chapter Twenty-five

The two shooters eventually ran out of cartridges and returned to the stables where they locked the Mauser in the tack room for use on another day. After rubbing down their horses, they fed and watered them and were heading up the path toward the house just as Sigrid and Karoline came into view, cutting across the lawns from the direction of the river, Nadia and Nurse Heller following close behind, carrying an empty picnic basket, wet towels, and a folded parasol. The girls, still in their swimsuits, were struggling with a large bucket splashing water over its rim with each step they took. And if one looked closely into the pail - something both Fritz and Peter were asked to do - tiny minnows could be spotted swimming in confused circles among blades of grass thrown into the water to make the fish feel at home in a habitat Karoline insisted would sustain them until they grew *this big!* She put down the bucket and held out her arms for emphasis. Fritz grabbed her, tossed her into the air, and hugged her fiercely.

After he put her down, squealing and begging for more, he gave Sigrid a hug as well. He couldn't throw a ten year-old into the air, even a spindly ten year-old, but Sigrid did not feel cheated because Uncle Fritz whispered *pretty princess* in her ear, which pleased her far more than a high flying tumble.

Rainy weather kept the girls inside most of the following day. They kept busy in Sigrid's room, redecorating her dollhouse and hosting elaborate tea parties for the dolls. When that wore thin, they played school. Sigrid, in the role of teacher, read books to Karoline who interrupted constantly, testing her older cousin's patience with dumb questions. Eventually, Sigrid grew irritable and called her "a baby."

"I am not!" Karoline pouted and retaliated by throwing her teddy bear at the tea set, breaking a cup.

Sigrid yelled at her and would have pinched her, but Karoline howled, alerting Nadia to trouble. Nadia rushed to the rescue and set up the Parcheesi board. But no sooner was a game underway when Nurse Heller came looking for her, explaining that Arina was asleep and that she was retiring to her room for a rest and wanted tea and buttered *schonbrot* sent up.

Leaving the girls with a warning not to argue, Nadia ran down to the kitchen, eager to oblige Nurse Heller who reminded her of the head mistress at the orphanage in Kungrad, a stern woman whose fickle moods she'd been conditioned to indulge.

The weather worsened, dark clouds rolled across the landscape with thunder, lightening, and heavy rain. Peter came in from his work, hoeing the orchards. Fritz stayed in the stables, showing the new groom around. Peter had barely set foot in the house before Sigrid and Karoline recruited him for a game. He hated Parcheesi and insisted on cards. The girls agreed and although he smelled abominably of wet grass, dirt and manure, chose to overlook the affront to their delicate nostrils in favor of his company. Of course as soon as the storm passed, he went back outside. Shortly Nadia came to fetch Karoline for her afternoon nap.

Left alone, Sigrid rearranged the dollhouse and placed her dolls - those that were made of porcelain - on a high shelf out of Karoline's reach in case she woke early and came around without supervision. That done, she went in search of *Oma.*

She found her in the library with *Tante* Lisbet and Arina. The baby was still asleep in the playpen and, knowing it meant she needed to be quiet, Sigrid picked up a book and curled up on the sofa, where she could eavesdrop on the soft conversation that passed between *Oma* and *Tante* Lisbet. They were discussing the Lundgrens' upcoming visit. Sigrid was looking forward to seeing Karoline's and Arina's Danish grandparents. They always brought such wonderful presents.

With the storm gone the clouds parted, and the sun soon poked through the windows of the library, bringing attention to a fine layer of dust on the black marble mantelpiece and other shiny surfaces. Dorrit sighed and decided she would have to dust. But first she and Sigrid ought to go outside to see if the heavy rain had damaged the rose garden. Sigrid's job this summer was tending the flowerbeds, something she loved, and she tugged impatiently on Dorrit's hand as they now left *Tante* Lisbet with the baby making squeaky noises with the rubber toys she chewed on.

They left the house by the front door, Sigrid running down the wide stone steps ahead of her grandmother, her auburn hair bouncing about her head, the skirt of her green-dotted cotton dress flying above her skinny knees. She stopped by the fountain in the courtyard and leaned over the reflecting pool, sticking her tongue under the water trickling from the marble nymph's urn.

"I hope the water is clean," Dorrit said, shaking her head with concern over the child's habit of drinking it.

"It tastes great," Sigrid said as if taste and clean were synonymous. She wiped her mouth on the hem of her dress and with a streak of mischief strafed the water's surface with her fingertips, scaring the goldfish under the lily pads. She now sprinted toward the greenhouse and tool shed on the far side of the courtyard near the kitchen and service entrance.

By the time Dorrit caught up, Sigrid had collected gloves, clippers, and a basket for the blooms she planned to cut. On account of the wet ground, she also found some rubber galoshes, which she and Dorrit pulled over their shoes before rounding the house to the flowerbeds by the terrace.

The beautiful gardens had gone to weed and, shaking her head, Dorrit explained that once the war was over they could again hire proper groundskeepers and everything would be as before. "For now we'll just have to do our best," she said, pulling at some stubborn thistles around the rose bushes while Sigrid began to tug at the dog fennel choking the peonies. The soil was soft, relinquishing the offending weeds with little persuasion. Still, Dorrit soon grew tired.

"I'll have to rest a minute," she grimaced, a twinge nipping at her back. She climbed the steps to the terrace and sat down on a wrought iron chair after first wiping it dry with a handkerchief. Removing her garden gloves, she tidied her hair, securing some loose strands with a tortoise-shell comb. The red roses growing against the house hung upside down, the blooms heavy and saturated with rain. They will need a thorough trimming, she realized. But that, too, would have to wait until after the war.

"Can I cut some flowers now?" Sigrid asked, having grown bored with weeding and pointing toward some pink rose bushes. "I won't take the buds."

"Sure. Go ahead. Just don't cut your fingers."

“I’ll be careful.” Sigrid reached for the clippers in the bottom of the basket, hung the empty hamper over her arm, and walked along the gravel paths separating the various hybrids. “These will look pretty in the hall,” she said, examining blooms the rain hadn’t damaged. “On the table under the mirror.”

Dorrit nodded. “It’s a large vase. You’ll need at least two-dozen.” She watched Sigrid clamp her lower lip between her teeth in concentration as she cut and counted roses, placing them in the basket. The child's energy pleased Dorrit. Her physical weakness was a thing of the past, and when she stopped a moment to push the hair off her forehead, the healthy glow in her cheeks was prettier than that on the pinkest rose.

Chapter Twenty-six

In September, shortly after returning to Berlin, Fritz received a letter from Robert Grantham that had miraculously escaped the censors. Linda had included several pages elaborating on the daily routines of her two small boys, so perhaps this mundane information had made the postal workers careless. Grateful with this bit of luck, Fritz learned that his American friend was on his way to Cambridgeshire to fly alongside RAF pilots. Robert groused about having to adjust to the notorious English rain and fog as well as his long absence from his family. In short, the letter was peppered with the usual wit and vitriol that characterized his writing. In closing he suggested a reunion as soon as the war was over. "Berlin or New York," he wrote. "What do you say? We'll raise some real hell. But for now, being that we're sworn enemies, for Christ's sake stay out of my sight!"

Toward the end of '42 air raid warnings over Berlin increased and people went to their basements with predictable regularity, some decorating their shelters with pictures, knickknacks, rugs and comfortable chairs. When British bombs fell on Alexander Platz in the heart of the city, optimism survived because Herr Goebbels' radio broadcasts promised the war was all but won. His assurances were supported by daily reports from the War Ministry, telling of decisive victories on all fronts.

With such good tidings, Berliners cheerfully traded rationing coupons for the steadily diminishing food supplies. Gasoline had been scarce for some time already and coffee and meat soon joined the list of rare commodities. Quantities of bread and vegetables remained acceptable and beer brewed locally at Kindl Brauerei was plentiful, while Fashinger mineral water, a household stable from the Alps, was not. People shrugged and made the necessary adjustments.

However, with each passing week, goods and services deteriorated. Items such as sugar and jam vanished and milk was only available to households with children. During the autumn, when coal for home heating was delivered in paltry amounts, Berliners braced themselves for an uncomfortable winter.

It became unrealistic to try to heat the entire house on Lindenstrasse. In November, Dorrit closed off the upstairs floors and along with Nurse Heller, Peter and Sigrid, moved into the guest rooms on the ground floor. This did not please Nurse Heller. After yet another insult to her comfort, that of spending an entire night in the damp cellar when consecutive false alarms sent everyone below ground, she gave notice, packed her belongings and was gone within a week, returning to the place of her birth - a small town on the Baltic that she felt sure would not attract bombs.

In December Fritz came to Grunewald to say good-bye. He had received his induction notice ordering him to report to Krampnitz, an officer tank training school outside Berlin that had recently been expanded to give crash courses in the rudiments of soldiering. Helmut Niemann had been drafted in October and was now on the eastern front, a destination Fritz assumed awaited him as well. Herr Hitler was determined to crush the Soviet Union and continued to throw all his might at Russia, depleting his forces in the west to do so. He referred publicly to the Soviets as subhuman and demanded that when his army reached Moscow, the city be pulverized.

Fritz walked into the entrance hall on Lindenstrasse, where Dorrit and the children were waiting for him. Stepping through the front door, his coat hanging casually over his broad shoulders like a cape, his eyes flicked over the high-ceilinged hall, crowned by a magnificent crystal chandelier casting light across the rare paintings on the walls. Suddenly he felt an icy draft and an eerie feeling that he was seeing his childhood home for the last time. The next minute he shrugged it off, realizing there was a perfectly good explanation for the chill. The house was cold. Dorrit was rationing the coal.

"Well, Peter," Fritz clasped the boy's hand firmly, "for the next couple of weeks, until your parents return for Christmas, you'll be the man in the family. Take good care of your sister and your *Oma* for me."

"I will," Peter promised and looked reverently at Fritz. He was proud to have his uncle go off to war. Most of his friends had already seen their fathers leave and it was getting difficult to explain why his own was absent from the war effort. Now with an uncle involved, he finally had something to talk about.

Fritz bent down to kiss Sigrid hopping up and down impatiently, her black patent slippers making clicking noises on the parquet. "Good-bye, pretty princess," he whispered in her ear. "You look particularly fetching today. Did you dress up just for me?" She nodded and Fritz took her small hands in his and admired her mauve dress with its round white collar and pearl buttons. When he let go, Sigrid executed a pirouette to show off the fullness of her skirt.

Peter rolled his eyes with her embarrassing display.

Dorrit walked Fritz out to the front gates, supporting herself on his arm as they left the house. The flower urns on either side of the footpath were devoid of greenery and the grass was a desolate brown, reflecting the season as well as her mood. She pulled a shawl tightly around her shoulders and ignored the biting December wind. Her heart was heavy and shaking with fear of what would face her son at the front. She remembered Johann's ghastly stories from Kapsukas.

On the sidewalk, Fritz stopped and turned to face her. As a child he had always believed that he had the loveliest of mothers and although he had never changed that opinion, he realized that she'd grown old without giving notice. Her formerly bright green eyes had dulled, creases marked her forehead, and as her chin quivered it drew attention to the lines around her mouth. But she was as slim and elegantly dressed as always. Her skirt was of the finest black wool and a lace collar - along with the emerald heart she always wore around her neck, softened the severity of her tailored blouse.

Dorrit's bearing crumbled the moment she spotted the taxi waiting at the curb; she hated the sight of it, for it would take her son away. But, determined not to show despair, she squared her shoulders. This painful parting must not rob her of her dignity. Fritz must not remember her as a teary old woman. "Take care of yourself," she said, forcing a smile even as her voice was breaking. "Our prayers, our thoughts will be with you day and night until you're safely home again."

Fritz bent down and kissed her cold cheek. "The war will be over soon," he said. "Stay well and don't worry about me."

An obstruction in Dorrit's throat was strangling her. She couldn't speak and simply clutched Fritz's warm hands to her face a moment before letting go.

Later that night on Uhland Strasse, Fritz went into the children's nursery. A small night light was burning and, quietly closing the connecting door to Nadia's room, he stood for a moment in the semi darkness, watching Arina sleep, wanting nothing more than to pick her up, feel her warm little body against his chest, and kiss her downy yellow curls. But he couldn't bring himself to disturb her dreams. She was sleeping so peacefully, lying on her stomach with her fat little legs tucked up under her, blissfully unaware of the war and of this painful separation.

Leaving Arina's crib, Fritz went over to Karoline's bed, fully expecting to find her asleep as well. However, her eyes were wide open and she immediately threw off the blankets and jumped up to hug him. She knew her father was leaving for the war in the morning before she'd be awake and, winding her arms around his neck, she cried and begged him not to go.

Pulling up a chair and putting his daughter on his lap, Fritz again told her why he must go and why he had no choice. Switching on a lamp, he explained, as he'd done before, the meaning of the word *induction*. Then he found her favorite book, *Struwwelpeter*, and read aloud until she fell asleep, her head lolling on his shoulder.

Much later that night when Lisbet was in his arms, Fritz interspersed his tender words with some sober advice in case the war lasted longer than expected, or in case he didn't return.

"*What!*" Lisbet sat up in bed, her blue eyes flashing in the darkness. "Don't you dare talk like that!"

"Darling, I have every intention of making it back in one piece." Fritz smiled at her outburst; her sense of drama had not diminished with her years away from the stage. "But, if the worst were to happen, I want you to remember that you and the girls can rely on Max. He can be depended on to keep the family holdings intact. He will always vouch for your financial security." Gingerly, Fritz also explained about a pact he had made with Helmut Niemann. "If only one of us returns from the front..."

Lisbet stopped him. She refused to hear any more *ifs*. "It's bad luck to talk like this," she cried. "Julianne and I forbid you or Helmut to get a scratch. Do you hear me?"

"Yes, darling," he whispered as he buried his face in her fragrant hair. Tonight was heaven. Tomorrow he had his orders, and whether or not he believed in Herr Hitler's cause was immaterial. His orders were to report for duty or be shot as an example to others. So, he would go to war, but he would not fight for the Third Reich, he would fight for the Germany he remembered, the Germany he loved and the country it would be again once the Nazi pestilence went down in defeat. For God help all of Europe if Hitler won and spread his personal brand of terror. Therein lay true disaster.

Contrary to the rosy propaganda that circulated in Berlin, Fritz knew about the chaos at the fronts, information he kept in his head because, since that night when his library was torn apart, he had ceased being a writer. But he had not ceased gathering information and had learned that while factories built plenty of spare parts, the transportation of these components more often than not broke down, leaving tanks and guns inoperable along battle lines. Likewise, interruptions in fuel deliveries left entire convoys stranded inside enemy territory unable to mount an attack. Fritz guessed that if the Allies knew how inefficiently the Nazi war machine operated, they would be amazed. But they didn't know because when it came to bluff and propaganda, the Nazis were professionals without equals.

Chapter Twenty-seven

Adolf Hitler lived in mortal fear of assassins, wore bulletproof clothing, surrounded himself with burly bodyguards, and built massive bunkers under Berlin and elsewhere so he could conduct the war in concealed safety.

A rash of attempts on his life proved unsuccessful, including an attempt to poison his food. When his personal chef fell ill while preparing the meal, and a manservant was reluctant to sample the dinner, everyone in the chancellery residence with the slightest knowledge of chemicals was rounded up. Three hundred people went to the gallows. As a deterrent to others, newspapers ran photographs of the executions.

Dorrit was dining with the Eckarts in their townhouse shortly after this event. It was just the three of them on this January evening, and the shocking front-page pictures immediately became a topic of conversation. Lillian was convinced that the collaborators were innocent, if only because she flatly refused to believe that anyone would want to harm Herr Hitler.

"It was foreign treachery," she said, lifting a morsel of fish roasted in butter, a treat for the palate, as were the mushrooms and creamed potatoes. "The Soviets must have infiltrated Herr Hitler's kitchen."

"No, my dear," Kurt said, reaching for the saltshaker. "The plotters were German. All of them."

Lillian looked at her husband as if he'd lost his mind. "All *three hundred?* That's preposterous, Kurt. How can that many people plot when meeting in large numbers is prohibited? If more than a handful of people gather, they're quickly dispersed."

"Just because three hundred were executed," Kurt said quietly, "does not mean all were guilty."

Lillian looked confused. “Well, I think the SS and the Gestapo, or whoever, are going too far. Power has gone to their heads. They're making too many arrests of our own citizens when they should be rounding up more foreigners. They are the ones who want to harm Herr Hitler. You ought to bring it up at the next meeting.”

“I’ll mention it,” Kurt said. Of course he had no intentions of doing anything of the sort. To suggest a slip-up on the part of the SS or the Gestapo was a ticket for oneself to the gallows.

“I wonder,” Dorrit mused, “if those who plot give any thought to who will pick up the reigns of government in the event their attempt is successful.”

Kurt stiffened, remembered the servants, and put a finger to his lips.

Taking the cue, Dorrit lowered her voice. “After all,” she whispered, leaning across the table, “Herr Hitler's designated successor, Hermann Goering, is hardly Santa Claus. I can't name a single soul at the chancellery who’d bring Germany back to its former democracy. A lot of corrupt men at the top will have to die before things change. Even a skilled assassin can't hope to kill them all.”

“My God, Dorrit!” Lillian gasped and clasped a hand over her mouth. “What are you saying?”

“It's all right, Lillian,” Kurt forced a chuckle. “I’m sure it was said in jest. We haven't lost our sense of humor, have we now?” His leniency toward Dorrit was rooted in an old friendship. He owed Johann’s widow protection.

“Yes, of course, I was only joking.” Dorrit laughed nervously, realizing she’d been much too glib. Prudently changing the subject, she commented on the absence tonight of Isabel and Philip. Both were ill and as Lillian had explained earlier, canceled at the last minute. “I am not surprised the von Brandts are sick,” she said. “It’s been a rough winter so far. I can’t remember ever being so cold. Anna and Enno were smart to head south last month.”

“I guess they’ll spend the entire winter in Greece,” Lillian said, scooping up a second helping of the creamed potatoes.

“And the spring,” Dorrit said. “Anna wrote last week that she and Enno plan to stay through June.”

This benign conversation was fortuitous because the door from the pantry opened without warning when the Eckarts’ housekeeper and a maid came in to clear the plates. Kurt's high position in the Nazi party accounted for the fact that amid a severe labor shortage his house was fully staffed.

"Gerti, we'll take our coffee and dessert in the library," Lillian told the housekeeper.

Kurt rose and helped the ladies from their chairs. "I think it's time we open that fancy cognac Elsie sent us from France," he said as he escorted Lillian and Dorrit across the hall and into the library carpeted in a maroon rug and furnished with a pair of gray tweed sofas and matching chairs. He went over to his desk and pressed a button; the paneled wall behind him rotated, revealing a well stocked bar. "Ah, here it is," he said, lifting the bottle from a shelf. "La Reine!" He held the amber vessel in his hands, rotating it reverently. "This cognac spent fifty years in a wooden cask buried deep in a French forest before being deemed fit to drink."

"That makes me curious enough to try it," Dorrit laughed. "Though, as a rule, I never drink brandy."

"I'm glad you're making an exception tonight," Lillian said. "In view of the unfortunate events in the chancellery kitchen, we must drink a toast to our Fuehrer's health." Settling into opposite corners of a sofa, she and Dorrit watched Kurt open the bottle with the precision of a surgeon.

"To our Fuehrer!" he said after he filled three snifters and passed them around.

"Our Fuehrer!" Dorrit and Lillian echoed. Silence followed, broken by sounds of *um* and *ah* as the cognac was sampled and appreciated.

"And now," Dorrit said, putting her glass down on the small marble table by the sofa, "I want to hear all about Elsie's new home in Paris."

"*Ach!* Paris." Kurt scoffed and remained standing, leaning his elbow against the mahogany bar counter. "All that can be said about Elsie's new home is that it's too far away. But I guess that's what we get for letting her marry a Frenchman."

"Did I tell you we're planning to visit?" Lillian turned to Dorrit.

"No, you didn't."

"Well, it's not certain yet." Lillian glanced toward Kurt; he was so frightfully busy that she hardly dared believe his schedule would allow for a pleasure trip.

"We'll go first thing next month," he promised her with a wink.

"I can't wait to see my newest grandchild," Lillian smiled wistfully. "Imagine," she leaned over to squeeze Dorrit's hand, "my little Elsie is now the mother of four sweet darlings. Two boys and two girls."

Lillian patted her silver-blond coiffure before pulling a handkerchief from her pocket as tears of joy welled up in her eyes. "Could anything be more perfect?"

"Yes!" Kurt laughed. "Elsie could have married Fritz. Then she would be right here in Berlin with us."

"Well, it wasn't for our lack of trying," Dorrit grinned, remembering how their matchmaking skills had fizzled years ago when Elsie was swept off her feet by a dashing French diplomat ten years her senior.

"We *did* try," Lillian sighed.

Gerti came into the library, carrying coffee and *petit fours*. Lillian put her handkerchief away, now turning her attention to the refreshments. "This is genuine coffee," she boasted as Gerti poured. "Not that awful substitute they palm off nowadays." Dorrit was not surprised. Along with servants, Kurt's position in the Nazi party meant he had access to luxury goods. "But now, tell me," Lillian said, leaning back in the sofa after Gerti had left. "Any news from Fritz? He's still at Stalingrad, isn't he? You must be so proud of him. I hear our troops are making great strides inside the Soviet Union and bringing the Soviets to their knees."

Sipping her coffee contentedly, Dorrit shared everything she remembered from Fritz's last letter. She was glad to report that he was well and that the siege at Stalingrad was going splendidly. Morale was high, rations and supplies were plentiful, and they were winning every skirmish. As she related this rosy news, she failed to notice the odd, dark look creeping into Kurt's face. Though seemingly attentive, his mind was locked onto something else - something known only to him - something he could not speak of.

Much later that evening, when Dorrit was saying goodbye, she lingered in the front hall, buttoning her sable coat and fastening her hat by the mirror in the slim hope that the evening might have had a double purpose: a lovely dinner with old friends and an opportunity for Kurt to slip her some desperately needed documents. But he gave her no papers, only a fond parting embrace.

His car and chauffeur were waiting at the curb to drive her home. As she went down the steps toward the uniformed, armed man, she shuddered an instant before turning around to wave to her friends standing in the open doorway, silhouetted in the yellow light of the foyer.

"Lunch next Wednesday!" Lillian called into the frigid January night. "At the Adlon. Don't forget."

"I'll be there," Dorrit assured her.

The chauffeur inclined his head respectfully, opened the car door and helped the Baroness von Renz into her seat. Watching as he walked around and got in behind the wheel, Dorrit wondered at his reaction if he discovered that the person in the back seat of Herr Doctor Eckart's luxurious black sedan - fueled with gasoline allotted only to high Nazi officials - had Jewish blood.

Chapter Twenty-eight

In response to Germany's bombing of London and the utter destruction of Rotterdam, Allied retaliation raids on German cities began in earnest. It was no longer false alarms that sent Berliners below ground.

In April Dorrit received a telegram from Istanbul with an unexpected message: Max and Cassandra were on their way to Berlin. In view of the escalating attacks, they had decided to come home and take Peter and Sigrid out of harm's way and bring them to Turkey.

Max and Cassandra spent only one night in Grunewald. After the children had eaten supper and gone to bed in preparation for an early departure the next morning, they sat down for a quiet dinner with Dorrit.

"You look lovely," Dorrit said as Cassandra came into the dining room. After saying goodnight to the children, she had taken time to change out of her travel clothes, now wearing a yellow short-sleeved dress, her long black hair tied in a neat ponytail. Still a beauty, her work in the various dust bowls of the world had yet to dry her complexion or etch a single line around her large black eyes.

"As you know," Max said to Dorrit, as he got up to pull out a chair for Cassandra, "I've turned forty. Still, there's a good chance the military will want me. No age or profession is safe any longer, which is why we're only staying one night." He sat down and took the linen napkin off the table, unfolding it across his lap. "Once I'm back in Turkey, it'll be difficult for the induction board to collar me. Herr Hitler's signature notwithstanding, I suspect both my gasoline vouchers and military deferment can be revoked at any moment. I certainly don't intend to hang around and make it easy for them to put me in the army."

"*My* son is in the army," Frau Mueller announced proudly, having overheard Max's comment as she brought in a platter of roasted potatoes and a dish of peas and carrots. "He volunteered. He's now in the *Afrika Korps.*"

"Congratulations," Max mumbled, glancing at the sparse meal she left on the table; the tiny pieces of meat among the potatoes looked like garnish and, though hungry, he avoided taking a large helping. He was aware of food shortages in Berlin but had expected his mother to have more adequate rations. Frowning, he looked at her. "I wish you'd come with us."

"You've said that a dozen times since you arrived."

"I'd still like to talk you into it."

"Well, forget it." Dorrit smiled at his persistence.

"As you know," Cassandra said in a bid to help Max convince his mother, "the von Steigerts are not returning to Berlin in June after all. They plan to sit out the war in Greece. They've rented a lovely house in Thessaloniki with a guest bungalow. When we stopped there on our way here, Anna begged us to persuade you to come. The von Brandts will be joining them shortly."

"Yes, I know." Dorrit nodded. "Both Isabel and Philip were ill much of the winter and now the constant sirens are getting on their nerves. But I'm all right. If the air raids keep up I'll move out to Bernau. Now that Peter and Sigrid will be with you, I no longer need to worry about their schooling."

"You should have gone to Bernau already," Max observed. "To hell with their schooling. Last summer Fritz told me about the rubbish they teach."

"Actually, I did consider going to the country on several occasions. But I can't buy anything of consequence in Bernau. My rationing coupons are redeemable only at food stores here in Berlin."

"Couldn't the Konauers help out?" Cassandra said.

"Oh, I suppose. But I wouldn't presume. They have their hands full now that Klara and her husband, including the in-laws from Eberswald, have moved in with them. Bombs destroyed their manufacturing plant *and* their home. Did you know that Gerlinde and Karl-Heinz have two grandsons in the war?"

Max looked up from his plate. "I haven't seen the boys in ages. Are they old enough?"

"Yes. They were drafted. Gerlinde is beside herself."

Max nodded. "I can imagine. She lost her son in the last war."

Frau Mueller came in to clear away the dinner plates and brought cups of vanilla pudding to the table, a bland dessert made mostly with water and very little sugar. The coffee was piping hot but it was *ersatz* and as tasteless as the custard. While Max and Cassandra pretended to enjoy it, Dorrit wasn't fooled.

"I know," she laughed, seeing their faces. "It's pretty awful. Please don't feel obliged to eat it." She put her spoon down, pushed her pudding aside, and tried not to grimace as she sipped the bitter coffee substitute. "I'll go out to Bernau as soon as possible. There's still sugar and coffee beans in the cellar and, come summer, there'll be fruit in the orchards. Unless Lisbet decides to take the girls to Denmark, they will come with me. In the meantime, I feel quite safe here. The Allies don't fly over residential neighborhoods."

"I still don't like it," Max muttered.

"It can't last much longer."

"Let's hope not." Max stretched unselfconsciously. "Anyway, we'll be shoving off in the morning. By then you may have changed your mind and decided to come with us."

Dorrit shook her head.

"At least think about it," Cassandra pressed her. "Sleep on it. We have plenty of room in the car and you won't have to pack much. You and Anna can shop for everything you need once you're in Thessaloniki."

But Dorrit remained unshakable. Only she and Kurt knew that travel was impossible. She couldn't leave Germany and she couldn't tell Max and Cassandra why not. If Max became aware of her vulnerability, he might do something reckless on her behalf.

Chapter Twenty-nine

Lisbet came over the following morning to see everyone off. She came without the girls. Both had colds and as she now witnessed the scene in the hall where the luggage was being assembled, she was glad they had stayed home with Nadia. Peter was exited about the trip and eager to help his father bring everything out to the car, but Sigrid was working herself into a full-blown tantrum.

"I don't want to go!" she sobbed, stomping her feet on the parquet and flinging off Cassandra's arm as she tried to coax her from the house. "I want to stay with *Oma!*" Yesterday she'd been happy with the idea of going to Turkey, but now that the time had come, she suddenly felt differently

Cassandra was at a loss. She had never before seen her daughter put on such an exhibition. She tried words of reason, then pleadings, all for naught. Finally, she took hold of Sigrid's arm and dragged her out the door and down the steps. Dorrit and Lisbet followed a few paces behind this classic display of a mother's will against a child's defiance. In retaliation of the rough handling, Sigrid suddenly went limp, collapsing along the footpath. But, although she was small for her age, Cassandra was not about to pick up and carry an eleven-year-old, and decided to wait for Max to finish with the suitcases so he could deal with the stalemate. Quick to take advantage of her mother's inattentiveness, Sigrid got on her feet and raced back to Dorrit.

Dorrit's arms went around the child's thin shoulders. She, too, felt a deep sadness with the departure and had to bite back her own tears. She would miss Peter and Sigrid terribly but she mustn't let on because it'd only add to Sigrid's despair. A stiff upper lip was needed. The children would be safe from the bombs and that was the only important thing.

"My dear girl..." Dorrit raised Sigrid's face. "Sweetheart, look at me!" Her eyes blurred with tears, Sigrid did as she was told. "When we got your parents' telegram, you could hardly sleep because you were so excited about this trip."

"I know, but I'm not excited anymore."

"But you will be. Once you're underway you'll have a wonderful time. You'll see so many new and interesting places. And before you know it, it will be August and you'll be back home again. If the war ends, you'll be back even sooner. Think of all the stories you can tell me. We'll have a great big celebration. We'll invite your friend, Gabriella."

"I don't want a party. And Gabby is in Hartzen. She moved there because of the bombs."

"Well, there, you see! Even Gabriella has left Berlin. Just like you and Peter are doing."

"Karoline and Arina aren't leaving," Sigrid sniffed stubbornly.

"Oh, but they will. If the bombing gets any worse they'll go to Copenhagen."

"I'm not afraid of the bombs. I don't want to go anywhere. I just want to stay with you." Sigrid's thin arms clutched at her grandmother's waist while a new wave of sobs drowned her. "Why c...can't I just stay h...here?"

"Save your tears, my precious," Dorrit said, fumbling in her pocket for a handkerchief to wipe the child's wet cheeks. "Save your tears for tomorrow. For, who knows? Tomorrow you may need them."

Sigrid managed a small giggle at her *Oma's* timeworn advice. It was oddly comforting and, although she was still weeping, her hysterics subsided.

Impulsively, Dorrit removed the emerald heart from around her neck that Johann had given her so many years ago. She held it in her hand for an instant before slipping the chain over Sigrid's head. Lisbet gasped in horror. Surely, Dorrit didn't mean to give that priceless gem to a *child!*

Cassandra protested openly. "Dorrit!" she cried. "You can't give that to her. Suppose she misplaces it?"

"She won't." Dorrit smiled, seeing her granddaughter's eyes sparkle. Sigrid was thrilled to have *Oma's* emerald and immediately forgot her tears.

"I'll never take it off, *Oma*," she promised, holding out the chain to admire the jewel. "That way I can't lose it."

"That's right. You'll wear it and know that I'm here at home, thinking about you and waiting for you."

Sigrid threw herself into Dorrit's arms, finally letting go in order to say goodbye to *Tante* Lisbet, whose practical mind was worrying itself sick about the emerald. "Tell Karoline," she said, hoping her younger cousin wouldn't learn about her hysterics, "tell her when she visits *Oma*, she can play with all my stuff except the porcelain doll with the real hair."

"I'll be sure she doesn't touch that one," Lisbet promised, hugging her.

Hiccupping from her outburst, Sigrid walked to the curb where, having finished helping his father arrange the suitcases, Peter said good-bye to Dorrit and Lisbet with a dignified handshake. But before getting into the back seat next to Sigrid, he, too, threw his arms around his grandmother.

As Cassandra embraced Lisbet, both women made elaborate promises about the wonderful time they would have in Bernau come August. Now turning to Dorrit, Cassandra embraced her as well and promised to send pictures of the children from the dig.

Oddly, a moment later as she prepared to get into the car, Cassandra shivered despite the pleasant April morning. Her suede jacket and lined gabardine slacks were no match for the goose bumps suddenly peppering her skin. She pivoted her head and looked at the grand villa. The windows - only moments ago reflecting the bright blue sky - were suddenly hollow and the entire house was shrouded in a strange darkness with brown and brittle foliage from a different season blowing across it, sweeping it away stone-by-stone until a black void yawned in its place.

Feeling dizzy with her vision, Cassandra reached out to steady herself on the car, all the while wondering why her childish notions of seeing the future hadn't gone the way of other youthful fantasies.

Seated in the back seat, Peter was rolling down the car window, now promising *Oma* that he would send postcards from stops along the way.

"Me too!" Sigrid hollered from the opposite corner.

Dorrit smiled and blew kisses to them both.

Cassandra gave herself a mental shake. Nonetheless, while Max was preoccupied with something Lisbet was telling him, and before settling into the front seat, she discreetly spit over her left shoulder to ward off evil.

"Last chance to come along." Max winked at Dorrit.

"Thanks, but no."

"Well, then don't delay going out to Bernau."

"Don't worry, Max."

"We might even scoot up to Denmark for a while," Lisbet added and linked arms with Dorrit, indicating they would stick together.

"Good." Max got in behind the wheel and switched on the ignition. "I left a letter for Fritz on the hall table. Could you drop it in a mailbox?" Dorrit and Lisbet nodded. "It will probably zigzag all over the front before reaching him. In the meantime, if he calls, tell him we said hello and Godspeed."

Lisbet almost laughed. "There are no telephones where he's at. We're just hoping for some mail. We haven't had any since the surrender at Stalingrad. Before that, his letters came pretty regularly. He numbers them. Something we agreed on before he left. The last one was marked number nine. The previous one was number seven. Which means number eight is still missing."

"I imagine a lot of mail goes AWOL," Max said.

"Or the censors eat it." Lisbet shrugged.

Max looked at his mother. "Keep that in mind and don't worry if letters from us are slow in getting here. As you know, we have no telephone at the dig. There's a telegraph station some thirty kilometers away in Istanbul but it's temperamental. Last week when I wired you, it was up and running. Next week? Who knows?" Max revved the engine, put the car in gear, and with a jaunty smile and a wave pulled away from the curb.

As the car sped down Lindenstrasse, Sigrid and Peter turned to look out the rear window. Sigrid had started to cry again and Peter noted with considerable irritation that her hot breath was fogging up the window. He could barely see *Oma* and *Tante* Lisbet standing on the sidewalk. He gave the window a swipe of his sleeve.

Now he could see them. *Oma* had stepped off the curb and into the street. She was waving a handkerchief that fluttered in the wind.

Peter and Sigrid both looked until she was lost from sight.

Chapter Thirty

Early in the morning on the second day of their journey, Max and his family left their hotel in Klagenfurt, Austria, and prepared to cross the border into Yugoslavia. The checkpoint at Jesenice was jammed with vehicles, most of which were heading toward Italy. But regardless of destination all were subject to painstaking searches by border guards determined that no undocumented person or automobile slip through their fingers. Passports were scrutinized and travel itineraries questioned.

"Leaving German jurisdiction is getting more difficult than entering," Max observed wryly as he and his family stood stoically by while their car and papers were being inspected. Although he was dutifully wearing his uniform, it didn't help him escape a thorough examination.

"Why are they taking the back seats apart?" Sigrid wanted to know, seeing the guards dismantling her father's car.

"They're looking for contraband," Cassandra said.

"What's that?"

"People," Peter spoke up. His teachers at school had explained that a great number of individuals wanted by the police were trying to flee Germany.

"People?" Sigrid looked confused.

"Yeah, silly! The border guards are checking our car for anyone who might have hitched a ride."

"Under the seats?" Sigrid looked at her brother as if he'd gone soft in the head. "If I were you, I'd be careful who I call silly." She stuck out her tongue.

"None of that, young lady!" Cassandra scolded and with a stern glance silenced Peter's ready retort.

Max was finally given permission to proceed. Everyone piled back into the car and, grinding the gears impatiently, Max turned east and drove across the border into Yugoslavia, unfriendly territory as it were, but he knew the main roads and would not need to bother any combative native for directions. Who could blame them for being hostile? German troops had invaded with Herr Hitler's demand that all resistance be crushed without mercy.

Hours later, after stopping in Zagreb for lunch, Max pulled into a gas station operated by the German military. He flashed his purchasing voucher and was allowed a full tank.

The soldier manning the pump removed a cigarette stub from between his teeth and ground it into the dirt before connecting the hose. “Where are you headed?” he asked as his eyes swept over the expensive black Mercedes.

“Turkey.” Max strolled around the car to check the tires.

“That's quite a trip.”

“Not really.”

“You’ve done it before?”

“Several times.”

Once the tank was full, the soldier released a scrap of cloth fastened to his belt and wiped the dust from the windshield. He spotted the lovely lady in the front seat and the two kids in the rear. “*Guten Tag!*” he said, grinning through the glass.

“*Guten Tag*,” Peter and Sigrid echoed. Cassandra simply smiled at the soldier who didn't look much older than Peter. Of course he would have to be at least eighteen, she reflected, for surely anyone younger than that was not drafted.

While Max paid for the gasoline, the soldier felt compelled to caution him. “Sir, I know you've driven through Yugoslavia before,” he said as he counted out the change and stamped the voucher.

“Yes. We came through here few days ago. On our way north.”

“Still, I ought to warn you...”

“About bandits?”

“Yeah.”

“Well, don't worry. I have no plans to travel after dark.”

“Good. Some stretches south of here are awfully lonely.”

“I know.”

“Once you're in the foothills,” the soldier persisted, “you can drive a hundred kilometers without seeing a soul. If you do see someone, I recommend that you floor the pedal. Whatever you do, don't stop. Even an old lady thumbing a ride can be a decoy for thugs waiting in the wings." The attendant smiled crookedly. "Sorry for the lecture, sir, but our superiors have told us to warn all motorists going south." He glanced toward the children in the rear seats. "One more thing..."

"What?" Max was impatient to get back on the road.

"If you notice anything suspicious, tell the kids to keep their heads down. Only yesterday a car was sprayed by gunfire a few miles south of here. The driver was able to get away, but it proves that thieves are getting more brazen. Yugoslav partisans along with various religious fanatics roam freely. To a man, they hate us. Of course they also hate each other. Each group has a different agenda and fight among themselves for turf. It's guerrilla warfare, if you know what I mean."

"I'll be careful." Max got into the car and turned the key. He smiled at the fellow, rolled up the window, and pulled away from the pump. "One car suffers a bullet," he mumbled to Cassandra as he merged with the traffic leading out of town, "and that chap back there would like to close all the roads."

Chapter Thirty-one

Later that afternoon Max stopped in Sisak to buy snacks and drinks before continuing on to Bos Dubica, a large town with a German military presence, where he again filled up the tank. Once back on the road, the terrain became steeper, more barren, and the road was less traveled. It was mid April but spring was slow in awakening this part of Europe. The ground lay brown and dormant as if waiting for peace before rolling out a green carpet.

"We're heading into the Dinaric Alps," he said after a while, directing the geographical information toward the back seats.

"I think they're asleep." Cassandra glanced over her shoulder. Peter and Sigrid were slumped down in opposite corners, their heads lolling on the padded armrests.

"That's why we've heard no squabbling since leaving Bos Dubica." Max grinned and reached for Cassandra's hand. He pulled it toward his lips and kissed the inside of her wrist. "I'm amazed they're able to sleep on this bumpy road."

"Boredom, no doubt. The landscape is pretty dull. There isn't much to look at in these foothills. Besides, it's been a long day. Are you tired?"

"A little. But we have plenty of daylight left. Still, I don't plan to push on much longer. We'll find a hotel in the next town."

Cassandra reached into the glove box for a map. "That will be Banja Luka," she said, her finger tracing their route. "It's only another forty or fifty kilometers. We've done well. And without speeding."

Max put an arm across the seat back and caressed her shoulder. "Speeding is unpatriotic," he grinned. "It wastes fuel."

"As if that would stop you." Cassandra smiled. "But please, do keep both hands on the wheel."

"There's no traffic, sweetheart. The gasoline shortage keeps people off the roads. We haven't passed another car in either direction for a while."

"Actually I'd welcome some traffic," Cassandra mused. "A German patrol car would be a comforting escort against any wild-eyed bandit who might be roaming these parts." She studied the rugged terrain on both sides of the road. "But I suppose rebels and partisans would have little interest in us. After all, we are civilians."

"I wouldn't count on it. Don't forget that we are *German* civilians. Plus I'm wearing this damned Nazi get-up."

"Surely no angry Yugoslav can see your uniform from the outside."

"No, but I imagine they can spot the license plate."

"That's not very comforting." Cassandra frowned and peered into the landscape with renewed concern.

"Relax, darling." Max stifled a yawn and stretched in the confines of his seat. "We'll soon be in Banja Luka. We'll stay at the same hotel where we stopped on our way north. As I recall it was a friendly place, considering we're the enemy."

Cassandra slipped out from under his arm; she felt more secure when Max had both hands on the wheel. She looked out the window, studying the pale gray sky. Twilight wasn't far off. Long shadows were spreading across the road surface. The wind was picking up, rustling through the stunted pines and prickly bushes growing along the edge of the road. Cassandra felt a pricking at the back of her neck, giving her chills. She was tempted to spit over her left shoulder.

"Thank goodness Banja Luka is close," she mumbled instead and, folding the map, put it back into the glove box. "How long will it take to get there?"

"It's hard to say. The road winds a lot. We ought to be there within an hour."

"Maybe I should wake Peter and Sigrid. Otherwise they might not go to sleep tonight. Of course, if I wake them, they'll complain of hunger."

"Didn't they eat something at our last stop?"

"Only some chocolate. It was a local brand and not very good. They threw most of it away."

"Well, in that case don't wake them. I don't want to spend the next forty kilometers listening to complaints." Max grinned and patted the space next to him. "Slide over," he said.

A piercing shot suddenly shattered the graying scenery, rousing a covey of partridges from their roost among the pines. Flapping wings not made for graceful flight, they flew low and clumsily across the road.

Along with the birds, Cassandra saw a large pattern - like a spider web on the windshield - an instant before her head snapped back with a sickening crack. She was clutching at a burning ache in her throat when her shoulders lurched forward in an involuntary movement. A dark trickle of blood was pulsing from her neck, staining her suede jacket.

The shot had come like a bolt of lightning from a clear sky. Max knew that a bullet had entered the car, but only when he saw Cassandra's head roll forward, did he realize she'd been hit. Horrorstricken, he slammed his foot on the brakes, agony ripping from his throat as he called out her name. The car fishtailed. Cassandra slid from the seat toward the floorboards.

"No! Oh, God, no!" Max reached over with his free hand to try to grab hold of her.

He was bringing the car under control when a second volley hit and he felt a thrust in his chest like the punch from a prizefighter. He glanced down, stupefied, to see a large red circle spreading on the lapels of his loden uniform. Keeping one hand on the wheel, groping the sticky softness with the other, he experienced a strange floating sensation and could now no longer control the car. It kept rolling. He willed his foot to stay on the brake, but it didn't respond. He was suffocating. He struggled to pull air into his lungs. The view ahead was obscured in a jumble of nothingness. Blinking to clear his vision, he turned his face toward the back seats. Peter was awake and attempting to sit up. Sigrid was squirming. They weren't hurt. Thank God! Max moved his lips to speak. No words came. Something else poured forth. It tasted salty and metallic in his mouth.

Rudderless, the Mercedes careened along the roadway, crossing to the opposite side, its wheels spinning in the soft dirt where the gravel ended. Skidding down a deep embankment, it tilted and came to a crunching halt on its side. The engine died.

Silence and a cloud of dust enveloped the car and its occupants.

Chapter Thirty-two

Peter's head hurt. It was throbbing something awful. He couldn't remember hitting anything but must have bumped his head. Except for that painful pounding, he felt strangely numb, yet knew that something was wrong, terribly wrong. The world was upside down. The car was pitched at an odd angle and he lay straddling Sigrid.

Suddenly it came to him. *Someone had shot at the car!* He'd been sleeping when a loud noise woke him. *Rifle fire!* He recognized the sound from last summer when he and Uncle Fritz had shot at targets in Bernau.

"Hey! Get off me!" Sigrid was whining and pushing at him. "Give me some room! What happened?"

Peter hauled himself up and peered across the divider to the front seats, immediately wishing he hadn't. He gagged, seeing his parents lying in a crumbled heap. There was blood everywhere. His father's opaque and unblinking eyes were staring into space, his expression one of shock. In direct contrast, his mother's face looked peaceful except for the odd angle of her head - like one of Sigrid's dolls after Karoline's rough handling. She appeared to be sleeping. Her eyes were closed. With the exception of some dead birds and on one occasion a cat, Peter had never before seen death. *It's only a nightmare*, he told himself, pinching himself to wake up. But with the sharp sting came the realization that he was awake. He knew where he was. He was on a road in Yugoslavia. Someone had fired at the car. His parents had been shot, and as this cruel reality sank in, it intensified the throbbing in his head. He wanted to scream, not because of the pain, because of his raw outrage at this horror. But he couldn't scream; a lump the size of a soccer ball was lodged in his throat, preventing him from uttering a sound. Through the haze of his agony, a practical thought entered his mind. He ought to close his father's eyes. He had once heard that the dead must have their eyes closed in order to be at peace. He wanted his father to look as serene as his mother. He lifted his arm, but it was trembling too violently to be of any use. To make matters worse, Sigrid was tugging at his jacket, shaking him further. *Sigrid?* Oh God, she mustn't see this carnage. She tended toward hysterics. A sight like this would throw her into a two-week tantrum.

Suddenly Peter heard noises from up along the road. He froze. *Voices? Yes!* Whoever had done this murder was coming to inspect their evil deed. He wondered what had taken them so long. In his stupefied state it seemed like an hour had passed since the car went off the road. But of course it had only been seconds and adrenaline was now surging through his body. He turned to his sister.

"We've got to get out of here!" he hissed between clenched teeth as he rolled down a side window where the roof should have been. "Hurry! Climb out!" Blocking the bloodbath in the front seats with his body, he grabbed Sigrid and hoisted her up. Thankfully, she was small and light. "Jump off on the side facing away from the road," he ordered breathlessly. "Don't make a sound!" He pushed her roughly through the open window. Much to his surprise, she did what he told her. Quick as the wind, he followed, crouching next to her in the dirt by the wrecked car, fumes from leaking gasoline burning their nostrils. Peter scanned the area for a place to hide. There were some dense bushes in a gully a stone's throw away, but an outcrop of boulders off to the left were a safer bet. When he heard running footsteps on the road above, he knew the boulders were too far away. Pulling Sigrid along, he dashed forward and went headlong into the spiny shrubbery.

"Ouch!" she protested, the thorns scratching her bare legs and tearing at her sweater. "Ouch!"

"Hush!" Peter pushed her into the ground under the thicket. "Be still and don't move a muscle." He flattened himself next to her. "Don't make a sound!"

Sigrid was baffled by her brother's hoarse whisper. But as the residue of sleep dissipated, her mind cleared. "Why aren't Mama and Papa climbing out of the car?" she whispered. "Aren't they coming?"

"They can't," Peter snapped. "We had an accident." He didn't dare say anything more. His sister would start to wail. "We were sleeping when it happened."

"Oh." Sigrid puckered her forehead. "They can't climb out because they're hurt. Is that it? Huh?"

Peter nodded.

"Are they real bad off?"

"I don't know," he lied. "Now be quiet!" He pressed his sister further into the ground. "Hush your mouth or those men will hear you." He pointed to a cloud of dust kicked up by several individuals sliding down the embankment. "I think they're thieves. They mustn't see us. Play dead and they won't hurt us."

Biting her lips, Sigrid was quiet as a rock, her fear of the men surpassing her immediate concern for her parents. Moreover, she clamped down her eyelids so she wouldn't see them. But after a moment, she decided that she needed to know what the bandits looked like because *Oma* would expect some details when told about this.

Opening her eyes, she saw five dirty and unshaven men toting rifles and ammunition belts. They approached the upturned wreck, surrounding it with guns poised. One stepped forward and, using the butt of his rifle, knocked out what was left of the broken windshield. The group now jostled each other for a look inside. Sigrid hoped her parents were playing dead so the bandits wouldn't hurt them.

Peter winced when he heard the men whistle and, swallowing convulsively, tried to block out the vision of his dead parents as the killers began looting. Papa carried a lot of money and of course they would strip Mama of her jewelry.

It didn't take long for the men to finish with the inside, after which they picked the trunk clean and attempted to right the car, their grunts and oaths distinguishable in any language. They were annoyed that it had run off the road and were arguing about the possibility of salvaging it; something they eventually gave up on because - strong as they were - they couldn't push the Mercedes back up the steep embankment.

It seemed an eternity before they left, scraping the leather suitcases on the rocks and gravel as they climbed up to the road. One of the thieves was carrying his mother's purse; another had taken the spare tire. Soon they were gone from sight, but their guttural laughter could be heard, trailing them into the hills on the other side where it eventually died away.

Chapter Thirty-three

For a long time neither Peter nor Sigrid stirred. Weighed down by the immense tragedy, Peter wondered if he'd be able to get up again. In truth, he didn't want to. Lying in the dirt was far better than anything else he could do at the moment; such as tell Sigrid what had really happened. Thankfully, she wasn't asking questions. The bandits were gone, yet she remained uncharacteristically quiet. Perhaps she had guessed the worst and was in shock.

Peter heard the sound of an approaching car but with bandits nearby, didn't dare run up and flag it down. It sped by, oblivious to the catastrophe that had taken place. Apparently, the Mercedes in the deep ditch was not visible from the road.

Suddenly Sigrid began to weep, tears were running down her face before violent sobs shook her shoulders, convulsions that felt like giant earth tremors. Peter let her cry. Surely the bandits couldn't hear her. Since they hadn't fired at the car that just went by, they were probably at their hideout deep in the hills.

Aimlessly, Peter began brushing leaves off his sister's cardigan and picking burs from her hair. Their mother had plaited it this morning before leaving Klagenfurt, tying each plait with a blue ribbon that matched the flower print in her smocked dress. Peter had always been proud of his pretty sister and had sheltered her from playground bullies in Grunewald Park. But how could he protect her from a disaster of this magnitude, a calamity so enormous that he couldn't bear to think about it, let alone make decisions about what to do next, such as go back to the car - which was really out of the question. He couldn't make himself look at all that blood again.

A pale orange streak across the gray sky was all that remained of the setting sun; it would soon be dark. Should he and Sigrid stay here till morning or was it better to walk along the road tonight and look for help? Would they risk running into more bandits, perhaps the same group? If so, and if the killers suspected that they were eyewitnesses, their lives wouldn't be worth a *pfennig*. Peter concluded that it was safest not to be associated with the death vehicle. Therefore, much as he hated leaving his parents behind, he figured he had no choice. He and Sigrid had to put some distance between themselves and this spot. Their lives depended on it.

Sigrid's sobbing began to lose steam. "I want to go back to the car," she whimpered. "The men are gone. Can we go back now?"

"No."

"But we have to help Mama and Papa."

"We can't help them."

"Why not?"

"Because…because there's nothing we can do. Do you hear me? Nothing!"

"Why?"

"Because they are dead. They were shot!" Peter said it so fast that he surprised himself.

Sigrid made a strange hiccupping sound. "What?"

"They're dead. You hear me? *Dead!*" He wondered how he managed to say it a second time.

"I don't believe you. Why do you say such awful things?"

"Because it's true. They were shot up along the road. That's why the car crashed. We were both sleeping when it happened. The bandits didn't see us. If they had, they would have shot us as well."

A dull look came into Sigrid's eyes. Her mouth went slack and she stared at her brother, mute as a stone, a godsend because Peter was so desperately near tears himself that it was a battle not to cry. Another question might tilt him over the edge. Mindlessly, he began drawing circular paths in the dirt with his fingers and watched in detached fascination as some ants tested the new terrain. Soon he was aware of very little except the ants, and the fact that Sigrid's vacant eyes were still staring at him. But eventually he also became aware of the fact that the longer he stayed prostrate on the ground the more he ran the danger of falling into apathy like his sister. So, although it took great effort, he finally stood up and dusted off his pants. His tan corduroy blazer was peppered with burs from the shrubbery, and the suede elbow patches were caked with dirt; only his plaid shirt remained clean. Brushing at his clothes, he glanced around. Black shadows were obscuring the landscape, a good thing because darkness diminished the chance of being spotted.

"If we go back down the road," he said after contemplating various options, "we'll reach one of the towns we passed earlier today."

"But what about the...uh, those men?" Sigrid stammered, pushing at the bushes, attempting to get up.

"From the sound of their footsteps, I think they headed south into the mountains. If we go north, back where we came from, we won't run into them. As long as we follow the road we can't get lost." Peter wished he hadn't been asleep earlier. He checked his watch. It was almost eight o'clock. How many kilometers had his father driven since their last stop? Had they passed a town in the last hour of driving? And, bandits or no bandits, was it better to continue south, the direction his father had been traveling? No, the road north led home. *Home!* Peter made up his mind and reached for his sister's hand.

Sigrid didn't argue. She generally let him boss her around, and he only hoped that she wouldn't be afraid once it got pitch black. Unlike the rough handling he'd given her earlier, he guided her slowly from the shrubbery, and was brushing some dirt from her cardigan, when he caught sight of the gem around her neck.

"Tuck the chain under your collar!" he ordered. "If anyone sees *Oma's* emerald they'll steal it for sure. Keep it out of sight till we're back home." Again Sigrid didn't argue and slipped the jewel under her dress.

Peter pulled her across the ditch and up the embankment so quickly that she had no chance to look at the wrecked car. He alone saw the pool of blood oozing from the front seats, the round glossy stain spreading in the dirt. He felt sick to his stomach. He tasted bile in his throat. He wished he had closed his father's eyes. It suddenly didn't seem right to walk away. Of course, once he got to a town he would tell the authorities what had happened and come back here with the police, perhaps within the hour. His parents would be sent back to Germany for a proper burial. *Oma* would insist on that. She liked visiting the cemetery in Bernau. He and Sigrid had often accompanied her, sitting on the marble bench inside the low fence enclosing the gravestones of their ancestors. There, under the poplars, *Oma* had told them such wonderful stories about their grandfather whose name was etched on one of the large headstones. *Oma* had explained that someday she would be buried right next to him. She had pointed at the spot, and looked as though she couldn't wait.

Oma? Peter slowed his steps. What would she say when told about this tragedy? Miserable with that thought, he was no longer in a hurry, because when he came to a town he would have to telephone *Oma*. Telling her about the killing would be as bad as experiencing it all over again.

Chapter Thirty-four

Peter and Sigrid walked quickly along the road, but after a while their steps slowed and eventually Sigrid began to lag behind. The black sky was now full of stars, which made it easy to see; still, Peter would rather have had some lights of the manmade variety, but there was not as much as a flicker on the horizon, indicating a town or a farmhouse, and no car had come along since the one that sped by earlier while they were hiding in the ditch. The night was eerily quiet and behind him on the graveled road, Sigrid's steps were growing fainter. He turned around and saw that she was nothing but a small wobbly shadow on the roadway. He stopped and waited for her to catch up.

"If you loiter," he said when she came closer, "don't blame me if we become separated."

"How can we become separated if we follow the same road, silly?" She stuck out her tongue and sat down to remove her shoes - pretty patent leather slippers not made for hiking. Peeling off her socks, she grimaced. "Look! My feet are swollen. They hurt!" She began rubbing them. "I'm tired. You walk too fast."

Peter leaned down and studied her feet. They'd be a mass of blisters by tomorrow. But never mind. Tomorrow she wouldn't have to walk because they would reach a town long before morning.

"Put your shoes back on," he told her. "We can't afford to dawdle. We have to get help and we won't find any sitting here. It's best to walk while it's dark."

"I can't take another step. Can't we rest a minute?"

Peter checked his watch. It was past midnight. They had hours of darkness left. Maybe a short break wouldn't set them back significantly.

"All right," he said. "We'll rest. But only for fifteen minutes." His eyes strained to see into the night and away from the road. "Over there." He nodded toward a large outcropping of rocks. "But I'm warning you. Only fifteen minutes."

"You don't have to shout. Do you want the bandits to hear you?" Sigrid made a sassy face as she followed Peter down into the ditch and over to the boulders where years of accumulated pine needles offered a cushion against the hard ground and a copse of stunted evergreens provided some cover. Peter felt sure that if any killers happened along the road, they'd never spot them among the rocks.

Sigrid plopped down and was instantly asleep. The night air was chilly. Peter took off his jacket and put it over her. Crossing his arms, he sat down and leaned against a boulder. He would stay awake, keep watch, and make sure their rest didn't last longer than agreed upon.

Chapter Thirty-five

Peter awoke with a start to find the sun on his face and in the first instant of consciousness, wondered why he was sleeping in the out-of-doors. Of course, yesterday's horror quickly dawned on him, after which he wanted nothing more than to go back to sleep and blot out the world.

Propped up against the rocks, his muscles aching after spending the night in an unfamiliar position, he was angry with himself for having wasted precious hours. Glancing at his watch, he groaned. It was mid-morning. And as if that wasn't bad enough, he didn't feel a bit refreshed from his long sleep. He was bone weary and hungry, something he could deal with, but an empty stomach was something Sigrid would make a mountain-sized fuss about.

He got up stiffly, lifted his jacket off her inert form, all the while praying that a town was close by; and if not, that a friendly motorist would come along and give them a lift. As he expected, Sigrid became difficult the minute she opened her eyes. She whined and insisted on going back to the car before she remembered that she was hungry and that her feet hurt.

"A car is bound to come along," Peter said. "We'll thumb a ride. In the first town we come to, we'll find some German soldiers. After we tell them what happened, they'll give us breakfast and put us on a train to Berlin. Remember all those soldiers we saw in Zagreb and Bos Dubica?"

"That was a thousand kilometers ago," Sigrid sniffed and tried to put her shoes on, her blisters making it painful.

"No, only about a hundred. Maybe less."

"Well, I can't walk that far. I can't even get my shoes on."

"Don't be an idiot! I'm not asking you to walk the entire way.

There'll be a town or a village long before we get to a big city like Bos Dubica. A local policeman will give us a ride." Peter sat down to help Sigrid put her shoes on, but saw that if he forced the issue her blisters would pop. "You'll have to carry them," he said. "You can walk in your socks for a while. It won't be long before we get a ride."

As a precaution against being seen by robbers, the children spent most of the day walking in the gullies that ran alongside the road, Peter listening for traffic and climbing up to the graveled surface the minute he heard a car. By late afternoon only four had come along; three were going in the wrong direction and the northbound motorist ignored his frantic waving. Peter couldn't imagine why the driver hadn't stopped. He grew worried about the odds of seeing another northbound car before dark. But at least he and his sister were now far enough away from their wrecked car to be associated with it. They could safely walk on the road where they made better time.

Chapter-Thirty-six

With each passing hour, Peter became increasingly uneasy. Not only was he surprised by the absence of traffic, but also by the fact that he and Sigrid had not yet come to a town. They must have walked ten kilometers since this morning and the only sign of civilization was a small farmhouse nestled in the hills some distance from the road. They had gone there, only to be disappointed when they found the house deserted. Looking through the windows they saw floors littered with old mattresses, empty wine bottles and spent cartridges. Concluding that it was some bandit's hideout, they quickly left but not before drinking some rainwater that had collected in a metal basin by the front door. The water took the edge off their thirst and their disappointment.

That evening, after their first full day of walking - their stomachs writhing for food - they again sought shelter away from the road. Before exhaustion claimed him, Peter decided that food had become a top priority. Town or no town, tomorrow they would have to find something to eat. But what? It was spring, too early for berries and nuts.

By noon on the second day, driven by hunger and a relentless thirst exacerbated by the sun beating down from a cloudless sky, the two children wandered away from the road in search of water. The weather had changed, and the sudden heat was debilitating and slowing their steps. Stumbling across a grassy and rocky field, looking for a crevasse or a clump of trees that might indicate the presence of water, they eventually found a shallow stream. The pools between the rocks looked stagnant and brackish, but it was drink or die. They also had to eat. Lack of food was clouding Peter's mind.

Their thirst quenched, they tempted fate and chewed on some shrubbery growing near the creek. But a while later, just as they found their way back to the road, they both retched, which left them weaker than before. Fighting nausea and overcome with a disabling fatigue, they shuffled on, pledging never again to eat vegetation or drink foul water. Long before darkness set in, Peter looked for a place where they could sleep off their misery.

The next morning Sigrid refused to budge. The bottoms of her socks were gone and her bare feet had taken a beating. Yesterday she had lost interest in carrying her useless shoes, discarding them. In no mood to again cajole her with promises about getting a ride, Peter hoisted her onto his back, carrying her like a knapsack - sheer desperation giving him the strength. But with each passing hour he suspected they would both die by the side of the road. When several cars roared by without slowing down, he was overcome by despair.

"Why doesn't anyone stop?" Sigrid asked, collapsing on the gravel when Peter put her down a moment so he could rest. He sat down next to her and took off his socks, wrapping them around her feet so she could try to walk on her own. He could no longer carry her. He would have given her his shoes as well, but they were far too big and would only make her trip.

"They probably think we are bandits," he said, standing up and taking her hand, ready to move on.

"Us? Bandits?" Sigrid frowned and would have laughed at that preposterous idea, except she didn't have the energy. "Is there such a thing as children bandits?" she asked instead.

"I don't know. Maybe. Even if motorists don't suspect you, they could mistake me for one. From the distance I might look like an adult."

"You have to be at least eighteen to be an adult. You're only fourteen."

"Is that so?" Peter said, irritated with her logic. "Well then maybe cautious travelers think we are bait."

"Bait?" Sigrid wrinkled her nose. "You mean like worms and stuff?"

"Don't be a dunce! I mean someone who pretends to look poor and pathetic in order to arouse pity and lure motorists to stop. Once they do, they find cutthroats waiting behind a tree, ready to rob them." Peter glanced at his sister, realizing they both looked genuinely pathetic. Her hair was a mess, the ribbons were long gone, and her blue dress was filthy. Because of the heat, she had tied her sweater around her waist, stretching the sleeves shapeless in order to knot them. That said, he probably looked worse. His knees were caked with dried mud from kneeling at the briny creek, and his blazer was torn where it'd snagged on some thorns. "We look like vagrants," he said in a dismissive gesture. "It scares people off. I remember hearing the soldier at the gas pump in Zagreb warn Papa to be careful. I bet all travelers are told not to stop for anyone."

"Well, Papa would stop. He wouldn't be afraid." Sigrid began to whimper softly; she had no strength left for loud outbursts.

"Yes, he'd stop." Peter began to walk, no small thing because without socks his heels would soon blister. The next time they found water they would have to soak their feet. To distract his sister from the long trek ahead, he began to talk about home; conversation didn't tax him nearly as much as carrying her. He talked about *Oma*, Karoline and Arina, Aunt Lisbet, and Uncle Fritz, whom Peter felt sure was a war hero by now. He talked about Karoline's and Arina's Danish grandparents, and he talked about Gabriella, Sigrid's friend. He also talked about his own friends, his soccer teammates, a tightly knit group of boys who were inseparable in school and on the playing fields. Peter talked until his tongue became a piece of leather in his mouth from lack of moisture. He talked until something in the distance caught his attention.

Chapter Thirty-seven

Unless his eyes were playing tricks on him there was a roadside establishment up ahead. Squinting against the sun, he saw a tavern - dilapidated - but unlike the farmhouse they'd come upon yesterday, it was inhabited; a man was sitting on a stool leaning against the building. Peter let go of Sigrid's hand and broke into a run. With deliverance in sight, he could safely leave his sister to plod along at her own pace. As he ran, he decided he would pretend to be something other than German. German soldiers had invaded Yugoslavia and were presumably very unpopular. It would be wise to speak French. As far as he knew, the Yugoslavs had no quarrel with France and, thanks to Mademoiselle Morisot, he spoke the language pretty well. First off, he would ask for a telephone. Initially it was more important than food because once he'd alerted the authorities to the wreck, and while waiting for them to arrive, he and Sigrid would have plenty of time to eat. As he neared the man slouched in the chair, a hat pulled down over his face, Peter slowed his steps and approached softly. There was nothing to be gained from startling anyone.

The place had seen better times, he noted; it did not appear to be a thriving business. Several windowpanes were broken and no sign hung on the rusty chain dangling from a pole above the door. His eyes traveled around the side of the building, where he spotted a woman in the fields some distance away. It appeared she was planting, but the rocky soil and the chickens pecking the ground around her probably defeated her efforts. Being careful not to make any sudden movements, Peter now stopped in front of the man, cleared his throat, and with a perfectly executed, "*Pardon monsieur, aidez-moi, s'il vous plait!*" announced his presence.

The man stirred, shoved his hat up on his head, blinked against the sun, and scowled when he realized that a mere boy had disturbed his peace. Waving him off, he folded his arms across his considerable chest and went back to sleep. But Peter needed help too desperately to ignore the dismissal. He might not find another living soul today. After two days of walking he had come to accept that this part of Yugoslavia was sparsely populated.

"Please, do you have a telephone?" he persevered in French.

Again the man motioned him off.

"Telephone!" Peter stood his ground, pantomiming to illustrate what he meant. "Please! A telephone!"

Peering from beneath his hat, the man finally interpreted the hand signals, rolled his eyes, and growled in his native tongue, "Telephones are for rich people living in cities."

Peter wondered if he ought to tell this man about the shooting. Maybe he'd be more helpful if he knew that he and his sister had been victims of a crime. But how could he make himself understood? How might one use hand signals to explain a double murder and a car wreck? In fact, it might be dangerous because, except for the absence of a rifle and gun belt, this man bore a strong resemblance to the bandits. Even if he was not a bandit, he might have a relative who, because of the war and general lawlessness, had taken to a life of crime. Peter decided not to mention the car or his parents. It was safer to simply barter for some food. If he and Sigrid got something to eat, they could continue walking. Surely a town with telephone service was nearby. This man and his wife obviously needed to shop for supplies. A rusty bicycle leaning against the building along with a motorized scooter, albeit with a flat tire, pointed to the fact that a town was within a reasonable distance.

Peter again began his creative gesturing.

The man looked at him and rubbed his fingers together - the international sign for currency. He was ready to make a deal.

Peter shook his head. He had no money.

The man waved him off, more annoyed than before.

Peter remembered his watch. It was an expensive Swiss timepiece *Oma* had given him last summer on his birthday. The case was pure gold, the band real alligator; he figured *Oma* wouldn't mind if he traded it for food when it was a matter of survival. He pushed up the sleeve on his jacket and pointed to his wrist, then to his mouth, indicating he was willing to make a trade.

The offer was sufficiently interesting to get the man off his chair. As he stood up and approached, he was so huge that Peter expected the ground to shake. The man bent down to study the watch. A moment later he returned to the chair, his snort indicating there was no deal.

Nonetheless, Peter forged ahead. "It keeps excellent time!" he said, again in French, even though he knew the man didn't understand a word of it. He removed the watch from his wrist and dangled it in the sun. “Look! It's pure gold. It’s worth a lot of money. It's practically brand new. It's an Omega! Swiss! The finest workmanship!”

The fellow pretended not to have the slightest interest and pulled his hat down over his face. But Peter suspected that he was plenty alert, his mind ticking sure as the watch.

Sigrid had caught up, her face flushed with excitement at the sight of an adult. She pulled at her brother's sleeve. “Look, biscuits! In there!” She pointed toward an open window where boxes of crackers stood visible on a shelf.

Peter, preoccupied with making a trade, forgot to warn her about speaking German. Now it was too late. The man had immediately recognized the language of the despised invaders and rose menacingly, his unpleasant expression turning positively ugly. Hissing a string of what Peter took to be Yugoslavian oaths, he fingered the handle on a knife in his belt and advanced like an armored tank.

Instead of doing the sensible thing, turning and running, Peter stood firm, his need for food so crucial he was willing to die for it. Boldly he held out his watch, all the while pointing toward the window. The crackers looked like they’d sat in the same spot for weeks but he figured they were still edible.

Precisely how edible, he and Sigrid would never know. With sudden and amazing dexterity for one so bulky, the giant reached out and grabbed the watch the same instant he turned around and took a bottle of mineral water from beside his chair. He shoved it into Peter's hands, pocketed the watch, moved a wad of tobacco from one side of his mouth to the other, spat, and took the knife from its sheath, running his thumb along its sharp edge. The message was crystal clear.

With the bottle under his arm, Peter reached for Sigrid's hand and backed away. Once he felt the graveled roadside under his feet, he turned and broke into a run, pulling his sister along, and only slowing down when a crippling exhaustion stopped him. He looked back, confirming that the man was not giving chase.

Panting, their lungs bursting, the children fell down on a patch of grass by the side of the road. After catching their breaths, they shared the water. Long greedy gulps soothed their parched throats and ran down their chins. The water was clean, bubbly, and made them belch, which in turn made them laugh at each other. They were having a wonderful time until the bottle was empty and Peter remembered he should have rationed it.

Chapter Thirty-eight

Later that afternoon, he and Sigrid were coming down out of the higher elevations, now walking along the road through a flat rolling landscape where tall deciduous trees encircled fields of grass. Believing they might find something to eat in the fields, they left the road and spent hours rummaging the vegetation, nibbling on anything that looked chewable. Feet dragging, heads bowed, they combed the terrain, swallowing wads of tasteless weeds that did nothing to satisfy their hunger and only succeeded in working up a blistering thirst.

Sigrid tripped. Peter heard dry twigs break as she fell and, turning around, saw that she made no effort to get up.

"Hey, come on!" he said, going over to where she'd fallen. Her eyes were closed. "You can't sleep here in the open. The sun will burn you."

"I don't care." She was licking her dry lips and moving her mouth like a beached fish, dying.

Peter could only stare at her. He had run out of incentives to motivate her. Lying on the ground she looked like a recently hatched bird that had tumbled from its nest. Her fragile condition scared him, but he didn't have the strength to pick her up. He looked around. There were some thick woods in the distance where they might find shade, water, and some edible mushrooms.

But talk of water and shade didn't tempt Sigrid. She just curled herself further into a ball. When neither scolding nor pleading roused her, he realized he had no choice but to carry her. Bending down, he mustered enough strength for the task, but might as well have picked up the giant who now owned an expensive gold watch. As Peter stumbled toward the woods, he had no way of knowing that if he'd gone in the opposite direction, crossed the fields and climbed a rocky hill, he would have come upon a homestead nestled in a small valley on the other side. It never occurred to him to head that way because it was arid terrain and he was looking for shade and water.

"We're almost there," he said, counting his steps in increments of fifty to urge himself on; even so, he began to think that the forest was a mirage because the more he walked toward it, the further it shrank into the distance.

"I can smell the pines," he said after a while, putting Sigrid down so he could rest. "They smell just like the ones in Bernau." Sigrid didn't respond and were it not for an occasional moan he might have believed her dead. "You know what? Once we find a nice cold stream I might catch a fish." He went on to tell her about people in Japan who eat raw fish and apparently enjoy it. "You like fish, don't you?"

Sigrid didn't answer.

Peter picked her up and again forged ahead, finally reaching blessed shade. Picking a path through the forest, he stopped to listen for the gurgling sound of a brook. He wished he had a knife so he could make notches on the trees to help him find his way back. Instead, he tried to remember distinctive patches of moss and trunks with unusual bark patterns. Carrying Sigrid like a rag doll, her feet dragging on the rotting leaves of seasons past, he finally happened upon a pond with evergreens growing around the edge of its muddy bank. Looking across the water, he saw that the opposite side had a small meadow fanning out from it. Walking through bog that tried to suck the shoes from his feet, he rounded the pond to this pleasant grassy spot.

"There! What did I tell you?" he said, carefully dropping Sigrid down on the grass, inches from the water. Although he knew he had wandered too far away from the road and too deep into the woods, finding this wonderful oasis was worth it. Notches or no notches, he'd find his way back. "I bet there is a sheep herder nearby," he said as he unwrapped the muddy strips from Sigrid's feet, all that was left of his socks. The smell of sheep hung heavy in the air and the grass had been trampled flat. "This is probably a watering hole for his animals. Maybe we'll run into him. If we do, remember to pretend you're French. Don't speak a word of German. We have to make sure he doesn't get mad and chase us off like that other man." Peter leaned over the pond and scooped water into his mouth.

Sigrid fumbled under her collar, fished out Dorrit's emerald heart, held it out on its chain and gazed at it. "I miss *Oma*," she said in a lifeless voice, her lips quivering, her dirty fingers smearing the priceless stone.

"I know. But it is no use crying about it," Peter said, realizing he mustn't even think about *Oma* right now or he, too, would cry. "Come on! Get up. I'll hold you so you can lean over and drink. But first, put that thing away." Sigrid obediently slipped the emerald under her collar, and once she was done drinking, she sat down on the grassy bank, drying her hands with a corner of her dress.

"You know what I wish?" she said as Peter again bent over the pond.

"What?" He lifted his head and looked at her, water dripping off his chin.

"I wish we'd stayed with the car. Maybe Mama and Papa weren't shot? Maybe they're waiting for us back there?"

"Stop it!" Peter sat back on his haunches and wiped his face and hands in the lining of his jacket. "They are dead. They were dead even before the car went into the ditch. I saw the whole thing."

"I don't believe you."

"It's the truth. I saw it!"

"I still wish we'd stayed. We wouldn't be lost."

"Who says we're lost? I know exactly where we are. The road is right over there." Peter pointed over his shoulder in a general northern direction. "I can have us back there in a matter of minutes."

"You also said there'd be a town and some German soldiers. You said they'd help us get home."

"Well, there *are* German soldiers. They are all over Yugoslavia. We just haven't gone far enough yet."

"I can't go any further."

"Sure you can." Peter stood up. "Put your feet in the water. Soak them while I go look for something to eat."

"No!" Sigrid cried, wild-eyed, anchoring her thin arms around his legs. "Don't leave!"

"I'm not leaving. I'll just look around the edge of the pond for some mushrooms. Maybe I can catch a fish. You'll be able to see me the whole time."

Sigrid let go of his legs and, dangling her feet in the water, watched him.

"I bet there's crayfish around here," he said as he moved along the bank.

"What's that?"

"It's like a small lobster." He didn't tell her that crayfish lived in the mud and were about as attractive. He had caught one in the riverbank in Bernau last summer. Of course he hadn't been tempted to eat it, but Nadia had sworn that crayfish were quite good when cooked. Raw, they'd probably be watery and chewy but he had passed the point of being fickle about anything he could put in his mouth.

"Um, lobster." Sigrid licked her lips dreamily and lay down on the matted grass. It felt soft as a bed. A moment later she was asleep.

Chapter Thirty-nine

Peter circled the pond, searching for mushrooms at the base of tree trunks and digging into the muddy bank, lifting large rocks where crustaceans might hide. There were plenty of water bugs and tadpoles, but nothing else. He spotted a frog and tried to grab it, but it got away. Empty handed he eventually walked back to Sigrid, washed the mud from his hands, pulled off his shoes and, huddling close to her, fell asleep, his feet in the water next to hers. His open blisters stung, but he was too tired to care.

He slept till stomach cramps woke him.

When he tried to sit up every muscle in his body screamed in protest. He was cold, stiff, and his head felt wooden and much too heavy for his shoulders. He fell back down on the grass and closed his eyes, tears suddenly streaming down his cheeks. He wished he were dead. Again he slept, woke, cried, wiped his eyes, and dozed off again.

Sometime later, being careful not to make any jerky movement, which sent jolts of pain through his body, Peter pried his eyes open and squinted through the canopy of trees overhead. Was it twilight or was it morning? He couldn't tell. The sky, what little of it he could see between the branches, was obscured in a gray blur. The weather had changed, he realized. There was no sun now, only clouds. He felt as if he'd slept an age, so it could very well be a new day.

What time had he and Sigrid gone to sleep? He missed his watch. Addled by deprivations, he had no inner sense of time and couldn't determine if it was dusk or dawn. The forest lay hushed and still. It must be toward evening, because if it were morning, birds would be twittering about, welcoming a new day, even a drab and dreary one.

Peter closed his eyes again; the grass felt comfortable, the water had numbed his feet. He questioned if he had the capacity to get up and leave this spot, or the wherewithal to find the road again. Suddenly he didn't care. All he wanted to do was sleep. He felt Sigrid stirring next to him and heard her talk, not to him, to *Oma. What?* Yes, he distinctly heard her talking to their grandmother and tried to listen but nothing she said made any sense. He turned his head and saw Sigrid, calm as a cucumber, sitting up and talking to someone a thousand kilometers away. Moreover, she was folding blades of grass and putting them neatly into the pockets of her dress. *She's losing her mind!* Peter struggled to sit up. He must shake some sense into her; flat on his back he could command no authority. They also had to get back to the road. Without it they were lost. The road was their only hope, their lifeline home. Slowly he pulled himself up on his elbows, reached for his muddy shoes and stuffed his wet feet into them. He found the scraps of his socks and without a word tied the material around Sigrid's feet as best he could. He stood up and reached for her hand.

"Come," he said, interrupting the splendid chat she was having with *Oma.* "Come on! We've been here long enough."

"Are we going to look for the shepherd?"

"No. We'd better get back to the road."

"But the shepherd might have some food."

"He could be far away and we need to find the road before it gets dark. The road is our only sure thing."

"But I'm hungry. Did you find some gray fish?"

"Crayfish? No."

"Then I can't walk. I don't feel so good."

"You might not have to walk. There's a good chance a motorist will stop."

"You've said that before."

"I know. But there's always a chance. We'll accomplish nothing, staying here. This spot will be cold and damp once it gets dark. Besides, there might be wild boars in the woods. They come out at night."

That stirred Sigrid into action. She had heard the story of their great-grandfather who'd been gored by a boar in Bernau, and it required no further coaxing to get her on her feet. Peter took her hand, turned his back on the pond, admittedly with half-baked determination, and started to walk, each step a hard won victory over buckling knees. Despite his talk about the importance of getting back to the road and the danger of boars, he'd much rather stay here where there was plenty of water. He felt dizzy and weak. Night was falling - he didn't need his watch to tell him that - and ribbons of mist snaked through the woods. He held Sigrid's hand tightly, afraid to lose her in the encroaching darkness.

He kept walking, but couldn't recall having come this far. Without daylight he lost his sense of direction. How long since they left the pond? Twenty minutes? An hour? Two? The mist was congealing into a dense fog that obscured all points of reference. He saw no familiar patches of moss, no gnarled branches, no bark pattern he recognized from before. It was as if the world was composed of nothing but identical tree trunks standing in a gray sea in which he floundered. He stopped a moment to get his bearings. Perhaps they should have stayed at the pond till morning. Peter fought a gnawing, panicky feeling that he was lost and despite exhausting footwork, getting no closer to the edge of the forest. He looked into the spreading darkness and suspected that he'd been walking in circles. He and Sigrid were trapped in a fog so thick that the moisture flattened their hair and made their clothes cling to their bodies.

Suddenly Sigrid stiffened.

"What?" Peter asked, believing something in the dark had frightened her. Visions of a mad boar roared through his mind.

"Smoke," she whispered, tugging at his hand.

Peter flared his nostrils and sniffed the air. He, too, could now smell the smoke along with the wonderful aroma of sizzling meat. Somewhere in this blurred world supper was being prepared on an open fire.

"Do you think it's the shepherd cooking his dinner?" A glimmer of life came into Sigrid's haunted face. "Do you think he'd share?"

"Maybe."

"Do you think he'll let us sit by the fire?" Sigrid's eyes were burning with dreamy visions of food and comfort.

"Sure. Why not? He's bound to be lonely with only the sheep for company. He'll probably enjoy having someone to talk to. But don't forget to speak French. Don't say a word in German. Better yet, let me do all the talking."

Sigrid nodded. She'd gladly leave all conversation to Peter because her mouth was going to be too full of food to say a word, except a polite *thank you.*

In wild anticipation, the two stragglers followed their noses, their steps quickening as they went. Soon they were running blindly through the night, pulled by the tantalizing smell of roasting meat. It wasn't long before they spotted the welcoming glare of a campfire in the mist between some tree trunks. Closing in, they could hear the low laughter of those gathered around its warmth.

"Sounds like there's more than one shepherd," Peter panted, slowing down to pick a path through the underbrush. "It means there will be more to eat."

Their minds consumed with thoughts of food, he and Sigrid stepped through the ring of trees that surrounded a clearing like a pole fence. However, barely had a dry twig snapped underfoot, announcing their presence, when six pairs of astonished eyes looked up at them with as much welcome as half a dozen cocked pistols.

Peter's heart stopped at the sight of the men sitting on rolls of bedding arranged around the fire. Remnants of meat hung over a crudely made spit, blackened ribs dangling into the flames. The head of a deer, its innards, legs, and skin, lay in a bloody heap off to the side. Several empty bottles and various eating utensils were strewn about. It appeared the meal was finished and that this was a temporary campsite meant to serve for one night only.

This was a cabal on the run!

Peter's joy of a minute ago turned to icy horror, plummeting his heart into a black abyss. Unintentionally, he squeezed Sigrid's hand so hard that she blanched. She turned and looked at him with eyes made huge by the alarm he projected.

"We've made a mistake. These men are not shepherds," he whispered with a sick feeling and realized that throwing caution to the wind had been a grave error. Unlike a shepherd who, having chosen a solitary life, might resent an intrusion but still offer comfort, these men would offer nothing. Their faces, grotesquely illuminated by the dancing flames, were the faces of brutality, similar to the ones who had killed his parents; outlaws who, because of the war, could ply their trade without repercussion or punishment. Men who were loyal to no one, no God, no country, and only to each other for as long as it suited their purposes to kill and plunder in packs.

Chapter Forty

The men remained seated, fingering their weapons and staring at the newcomers, their eyes narrowing and soon settling on Sigrid, ugly grins spreading on their bearded faces. With paralyzing horror Peter guessed what was going through their minds. But even if he could bargain for his sister, he had nothing to trade except *Oma's* emerald and worn by a girl in a dirty and torn dress, these men would probably think it was a worthless trinket made of bottle glass. Or they would simply take it and give no mercy in return. Peter had seen what bandits were capable of. His only hope now was to distract them long enough for Sigrid to get away.

"These are bad men," he choked on the words, still holding her hand in a viselike grip.

"Bandits?"

"I think so."

"What'll we do?"

"You're going to run."

"Huh?"

"You're going to run as far away from here as you can. Hide in some shrubbery till morning. Then find your way back to the road."

"Aren't you coming?"

"Not right away. I'm going to stall them."

"I won't go without you."

"You have to. I'll catch up with you along the road. Promise me you'll run when I let go of your hand."

"But it's so dark."

"Never mind. Run and you'll be safe. Run like a rabbit. And don't look back."

The men were getting up, approaching clumsily, the vile odor of stale tobacco, cheap wine, and unwashed bodies preceding them. The smell would have caused both children to hold their breaths if they weren't already doing so in abject terror.

Peter began backing up, pulling Sigrid along with him, all the while talking to the men in French. He explained that his family was nearby. He and his sister had gotten lost during an outing in the woods. A large search party was looking for them. So if they could just be allowed to leave the same way they'd come, there would be no trouble. When the men kept advancing, he tried his plea in what little English he knew and in utter desperation finally resorted to German. With that switch he also changed his story, telling the men that he and his sister were hiding from a battalion of armed soldiers. He had been caught stealing and expected to be shot. "It will be in your best interests not to be associated with us. We are thieves."

But no matter what language Peter used, the men understood only one thing: a pretty female had entered their lair and her age was of no concern because they were not particular about details.

As the slovenly individuals kept coming, the forest spun in dizzying circles around Peter. *Please, don't touch my sister*, he begged silently. This was as bad as seeing his parents shot. For the second time today he wished himself dead. *Kill us both! Just shoot us!*

One of the less sure-footed men tripped over a log and fell flat on his face. The others were quick to turn on him with ridiculing laughter. It was all the distraction Peter needed.

"Run!" he said, letting go of Sigrid's hand. "Now!"

He heard her sprint through the trees behind him and stood his ground a moment before he dove forward head first into the bulky flesh of the person he judged to be the leader. Thrashing and kicking, Peter held on so tightly it required the rest of the men to pry him loose; something he hoped would buy Sigrid time to get away. However, as ferociously as he fought, he was soon thrown down, his arms pinned behind his back, his face ground into the dirt by a foot planted on his neck. He heard a harsh command and the sound of heavy boots running through the underbrush.

It wasn't long before Sigrid was caught.

"Peter!" she screamed as she was brought back to within the ring of trees and thrown down on the ground next to the fire.

His mouth grainy with dirt, Peter pleaded for his sister, telling the men she had a priceless emerald they could have. He mixed languages together because in his torment he was no longer clear headed. But it didn't matter. The pack didn't understand a word he was saying and only laughed at him. He attempted to free himself in a contest so savage that it required several men to subdue him.

The rough handling had knocked the wind out of Sigrid and, heaving for air, she looked wildly around the campsite for her brother, finally seeing him pinned in the dirt nearby. She called out to him before a greasy hand came down over her face, shutting off all sound except a gurgling in her throat, stemming from a violent need to retch. She felt her underclothes being torn from her body, and shrieked in primitive protest but the sound was trapped in her chest by the unrelenting hand over her mouth. She shut her eyes and blindly kicked at everything around her until - spread eagle - her legs were immobilized by someone of a powerful strength. With renewed desperation, her fingers clawed at the hand covering her mouth. Someone grabbed her arms and pulled so violently that one snapped.

"Peter!" she screamed against the hand covering her mouth. "Help me!"

An instant later, a large individual was straddling her at the same time hands were exploring her most private parts; her immediate and monstrous outrage was followed by an excruciating and disabling pain in her abdomen.

"Peter!" she cried out again. "They are hurting me!" She tried to sink her teeth into the foul flesh, but only managed to bite her own lips.

The heavy body rolled off her but someone else was still holding her down. She couldn't move but could hear a brawl taking place nearby. Was Peter fighting with the men? Were they hurting him like they were hurting her? Dust was being kicked up and she heard Peter utter a string of profanities. In the next instant she heard him moan, a gurgling moan representing such agony that even the men momentarily stopped what they were doing. It became very quiet where the struggle had taken place. Something fell to the ground with a sickening thud. Sigrid jerked her head. The hand covering her mouth slipped. Peter's name ripped from her throat.

A moment later, a repugnant body was again crushing her. Again she felt a terrible pain and could do nothing but endure it. She closed her eyes. When the torment was repeated over and over, she began drifting in and out of consciousness.

Much later, surfacing from a black void, Sigrid sensed that her ordeal was over, if only because hands were no longer holding her down. Still, she couldn't move and she couldn't pry her eyes open. She heard rattling noises and hurried footsteps. It sounded as if the men were gathering up their belongings.

Were they leaving? Someone doused the fire, sending hissing steam into the air. It carried the smell of burnt meat; a smell that had been so inviting earlier now revolted her. Her stomach swayed, she gagged with spasms of dry heaves.

The noise of boots trampling between the trees and through the undergrowth grew faint, soon disappearing altogether. Shortly, all trace of the men vanished, except a lingering odor. It became quiet and, without the fire, cold. A chilly mist penetrated the ring of trees, hovering just above the ground like witches' brew.

Sigrid lay very still. She had no choice; movement was impossible. Her bones felt like pulp and her insides hurt with every breath she took.

Peter? Her lips formed his name. She couldn't utter a sound, but could finally open her eyes. She looked up toward the sky. The mist obscured everything. Where was Peter? Why was she alone? What had he told her? Suddenly she remembered. He'd said that she must find the road and that he would catch up with her.

Looking around, she attempted to raise her head, but a sharp pain in her stomach - like a knife twisting inside her - stopped her. Her head fell back down as a warm river left her body. Burning cramps followed. Oddly it didn't disturb her. She had believed that the bandits would kill her, but since she hadn't died and since they were now gone, she was no longer afraid. She was not even afraid of the dark. She was only afraid of being alone.

"Peter!" she called out softly.

There was no response.

The woods were quiet and she felt a strange peace. She slipped the hand that didn't hurt under her collar, extracting *Oma's* emerald heart, her fist closing around it. Gazing skyward, she saw her grandmother so clearly. *Oma* was dressed in a green suit of the finest mohair with a ruby broach fastened to the collar of her blouse. She was smiling and her eyes were full of love and comfort. It caused Sigrid such happiness that she experienced a pleasant floating sensation and discovered that she could now lift her head. Soon she could prop herself up on the elbow that didn't hurt. She looked toward the spot where Peter had grappled with the bandits, and as her eyes adjusted to the inky darkness, she saw him. *He was still there!* He'd been there the whole time. He had stayed with her. He hadn't run away.

"Peter," she cried feebly and with great relief. His face was turned toward her, his long legs were sprawled and one arm lay across his chest. Why didn't he answer? Was he sleeping so soundly that he didn't hear her? Yes, of course. They had done so much walking and he had carried her so much of the time that he was tired, too tired to talk.

Sigrid let him be. He needed rest. In the morning they would find the road together. The road home to *Oma*…

Thinking about the coming morning caused hot and happy tears to form on Sigrid's lashes. She blinked them away. "I'll save my tears, *Oma,*" she whispered. "I'll save them for tomorrow because tomorrow..." Her voice trailed off, the tears were choking her and, much as she tried, she couldn't stop them. But it was all right to cry tonight because tomorrow she wouldn't need her tears. Tomorrow she and Peter would be home.

She sank back down on the ground. She was cold but didn't mind it because *Oma* was smiling and waving to her from the garden gate. The sun was shining and the purple wisteria clinging to the wrought-iron fence along Lindenstrasse was in full bloom. A lace handkerchief fluttered in *Oma's* hand as she stretched out her arms to welcome the children home.

Chapter Forty-one

A farmer rounding up his sheep with the help of a dog long past its prime, happened upon the clearing the following morning, his mangy cur having growled from afar before bounding eagerly ahead and disappearing in between the trees. Figuring the worthless canine was finally on the scent of a lost sheep, the man followed.

Finding the two bodies didn't surprise him. He had seen bodies before; too many tribal groups divided the country; killings were commonplace, and since the invasion from the north, it had only gotten worse. Besides, he was a pragmatic man, not particularly disturbed by death unless it happened to one of his sheep, then he mourned because it impacted his livelihood. Other tragedies were quickly forgotten as he went about his daily chores.

However, this morning he could not turn away. These two casualties were so young and so horribly brutalized that it touched a nerve deep in his heart, a nerve long anesthetized by endless struggles against nature and man, now roared to life and refused to heed any amount of wisdom. The fact that there was no time for the dead when there were live sheep to round up went unheeded. The farmer stood silent and confused in the clearing while his dog, equally confused, ran back and forth between the bodies of the children and the partial carcass of a deer.

The dog ultimately settled on the deer, pulling on some entrails while the farmer bent over the nearest body. It was obvious that this boy had been badly beaten before his throat was cut. What on earth had he done to deserve such a cruel fate? He was a handsome lad and didn't look like a sniper or a thief. Dirty, yes, and his clothes were torn, but they were of a good quality - even an unschooled person could see that. It was also obvious that he didn’t hail from these parts. He was no peasant. His hands were too fine, his fingers long and slender and bearing no calluses. This was a city dweller probably from Sisak. But how had he ended up so far from home? Was this killing the work of some local thugs hiding out in the woods or those damned Germans? The size of the cold campfire and the tracks of many boots bore witness to the fact that a handful of miscreants had been in on this foul deed.

"I ought to inform the authorities," the farmer muttered out loud, but immediately thought better of it because they might detain him with questions, something he had no time for. Suppose he was asked to fill out a report. He couldn't write. He was not a man of letters any more than he was a man of leisure. He could not afford the luxury of a trip to town to spend time with something that was none of his business. However, he could spare a few minutes and bury these youngsters before predators in the forest tore into their flesh.

After establishing that the boy carried nothing of value, the farmer dragged him over to the edge of the clearing where a tree had fallen over, its roots pulled up, exposing a cavity large enough for two bodies. He slid the boy into it. Now walking back to the girl, he saw that his dog had lost interest in the animal carcass and was sopping up the blood she had hemorrhaged.

"You worthless idiot!" he yelled. "Get away! Go find some sheep!" He picked up a stick and chased the dog off before bending over the girl. She was exceptionally lovely. Her tragic eyes were open and fixed on the sky. It required no formal education to deduce what had happened to her. The revitalized nerve in the farmer's chest trembled anew with hot contempt for the perpetrators of such depravity.

As he prepared to pick her up, he blocked out the morning light filtering through the trees. She blinked, and her eyes, green as the glass trinket around her neck, settled on his face. *What?* The farmer scratched his head. She wasn't dead. Unfortunately, that complicated things. It was every person's nightmare to be buried alive and this child had already suffered a mortal atrocity. He tested her limbs. They were cold and stiff, but not with the firmness of rigor mortis - a condition he was familiar with in dead livestock. He felt her wrist, couldn't detect a pulse, but what did he know? He was no doctor, but he knew enough about life and death to guess that this girl was hovering somewhere between and betwixt, and if he didn't bury her, critters would soon enough come around and finish her off. His dog was not the only misbegotten scavenger in the woods.

Perhaps he could carry her home. It was a long way, but she was just a slip of a girl and it didn't look like she weighed much. She probably wouldn't last the trip, in which case he could bury her somewhere in the woods without qualms. On the other hand, why trouble himself? He had enough to carry on his worn shoulders. God had given him a far greater load than he could handle. His land was barren. His wife was fertile. He had too many children and too few sheep. While arguing with himself, listing his grievances with his Creator, he decided that the girl was as good as dead. He'd put her into the pit with the boy and be done with it.

He picked her up. One of her arms fell back at an odd angle. She didn't flinch. She felt no pain. She was dead. He could get this over with and go back to rounding up his herd. He carried her over to the pit. In his hurry, he tripped. A small cry left her lips. Exasperated, the farmer raised devout eyes toward heaven. The die was cast. Carefully shifting the girl to support her broken arm against his chest, he whistled to his dog and trudged toward home, carrying his new burden.

The mist had lifted. The morning sun was shining through the tops of the trees where birds flittered from branch to branch, their cheerful chirps welcoming the new day.

Chapter Forty-two

The month of May slipped by with no letters from Turkey. Dorrit experienced moments of concern but realized the war was responsible. Mail was notoriously slow, particularly international mail, and if Max had written anything that could be construed as war sensitive, mail examiners deleted the bulk of the letter and then found no reason to bother the beleaguered postal service.

In June - along with Lisbet, Nadia, and the little girls - Dorrit rode the *Ring-bahn* to Bernau. Persistent air raids over Berlin made everyone jumpy and they hoped the quiet in the country would restore their bomb-frayed nerves.

They had barely settled in when the military appropriated the remaining three horses and both cars, giving Dorrit promissory notes. She shrugged. Without gasoline, the cars were useless anyway. She was, however, saddened by the empty stables. Peter would be disappointed when he returned in August to find his pony gone. The Konauer stables were stripped as well, except for one old nag that Karl-Heinz rode to get around the countryside when bartering for provisions for his large household. Whenever he got lucky and was able to buy more than one chicken he always brought one over to Dorrit.

"If only I could get my hands on a live rooster," he said one morning as he walked into the kitchen at the barony with a scrawny hen under his arm, "I'd raise my own flock and have a hundred plumb pullets in no time."

"A lot of good it'd do you," Dorrit said. "The military would soon enough get wind of your industry and crate them off for the army."

"You're right." Karl-Heinz grinned at Dorrit's brood of females gathered in the kitchen; he personally made these deliveries because he trusted no one with anything as valuable as a chicken. "I'm afraid this bird is more feather than flesh," he added, handing the fryer to Dorrit.

"And no doubt cost a king's ransom," Lisbet remarked, becoming more and more practical with each new hardship.

Dorrit put the bird down on the kitchen counter. "It's wonderful. Thank you!" She hugged Karl-Heinz. "It'll make a great meal." Releasing her old friend, she went into the pantry and wrapped up several scoops of coffee beans. When Karl-Heinz refused her offerings, she insisted, saying, "Klara's oldest boy will be home on furlough next week. She and Gerlinde are planning a celebration. I'll be there and if I've contributed the coffee I won't be shy about drinking it."

Karl-Heinz relented and took the package; he very much wanted his grandson to have a cup of real coffee when he returned from the front.

"The bones will make a good soup once we've eaten the meat," Nadia said, taking charge of the chicken after Herr Konauer left. She immediately started plucking it. Karoline helped her by collecting the feathers floating around in the kitchen, while Arina sat on the floor, amusing herself with a couple of tail plumes. Dorrit and Lisbet took a basket and went outside to dig up some onions and potatoes from the vegetable patch behind the greenhouse. Later in the afternoon the whole family would walk across the fields and into the woods to pick wild blueberries. Gathering food was a daily routine. Lisbet's parents did not visit this summer. But in lieu of a visit, the Lundgrens sent food packages containing jams and jellies and other luxuries nonexistent in Germany.

Chapter Forty-three

A morning in July, an elderly postal worker on a rusty bicycle struggled up the long graveled driveway to the barony, rang the bell on his handlebars - a sound Dorrit and Lisbet had been waiting for. Hearts pounding with happy anticipation they ran into the courtyard where he handed them a letter. *Just one?* Though disappointed, both women rejoiced the minute they saw it was from Fritz. Mailed from Stalingrad, it had taken six months to reach them but had made it intact and had even been forwarded from Uhland Strasse in Berlin, something Lisbet credited to the kindness of one of her neighbors. In her excitement, she offered the postal worker some coffee, which he gladly accepted. She hurried back into the house, returning with a steaming cup.

The man sat down on the steps to savor his windfall. Climbing roses scented the air, which, combined with the sound of the trickling water in the courtyard fountain, made the morning exceptionally pleasant. Were it not for the mail pouch hanging on his bicycle, reminding him of his responsibilities, he would have stayed longer and chatted with the delightful baroness and her daughter-in-law. Instead, he finished the coffee, handing Lisbet the empty cup with a flurry of thanks. Just before he mounted his bicycle, Dorrit asked him to check the contents of the mailbag once more, explaining that she was expecting a long overdue letter from Turkey. With the taste of real coffee still on his tongue, the old man was happy to oblige her, went through his bag again and confirmed there was nothing further for this household. Tipping his cap, he pedaled to the gates and coasted down the driveway under the dappled shade of the ancient poplars.

Dorrit and Lisbet went back inside to the library where they'd left Arina asleep in the playpen. Lisbet ripped open Fritz's letter, saw the number eight in the upper right hand corner, and realized this was the one she'd given up for lost after receiving number seven and number nine. Sitting down on the sofa, devouring each page, she handed the sheets to Dorrit.

Nadia and Karoline returned from the orchards where they had gone to gather whatever fruit remained after military officials with crates had visited earlier in the week. Carrying some small green apples in her apron, Nadia walked into the library to check on Arina before going to the kitchen to make applesauce. Curled up like a cat in a playpen she had long since outgrown, the toddler was happily sucking her thumb.

"There's mail from your papa," Lisbet said, waving the envelope as Karoline appeared in the doorway behind Nadia, a half-eaten apple in her hand.

"Read it to me!" Karoline ran over and, clamping the apple between her teeth, grabbed the envelope, looking reverently at it while waiting for *Oma* to hand back the pages.

Her Papa wrote about snow, an icy landscape, and meeting Soviet troops face-to-face and living to tell about it. He described every ordeal associated with the siege at Stalingrad in a calculated casual vein, making no references to bleak and dire hardships. The military censors were harsh; mail containing bad news would not be delivered. Fritz complied, concluding that it was more important that his family hear from him, than hear the truth. Besides, he had absolutely no wish to distress anyone back home.

Working on his correspondence was the one activity that kept him sane during the final weeks at Stalingrad, where, half starved, numbed by cold and propped up against the bricks of a toppled chimney during a lull in the fighting, he wrote until his fingers froze around the pencil or until a renewed barrage forced him to put his writing away and pray that the Soviets, like the Germans, had run out of the really lethal stuff. By mid-January, following several disastrous battles where the Soviets showed surprising strength, Fritz suspected that a German surrender was inevitable and was not surprised when it came on the second day of February. He was only surprised that, among the mind boggling numbers of dead and dying, he had managed to stay alive. Bullets, mortar shells, dysentery, and influenza killed with equal determination. Of course he made no mention of any of this in the letters. Likewise, he didn't mention red snow littered with human body parts, nor did he disclose the fact that he and his comrades were eating the putrid flesh of dead horses.

Chapter Forty-four

Toward the end of August, after Dorrit and Lisbet had pulled up the last of the carrots and potatoes, it became a choice of hunger in Bernau or bombs in Berlin. They decided to return to Berlin. Max and his family had not arrived for their regular August visit and there had been no letters, so Dorrit was eager to return to Lindenstrasse and the mail she expected to find there. After reserving a taxi to take them to the train station the following day, she called Gerlinde and Karl-Heinz, inviting them over for one last visit of the summer.

They came that afternoon, arriving in an old buggy pulled by the single swaybacked horse left to them. The minute Dorrit heard wheels in the courtyard she rushed from the house to greet her dearest friends. Gerlinde had let her hair go gray, her face was deeply lined; all that remained of her former self was her slim, petite frame. But as if in defiance of the cruel and difficult times, she wore a bright red cotton skirt with a frivolous lace blouse. Karl-Heinz was in his usual riding garb. He was still a large individual but his shoulders were permanently bent. Were it not for a perpetual, amused gleam in his blue eyes he might be mistaken for a humbled man.

The three old friends went into the house, picked up some cold drinks from the kitchen, and walked through the center hall out to the flagstone terrace, where they sat down around the glass-topped table. They reminisced about the good old days, speculated on the war's imminent end and of better days to follow. Leaving Nadia with the children, Lisbet joined the threesome on the terrace, bringing out a treat Nadia had concocted with blueberries baked in shells made with the last of the flour and sugar.

Talk of *after the war* dominated the conversation as everyone made plans for next summer - Gerlinde making extravagant promises to once again host a Midsummer Night's festival. But for all their lighthearted talk, when the Konauers eventually left, everyone parted with heavy hearts and untold fears that couldn't leave their lips. A cruel fate with a twisted sense of purpose might breathe life into their most dreaded forebodings.

The following morning after a final trip to the cemetery to visit Johann's grave, and before the taxi arrived to take them to the station, Dorrit busied herself in the kitchen, carefully wrapping up any remaining comestibles that could be taken to Berlin. Lisbet and Nadia had gone to the river with the girls for their last swim of the season. It was a warm and sunny day without a cloud in the sky; surely a good omen, Dorrit thought, as she cleaned out the shelves. There had been no reports of air raids over Berlin for several weeks. Perhaps the worst was over. Perhaps it would be quite safe in the city and, if it remained so, Max and Cassandra would soon bring the children back. Dorrit sighed with that happy prospect and stopped her labors a moment to gaze out the window, half expecting to see Fritz and Peter ride home after a day of working in the fields, such as they'd done last summer.

Her eyes swept the unkempt lawns sloping toward the neglected fields in the distance. To the left, the orchard was a pitiful sight. The last time the military stripped it of fruit they broke so many branches it was as though a storm had ripped through the trees. Would the house be next? Would the regime begin to appropriate antiques and paintings to raise money for the war? Would they establish a military headquarters within these stately walls?

A thousand employees could not guard the estate from a Nazi command and - come September - Dorrit would only have one custodian on the premises. Marina, a local woman who worked for Gerlinde during the day had promised to spend nights at the barony.

Chapter Forty-five

Several pieces of mail awaited Dorrit when she arrived home on Lindenstrasse. She spotted them on the floor under the mail slot the moment she unlocked the front door, the same moment she was greeted by a musty smell, reminding her that the house had been closed up all summer. Frau Mueller had left her employ in June after her husband was called up for military duty and she had to fill the vacancy at the ball bearing factory.

Shutting the heavy oak door behind her, Dorrit felt the emptiness of the house as never before. Whereas formerly Peter and Sigrid would have raced up the stairs to reacquaint themselves with their rooms, now there was only a hollow silence in which her own movements echoed eerily. She dropped her bag on a hall chair and bent down to pick up the envelopes; surely one was from Turkey. However, leafing through them, she merely found some business correspondence and a letter from Anna von Steigert. Groping for some reading glasses in her purse, Dorrit walked into the library. The entire nation was under strict orders to conserve electricity, so she sat down by the Queen Anne desk near the windows to take advantage of the lingering daylight.

The censors had pretty much left Anna's letter alone. In the opening paragraph, she wrote how much she and Enno enjoyed having Isabel and Philip with them, before lamenting that Dorrit hadn't also come to Thessaloniki. Plus, she made no bones about her disappointment that Max, Cassandra, and the children hadn't seen fit to visit on their way back to Turkey. Puzzled, Dorrit looked up from the letter. Both had said that they would be stopping over at the von Steigerts on their return trip. Of course, since she had not come along, they might have skipped Greece altogether. Dorrit put the letter down, got up and went over to the globe on Johann's desk. Using her finger as a pointer, she traced various ways of getting to Istanbul. After driving through Yugoslavia, Max could have decided to go straight toward Zanthi and the Turkish border. Knowing his impatient nature, Dorrit concluded that was precisely what he'd done.

Finishing Anna's letter, she put it aside and was opening another envelope when heavy raindrops began pelting the windows. Driven by sudden strong winds, branches on the birch trees outside swished against the glass. The sky darkened and in the distance she heard the roll of thunder.

Thunder? Or bombs?

Dorrit got up and peered nervously through the leaded glass panes. Flashes of blue lightning, followed by violent claps and deep rumblings shook the windows. It was thunder, thank God, a late summer storm of natural origins.

She remained standing by the window and prayed the rain would last the night. The Allies never flew bombing missions in bad weather. A good downpour meant Berliners could sleep in their beds, not in their basements.

Chapter Forty-six

A week later a blaring sound pulled Lisbet from a deep sleep. She heaved herself up on one elbow and squinted at the bedside clock. It was too dark to see; the blackout shades were drawn and it was forbidden to use electricity during an alert. Groggy and disoriented, she closed her eyes and sank back down on the pillow, pinning her hopes on the fact that false alarms were quite common.

The sirens persisted.

She threw off the covers, sat up and raked her hands through her sleep-matted hair, wondering why in heaven's name the Allies couldn't do their dirty work at a more civilized hour. She heard a door open, followed by whining noises and running footsteps in the hall. Nadia and the children were up. Lisbet swung her feet out on the cold floor and, getting down on all fours, poked around in the dark for some slippers.

The sirens grew louder, the blasts came more frequently, signaling the bombers were nearing Berlin. Any hope that this might be a false alarm died in Lisbet's chest and, locating her fleece-lined moccasins, she staggered from the bedroom and into the foyer where she collided with Nadia, who was carrying Arina and had Karoline by the hand. Both children were sniveling and rubbing their eyes.

"Mama, it's dark. I can't see," Karoline moaned, now clinging to Lisbet. "Nadia says we have to go to the basement." Having just spent a peaceful summer in Bernau, Karoline had forgotten about these drills. "I don't want to…"

"Hush!" Lisbet said sharply. "We have no choice." Rummaging in the hall closet, she found the children's cloaks and dressed them before grabbing her own coat. Karoline fell silent. She was afraid of the dark, the screeching sirens, and now of her mother's voice.

"I'll carry Arina," Lisbet said, taking the child from Nadia. "Hurry up! Get your wrap. It's cold in the cellar."

Nadia found her coat, threw it over her nightgown, and took Karoline by the hand as Lisbet led the charge through the front door.

Guided by the banister, the small, frightened group went down the three flights of stairs as fast as they dared in the pitch black. Once in the lobby, they felt their way along the walls for the door leading down into the bowels of the building and the designated bomb shelter, a windowless room where a single low-wattage bulb was permitted to burn. Someone had gotten there ahead of them. The light was on and, though weak, made the climb down the narrow basement steps less death defying.

Tottering into the shelter, Lisbet nodded politely to her fellow tenant, a retired Reich Minister, who lived on the ground floor. Seated on one of the benches provided by the management, he was wearing his Nazi armband on the sleeve of his dressing gown as if afraid to be caught dead without it. He inclined his head, too aggravated with this nocturnal inconvenience for any conversation. By the same token, he regarded Karoline and Arina with a frown. They were the only children in the building and he sincerely hoped they would sit quietly for the duration of the air raid. As unpleasant as this was, crying children would make it even more so.

Putting Karoline between them, Lisbet and Nadia took their seats on a hard bench opposite the Reich Minister. No one thought to add any comfort because each air raid was expected to be the last; the press insisted the Allies were ready to call it quits. Knowing it calmed the nanny to have Arina on her lap, Lisbet handed the child back to her. As Nadia's arms closed around the warm bundle, she began to hum Ukrainian folk songs, her falsetto voice a pleasant sound compared to a dozen others one could expect to hear tonight.

The dowager, who lived a floor below Lisbet, entered the shelter a moment later, wearing a wool coat over her nightclothes. She was carrying her two pampered Persian cats; one was gray, the other black. Both wore real jewels in their collars, and as she sat down next to the Reich Minister, she gave the gray one to Karoline. Karoline smiled, stroked the long glossy fur, and lost her fear of the sirens.

The white Russian aristocrat Count Vaslav Golovkin, who occupied the garret apartment in the building, climbed down into the basement last. A debonair red velvet smoking jacket was draped over a richly embroidered black silk robe. His blond hair was slicked back with a fragrant tonic. He had clearly taken pains with his grooming before making his appearance and was, moreover, carrying a champagne bottle and four crystal flutes laced between his fingers. He was a well-known gay blade around Berlin. An array of pretty women regularly stayed in his apartment, and Lisbet was surprised to learn that he was home alone tonight. She felt conspicuous in her wrinkled nightgown, clumsy house shoes, and trench coat, and wished she'd taken time to brush her hair and apply some lipstick.

After greeting everyone with an easy smile, Count Golovkin asked the Reich Minister to hold the champagne while he pulled a wooden crate from a corner of the room to use as a table. Then he sat down, placed the long stemmed glasses on the crate, and popped the cork.

"Who'll join me in a toast to the Allies' poor aim?" He winked at the small stony-faced assembly, poured the first glass and offered it to the dowager; after all, protocol had to be observed even under these inelegant circumstances. She declined and gave him a quelling look. She didn't approve of the building's resident bachelor and his immoral ways, which included mocking this life and death situation.

The Reich Minister, whose wife hyperventilated whenever a tenant closed the lobby door with more than a polite click, was experiencing a touch of nerves himself tonight and gratefully accepted the champagne the dowager had refused.

"Where's your *gnadige* Frau?" Vaslav Golovkin asked as he passed the glass to him. "I trust she's not still upstairs."

"No, no. She's in the lake country. I sent her to stay with our married daughter in Plauersee. She left this morning."

"Good timing," Count Golovkin remarked. "I dare say the Allies mean business tonight. Judging from the intensity of the alarm, our spotters must have caught sight of a hundred bombers. Maybe more? I'm afraid we're in for some fireworks." He poured another glass of champagne and held it out to Lisbet.

She shook her head.

Vaslav Golovkin grinned at the Reich Minister. "Well, since the women refuse to join us, there'll be more for us. *Prosit!*"

"Heil Hitler!" the Reich Minister responded, taking a sip.

"Yes, to victory," Count Golovkin muttered with a sudden and abysmal expression.

Chapter Forty-seven

The blaring sirens stopped as abruptly as they began. A tense silence followed. Conversation in the basement died. All raised their eyes skyward as if expecting to see something besides the lone electric bulb dangling on a wire from the dirty ceiling. Everyone prayed the power would stay on because the light, though meager, was comforting.

The droning sound of enemy aircraft could now be heard. Count Golovkin's eyes caught and held Lisbet's. He looked repentant. His pretty neighbor had two small children, a husband at the front, and a scared nanny who looked as if she'd just been thrown to the lions.

"This is serious business," he apologized for his comment about fireworks. "I should not have joked about it."

"Maybe I'd better have a bit of champagne after all," she said, realizing she needed a drink. The humming in the sky over Berlin, which had replaced the sirens, was suddenly a thousand times more ominous.

Count Golovkin smiled, filled a glass, and magnanimously offered to pour one for the nanny as well.

"Thank you, no. We'll share this one." Lisbet took a sip and held out the glass for Nadia to have a taste.

As the planes flew lower, the basement walls vibrated. Lisbet took a second sip of champagne before putting the glass down on the crate. The Allied formation was directly overhead. *Count Golovkin is right*, she thought with mounting fear, *there's a hundred planes tonight.*

Again, everyone looked toward the ceiling, one and all praying the light would stay on. Their prayers weren't answered. The bulb flickered and went out at about the same time they heard the whistling of bombs hurdling down, followed by explosions in the neighborhood.

"*Mein Gott!*" the Reich Minister mumbled. "That was close."

In the dark Lisbet could hear him gulp his champagne.

Count Golovkin made a comment, but it was lost to the concussive blasts outside on the street. The basement walls shook; ears were buffeted, the cats meowed plaintively. Upstairs windows shattered.

Nadia was suddenly humming a gutsy Horst Wessel march, nothing like her Ukrainian folk melodies, and Lisbet was about to tell her to stop when anti aircraft gunners on city rooftops drowned out everything, including Nadia's burst of German patriotism.

A second wave of aircraft flew overhead. Rapid eruptions followed and were so deafening that the frightened group in the basement could no longer hear the whistling of individual bombs. Again the cellar walls shook, sending cement dust raining down from the ceiling.

Vaslav Golovkin lit a match. Eight pair of glassy terrified eyes, including the cats', stared back at him from the darkness. He changed his mind about pouring more champagne; it was no use asking anyone to hold the match while he refilled. His fellow tenants were holding their breath, all they could manage at the moment.

Suddenly, there was a sickening thud. Something hit the roof with a jolt that shook the entire building. Hearts stopped, all ears listening to the groan of beams breaking overhead.

A heavy object was plunging through the individual floors above them!

Chapter Forty-eight

Lisbet stiffened, the blood curdling in her veins. The hair rose on her scalp. A bomb this close was catastrophic. There would be no escaping it. Even if the swiftest among them clawed a way up the cellar steps it would be too late. The bomb would explode long before anyone reached the lobby. Any path to safety would be engulfed in fire.

Dear God! Her heart lay like a stone in her chest. Had it finally come to this? Entire families had died in previous attacks. Would she and her children be among tonight's victims? Like a fish on a boat deck, she was gasping for air, her lungs incapacitated with unspeakable fear, the thought of dying paralyzing her. Would death be mercifully quick? She couldn't bear for her children to suffer, to survive the impact, only to be burned alive. *No! Dear God! Anything but that!*

She clutched Karoline's head savagely against her breast and groped in the dark for Arina, her arm circling Nadia's trembling shoulders as well. On the fringes of her panic, she heard the dowager mumble the Lord's Prayer. Count Golovkin set his glass down on the crate. The Reich Minister was making odd wheezing noises. Lisbet wondered if he suffered from asthma. She also wondered how she was able to hear these trifling sounds, given the noise above her head.

There was another crash. The bomb had reached the lobby. The ceiling above the immobilized group in the basement caved in. Debris in the form of floorboards, lath and plaster, rained down on them along with a huge black metal object - the size of a bathtub - that smashed to the floor a few feet from where they sat in disabling terror.

A thick cloud of rancid dust filled the room.

No one moved.

As the dust particles slowly began to settle, all eyes were fixated on the blunt nosed object lying in the deep crater it had dug in the cellar floor.

There was no explosion, no fire, and everyone was wondering the same thing: was this a delayed-action bomb? Would a noise or sudden movement set it off? If so, it would never detonate in this cellar. The room was quiet as a tomb. Not a ripple of breath stirred the air. Everyone had turned to stone, everyone except the cat on Karoline's lap. It leapt into a dark corner far from the offending object.

Agonizing moments of a tense silence hung over the group before everyone slowly and very carefully began to crane their necks and glance around. The hole in the ceiling let in some light from the vestibule above, illuminated by fires in the neighborhood. But light was not needed. Everyone's pupils were dilated by shock, and, still expecting disaster, all remained in their seats, again staring at the bomb embedded in the floor. Every soul was thinking the same thing: would it be possible to ease out of the room without setting it off?

Chapter Forty-nine

The anti aircraft guns had silenced. There were no new explosions, and the droning in the night sky grew faint as the bombers left the airspace over Berlin. Eventually the all-clear whistles blew. Still, no one below ground at number 137 Uhland Strasse moved a muscle.

After what seemed like an eternity, the Reich Minister cleared his throat. First to speak, he did so with great difficulty. "I believe it's a dud," he said.

"A dud? How do you know?" Count Golovkin's voice was tight and uncharacteristically feeble for such a flamboyant individual.

"Because if it isn't, it would have detonated long before crashing through the floors above us. Certainly upon impact in this cellar."

"I see." Vaslav Golovkin didn't sound convinced.

"Believe me. We're quite safe. I know a bit about these things. This bomb is a dud. I guarantee it."

"Well, if it truly is..." Count Golovkin said with a nervous jiggle in his throat as he brushed at the wood chips and dust particles on his velvet jacket, "the Allies need to work on quality control."

No one laughed.

"It's a dud," the Reich Minister repeated, also brushing off the ceiling debris that had landed in his lap. He stood up. "We're perfectly safe."

"Then I suggest we leave." Vaslav Golovkin got to his feet, eyed the two children, and was amazed they hadn't become hysterical. His own nerves were jumping like static electricity in his body. "I suggest we move slowly and very quietly."

"Don't worry. You can kick it. It won't explode," the Reich Minister insisted and produced a candle from his pocket. He lit it, stepped over the debris littering the floor, and approached the crater.

Fearing the man was about to prove his point, Count Golovkin held up his hands, blurting, "All right! All right! I believe you. We all believe you. Now, let's get the hell...uh, pardon me ladies, let's get out of here." He motioned Lisbet toward the stairs. "Women and children first," he said with a gallant nod.

"I'll notify the bomb squad in the morning," the Reich Minister assured his neighbors. "They'll come and remove it. It's not the first dud to fall on Berlin."

The dowager called her missing cat out from the corner and, carrying both animals, followed Lisbet and her brood up the steps. Disbelief in their luck made the temptation to pinch each other unanimous. Of course, once upstairs in the lobby, any foolishness was checked by the sight of the gaping puncture wound in the roof high above the stairwell where a broken piece of the balustrade was swinging like a garden gate. The cavity in the lobby floor where the bomb had plunged into the cellar was equally disquieting, as was the smoke seeping through the front door, its stained glass panels shattered and reduced to a glistening heap on the floor. Of course this damage was immediately forgotten as everyone bunched together and peered outside where true disaster met their eyes.

The building across the street had suffered a direct hit and was burning out of control, thrusting billows of black smoke into the night sky. Residents in the structures on both sides of this inferno were leaving their basement shelters and running back up into their apartments to collect valuables and throw bedding from the windows because the fire was sure to spread. Other neighbors were standing on the street, screaming for those who were trapped, some braving the flames to enter the burning building.

The instant he spotted the inferno, Count Golovkin swore without apology, dropped the champagne bottle and glasses on the floor among the other debris, and pushed his way out the door to help with the rescue. His velvet jacket and silk robe flying about him, he sprinted across the street, dodging the small firebombs lolling about, clusters of incendiary devices the Allies dropped to help fan the fires.

The dowager sniffed approvingly at his quick action and agreed to let the Reich Minister help her return to her apartment. The glare from the fire made it easy to see but the smoke made it difficult to breathe, and she was glad to have a strong hand on her elbow.

"As long as it doesn't rain, I suppose we will be all right for the time being," she sighed wearily, bidding Lisbet and the girls a good night and again eyeing the gaping hole at the top of the stairwell. "I can't imagine workers will be available anytime soon to make repairs." She started up the stairs. "Are you absolutely sure that thing in the basement is a… What did you call it?"

"A dud," the Reich Minister said, taking her arm. "It won't explode."

Lisbet turned her attention back to the fire across the street and took comfort in the fact that Uhland Strasse was a wide boulevard; burning cinders would extinguish themselves before the wind could carry them over to this side. In the next instant she remembered that she knew someone in the burning building: a small boy about Karoline's age. They often played together in the park. He had an older sister, a sweet girl of about twelve, who watched him while their mother ran errands. *Oh, God! Those poor children!* Lisbet shivered and made a snap decision. She could no longer stay here. It was too close to the center of Berlin. The bombers would be back. She was moving in with Dorrit tonight.

She turned to Nadia. "Bring the girls upstairs!" she said, her voice raspy with stress and smoke. "I don't care what the Reich Minister says. We are not going to sleep here with that thing in the basement. Dress both girls and pack some clothes."

"Where are we going?" Nadia looked bewildered. The dowager had gone back to bed. Surely it was safe.

"To Grunewald. To my mother-in-law." Lisbet turned to Karoline. "Be a good girl and help Nadia. You're big enough to pack your own things. Just a small bag. We'll come back for more stuff in a few days."

"Aren't you coming upstairs?" the child wanted to know; her voice shook, the smoke and the raging blaze across the street frightened her far more than the bomb lying in the basement.

"Not just now, sweetheart. While you pack, I want to see if anyone needs help." Lisbet nodded in the general direction of the disaster, hoping Karoline wouldn't pick this very moment to remember her friend and start a commotion. "Now, get going!" Lisbet handed Arina to Nadia and turned back to Karoline. "The faster we get ready, the quicker we'll get to *Oma's* house." She prayed there was no disruption of the city's streetcar rails.

Karoline became cooperative. She loved going to *Oma's*, and surprising her in the middle of the night was bound to be an adventure.

She decided to help pack her sister's clothes along with her own.

Once Nadia had taken the children upstairs, Lisbet buttoned her trench coat, dashed across the street and went into one of the basements next to the burning building, joining rescuers already there. Everyone was feverishly digging a tunnel through the foundation, because if anyone was still alive in the shelter under the burning building, they needed an escape route. It was a race against the clock. The fire sucked up the oxygen and survival for those trapped in the airless spaces below ground wasn't very long. Smoke and blistering heat choking her, Lisbet clawed at the bricks and thought of nothing except digging the people out, two children in particular.

A fire truck came by. The men ordered all diggers out of the basements because carbon monoxide poisoning posed an acute danger. They doused the flames as best they could - given the low pressure due to damaged water mains - got back on the truck and sped off. There were other fires worse than this one.

A rescue vehicle came by a short while later and pumped air into the rubble of the now smoldering ruin. No sounds came back; there was no tapping on the walls, no faint cries. Behind her, Lisbet heard the retired Reich Minister talking to one of the rescue people. After walking the dowager upstairs, he had apparently wasted no time coming to help. She turned around and saw that he was covered with soot and that his clothes were singed; he must have tried to enter the burning building. She warmed toward him and almost forgave him his Nazi affiliation.

The rescue vehicle left. Nothing more could be done here. People, too, eventually began to disperse, heads bent, hearts heavy. Some went back into their damaged apartments while others walked away in search of family or friends where they could spend the night.

The Reich Minister took a piece of chalk from his pocket and scribbled a grim report on a charred building column: *All in this cellar perished*. The message was for relatives who were bound to come by in the morning. He added the date and as many particulars as he could collect from people before they scattered.

Lisbet gave him the names and ages of the two children before sadly realizing that she didn't know their mother's name.

Shrugging, the Reich Minister simply added: *And mother*. Underneath in parenthesis he wrote: *Father believed to be at the front*.

Chapter Fifty

As autumn of 1943 wore on, German cities experienced saturation bombings. The Luftwaffe was no longer able to scramble a sufficient number of fighter planes to intercept the Allies' airborne fleets. Most of Herr Hitler's feared Messerschmitts sat idle on runways, waiting for nonexistent spare parts.

Daily life in Berlin changed dramatically. Heavy losses, both at the fronts and at home, affected everyone. Former optimism was replaced by despair. Life became a constant struggle against heartache, political tyranny, hunger, and bombs. People left homeless moved in with friends until they, too, were bombed out. Subway stations became home to many, except near the Zoological Gardens, where people discovered venomous reptiles seeking shelter after their cages were damaged. A dozen crocodiles tasted freedom along with the snakes and were painstakingly hunted down in the city's waterways. Several of the huge creatures remained unaccounted for, striking a new kind of terror into anyone living near the canals. All zoo cages were now meticulously emptied, some of the animals dispatched to various butcher shops around town.

November came and with no coal for heating, Dorrit again closed the upstairs rooms, moving everyone into the guest quarters on the ground floor. Nights grew bitterly cold, and she and Lisbet regularly huddled by the fireplace in the library long after Nadia and the girls had gone to bed under mountains of blankets. The two women stayed up to enjoy the last glowing embers because nothing was wasted. Admittedly, they were also reluctant to go to bed because their sleep was bound to be disturbed. In fact, if an entire week passed without alarms, false or otherwise, the silence alone was so menacing that it woke them. Pacing the house in the wee hours of the night while imaginary noises roared in their ears, they often met up in the kitchen for a cup of tea to help settle their nerves.

On one such sleepless night, standing over the slow boiling kettle, Dorrit said for the umpteenth time, "I wish you and the girls would go to Denmark."

"We would if you and Nadia could come along," Lisbet answered wearily, placing two cups and saucers on the blue-tiled kitchen table. They had discussed this subject many times, and again yesterday after getting a letter from Lisbet's parents begging them to come home.

"I'd go in a minute if I had a passport," Dorrit said. "As it is, I'm lucky to be left alone. Nadia as an imported foreign worker can't travel either, but nothing keeps you and the girls here. A few weeks of uninterrupted sleep and some nourishing food would be good for you."

Lisbet couldn't argue that point. She'd love a square meal and a decent night's sleep in a heated house. But she had a good reason for not leaving Berlin. "Suppose," she sighed, sitting down at the kitchen table, wrapping the thick terry cloth robe securely around her, "suppose Fritz gets a furlough. He's entitled to one in December. What if he has written to tell us but the letter has gone astray? What if he suddenly comes home and I'm in Denmark?"

"I'd tell him. He'd call you immediately."

"What if the wires are down? More often than not the telephones are dead. His furlough could be used up before I got word of it." Lisbet shivered, not from the cold but from the thought of Fritz arriving home to find his wife and daughters gone.

Truth be known, Dorrit was glad Lisbet wanted to stay in Berlin, at the same time wishing she wouldn't because, frankly, it wasn't safe.

"Maybe you and the girls could go to Denmark for just a week," she mused out loud.

"Are you so determined to be rid of us," Lisbet laughed, "that you want me to take a long trip with two children for a measly week?"

"Of course not. But the girls are getting thin. It worries me. And if there's cream and butter in Denmark, I want them to have it."

"And they will. We all will. This war can't go on forever."

"I hope you're right." Dorrit turned off the gas burner, poured hot water into the teapot and brought it over to the kitchen table, sitting down opposite Lisbet.

They drank their tea in silence and without sugar or milk; what little they had was saved for the children. The heat of the steaming brew alone was a panacea against the cold and the inability to sleep. A November wind was blowing outside, rattling the windows behind the blackout shades. Dorrit rolled up the collar on her navy velour robe to shield her neck from the draft.

"Let's check Gertrude's garden tomorrow," she said after a while and poured more tea into their cups. "We might find some apples. I've been meaning to go and have a look. I should have done so long ago. I'm becoming absentminded."

"Don't you think others have already picked the trees clean?"

"Maybe. If we don't find any, we'll eat the brandied plums your parents sent."

"I thought we decided to save them for a special occasion. Such as Fritz's furlough." Lisbet took a sip of tea and shook her head. "Imagine, two perfectly sane women sitting in the kitchen at midnight, discussing when to open jar of preserves."

"It's a treasure. I'm sure it's the last jar in Berlin."

"All the more reason to save it. Imagine what it'll fetch on the black market come Christmas," Lisbet grinned.

"Christmas," Dorrit echoed dreamily. "It would be wonderful to have the family back together by then. Maybe Fritz's furlough will coincide with everyone's return from Turkey. What a holiday we'll have."

"Yes," Lisbet agreed. "Hardly a day goes by without Karoline asking when Sigrid and Peter are coming back. She misses them terribly. It won't be a real Christmas without them."

"I pray they'll be here. Surely, this incessant bombing can't last."

"If it does, if they can't come home, you will get a letter. Surely in the spirit of the holidays the post office will be motivated to let more mail through."

"A letter would be wonderful. Sometimes I worry so."

"You shouldn't. Julianne Niemann has family in Italy on her mother's side that no one has heard from in over a year. Max and Cassandra and the kids have only been gone for what? Six months?"

"Seven."

Chapter Fifty-one

"Come on down!" Dorrit called anxiously up into the gnarled branches of one of Gertrude's prized apple trees. "We don't need any more." She looked into the basket she was holding, counted seven apples, and although several were bruised and damaged by frost they would make a delicious puree. "Do come down!"

"In a minute."

Dorrit stepped out from under the tree and looked around the barren garden and the brick terrace where she and Gert had enjoyed many an afternoon.

"There are some really big apples up here," Lisbet hollered and inched further out on a limb, the bark discoloring her gray slacks. "If I can't reach them, I'll shake them loose." She yanked at a branch above her head, causing the entire top of the tree to sway. "Why are they so stubborn?" she grunted, struggling with the branch. It broke off. She lunged for another and shook it violently. "If these apples don't drop, I'll scream."

The apples dropped. Someone screamed and Lisbet looked down, wondering if one had hit Dorrit.

"Hey, *you!* What do you think you're doing?"

Quick as a flash, Lisbet shimmied down and bounced to the ground, brushing at the bark stains on her slacks and cable-knit sweater. "Did you say something?" she asked Dorrit picking up the apples.

Dorrit shook her head.

"*Hey!* You down there! Are you deaf?"

Dorrit and Lisbet stepped out from under the tree and glanced up toward the Tarnoffs' balcony, dumbfounded to find a woman hanging over the railing. Her long hair, the color of brass, was swept back from her face with silver combs, displaying huge red rhinestones dangling from her ears. A black feather boa was wrapped around her neck, and what little was visible of her dress, told them it was a shiny satin, a metallic color, and hardly morning attire.

Dorrit was about to inquire what on earth *she* was doing up there, when a man in Schutz-Staffel raiment materialized behind the woman, rising into view like a storm cloud on the horizon. Dorrit bit her tongue. She couldn't question him. One *never* asked an SS officer to explain himself.

"Don't say a word," she whispered, frantic, because the man on the balcony would not be amused by any of Lisbet's coy and saucy comments. This situation called for groveling. Nazis loved nothing more than to see people cringe. Snivel and lick his boots, Dorrit reminded herself; convince him we hold nothing but the highest regard for his officialdom. *And please dear God don't let him ask for identification!*

"*Bitte*," Dorrit began and almost sank to her knees, but that might be overplaying her part. "Forgive us." Meekly, she looked up at this menacing individual who could take his revolver, shoot at whim, and never be asked to justify his action. People were killed for lesser crimes than stealing apples. "I had no idea that anyone lived here," she said. "You see, I used to know..." she stopped herself in the nick of time. She couldn't mention the Tarnoffs. To admit association with anyone Jewish would put oneself under suspicion. Kneading her hands and lowering her eyes humbly, she prepared to correct herself.

"Who did you know?" the officer demanded.

"Ah, just someone in the clinic." Dorrit pointed toward the ground floor of the building. She didn't dare say she was the widow of its founder because hatless and wearing an old black coat with a dirty apron, the man wouldn't believe it and demand that she prove her claim with identification. "I was friendly with a nurse who worked there," she lied staunchly. "She's at the front now. At a war hospital. Before she left, she told me that this garden was no longer being maintained so I ought to harvest some of the fruit. I'm caring for my son's family. He's also at the front. In the Soviet Union." Dorrit knew this would please the officer and to further please him, she raised her voice declaring loudly, "Heil Hitler!"

"Heil!" the man responded and peered down at her as if he wanted to hear more.

Dorrit forged ahead. "My son's wife," she put her arm around

Lisbet as if to guard a certain frailty, "is expecting a baby and experiencing cravings. She must have apples. They ease her nausea. Her sickness this morning made us bold. She wants very much to have a healthy child for our Fuehrer." Dorrit eyed Lisbet's blue sweater, glad of its bulk, and prayed the man wouldn't inquire how long her husband had been at the front, which would necessitate another lie. To distract him, she said, "Of course, since you are now living here, *mein Herr Oberstleutnant*, the garden is obviously no longer deserted. So I'll leave this fruit for you and your wife." Dorrit held up the antique French wicker basket, indicating she was willing to throw it in with the apples.

Ignoring her offer, the officer addressed himself to Lisbet; there was little that pleased a Nazi more than a blond woman expecting a baby. "Let me give you some advice," he said in a less hostile tone. "Don't climb trees. You might do harm to the child."

"You're right. It was silly of me. I won't do it again." Lisbet flashed him her prettiest smile.

"I need a light, *Liebchen*." The woman, toying with a cigarette in a long slender holder, purred seductively and plucked at the officer's sleeve. She had lost interest in the trespassers, one of whom was far too attractive. "Let them keep the silly apples, Rudger." He lit her cigarette. She inhaled and playfully blew smoke at him. "Come on!" she said. "Let's go inside. It's cold out here."

The officer dismissed the women below with the wave of his hand. "Eat the fruit in good health, little mother," he said to Lisbet before he turned and disappeared into the apartment.

Pulling Lisbet along, Dorrit bolted for the garden gate, her heart pounding from the strain of dancing attendance to such people. Besides, Lisbet was about to explode with laughter, which would never do.

"Dorrit, you missed your calling," she sputtered once they were out on the sidewalk. "You could have had a career on the stage." She laughed and patted her stomach. "I wonder if Fritz will be pleased about this baby in view of the fact that he hasn't been home in eleven months."

"I had to say *something* to that uniformed beast. He could have charged us with trespassing. They shoot people for that."

"How did you ever come up with such a story?"

"I've heard Herr Goebbels claim that it's every woman's duty to provide children for the Fatherland." Dorrit took hold of Lisbet's arm to steady herself; she was sixty-two, too old to stoop and lick boots, too old to test a Nazi's gullibility.

"Don't tell me you're listening to his broadcasts," Lisbet teased and took charge of the heavy basket as they walked toward home.

"Heavens no! We had electricity early this morning so I turned on the radio. He interrupted the program with advice for the nation. Some of his rhetoric finally paid off."

"I guess so. Anyway, what were those two characters doing in the Tarnoffs' apartment? What right did they have to chase us away? It seems to me that *they* are the trespassers. It's still the Tarnoffs' place, isn't it?"

"No. The old order has changed. Laws have been turned upside down. Those in power confiscate the property of those they condemn. This couple was probably bombed out elsewhere and because of the man's position in the SS, given nice new lodgings. I imagine others have occupied the apartment since the Tarnoffs were arrested. I used to come by to check on things. But after I learned that Gertrude and Ben were dead, I stayed away."

"Somebody told you they died?"

"Yes."

"Who?"

"I can't say. I gave my word. I shouldn't even have mentioned it."

"If the Tarnoffs are dead, doesn't the property revert back to you?"

"Yes. But I hope poor Gertrude and Ben are never declared dead. I wouldn't want any official to examine my late husband's papers, titles and deeds, and perhaps discover that he married a Jew."

"Half," Lisbet grinned.

"It's all the same to the Nazis."

Chapter Fifty-two

Lillian Eckart called Dorrit on a Friday morning in early December to report that Kurt was missing. She was beside herself with worry and was about to pour out her fears when Dorrit stopped her, suggesting they meet in town for lunch. Since the telephones were working today, the wiretappers were back in business as well.

Two hours later in the elegant dining room at the Bristol Hotel on Unter den Linden, Lillian told of how she and Kurt had been awakened Tuesday at midnight. "Kurt cursed poor old Dieter," she said with concern for a butler of long employ who'd answered the doorbell and roused them from sleep. "Of course the minute Kurt learned that two Gestapo officers were at the door, he threw on a kimono and went downstairs."

"Gestapo?" Dorrit said, feeling a chill at the very mentioning of that dreaded corps. "What did they want?"

"I have no idea." Lillian began twisting her napkin as if wringing water from it. "They just asked him to come with them."

"Did he know them?"

"He must have. They chatted like old friends. I heard them tell Kurt he needn't trouble himself with his car. They would drive him. I suppose they didn't want him to waste gasoline. He came back upstairs and while he was getting dressed and collecting his briefcase, he told me that he'd been called to the Fuehrer's bunker. Night meetings are common, of course, and I wasn't alarmed until after he left. I pulled back the drapes to look out and saw two cars parked on the street with several more Gestapo officers standing about on the curb. I noticed Kurt tense the minute he spotted the additional escort. He slowed his steps, stopped, and turned back toward the house. He glanced up and saw me at the window. He waved. It made me nervous. I couldn't sleep the rest of the night."

"Because he waved?"

"No, because it wasn't a real wave. It was more like a sad gesture. I could tell by his face that something was suddenly very wrong."

"You could see his facial expression in the dark? From your bedroom window?" Dorrit suspected Lillian's imagination was getting the better of her.

"Sure. There were no blackout orders Tuesday night. Dieter had turned on the lamps along the walkway. And I'm telling you, Kurt looked odd. For the first time in his life he looked afraid." Lillian bit into an oyster and chewed distractedly; fortunate to have found seafood on the menu today, she unfortunately had no appetite. She swallowed with some difficulty. "Believe me, meetings in the Fuehrer's bunker can easily last three hours. Three days? Never!"

Dorrit didn't know what to make of it. She ate her oysters and tried to think of something to say. "Maybe he was sent away on one of those official trips you often complain about. He could have left right after the meeting."

"Without a suitcase? Besides, a trip has never before prevented him from calling home." Lillian stabbed at a carrot on her plate. "Yesterday I went to Gestapo Headquarters on Prinz Albrecht Strasse. I figured they could tell me where he was. I should have known better. They've become so secretive. I went home and called the Reich Chancellery."

"What did they say?"

"Oh, some tart receptionist said that Herr Doctor Eckart was on assignment in Munich. She acted as if it was none of my business. *None of my business!* I'm his wife. Can you imagine such gall?"

"Well, Lillian, if Kurt is in Munich. What's the problem?"

"The problem is that he hasn't called."

"Perhaps he's on a sensitive assignment. One he can't talk about."

"He's been on those before and he has always managed to call. Besides, I didn't believe the receptionist."

"What reason did she have to lie to you? And have you considered that the telephone lines in Munich might be down? Allied bombers strafed the city last week. Maybe the wires haven't been repaired yet."

"I thought of that. Right after talking to that sour receptionist, I called the hotel where Kurt always stays. He hadn't checked in and the connection was fine. I tell you, a summons in the middle of the night might not be unusual, but a double escort is."

"I can't imagine Kurt has done anything to bring trouble on himself."

"Of course not!" Lillian snorted at the very idea. "But he might have been framed by some jealous colleague. He's told me more than once that there's plenty of envy and back-stabbing going on."

"Kurt's too smart to be framed."

"Yes, but what am I to think? The way he was summoned reminds me of something else he's told me." Lillian drew her lips into a tight line and looked around for anyone who might overhear. Nearby tables were empty. The Bristol was not busy today.

"What?" Dorrit prodded when Lillian hesitated. "What else did he tell you?"

"I'm not supposed to talk about it." Lillian dabbed the napkin across her mouth as if reminding her lips to be silent.

"You know I won't breathe a word to anyone."

"You swear it?"

"Of course."

Lillian couldn't resist sharing a secret and, leaning across the table, lowered her voice to a whisper. "Kurt told me that arrests of innocent people are deliberate and commonplace."

"Oh, I know that," Dorrit said. "Gert and Ben were arrested. I never told you this, but I was there the day they were taken away." Dorrit spilled the particulars of what she'd witnessed, but stopped short of disclosing her subsequent telephone call to Kurt and his fact-finding efforts. Lillian would be horrified that she had involved him. "I learned later that Gert and Ben were sent to some hideous camp," she finished.

Lillian waved her hand in the air as if her friend had lost her mind. "Hideous camp? Really, Dorrit, where do you get such nonsense? Some foreign-born citizens have to be isolated. It's not an unusual wartime practice. Every country does it. Our centers are comfortable and cheerful."

Dorrit remembered Kurt using those very same words, but didn't say anything. She had known Lillian for over forty years, loved her like a sister, was aware of her loose tongue, and yet Lillian had never revealed to anyone within her elite Nazi clique what she knew of Dorrit's ancestry. It was probably the only secret she'd ever kept and Dorrit owed her for that.

"You know what else Kurt said?" Lillian glanced around to make sure no waiter was nearby. "Again, this is just between you and me."

"Of course."

"He compared Herr Hitler to a monster. He called him a dragon we had breathed to life only to have its fire devour us."

Dorrit sucked in her breath. "Did anyone hear him say that?"

"Maybe one of the servants."

"Dieter?"

"No." Lillian looked pensive a moment. "I think perhaps it was Gerti."

"Your housekeeper?"

Lillian nodded. "She left our employ rather suddenly."

"With servants in the house, I am surprised Kurt was not more careful."

"Me too. He always warned me to watch my tongue." Tears suddenly flowed from Lillian's eyes, streaking her face powder and ruining her mascara. "And now he's been arrested. I just know it."

Chapter Fifty-three

In the taxi on the way home, Dorrit fixed her eyes on the streets to discourage the elderly driver from initiating small talk as he drove along the Kurfurstendamm, following it west to Koenings Allee and passing a building damaged in the last bombing raid, that had suddenly collapsed, spilling tons of rubble into the street, leaving only a single lane for traffic.

The taxi inched along and eventually got stuck behind a car that had run out of gas. Dorrit paid the driver and got out. It would be quicker to walk home and the exercise might help settle her mind. Kurt's disappearance lay heavy on her chest. For if, indeed, he'd been arrested any hope of getting a new identity was gone. And suppose he'd been caught while attempting to secure her new documentation? A terrible guilt assailed her with the thought that she might have been at the root of Kurt's arrest before a more desperate worry pushed it aside. Would he be forced to talk? Would they come for her next?

After several blocks, she cut across to Hagen Strasse and saw that a queue had formed on the sidewalk in front of Solms Seafood. It meant fish was available. She had a rationing coupon and immediately joined the long line. Shuffling her feet to keep warm, she forced her worries from her mind, instead visualizing the happy faces around the table tonight when something besides vegetables was served. In hindsight she wished she hadn't eaten her oysters at the Bristol. She should have taken them home. Lisbet was housebound with a cold and needed nourishment.

The wind picked up and the sky grew dismal. Dorrit buttoned her coat securely and pulled a scarf from her pocket, wrapping it around her neck. Her hat, a small black pill box with a pretty net, was perfect for lunch at the Bristol, but not designed for warmth. Her feet were growing numb from standing on the cold sidewalk, and a pain shot up her back; both could be ignored, not so the fifty people ahead of her. Of course in the last half hour dozens more had lined up behind her. Surely Solms had enough fish for everybody or the proprietor would make an announcement.

Inching forward, Dorrit tucked her purse under her arm and stuffed her hands into her pockets. Her supple kidskin gloves were as useless as her hat. She had dressed expensively today, wearing a butternut suede coat over her black suit. Her hair was twisted into a neat chignon and large luminous pearls adorned her ears. On the heels of her encounter in Gertrude's garden, she had decided never again to leave the house unless she was well dressed. Without documents, she needed to look her best in case of a confrontation with a Nazi official.

Another half hour passed. Dorrit glanced around for a familiar face. She recognized several neighbors, but everyone waited silently with eyes downcast. Days of frivolous chatter were gone; nerves were frayed, minds dulled from continued stress, fear, and bad news. Even young women and the children they wheeled in perambulators wore tired expressions. Food lines were no longer an inconvenience; they were a matter of survival.

It began to rain. No one left the line. People simply huddled closer together as umbrellas popped up. Dorrit didn't have one but an old gentleman behind her shared his without comment. Nodding her thanks, she was again reminded that Berlin was now a city of women, children, and old men, plus the dreaded Schutz-Staffel. The young, the healthy - men like Fritz - were at the fronts. Again, and as she did many times each day, she offered up a silent prayer for his safety. She also offered thanks that Max and his family were in Turkey, removed from this bitter war. Suppose Max had also been inducted. How could she endure having both sons at the front? Yet such was the lot of many of her contemporaries.

Dorrit was inside the store and within an arm's length of the counter when a "Sold Out" sign was posted. Sounds of disappointment rippled through the crowd as everyone turned and left the shop. Back outside on the rainy sidewalk, Dorrit decided that if Lisbet was feeling better tomorrow, they would have lunch at the Bristol, even if it meant using up an entire week's worth of rationing coupons. Walking toward home, she took a detour in order to stop at the dairy shop on Taubert Strasse. She had a coupon for half a pound of cheese, which, melted, would flavor tonight's potatoes. Hopefully, Nadia had remembered to go to the public milk distribution center on Bismarck Allee to pick up the children's daily allotment.

As Dorrit trudged along, her hat and coat dripping, strands of wet hair plastering her face, her predicament pricked her like a thorn in her side. She had plenty of money but was as poor as when she'd been a child in Bialystok. Today, without coupons, she could no more buy meat or chicken than she could back then without money. She and her father had often survived on potatoes. Tonight her family would as well, and be grateful. The sad irony fueled her depression, as did the rain and the prematurely dark December day. As she approached Taubert Strasse, she found herself following a woman who, judging from the packages under her arms, had met with some success in various food lines. In fact, Dorrit recognized her as one of the lucky customers at Solms Seafood. She felt a twinge of anger because that woman had bought *two* fish. It seemed unfair.

As the woman prepared to cross the street, she stopped briefly to rearrange her rain soaked packages before sprinting to the opposite corner against a traffic signal that wasn't working. As she stepped off the curb and ran, something slipped from one of the soggy wrappings under her arm. A van roared by, preventing Dorrit from calling the woman's attention to the lost article. Once the truck had passed, Dorrit looked down into the gutter and saw a beautiful brown-spotted lake trout, big enough for a family feast. She decided she had two options. She could pick up the fish, catch up with its rightful owner, and return it. Or grab the trout and go home. The second option seemed the more attractive of the two, and before she could wrestle with guilt and other useless emotions, the fish was tucked head first into her coat pocket. She would smell like the docks in August, but so what? Tonight her family would have a real meal.

Turning and hurrying away from the curb, Dorrit was glad of the rain, because pedestrians who might otherwise have witnessed her thievery had their heads under umbrellas, watching for puddles, not each other. Still, she decided to take a different route home. Nothing would be gained by a chance meeting with the woman who had probably discovered her loss and was in the process of retracing her steps.

Chapter Fifty-four

Startled by a deep male voice behind her, she stopped and whirled around ready to face an honest citizen who had witnessed a dishonest act. However, her humiliation at being caught immediately turned to horror when, instead of a fellow citizen, she saw a man in the dreaded SS uniform approach with long determined strides, his boots clicking menacingly on the wet sidewalk.

She froze. This officer had no umbrella so had obviously seen the woman drop the fish and watched Dorrit take it. But surely he had also seen that she had not deliberately robbed anyone. Of course, to stage a defense was a heady task. Members of the Schutz-Staffel did not stand around on street corners, listening to excuses. They made arrests. *Dear God!* She would be escorted to the nearest police station and like so many others vanish without a trace. If only she had stayed in the taxi. Kurt had warned her not to draw attention to herself, but again she had done precisely that and right on top of the close call in Gertrude's garden. Could she grovel and play on this officer's vanity? No, Lisbet was not here to give her courage; besides, to demean oneself on a public street was unthinkable.

The wet fish weighed a ton in her pocket, and though guilt burned like red flames across her cheeks, Dorrit managed to summon a dash of dignity. After all, she was the Baroness von Renz, and let no one - least of all the corrupt SS - see Johann's widow crawl in public. Fashioning an expression of pride mixed with offended virtue, she faced the officer, thankful that at least this confrontation was one-on-one; the SS generally patrolled in pairs. She clenched her fists and called upon her deep loathing of the corps, hoping it'd stiffen her spine because her fear of them was not diminished with the repetition of her encounters.

"My dear Baroness." The man was smiling as he reached for her hand, pumping it enthusiastically. "It's so good to see you!"

Dorrit was speechless. This was a distinct breach of conduct. Members of the SS did not shake hands with their victims.

"I turned the corner and saw you at the curb," he said, still smiling. "I'm glad you picked up that fish before others could spot it. It might have caused a stampede and I would have been obliged to keep order."

Dorrit's hand flew self-accusingly to the bulge in her pocket. He had caught her in the act, so why was he smiling? It made him look handsome, diabolically so, being that he was in that detested uniform.

"*Gnadige* Baroness," he studied her face with concern. "Don't you recognize me?"

"No," Dorrit croaked. She positively did not know anyone in the SS.

"It's me!" He removed his officer's hat, tucked it into the crook of his arm and ran a hand over his sand-colored hair. "Helmut. Helmut Niemann."

"Helmut? Oh my God!" The air rushed from Dorrit's lungs with relief. It was Helmut, Fritz's closest friend, someone she'd known since he was a boy. "Forgive me!" she stammered. "Of course I recognize you. But what on earth are you doing in that ugly uniform? Uh, I mean…oh, *Gott im Himmel*, what did I just say?" Dorrit clapped a wet, gloved hand over her mouth, aghast at hearing herself denounce the Nazi symbol of authority.

"What am I doing in this get-up?" Helmut shrugged, taking no offense. "It's a temporary job. I've been at it only a few days. I was wounded in Russia, sent home for a couple of weeks and assigned to law enforcement. I do foot patrol and watch for price gouging and other illegal activities among merchants. As soon as I'm declared fit, I'll be going back to the front."

"Where were you wounded?"

"In the shoulder. It wasn't life-threatening but I developed an infection so they sent me home."

"With all due concern for your convalescence, Helmut, I meant *where* were you when you were wounded?"

"Oh? Near Kiev. Crossing the Dnieper River we took a lot of sniper fire."

"How awful!" Dorrit shook her head. "Did you know that Fritz was at Stalingrad with General Paulus' Sixth Army at the time of the surrender?"

"Yes. But I know nothing beyond that. No one is talking about it.

Retreat is not in Herr Hitler's lexicon."

"I know. Lisbet and I have no idea where Fritz is. We are hoping he'll come home on a Christmas furlough."

Helmut frowned; furloughs were rarely given now except for the wounded. But he kept quiet about that. "When did you last hear from him?" he asked instead.

Dorrit tried to recall; her memory was failing her, something she blamed on poor nutrition. "We got a letter this past July in Bernau," she finally said. "And I believe Lisbet received another one when she returned to Uhland Strasse after the summer. She drops off a weekly letter for Fritz at the Potsdam military depot. We have no idea if he gets any of them."

"Look," Helmut said, "I'll be going east again shortly. Why don't I stop by the house before I leave? I'll be glad to carry some letters. They'll have a better chance of reaching Fritz if they're brought to one of our headquarters inside Russia."

"That would be wonderful! Yes, do come by. I know Julianne and Lisbet see each other regularly, but with the constant air raids it's getting difficult. Bring Julianne and your darling boys. I haven't seen the baby. I guess he's only a few months old."

"And already a tiger," Helmut laughed. "He has to be to keep up with the other two."

"Then it's settled," Dorrit said. "We'll look forward to your visit. I'm sure Lisbet knew you were back in town and probably told me but I tend to forget things. The bombs rattle me. There are times when...oh, never mind." In lieu of more conversation, Dorrit hugged Helmut, deciding that the brandied plum preserves would be served the day of his and Julianne's visit.

As she released him, she stepped back in shocked amazement that she had embraced an officer of the Schutz-Staffel. Of course, the person in that vestment was Helmut Niemann, which made all the difference, for although he wore the regimentals, he was not one of them - he could never be one of them. Helmut would die before abusing his frightful powers. The SS trappings cloaked his body, but not his soul. It occurred to Dorrit that perhaps Helmut was not the only one. Perhaps there were others like him? It might stand to reason that not everyone in the SS was certifiably heartless. This notion came as a pleasant awakening causing her to experience new hope. The uniform that kept a citizenry hostage was suddenly less threatening because all who wore it were not necessarily Nazis. Some of them were Germans like Helmut Niemann. As her heart swelled with this new concept, her head filled with good omens for the future. Germany would survive despotism. Oppression and tyranny would lift like bad weather. The country would be restored and be there for her sons, their wives and children long after the present scourge had been wiped from its soil.

Chapter Fifty-five

"I can't for the life of me imagine why we've not had a letter from Max," Dorrit mused that same evening after their delicious trout dinner, and after Nadia and the girls were in bed. Dorrit and Lisbet were again staying up late, keeping warm by the fireplace, burning some dead branches they had collected in the garden. Going over the events of the day, they were discussing Kurt's unexplained disappearance, Dorrit's meeting with Helmut, and again the lack of mail from Istanbul. Lisbet was sipping hot chamomile tea to ease the congestion in her chest, while Dorrit drank coffee ersatz. "I feel that something is terribly wrong. It is so unlike him not to write. And the children promised to send postcards. I don't understand it. After all, we've had mail from your parents."

"Denmark is right next door," Lisbet reminded her as she'd done each time the subject came up. "Max's dig is in a remote spot. Turkey is far away. You haven't heard from Greece either. When did you last get a letter from Anna von Steigert?"

"I believe it was back in September."

"That proves my point."

"You're right." Dorrit got up from the sofa to stoke some life into the fire. The library had always been her favorite room, except now that it was perpetually chilly. "I hope the girls are warm," she said, and sat back down in the red leather sofa, pulling an Afghan over her knees.

"If we pile another blanket on top of them, even Nadia will suffocate," Lisbet said, stretching her feet out toward the hearth.

"Sigrid?"

"No." Lisbet frowned. "Nadia."

"Yes, of course, the children are nice and warm. The weather in Turkey is not at all like here."

Lisbet looked queerly at her mother-in-law. Dorrit seemed confused. "Look," she said, "maybe it's time we take some action. How about if we go into town and talk to someone at the university? The archaeology department should be able to help us."

"I would have done so already," Dorrit said. "If not for something Fritz once told me."

"What did he tell you?"

"That the university is not what it used to be. Nazis are at the helm of every department. They'll ask to see my government ID card before giving me any information."

"Well, I can go." Lisbet huddled her shoulders inside the blanket she'd wrapped around her. "I have the required ID."

"I don't know. I wouldn't want you to go into town until your cold is better."

"It *is* better. We were talking about having lunch in town tomorrow. Remember? I could leave a little early, go to the university, and then meet you and the girls at the restaurant. Where do you want to eat?"

"The Bristol. They had such a nice menu today."

"Perfect! It's close to the university." Lisbet finished her tea, got up, stretched, and announced that she was going to bed. "Tomorrow we'll put an end to your worries." She smiled over her shoulder as she waddled from the room, clumsily swathed in the bulky wool blanket.

The next morning, warmly dressed in a red fox coat and matching hat, Lisbet made her way to Humboldt University and went directly to the Archaeology Department. The office was staffed by a lone middle-aged secretary, who checked Lisbet's ID card before telling her that all records, correspondence, and information was stored below ground in bomb proof cellars that could not be opened for civilian inquiries for the duration of the war.

"But I need information about my brother-in-law. He's in Turkey. He's an archaeologist. We haven't heard from him in ages," Lisbet pressed her.

The woman waved her hand dismissively; everyone had the same complaint. "I'm sorry, I can't help you," she said.

"There must be someone around here who has knowledge of his dig. It's a very large and important site."

The woman got up from her desk, motioned Lisbet out into the hall, and pointed down a long corridor of lecture rooms. "You're free to ask one of the professors," she said. "I don't know what else to suggest. But don't interrupt a class. Look through the glass panel before you go in."

Lisbet thanked her and walked down the hall. Most of the rooms were empty, only a few classes were in session. She finally found a professor sitting alone at his desk. She went in, introduced herself, and happily discovered that he was familiar with the dig near Istanbul. Moreover, he had visited it in the past and knew both the principal archaeologists, Herr Doctor Maximilian von Renz and Herr Doctor Ernst Horstmann. He told Lisbet that as long as Turkey remained a neutral country, he saw no reason why their work shouldn't continue.

"So you are saying that my brother-in-law is there, working?"

"Yes, of course."

The professor's assurances made the luncheon at the Bristol a festive affair. Later that day, Dorrit wrote a long letter, telling Max and Cassandra not to attempt to come home to Berlin for Christmas. *We will miss you terribly*, she wrote in closing, *but it is still not safe for the children. Youngsters are increasingly being sent away from the cities. We pray the bombings will end soon.*

Fritz did not come home on furlough and, with the exception of a food package from Lisbet's parents no mail was delivered to number 77 Lindenstrasse.

Chapter Fifty-six

Hungry in unheated houses, sons and husbands at the front, Berliners wanted an end to the war and were desperate for news to that effect. Headlines proclaiming that the Allies' struggle against the Third Reich as futile were no longer believed. Bomb victims from Hamburg and other cities told the real story as they milled around Berlin's railway stations, waiting for connecting trains. Their haunted eyes told of defeat, their wounds and burnt clothing told of untended misery, as did lost children who attached themselves to strangers. *Berlin will be leveled next,* these refugees were saying as they waited for crowded trains. Direction didn't much matter as long as it was away from vulnerable cities.

There was another unsuccessful attempt on Herr Hitler's life. When it was discovered that several from his inner circle and some high-ranking Gestapo officers were involved, the enraged Fuehrer chose a dozen of these prominent suspects for a public hanging on Alexander Platz - his insatiable appetite for the ghoulish now indelibly etched on all who passed the corpses swaying in the wind until the rotted flesh peeled away from the bones. The once grand platz, glamorous pedestrian concourse and parade ground of emperors, had become a feeding place for carrion crows by day and rats by night.

It was around this same time that Lillian was finally notified of Kurt's whereabouts. The official telegram she received was short: *Herr Doctor Kurt Eckart remains at Lehrterstrasse Prison, facing charges of treason. Interested parties will be informed of the outcome of his trial.* Lillian was not fooled. She knew Kurt was dead and avoided going anywhere near Alexander Platz. To help ease her torment, Dorrit stayed with her for a few days until Elsie arrived from France. Elsie came with the intent of bringing her mother back to Paris but learned that the wife of an indicted official had to remain in Berlin under surveillance. Lillian could count herself fortunate that she was not arrested.

Chapter Fifty-seven

Sections of Charlottenburg were hard hit last night, the radio blared on a morning in late January. *The great number of bombers proves that this was the Allies' final and desperate strike! Berlin can expect no further missions of a destructive nature!*

A grim chuckle went up among listeners across town; no one with a grain of gray matter bought that logic anymore.

That afternoon, as soon as it was safe to venture into town, Lisbet headed for her apartment on Uhland Strasse. Since leaving last October, she'd gone back once a week to check for mail and water the plants. Now, riding the bus along Kurfurstendamm, she saw the smoke hanging over the entire area and her heart sank. Stepping off the bus, dodging people pushing handcarts of salvaged belongings, she stood and stared at the wasteland. Uhland Strasse lay in rubble.

Her eyes smarting from the smoke, she drew small shallow breaths and pulled her scarf up over her nose and mouth before picking her way along the once fashionable street. Finally stopping in front of a fire-gutted shell, she gaped at the blackened stone and twisted metal all that remained of her apartment building. *Maybe this isn't it?* she thought, pivoting her head; all the ruins looked identical. She scrambled over a rock pile to the carnage next door.

"Is that number 137?" she asked an old man resting on a cement block and pointed over her shoulder.

"Yes," he said with some difficulty, wiping gray cement dust from his face with hands raw and bloodied from digging.

"Do you know if anyone survived?"

"No."

"No one survived?"

"I don't know." He dropped his head in his hands and choked down a sob.

Not wanting to intrude on his personal grief, Lisbet turned and crawled back across the rubble to her own ruin, scuffing her boots and soiling the hem of her coat. Sounds of activity could be heard along the entire block, the familiar clatter of bricks tossed into the curb, the melancholy sound of friends and families of the missing who'd come, hoping to dig them out. Why was no one at this site? Of course she knew the answer: nothing was astir here because her neighbors had all perished. She thought of Count Golovkin. Had he toasted the Allies' poor aim last night? What about the dowager? Had her Persian cats died in her arms? Was the Reich Minister's wife still in the lake country? An icy wind whipping at her coat, Lisbet dropped her head in her hands and wept. She wept for her neighbors and, yes, she wept with overwhelming relief at her decision to move in with Dorrit. She had shown uncommonly good sense. Fritz would be proud of her. He had worried about her welfare before he left for the front. Well, he needn't have. Her survival instincts were intact. Wiping her face, she retied her scarf around her nose and mouth and again looked at the scorched ruin. Everything was gone. The exquisite furniture she and Fritz had picked out together, treasured collections of music and first edition books, paintings and photographs. Even if there was something to salvage, she couldn't bring herself to dig into the rubble. Suppose she came upon the tomb of her neighbors?

Choking on rancid smoke, Lisbet was again blinded by tears, tears of gratitude for what was left. She had her daughters and she had Fritz. With all of their worldly possessions gone, God would surely spare him. No harm would befall him at the front. After all, fairness dictated that only so much could be taken from any one individual. She had lost her home but Fritz would return. They would pick up the pieces and start over. It was as simple as that. She turned away from the ruin and began to make her way back to the Kurfurstendamm, coughing into the folds of her scarf and hugging herself to stem a trembling she couldn't control. The smoldering piles of rubble gave off heat, but she felt chilled to the bone.

At a newspaper kiosk on the corner, she spotted an all too familiar sight: a military official posting casualty lists. She stopped and watched until he was done and had walked off to repeat his sorry task elsewhere. Staring at the fluttering sheets nailed to the side of the kiosk, they seemed to be waving her on, but she couldn't move. Pedestrians brushed past her, some muttering that she was blocking the sidewalk - narrowed by rubble - others inquiring if she was lost and needed direction.

Lisbet glanced down the Kurfurstendamm, saw no sign of a bus and knew she had time to check the lists. In fact, she had to check them because mail would not be delivered to a ruin. Like it or not, she was now dependent on public notices and might as well get used to it. Besides, she had nothing to fear from those wretched sheets. She had lost her home today and would not be dealt a double blow. That much was already established.

Approaching the kiosk, she put out her hand to hold down the pages against the wind. The names were listed in alphabetical order, and as she quickly skipped to the end of the alphabet, her heart began beating abnormally. The thought of walking away in blissful ignorance was tempting, but she couldn't. Perhaps she was a coward, but she was also an actress, and if the assortment of women now lined up behind her could face the music, so could she. Moreover, she had to be swift about it because it was too cold to keep the others waiting.

Forcing her attention back to the names, Lisbet continued. *Wait a minute!* Helmut Niemann had returned to the front right after Christmas. Was he listed? She scanned the Ns, reached the Os, and knew Helmut was alive. Fortified by this good news, she continued. However, by the time she passed U and came to the first V, she was swallowing convulsively. Of course, the War Ministry made plenty of mistakes. Even if Fritz's name appeared, it could be an error, and, bracing herself with that thought, she continued until she was reading names beginning with W. She had passed all the vons. Gustav von Posen was the last. *Fritz was not on the list!*

Lisbet's heart raced with a happy violence while uncontrollable giggles bubbled up inside her like the swarming butterflies she remembered from her days on the stage. She wanted to shout, she wanted to sing, but instead turned and ran toward an approaching bus.

Chapter-Fifty-eight

In February, Dorrit received an unexpected letter from Turkey, unexpected because it was from Ernst Horstmann, not from Max or Cassandra. Fraught with curiosity, she tore open the envelope. The letter had been written in December, had been underway for more than two months, but had miraculously escaped the censors' black ink.

My dear Baroness:

I begin by asking your forgiveness. I committed a grave breach of privacy today when I opened your Christmas letter to Max and Cassandra, my justification being that I was becoming concerned about their whereabouts and hoped your correspondence would shed some light on their itinerary. Needless to say it did not, and only made it clear that you are not aware of the fact that Max and his family haven't arrived yet.

Please do not be alarmed. Let me stress that I am not unduly concerned, only puzzled, because Max has always in the past communicated any change in his plans. He is, as of this writing, many months overdue. Perhaps he has been frustrated in his attempts to contact us. Neither the wire service in Istanbul nor our local mail delivery is dependable.

My personal hunch points to the idea that Max and Cassandra decided to travel to Aiyina to show Peter and Sigrid their mother's birthplace. Perhaps they are stuck on the island. In view of the war, I imagine the ferries run infrequently, if at all. I also know they planned to stop and visit the von Steigerts in Thessaloniki. I have now contacted Ambassador von Steigert and hope to hear from him soon. We all understand that travel is getting increasingly difficult. Another one of our colleagues is missing as well. People all across Europe become stranded for months and for any number of reasons. I remain confident that Max will soon be here.

I close with the hope that you are enjoying good health.

Cordially,

Ernst Horstmann

To alleviate Dorrit's anxiety, Lisbet went back to the university the following day. She combed the Archaeology Department, but couldn't find the professor she'd spoken to before. Nor could she find anyone else with reliable information about the dig outside Istanbul.

Chapter Fifty-nine

A few days later there was a loud knock on the door at 77 Lindenstrasse.

"Who on earth is that?" Lisbet's eyebrows shot up as she glanced around the kitchen table where the family had gathered for breakfast - oatmeal cooked over a small alcohol burner. The gas had recently been cut off in the entire neighborhood and it was anyone's guess when it might be turned back on. A weak winter sun peeked through the window over the sink, filtering its pale light through the feathery frost on the glass. "What can anyone want at this hour?"

"Maybe it's a telegram," Dorrit said, putting down her spoon. She'd been nibbling slowly at her porridge, trying to make it last. Pushing back her stool, she wrapped her quilted morning coat around herself and got up from the table.

Lisbet took off her apron, straightened the collar on her terry cloth robe, and ran her hands through her hair to give her curls some bounce. Despite present hardships, she wanted to look presentable for company, even if it was just the mailman.

Leaving Nadia in the kitchen with the girls, the two women left to answer the knocking which had grown more persistent.

"Maybe it is from Fritz?" Lisbet suddenly ran ahead of Dorrit. "Suppose he's finally gotten a furlough." With that happy thought, she flew crossed the parquet and threw back the latch on the front door, flinging it wide open. Her face fell the minute she saw the two SS officers, one cradling a clipboard, standing shoulder to shoulder outside.

"Heil Hitler!" They clicked their heels together.

Lisbet shivered in the draft. "Uh...Heil," she mumbled, disappointed.

At the sight of the officers, Dorrit paled, stopped half way across the hall and took a few clumsy steps backwards, shrinking into a corner behind a high-backed chair, her knuckles showing white as she clutched it. Her mind went back to that terrible afternoon at the clinic when Ben and Gert were arrested. *Was it now her turn?* Standing paralyzed in the shadows, a desperate *deja vu* assailed her; the only thing missing this morning were the dogs. Ironically, she had slipped the noose at her other encounters with the Gestapo and the SS, yet now, when she had done nothing to provoke them, they had come for her. Had some zealous bureaucrat uncovered her past? Had Kurt talked before he went to the gallows? Had an unguarded word slipped from Lillian's lips? She socialized with Nazis and had plenty of opportunity. Of course, since Kurt's arrest and word of his execution, no one had gone near her. Dorrit was the only one who visited her now and she refused to believe that Lillian would betray her. Besides, Lillian was a wreck. She could not get out of bed, let alone make reports to the SS.

"Can I help you?" Frowning, Lisbet looked from one officer to the other.

"We're collecting fur coats," one of them said, glancing past Lisbet into the elegantly appointed hall. A fancy house like this was bound to have more than one in the closet, he figured, and if this woman wasn't cooperative, he and his partner would search the premises and find other valuables the military needed, including a trinket or two for their wives.

"Fur coats?" Lisbet said, dumbfounded. "You're collecting furs?"

"Yes. For our soldiers fighting in Russia."

"Oh?" Dorrit emerged bravely from her spot behind the chair; these officers had not come to make an arrest. "Furs for the military? I heard about the fur drive and you're certainly welcome to take mine." She rushed to the closet, almost tripping over her own feet in her hurry to give them what they wanted so they'd leave. "I have several. One is a black Persian lamb. Two are sable." She reached into the closet and took all three off their hangers. "Here you are," she said, turning around and all but colliding with the men who had followed her. *Of all the nerve,* she thought, *no one invited them in*. But, forcing a disarming smile, she handed over the luxurious bundles.

"Whose coat is that?" the officers pointed toward Lisbet's pride and joy still hanging in the closet.

"That's mine." Lisbet hated to lose her fur. It would be a cold winter without it. "I suppose you can have it," she said, all the while thinking that Dorrit's donation should have been enough. "If you really need it."

The men took it.

"You can have mine too." Karoline's small voice resonated from the back of the hall, startling everyone. Curious about the early morning visitors, she had left the kitchen and, hearing talk about furs for soldiers, was now approaching the officers, clutching her white ermine with the pompom tassels that she'd fetched from a back closet where the children hung their coats. "Maybe it'll help keep my papa warm. He's a soldier in Russia. It's very cold there. Isn't it *Oma*?"

Dorrit nodded, her heart constricting with the child's sweet offer.

Lisbet fumed, hoping the officers would reject Karoline's coat.

They took it.

"Thank you," one of them said and wrote down the number of furs collected at this address. "You are a credit to our Fuehrer, little one." Executing a brisk "Heil Hitler," he and his partner left.

Karoline watched the officers disappear down the walkway, her white fur glistening in the winter sunlight. Papa had bought her that wonderful coat during one of their outings on Tauentzienstrasse just before he went off to war. Karoline remembered that after buying the coat, Papa had taken her to the Operncafe on the Kurfurstendamm. "A favorite spot for celebrities," he'd said, bending down and whispering in her ear as the *maitre 'd* showed them to a table.

Karoline was proud that her father was taking her to such a grown-up place, and felt very special because people were looking at Papa as if he were a celebrity as well. Karoline wondered if he noticed that all the ladies were staring at him.

Once they were seated, Papa ordered a cream puff and hot chocolate for her while he had coffee with brandy and smoked a thin cigar - the kind that smells spicy, not at all nasty. While Karoline was enjoying her refreshments, Papa nodded discreetly toward a beautiful Japanese lady seated among several individuals at the table next to theirs.

"She's the wife of the famous actor, Victor de Kowa," he said so quietly that only Karoline could hear.

"Really?" Knowing it was rude to stare, Karoline pretended to look at the pictures on the green damask walls, while surreptitiously studying those at the next table. "Which one is Victor de...de...?" she whispered. She had never before seen a movie star.

"He's not among them. I would guess he's on location. Would you like to go see his next film?"

"Oh, yes!" Karoline bit into her cream puff, her eyes dancing with excitement.

"Then it's a date," Fritz winked as he leaned across the table and used his napkin to wipe custard from around his daughter's mouth. "But only if the subject matter is appropriate for little girls."

Karoline wrinkled her nose with that comment because she knew that her more practical minded mother would probably think it wasn't and spoil their plans. However, when she nudged her toe against the lovely box under the table that held her white fur, she instantly felt happy again.

She never learned if Victor de Kowa's next film was appropriate because it was only two weeks later when her father left for the Russian front. And as she now went back to the kitchen to finish her oatmeal, she felt a sudden hollow sensation in her stomach, not because she was hungry but because she missed him so.

Chapter Sixty

As the winter of 1944 wore on, the Lundgrens could no longer sit by and wait for their daughter to come to her senses and bring her family to Copenhagen. Widespread destruction inside Germany was well documented in the Danish press, prompting Harold and Gitte Lundgren to make plans to drive to Berlin and force the issue. However, no sooner had they decided on this perilous journey when a ban on travel in and out of Germany took effect.

Lisbet was battling one illness after another, eventually developing a chronic cough. But she could take no bed rest, because Nadia was no longer any help as a nanny. The bombs were unhinging her. She suffered long spells of total withdrawal and could not be relied upon to watch the children. Any noise, even a truck rumbling past the house, sent her scurrying to the cellar where she would remain for hours. Soon it was the only place she dared sleep.

On the last day of February bombs again rocked Berlin. The attack was widespread, came at night and without warning. Habitually a light sleeper, Dorrit woke around midnight to a buzzing in her ears like a swarm of mosquitoes. Wondering why no sirens had sounded, she threw a robe over her nightgown and ran from her room to rouse Lisbet. Holding a child in each hand, they made their way to the kitchen and down the cellar steps. No sooner had they plunked down on the chairs and cots, joining Nadia, who, for all practical purposes lived in the basement, when the first explosion could be heard.

"Are they crazy?" Lisbet said, lighting the candle that always stood ready on a shelf. "Why target Grunewald? There are no factories or government buildings out here." In an instant of childish absurdity, she stuck out her tongue at the ceiling as the roar of planes intensified.

Dorrit couldn't think of anything to say that wouldn't alarm the children, but it was clear that the Allies meant to raze Berlin and the suburbs in order to demoralize Herr Hitler. "I guess they are becoming impatient," she simply said. "Herr Hitler refuses to capitulate so they're trying to force his hand."

"Don't they know he's mad?" Lisbet said tartly. "Don't they realize they're dealing with a lunatic who will never give up as long as there's breath in his body, a bunker to shelter him, and a single soldier left to salute him. Not to mention a..." The all too familiar whistling in the night sky drowned out her voice.

Instinctively, everyone in the cellar buried their heads in their laps as their ears were boxed by a series of eruptions in the neighborhood. Nadia chewed on her bedding and whimpered incoherently, something that irritated Lisbet past endurance.

"Do be quiet, Nadia!" she spoke sharply. "Get a hold of yourself!" Reproaching the nanny was something she rarely did, but tonight her own fears flamed her temper and she couldn't stop herself. "Your silly babbling is upsetting the children." Suddenly Lisbet was alerted to the smell of smoke. "What's that?" She looked at Dorrit.

"Smoke."

"What's burning?"

"I don't know. But it's not us."

"How can you tell?"

"If the house was burning we would hear it. Some trees in the park are probably on fire."

Time stood agonizingly still. Finally, there were no new explosions. The bombers left the airspace over Berlin. Across town, survivors below ground held their breaths, savoring the blessed silence, before climbing out of their shelters to face the carnage above ground. The night sky had turned blood red with the reflection of hundreds of fires. The glare could be seen out in the countryside where farmers and villagers gathered, shaking their heads sadly. "Berlin is burning," they said, pointing to the red glow across the heavens and bracing for the expected flow of homeless come morning.

Leaving Nadia on her cot, Dorrit and Lisbet climbed out of the basement to put the children back to bed before checking the house for damage.

As Dorrit had guessed, smoke from burning groves in Grunewald Park was seeping through several second floor windows shattered by bomb vibrations. Guided by the light from the fires across the street, she and Lisbet stripped blankets and comforters from the beds and hung them over the broken panes, propping dressing screens and chairs up against the windows to hold everything in place.

"It'll keep some of the smoke out," Dorrit sighed, once the job was done and they trudged like battle weary warriors back down the long curved staircase. "It'll have to do till after the war. I don't expect to be able to order new plate glass until then."

Early the following morning, Dorrit ventured out in search of food. A depressing sight greeted her. The majestic trees in the park resembled huge blackened matchsticks, but better the trees than homes she sighed.

An elderly neighbor, Herr von Holstein, wearing a Tyrolean hat and loden cloak, was out for his morning constitutional. Happy to see the baroness, he tipped his hat. "We should leave Berlin," he said, shaking his head sadly. "But maybe with this attack on the suburbs, we've finally seen the last of Allied planes."

"Let's hope so." Anxious to be off, Dorrit kept her comments brief and after a few moments took her leave. Herr von Holstein continued toward his home, tapping the cracked pavement with his walking stick.

Dorrit reached the Halensee and saw that Johann's clinic and the two adjacent buildings had been reduced to piles of charred brick in last night's attack. A crowd of people had gathered, some probing the rubble, others standing in the middle of the street, talking in hushed tones over several bodies pulled from the rubble. Dorrit bowed her head in anguish.

"Johann," she whispered, "I'm glad you are not here to see this *Gotterdammerung*."

Chapter Sixty-one

Telephone lines were down. It was a week before Karl-Heinz was able to call Dorrit and, when he did, the blow was so devastating she experienced actual physical pain; the kind she had not felt since Johann died.

Hit by a phosphorus shell, the most dreaded in the Allies' weaponry, the von Renz estate had gone up in flames. As Karl-Heinz delivered this tragic news, he speculated that a pilot making a U-turn back toward the west after bombing Berlin had jettisoned the last remaining shell in his cargo bay with unfortunate accuracy. Standing large and tall on a gentle hill, helped by a full moon, the barony had been an easy target. Marina, the nightly live-in, had escaped with her life, a down comforter, and a bag of potatoes.

Disconsolate with this unimaginable loss, something in Dorrit's mind snapped. Any hope that the war would end soon died in her heart. Plunged into a deep depression, she did not hear Lisbet's talk of rebuilding after the war. *After the war.* It was all anyone ever talked about. Dorrit no longer believed in an *after the war.*

Days later, as she slowly emerged from the depth of her shock, she knew only one thing: she must save Fritz's family. Lisbet must flee with the children. They must go to Denmark. They could no longer wait for his furlough. It was only a matter of time before Berlin was wiped from the map and if the bombs didn't kill them, disease would. Weakened by starvation and fear, people from all walks of life were falling victim to an assortment of illnesses. The common cold had become a killer.

If joy was possible during these bitter days, Dorrit experienced it the morning Lisbet was well enough to go to midtown to obtain the necessary travel permits for herself and her children. Dorrit stood by the windows in the library and watched her walk through the gates and down the street. It was mid March. The gnarled wisteria clinging to the fence that ran the length the sidewalk showed no sign of life; no purple bud or hint of a new leaf; it was as if the vines remained dormant in reverence of the burned wasteland across the street. Dorrit prayed that it was still possible to get travel visas. Borders were closed but surely a Danish-born citizen would be allowed to visit her parents. And merciful God, let there be no air raid today. Berlin was due for one. Rarely did more than a week pass between bombings, and she shuddered to think of Lisbet alone in central Berlin, the worst possible place to be in the event of an attack. If only they could have called for a taxi, but lack of gasoline had taken all taxis off the streets. Hopefully buses were still running on a quasi-normal schedule. In a state of great anxiety, Dorrit continued staring out the window. A benign wind was rustling through the beech trees, sadly deformed after she and Lisbet had sawed off many of the branches for firewood.

Lost in thought, fingering the red velvet drapes, Dorrit wondered if it was time to pick up Peter at the Koenings Allee School. The clock on the carved oak mantel was jingling a little tune, reminding her that time was passing. She had better go find Sigrid. A brisk walk would do them both good. Sigrid had been ill, but was much better now and Ben insisted she must have plenty of fresh air.

Dorrit felt a small hand tugging at her skirt.

"*Oma*, will you read me a story?"

Turning away from the window, Dorrit looked down and saw Sigrid's beautiful face. "Of course, sweetheart," she said and reached out to caress the thick auburn hair tumbling over the child's shoulders. *What? Oh!* Startled, she realized it wasn't Sigrid tucking at her skirt, it was Arina, equally precious with her sweet angelic face and short blond curls.

"Can we read Hansel and Gretel?" she was wheedling.

"Yes, darling." Dorrit pulled a chair close to the window to take advantage of the natural light and lifted the small child clutching a book of Grimm's Fairy Tales up on her lap.

Sucking her thumb, Arina opened the book to the beginning pages of Hansel and Gretel. As Dorrit began to read aloud, she marveled that a two and a half-year-old wasn't frightened by a tale of children abandoned in the words and taking shelter with a witch who planned to eat them. Suddenly she felt a cold draft as if someone had left the front door open. She shook it off and continued reading, her eyes skimming the illustrations. How pretty and inviting the gingerbread house looked. The children were running toward it in happy anticipation. “No!” Dorrit called out all of a sudden. “Don't go there!”

“*Oma*, that's not what the book says.” Arina giggled. She couldn't read but had heard the story so often that she knew it by heart.

“Oh? You’re right.” Dorrit squeezed her little granddaughter. “I guess my mind is playing tricks on me. I'm glad you can set me straight.”

Karoline walked into the library, looking for Arina. She’d become bored, playing alone and decided to invite Arina to her tea party; a little sister was better than nobody. However, when she found *Oma* reading, Karoline pulled up a chair and sat down to listen. To interrupt would infuriate Arina, who would then insist on going back to the very beginning of the book. Karoline was not so bored that she wanted to hear the entire story of Hansel and Gretel.

By the time *Oma* finished reading Arina was asleep. “Well, it's time for her nap anyway,” Dorrit said and put her down on the sofa, spreading the woolen Afghan over her. Karoline looked disappointed. There would be no tea party now. “When your mother comes back from town,” Dorrit said to cheer her, “I'll go out and get us something nice for supper.”

“Can I come with you? Please, *Oma*, can I?” Karoline was eager for any diversion, any at all.

“I think not, darling. Shopping is a tedious task. The lines are long and you'd become impatient.”

“No, I won't! Really, I won't. I'll be good. I promise!”

“I know. But I'm worried you might catch something. So many people are sick and…” Dorrit stopped herself before the word *dead* slipped out. How could she tell a child about the appalling number of corpses lying on the sidewalks? “I’ll tell you what. We’ll go into the garden later and look for crocuses. Some might have pushed through the soil. We can also clip some forsythia. If we bring the branches inside and put them in a sunny window they'll turn bright yellow right before our eyes.”

Karoline was somewhat mollified by that suggestion, but knew it, too, had to wait because *Oma* wouldn’t leave Arina alone in the house. She wished Peter and Sigrid were back home. Peter knew so many games and Sigrid dressed her dolls so prettily and hosted the best tea parties in the world. Again Karoline fell into wondering when her cousins were coming back, but refrained from asking because the last time she'd asked, *Oma* had become so sad and had only answered, "Soon, my dear. Very soon." That told Karoline absolutely nothing, because *soon* was a word adults used for everything nowadays. It could mean tomorrow or next month. Even next year was "soon" to adults.

Chapter Sixty-two

"Borders are closed!" A female passport official said, ignoring the documents Lisbet placed on the counter.

"Closed?" Lisbet pretended surprise.

"Haven't you heard?"

"No," Lisbet lied. Of course she knew why her parents' trip to Berlin had been aborted but she had come here today, hoping for an exception.

"Well, now you know."

"But I am Danish-born," Lisbet persevered. "My father is ill. I need to visit my family. Closed borders can't possibly apply..."

"To you *personally*?" the woman asked sarcastically and looked over Lisbet's shoulders. "Next!" she barked, motioning to the person behind Lisbet.

"No, wait! Wait a minute! Please!" Lisbet was not about to relinquish her spot in line; she had waited an hour to get this far. "If borders are closed," she glanced around the crowded office, "why are all these people here?"

"They're applying for travel permits."

"To go where?"

"Other parts of Germany."

"One needs a permit to travel within Germany?" Lisbet asked, incredulous.

"That's right. Some areas can no longer accept refugees. Needless and frivolous travel must be avoided."

Bureaucratic red tape, Lisbet fumed inwardly. This was precisely what Fritz meant when he said that a police state keeps its grip by intimidation. She glanced at a map taped to the counter and noted the red line marking the Danish-German border. "Is Flensborg accepting refugees?" she asked, knowing it was within spitting distance of Denmark, and if she could get that far, she'd think of a way to get across.

"Let's see..." The woman consulted a chart before declaring that it was not yet on any restricted list.

"Good. I'll take three permits to Flensborg." Lisbet pushed her pile of documents back across the counter.

The woman studied Lisbet's papers and her children's birth certificates before passing them on to a male official who searched for signs of forgery. Using a magnifying glass, he compared the photograph on Lisbet's passport with that on her government ID card. It seemed an eternity before he handed the documents back to the clerk.

"What's your reason for going to Flensborg?" she asked, pulling some sheets from a drawer, her pen poised.

"Reason?" Lisbet hesitated. She couldn't very well admit that she was planning to sneak across the border.

"Yes. Why are you and your children leaving Berlin?"

"We were bombed out," Lisbet blurted quite truthfully, drawing the woman's attention to the address on her papers. "Our apartment building on Uhland Strasse no longer exists."

"Since when?"

"Last October."

"I see. Where have you been staying since then?"

"Uh, here and there. Mostly with friends, but they are now homeless as well. Lately my daughters and I have been sleeping in subway stations." Lisbet had to lie. If she told the truth, the official would decide that her living arrangement in upscale Grunewald was more than satisfactory and deny her the permits. Besides, Nazi bureaucrats were exceedingly nosy. It would be dangerous to drag Dorrit's name into this.

The woman stamped the permits.

Chapter Sixty-three

Leaving the passport office, Lisbet walked along Voss Strasse, passing rows of buildings still standing but punctuated by black ruins like missing teeth. She needed to send a wire to her parents, alerting them to her arrival in Flensborg tomorrow, and finally found a telegraph office near Leipziger Platz, sent the cable, and caught a trolley heading west. Her luck ran out when it got stuck short of the Hohenzollerndamm by debris forced into the street by a sudden gush from a broken water main. Without a word, the motorman and the passengers got out to clear the tracks. Figuring that walking was less taxing than tossing bricks, Lisbet left the area and went over to Konstanzer Strasse in the hope of finding a bus to Grunewald.

She had walked a few blocks when she spotted a Red Cross stand on Fehrbelliner Platz, serving coffee to the homeless. Her nose twitched with pleasure at the wonderful aroma filling the entire square - a king's ransom couldn't buy real coffee nowadays - and she wondered how the Red Cross had managed it. Swallowing her pride with shameful ease, she got in line; glad she was hatless with a soot-stained coat, which enabled her to masquerade as a bomb victim.

A full cup securely between her palms, Lisbet sat down on the marble rim of an empty ornamental fountain along with scores of others enjoying their windfall. Children sat with their mothers who allowed them a sip or two of the coffee. The sun felt almost balmy and, getting quite carried away with this blissful respite, some began to strike up pleasant conversations. An old man took a bread crust from his pocket, crumbled a piece for the sparrows flitting about, before dunking the rest into his cup.

Suddenly this heady peace was shattered by the sound of aircraft. Instantly alert, everyone stood up and prepared to run. Lisbet gulped the rest of her coffee, left the empty cup on the rim of the fountain and like everyone else ran toward shelter, a U-Bahn tunnel a block away.

However, as abruptly as the stampede began, it ended. There was something different about the sound of the planes circling overhead. It was not the droning of heavy bombers but the light buzz of low-flying smaller aircraft. Everyone on the ground stopped and looked skyward. There were only two planes, both American, and instead of bombs, sheets of paper now floated harmlessly down toward Fehrbelliner Platz. The pilots tipped their wings in a friendly gesture and left for others parts of the city.

Leaflets?

There was a mad scramble to catch them as they fluttered to the ground. People scooped them up and read them aloud. With her heart in her throat, Lisbet listened as the message echoed across the square.

Women and children must evacuate the city!

Herr Goebbels went on the radio that night to minimize the threat, ordering all women involved in the armaments industry to remain. “Additional antiaircraft gunners have been put in place,” he declared in an attempt to forestall a mass exodus. “Additional Luftwaffe patrols have been engaged.” Raising his voice to a new pitch, he shouted, “Berlin is safe!”

People switched off their radios and braced themselves for a cataclysmic attack.

Dorrit helped Lisbet pack.

Later that evening when Nadia and the children were asleep, the two women talked long into the night. They spoke of the future with guarded optimism, no longer pretending that the war had run its course; such talk had worn thin. The only hope now was to get on a train tomorrow and only if there was no attack tonight. Lisbet worried there might be.

“I don't believe the Allies will bomb right after dropping leaflets,” Dorrit insisted in her acute wisdom. “Since they went to the trouble of warning us, they will give us a little time.”

“How much?”

“Probably a day or two.”

“Is that long enough for you to get out to the Konauers?”

“Yes. Don’t worry. As soon as you and the girls are on the train tomorrow, Nadia and I will pack up and go. Lillian will come with us. Thank goodness we don't need permits to ride the *Ring-bahn*.”

Chapter Sixty-four

The following morning Lisbet found herself among thousands at Anhalter Bahnhof. The once beautiful train station had suffered bomb damage; blue sky peered through several holes in the domed roof, and a portion of the south wall was propped up with wooden braces. Crossing the concourse through a maelstrom of anxious travelers looking for transportation out of the city, Lisbet felt hot in her practical brown wool suit as she lugged the valise and carried Arina. Dorrit was in charge of Karoline and Lisbet's overcoat, which she'd kept folded over her arm since leaving the house.

All the booths were closed, indicating tickets would be sold en route. Handwritten signs informed travelers of departures and arrivals, but the information was sketchy. A southbound train - no time schedule listed - was departing from platform number eight. The noon train to Hamburg and points further north would depart from platform number five. People wishing to travel east were directed to Lehrter Bahnhof since Potsdam Platz Station was closed due to bomb damage. A number of placards asked civilians to give priority to convalescing soldiers, while several signs warned that no one without valid travel permits would gain access to the platforms. Both the SS and Gestapo officers guarded the station, so Dorrit suspected that particular rule would be enforced, which meant she wouldn't be able to see Lisbet and the girls off. That was unthinkable. They might have a long wait. It was now eleven o'clock, the Hamburg-bound train was due in at noon, but would probably run late. Moreover, if this teeming concourse was any indication, the platform could be dangerously crowded. Suppose Lisbet became separated from her children? What if Arina wandered off? Suppose Lisbet didn't get on the train? Dorrit had heard of mothers handing their small children through open windows of jam-packed trains, into the arms of strangers, only to fail to get on when the train suddenly pulled away. She made up her mind. She had to get out on the platform.

"Let me carry Arina." She tapped Lisbet on the shoulder as they pushed their way toward Gate 5. "You have enough with the heavy suitcase. I'll take charge of the children." Dorrit was hoping that, carrying Arina, she might shield Karoline from view and their group be counted as three. As they inched toward the gate, she saw that the attendant was not an SS officer, but a retiree who probably hadn't worked for the railroad in twenty years. Old and frail, he looked overwhelmed. What luck! Just before Lisbet was asked to show her papers, and knowing the child loved attention, Dorrit whispered in Arina's ear. "I bet that nice gentleman would love to hear you sing the alphabet song. He'll think you are such a clever girl."

As her sister's voice began hammering out the alphabet, Karoline looked up and eyed *Oma* oddly. She always asked Arina to be quiet around old people.

Pleasantly startled, the attendant looked up from his task. He smiled at the pretty child in the older woman's arms. "*Ach!* My own little ones used to sing that song," he said, a grin spreading on his wrinkled face as he reached over to stroke Arina's cheek.

"How old were they?" she asked, stopping her song momentarily.

The man scratched his neck. "I'd say they were maybe four or five at the time."

"I'm almost three!" Arina announced and held up three fingers to show that she also knew her numbers.

It worked! The attendant smiled and returned the papers to Lisbet without checking them. Dorrit nudged her to hurry before he could realize his neglect; fellow travelers inadvertently helped the subterfuge by shoving impatiently. Slipping through the gate, Dorrit heard him address the line behind her.

"One at a time!" He put up his hands to hold people back. The shuffling feet stilled. "That's better," he said. "Now, who's next?" He was handed some documents. "All right, let's see. How many have we got here?"

Chapter Sixty-five

The benches on the platform were occupied, so Dorrit and Lisbet sat down on the suitcase, each holding a child. It was anyone's guess when the northbound train would arrive, but at least the tracks were intact. On the opposite platform a crew of foreign workers, policed by SS officers, were reassembling a stretch of bomb-damaged rails, the anxious southbound travelers eying the progress, wondering if the job would be done before their train came.

Two agonizing hours passed. The growing mass of people finally forced Dorrit and Lisbet to stand up or be denied oxygen. Wedging the suitcase between them, Lisbet picked up Arina while Dorrit held Karoline's hand and Lisbet's coat. The crowd began questioning if the promised train would, indeed, arrive before the Allies made good on their threat. No one wanted to be caught on an open platform. Transportation hubs were the Allies' favorite targets.

Another hour had passed when a sudden hush fell over the crowd. A whistle could be heard in the distance. A train was coming. Unanimous relief rippled through the waiting passengers, followed by a wild frenzy as everyone gathered up children and belongings.

"Thank God!" Dorrit said, looking at the slowly approaching locomotive. Battered and soot covered, it was nonetheless a beautiful sight. "Once the train stops, don't hesitate," she said to Lisbet. "Take a firm hold of both girls and climb on any way you can. Don't worry about the suitcase. I'll hand it in right behind you. People will assume that I'm boarding and will hopefully give an old lady some room. We can expect a mad charge for the doors. There are far more people on this platform than the train can hold. The trick is to get on fast and find some seats. I'd be terribly distressed if you and the girls have to spend the long trip standing in a drafty corridor." Dorrit pivoted her neck and saw the entire length of the train as it rounded a curve in its approach. "Or, God forbid, ride in one of those." She pointed to the last few cars of the train. "Why, they are nothing but boxcars!"

Putting Arina down, Lisbet threw her arms around Dorrit. "We'll get seats," she cried. "Please don't worry. I only wish you were coming with us."

"So do I, my dearest girl. But it can't be helped."

"Promise me you won't delay going out to Bernau." Lisbet's voice was breaking. The two women had sat together on the suitcase for more than two hours, keeping the children occupied with stories and games, but suddenly there was so much she wanted to say to Dorrit and no time left in which to say it. "Get going this afternoon."

"I will."

"Thank you for everything…" Lisbet's throat closed, tears welled up in her eyes. "For all you've done for us."

"There's no need to thank me. You and the girls were a great joy. More than you'll ever know. I will miss you terribly, but I'm so happy you're getting out of Berlin for a while. Give my regards to your parents. Tell them I look forward to seeing them again once the war is over."

Lisbet nodded, fumbling in the pocket of her suit jacket for a handkerchief.

"Oh, I almost forgot. Here's your coat." Dorrit managed a sly wink as she draped it over Lisbet's arm. "Take good care of it on the trip."

Puzzled, Lisbet looked at it. It was her coat, of course, but it felt strange. It was so heavy.

"I meant to tell you," Dorrit whispered, leaning close so not even the children would overhear. "Last night after you were asleep I sewed the family jewels into the lining. I saved some for Cassandra, but this," she stroked the coat on Lisbet's arm, "is your share. I want you to have it now because it seems like a good time to get it out of Germany. Like fur coats, who knows when the Nazis will start collecting jewelry."

Lisbet was speechless, but even if she'd been able to argue against such generosity, it was too late. Boarding a train in a frantic crush of people was not the time to probe her mother-in-law's logic. Surely she knew that jewelry could be buried in the garden. A great many people concealed their valuables under rosebushes and sods of grass. Apparently, she had chosen not to.

"The Gestapo will search your suitcase at the border," Dorrit added hurriedly. "Items of value are not supposed to leave the country. Hiding jewels in the lining of a garment is a very old trick, of course, but if you are wearing the coat and carrying Arina, I can't imagine they'll think to search it. Hand them your purse and the valise. Look them straight in the eye and tell them the truth: you have nothing to declare except the contents of the suitcase and the clothes on your back." Dorrit patted Lisbet's tearstained cheek. "Good luck, my dear, and have a safe journey. I pray your parents received your wire and will meet you at the border."

"They'll be there." Lisbet felt a stab of guilt that she had not been completely candid with Dorrit. Yesterday, when she returned from town, she had shown her the three permits to Flensborg, explaining that it was the train's last stop and that she'd been told to cross the border on foot. This little deception was necessary because she couldn't bear to burden Dorrit with any uncertainty about the trip. Besides, she *did* expect to walk across the border, with or without assistance from her parents.

Karoline was pulling at Dorrit's skirt. She wanted to hug *Oma,* and as she did so, began to cry. Not one to be outdone, Arina pushed out her lower lip, stamped her foot and whimpered, "My turn! My turn!"

Suppressing her own tears, Dorrit embraced each of the children and made them promise to be good on the trip.

"I'll get word to you the minute we arrive in Copenhagen," Lisbet said, prying the girls loose from Dorrit. "I'll send a telegram to you at the Konauers. Stay with them till we come back."

"I will."

The train had come to a full stop. Luck was shining on Lisbet. A door swung open right where she was standing and as she turned toward it, her children securely in hand, someone of immense strength jostled the crowd around her. An awesome force was at work, pushing her and the girls up the steps and onto the train ahead of the riot. And, sure enough, the suitcase came up right behind her.

Safely on the landing, Lisbet looked back over her shoulder and saw Dorrit step away from the train and be swallowed by the multitudes surging for the doors. Had she held back the mob, Lisbet wondered? Did a single individual possess such super human strength? Yes, she decided, Dorrit did.

A soldier on the train offered to carry Lisbet's suitcase as she made her way down the narrow passageway, anxiously peering through the compartment doors, searching for vacant seats. The train had taken on passengers at stations en route to Berlin, but she finally located two seats and decided to make do. Small children like Arina were expected to be lap sitters anyway. She thanked the soldier, placed her valise and coat across the seats - indicating they were now occupied - and left the compartment to let Dorrit know that they were nicely settled. Squeezing through the people filing along the corridor, she pushed herself and her children up against a window. How quickly the platform had emptied, she thought - amazed that everyone had managed to get on - everyone except one lone figure; a woman standing alone and forlorn, anxiously eying the train from the deserted platform. Lisbet rapped on the glass to get her attention.

Dorrit's face brightened the minute she spotted her. She ran toward her.

Without warning, the train began to move. Lisbet pulled down the window. "We have seats," she called out. Karoline pressed her nose flat against the glass and waved to *Oma*. Lisbet picked up Arina so that she, too, could see her grandmother.

"Wonderful," Dorrit said, running along with the train as it gathered speed. At the end of the platform she had to stop.

Lisbet craned her neck and continued waving. Dorrit was wearing a smart green suit with a jaunty feathered fedora and, standing alone against the dismal bomb-damaged backdrop, the fashionable ensemble was a foil for the depressing surroundings.

"We'll be back soon." Lisbet mouthed the words as the tracks curved, allowing one last view.

Nodding and smiling, Dorrit raised her arm to wave; a white silk handkerchief unfurled and fluttered in her hand moments before she was lost to sight. Lisbet did not see her posture crumble, nor did she see her sit down heavily on a deserted bench.

On the opposite platform, the workers were still repairing the rails, metal clanging against metal, the anxious would-be travelers still eying the progress.

No one saw Dorrit cry.

Chapter Sixty-six

Not an inch of space on the train went begging; people stood in the corridors without complaint. They were leaving Berlin and were grateful.

Lisbet went back into her compartment, heaved the suitcase up into the luggage net, told Karoline and Arina to share a seat, and sat down next to them by the door. Dorrit had done an excellent sewing job, she realized, as she folded the precious coat across her lap, leaving her purse on top of it. There was not the slightest rattling noise or scraping of stone against stone, nor were there any visible bulges.

An hour into the trip, a female conductor peeked through the glass panel in the compartment door and, spotting newcomers, walked in, followed by one of the SS officers patrolling the corridors.

"Tickets?" she looked at Lisbet and her children.

Lisbet dug into her purse for the money. "One adult and two children to Flensborg, please."

"Your youngest rides free." The conductress nodded toward Arina who had fallen asleep, her head in her sister's lap, her feet dangling above the floor. Punching out two tickets, the woman handed them to Lisbet along with her change. "Flensborg will be our final stop," she added before squeezing her large frame back into the passageway, giving the SS officer more room.

Lisbet put the tickets into her purse, fished out her travel documents and gave them to the man, a short wiry individual.

"You're going to Flensborg?" He examined her papers.

"Yes."

"You have someone who can house you?"

The question gave Lisbet a chill. He was clearly curious as to why a Danish-born citizen of the Third Reich was traveling to within an inch of the border. Lisbet called upon her skill as an actress and looked at him, wide-eyed, with a perplexed frown that he should ask. No one with an ounce of sense would travel to a strange town and not have a place to stay. "I have a relative," she said evenly.

"Who?"

The color was rising in Lisbet's cheeks. Lying didn't come easy. "A cousin on my husband's side," she invented hurriedly.

"Can you be more specific!" he snapped, still holding her documents.

"Uh...yes, of course. Her name is Gisela Wegener." Gisela had been a friend long ago at the Berlin Music Conservatory; she was not from Flensborg but for some reason her name rolled off Lisbet's tongue along with a silent prayer that the officer wouldn't ask for her address. To circumvent that possibility, she quickly added, "Her husband is serving in Russia along with mine. We will be good company for each other."

That seemed to satisfy the man. He initialed Lisbet's papers, handed them back without a word, and returned to the corridor to interrogate others.

Karoline couldn't contain herself any longer. "Aren't we going to visit our Danish grandparents in Copenhagen?" she said. "Where's Flensborg? Do we have a cousin there?"

Lisbet's eyes darted nervously around the compartment; there might be a Nazi informer among her fellow passengers. She put her mouth right up against Karoline's ear and whispered, "I had to tell a little lie because it's important that we keep our real destination secret."

"Why?"

"Because people are not supposed to leave the country."

"Why?"

"I'm not really sure. But I know this much. If that officer thought we were planning to go to Denmark, he'd set us off at the next stop. You wouldn't want that to happen, would you?"

Karoline shook her head.

"Can you help me keep our little secret? It's very important."

Karoline nodded, happy with the fact that her mother trusted her with a secret.

"Now, no more questions." Lisbet kissed her cheek. "Why don't you take a nap like Arina and that nice gentleman?" She nodded toward a well-dressed elderly man seated opposite her by the door. Head on his chest, leaning into the corner, he'd been asleep when she and the girls boarded and had not stirred when the door opened and closed for the conductress and the officer.

"I'm not sleepy."

"Then read a book. You brought along *Struwwelpeter*, didn't you?"

"Will you read it for me?" Karoline looked hopeful.

"Not now. I'm awfully tired. Later."

Disappointed, Karoline meowed like a cat and was about to pinch her sister whose head was too heavy in her lap.

"Don't you dare!" Lisbet spoke sternly. "If you wake her, we'll have no peace at all."

Karoline crossed her arms, pushed out her lower lip, and sulked.

Chapter Sixty-seven

Lisbet sank into her seat and tried to relax. With no adult conversation to help pass the time, it'd be a long journey. The two uniformed nurses occupying the seats next to Karoline and Arina were dozing, and the woman traveling with two glassy-eyed boys in the seats opposite Lisbet, kept her eyes averted and her mouth drawn into a tight line, indicating she was in no mood to talk. Lisbet figured she and her sons were refugees; there was no luggage in the net above their heads, and their clothing looked as if it had been slept in. The towheaded boys appeared to be twins, eight or nine years old, and were so thin they shared a seat with no trouble. They were remarkably quiet and - heads turned toward the window - seemed content to watch the landscape passing by. The middle-aged woman occupying the window seat was bent over her knitting, her eyes inches from her work, her hands moving like a nervous habit.

Lisbet checked her watch. It was three o'clock; it had already been a long day and she was exhausted. She closed her eyes and promptly fell asleep. Suddenly, she found herself in Bernau, riding Buttercup behind Fritz and Peter who were teasing her about her dawdling pace and telling her to hurry. The sun was shining, the day was warm, swallows were diving in the endless blue sky, and the three equestrians were cutting across a lush green meadow and heading toward the river. Fritz stopped his horse, turned in the saddle, and grinned at her.

"We'd like to have lunch before sundown," he teased. "You might try digging in the spurs."

"If Buttercup is slow, it's not my fault," Lisbet hollered back at him. "You give me an old mare to ride and then load her down with the picnic basket. It weighs a ton."

Laughing, Fritz offered to take it.

"No!" Lisbet waved him on. She was not about to entrust the sinful delicacies to his rough riding. Fritz's horse jumped hedges and she had to safeguard the food. The girls were at the river beach, swimming under the watchful eye of Nurse Heller and Nadia, and would be hungry as bears. While lagging behind, Lisbet reveled in the beauty of the countryside. The meadow grass was sprinkled with wildflowers in the colors of the rainbow. She ought to stop and pick some. A bouquet placed in one of the children's water pails would look lovely on the blue-checkered picnic cloth.

Suddenly she heard Arina wailing; Sigrid and Karoline were probably squirting her with water. Had she ruined their sandcastle? Why didn't Nadia intervene?

Lisbet was urging Buttercup to hurry as consciousness dawned. The picnic basket, the river, the sunny day, Fritz's wonderful laugh vanished. Squinting through heavy lids, Lisbet opened her eyes. Nothing looked familiar. Confused, she rubbed her neck, trying to remember where she was. The minute her drowsy mind recognized her surroundings, she wanted to go back to sleep. Her dream had been so excruciatingly pleasant. She wanted to recapture it. She wanted to go back to Bernau. She had seen Fritz so clearly, and her heart ached with the cruel reality that he was somewhere in the Soviet Union while she was on a battered train going in the opposite direction. Why had she left Berlin? Suppose he got a furlough. What if he were on his way home right now? Lisbet sighed with overwhelming sadness. She should have stayed put.

Again, she heard wailing and realized it had not been part of her dream. She turned her head and saw Karoline pinching Arina. In no mood to scold, Lisbet simply separated the girls, putting Arina on her lap. The indignant child pulled down her knee socks, lifted her red plaid skirt, and pointed at a hundred nonexistent pinch marks on her legs. Lisbet clucked her tongue, looked severely at Karoline, and warned her to busy herself with a book. *Or else!*

Pouting, Karoline stood up in the seat, reached into the luggage net, fished *Struwwelpeter* from the suitcase and sat down, consoling herself with the fact that at least now she had the seat all to herself.

Chapter Sixty-eight

Sometime later, checking her watch, Lisbet saw that it was after five o'clock, which meant the train should be nearing Hamburg. She glanced toward the window. They were passing slowly through a badly destroyed station, the wheels making an awful racket on the rusty rails. She noticed a lopsided sign on the broken platform. *Havelberg?* That was only some sixty-plus kilometers from Berlin! Something was wrong. They had been underway for three hours. There must have been a delay while she slept. Had the train stopped? She wanted to ask one of her fellow travelers but all eyes were closed, signaling they didn't want to be bothered. The war had drained peoples' energy, there was nothing left for idle conversation. At this rate we won't be in Flensborg until midnight, Lisbet realized and felt cramped. She needed to stretch her legs. A walk in the corridor might help and it'd be prudent to bring the girls to the bathroom.

"Let's take a walk," she said, putting Arina down on the seat while she stood up and put on her coat. Although her travel companions did not look like thieves, Lisbet didn't dare separate herself from Dorrit's jewels for any length of time.

"Are we going to the dining car?" Karoline asked expectantly, remembering former trips to Denmark with her parents that had included eating in the dining car where stewards served all sorts of delicious things.

"I don't believe this train has one."

"Why not?"

"There is no room. There are too many passengers." Lisbet took Arina by the hand and herded Karoline out the door ahead of her.

"And not enough food for everybody, huh?" Karoline remembered *Oma* telling her about shortages and long lines. But even without the prospect of a dining car, she was happy to leave the compartment and stepped gingerly around the people sitting on their suitcases in the passageway.

The line to the lavatory was long. While waiting, Lisbet struck up a conversation with the woman in front of her and learned that the train had not made any stops since leaving Berlin.

"We must be traveling unusually slowly," Lisbet said, voicing her concern about the lack of progress.

"I guess the locomotive is in bad repair." The woman shrugged. "Or it's pulling too many cars. More than it's supposed to. Be glad you're not at the end of the train."

"People are actually riding in the boxcars?" Lisbet remembered Dorrit's glum expression when she saw them.

"Of course."

Lisbet thought of her compartment and felt extremely fortunate.

It was half an hour before she and the children returned to their seats. No sooner did they sit down, when both girls began complaining of hunger. Breakfast had been a long time ago and there had been no lunch, which in itself was not unusual, two meals a day had been the norm for months. Lisbet dug into the suitcase for the food Dorrit had packed for the trip and, sniffing appreciatively, unwrapped Kaiser rolls, large slices of cheese, several sausages, carrot sticks, a bottle of fruit juice, and of course the predictable cold boiled potatoes. Looking at the veritable feast, a lump swelled in her throat. This included Dorrit's rations. What would she and Nadia eat tonight? But as Lisbet handed a roll to each of her daughters, she remembered that Dorrit and Nadia were in Bernau by now. Karl-Heinz hunted game in the woods, and if he got lucky, a good-sized deer would feed them all for a week.

Lisbet was about to bite into a piece of cheese when she noticed the refugee woman and her sons watching her. Caught staring, the woman flushed a deep red and looked down at the floor, but the boys' hunger was so acute they couldn't draw their eyes away. Putting the cheese back down on the parchment paper, Lisbet lost her appetite. She couldn't eat in front of starving children. A moment later, grudgingly deciding that it was better to eat a little rather than nothing, she split her rations, all the while telling herself that sausage didn't agree with her anyway. Assembling the food on a napkin, she offered it to the boys' mother.

The woman shook her head. "*Nein dank*," she said.

"For your children," Lisbet kept her hand extended. The boys were regarding their mother with a strange light blazing in their glassy eyes. "Take it. Please! I'm actually not all that hungry. I had a big meal before leaving Berlin."

If she'd had the strength, the woman would have laughed at such a preposterous lie. As it were, it required all her energy to lift her bony hands and reach for the napkin, her pride going down in the face of starvation. "You're very kind," she said, handing the food to her boys. She herself ate nothing.

Lisbet bit into a cold potato. God, how she hated potatoes, but at least they filled the void in her stomach.

The train lumbered on into evening. No lights came on; blackout rules applied to trains. The woman by the window had relinquished her knitting to the darkness and was digging into her bag for a piece of black bread. The two nurses were sharing a thermos of *ersatz* and a cigarette. The old gentleman opposite Lisbet appeared to be neither hungry nor thirsty, just tired.

The conductress could be heard opening and closing doors along the corridor. "Shades down!" she hollered and, reaching Lisbet's compartment, barked at the two nurses. "No smoking! This window has no blind!" She pointed at the metal glider where a shade had once hung. "Do you want to draw enemy planes?"

"Huh? No. Of course not." The nurses apologized and extinguished their cigarette, saving the stub for later use; nothing was wasted. As soon as the conductress left, Lisbet heard them whisper to each other. "Who's she kidding? Does she actually believe Allied pilots can spot the glow of a cigarette?"

The train pulled into Domitz. The town and the station lay in total darkness and there was considerable turmoil as passengers disembarked, blindly, as it were, risking life and limb on an un-illuminated platform. No one in Lisbet's compartment left. She saw several SS officers get off. They were easy to spot because they were using flashlights, clearly more worried about breaking their necks than drawing enemy fire.

The space vacated on the train was quickly filled with soldiers, most settling down in the corridors, sitting on their knapsacks. The majority were boys. Lisbet thought of Peter. Good thing he was out of the country or he, too, might be in uniform.

Without sounding its whistle the train pulled away, keeping the same exasperatingly slow pace, but at least it moved and each stretch of rail brought it closer to Denmark. Lisbet hoped her parents were on their way to the border. They were resourceful and could be trusted to have a plan to get her and the girls across. Her telegram had, unfortunately, not been specific. All she'd been able to say was: *Leaving Berlin on a noon train to Flensborg.* The length of the message was restricted by the wire service, the contents by the censors, and if she'd hinted that she needed help slipping across the border, the telegram would not have been sent and she would have been arrested.

Chapter Sixty-nine

Nerve-jangling blasts suddenly blared throughout the train. It came to a screeching halt. Recognizing the alarm, everyone scrambled to their feet and headed for the exits, soldiers rushing to the aid of mothers traveling with small children.

Seated by the door, grabbing a child by each hand, Lisbet was first to leave the compartment but could barely conquer her shaking knees in the stampede. At the end of the passageway she handed a screaming Arina out into the arms of a soldier on the ground before she and Karoline jumped free of the train. With no platform to alight on, it was a long leap of faith down to untested soil. The sickening thuds and shrieks of pain all around her attested to many awkward landings. With her heart in her throat, Lisbet pulled Karoline by the hand as she now followed the shadow of the soldier carrying Arina. Dashing blindly through puddles and thorny bushes, she ran in a desperate fear of separation, repeatedly calling for the soldier to slow down. But her pleas were lost to the noise of running feet and crying children. Continuing through the darkness, she was guided by the stubborn sobs she took to be those of her younger daughter.

Flares floating down from the planes droning overhead illuminated the train and the surrounding countryside. The eerie yellow glow was followed by the all too familiar whistling sound of falling bombs. Everyone hit the dirt. All had previous experience with Allied attacks.

Lisbet was reunited with Arina and, wrenching the frightened child from the soldier's arms, she too fell down, shielding her children with her body as explosions shattered the darkness. In her haste to get off the train she had left her coat behind, her practical mind now wondering if the jewels would be salvageable in the event the compartment took a hit. As her knees sank into the cold wet ground, the irony of her situation sank into her heart. She had left Berlin to escape air raids only to now be caught right in the middle of one with nothing above her head for protection. Tall swamp grasses were all that stood between her and disaster, and God knows what slimy vermin crawled in the bog beneath her. And when the enemy planes dropped to a lower altitude, circling the train like buzzards over a carcass, her terror was complete.

After an eternity for those huddled on the ground, the planes suddenly flew off, disappearing into the night sky. No more bombs fell. A thick silence settled over the swamp, a silence from which everyone drew grim pleasure and the same summation: the Allies had decided it was a civilian train and not worth bothering with. The absence of gunners responding to their attack had told them it was not an ammunitions convoy.

People rose from the bog and began plodding back toward the train, flexing their joints and brushing clumps of mud from their clothes. Bonfires touched off by the bombs dotted the landscape but would soon burn out in the damp terrain. For the time being, however, the fires were a godsend because they made it easy to see. A soldier came along and offered to carry Arina, a favor Lisbet gladly accepted though Arina made a mountain- sized fuss about it, hollering all the way back to the train.

The last boxcar was reduced to a sprawl of burning wood lying across the tracks, a huge section of which had been destroyed as well. Braving the heat and the flames, a group of soldiers helped the train personnel uncouple the burning wreck while others threw handfuls of wet dirt on the fire. With nothing to salvage, the passengers who'd been riding in that last car simply climbed aboard other cars, glad they had their lives. The chief engineer walked around the length of the train, inspecting it for any damage, which might preclude continuing on. There were many blown-out windows, a good deal of scorching, but nothing to prevent him from firing up the locomotive. More importantly, there appeared to be no disruption of the rails in front of the train. Still, as a precaution, he asked several soldiers to hike ahead to check the spoors and trestles.

Returning to her compartment, Lisbet found her coat and purse. Both were right on the seat where she had left them. The old gentleman was also right there. It appeared he hadn't moved. She mentioned it to the two nurses walking in behind her.

One said, "We should have roused him and made sure he got off the train."

"Yes. Suppose this car had been hit," the other one added. Both looked chastised.

"I can't imagine how he slept through all the commotion," Lisbet said.

One of the nurses bent down, eyed the man more closely and, being careful not to startle him, touched his hand gently. Suddenly she grasped his wrist with unbefitting roughness. "My God!" she uttered. "He has no pulse." She looked at her friend. "He's dead! He must have been dead for hours. He's stiff as a board. Quick, go get the conductress!"

Dead? The color drained from Lisbet's face. *Dead for hours!*

Thankfully, Arina was more curious about the fires burning outside in the swamp than anything else. Lisbet let go of her hand so she could stand by the compartment window and look out. This left her free to deal with Karoline, whose eyes were round with horror.

"He was very old," Lisbet whispered, sitting down and putting her arms around Karoline's small shoulders. "It was his time to go home to God."

The middle-aged knitter and the woman with the two boys came into to the compartment. The nurse standing guard over the deceased explained the situation, but neither the knitter nor the refugee raised an eyebrow between them. Death was far too commonplace. Unperturbed, they both sat down, the refugee woman taking her seat next to the body without hesitation. Her sons also sat down, eying the man with scant curiosity.

Soldiers arrived to remove the corpse. It was anyone's guess what they did with it. The conductress retrieved the man's briefcase and other personal effects from the luggage net; presumably she would contact his next of kin. No one spoke, no questions were asked. A young woman carrying a year-old child and no belongings immediately claimed the vacant seat. Lisbet assumed she had been a passenger in that last boxcar.

The train lumbered on.

Chapter Seventy

Faint traces of gray daylight spread across the landscape. It would be a dreary dawn; there was no pink tint in the sky, no promise of a rising sun. Of course, cloud cover was something to be grateful for. It meant there would be no enemy planes. Shortly, the train rolled into another bombed-damaged station, but it didn't stop. No one was getting off and no one was waiting to board.

Lisbet wiggled her toes inside her soggy shoes; her feet were ice cold and she'd never felt more dirty or hungry. Her brown suit was wrinkled and smeared with swamp mud and both of her silk stockings had holes in the knees. The girl's matching red plaid outfits and beige wool sweaters were muddied as well, their shoes a mess. But she counted her blessings. It was morning. They had made it through the night.

Diverted from damaged tracks, the train lurched and groaned as it approached Hamburg's main station. Lisbet craned her neck to look through the sooty window of her compartment. The city lay in ruins. She was horrified. This was far worse than the destruction in Berlin. The train finally squeaked to a halt in the once impressive twin domed station, now a wasteland of blackened cinder blocks. In former times, happy crowds would be gathered on its marble mezzanines to await arriving passengers. This morning only a handful of Red Cross nurses were gathered on some planks stretched over bomb craters, eying the arrivals with no enthusiasm whatsoever.

The locomotive came to a jerky stop.

People left the train in droves, and Lisbet was aghast when her compartment emptied. Was this their final destination? Had everyone endured the long trip only to arrive at this barren city of rubble?

At the door, the refugee woman turned to say goodbye and again thanked Lisbet for the food she had shared. The boys, too, thanked her.

"Don't mention it," Lisbet said. "But tell me, are you really getting off here?"

"Yes. Hamburg is our home."

"There's nothing left. Where will you live?"

The woman shrugged. "I don't know. At least the Allies won't waste any more bombs here." She turned and was gone.

A moment later Lisbet caught sight of her through the window and saw her trudge like a sleepwalker across the boards connecting the broken platforms, her boys following like awkward goslings. The two nurses, the knitter, and the woman with the baby had also gotten off. Lisbet guessed they had left Hamburg - escaping bombs and fire - to take shelter with family elsewhere, only to discover that these relations had momentous problems of their own, and new burdens were not welcomed. So, back home they went. It was better to live in one's own ruins than grovel elsewhere.

"Mama, when are we getting off?" Karoline felt abandoned in the empty compartment; no new passengers got on and the soldiers who had boarded in Domitz remained in the passageway.

"Soon."

Soon? There was that word again. Karoline decided not to press the point.

Chapter Seventy-one

The next stop was Elmshorn. The train emptied of civilian passengers and only soldiers boarded. Lisbet wondered if she had missed an announcement about transferring to another train, for she doubted that she and the girls were supposed to be riding a troop transport.

She stuck her head out into the corridor. "Do we stay on this train till Flensborg?" she asked the conductress standing by an open window, smoking.

"Unless you'd rather walk."

"Oh, uh, no." Lisbet retreated back into her compartment as the train began to shake under the heavy boots of soldiers boarding.

As if by unspoken agreement, young recruits settled down in the passageways among their counterparts who had boarded in Domitz, while seasoned men - those who had seen the front - got first crack at the seats. Several of these veterans filed into Lisbet's compartment, removed their hats and placed them in the luggage net, leaving their heavy gear on the floor. They acknowledged Lisbet with a quick nod but didn't smile; one and all looked like they needed a good night's sleep as badly as they needed a meal.

As the train pulled out of Elmshorn, Lisbet consulted her watch. It had been eighteen hours since they left Berlin. Again she counted her blessings, one in particular: the train was moving. Yesterday, they had passed several that were not so fortunate. One had sat idle in a small station, waiting for a crew to tend its silent engine. Another was stuck on bomb-damaged tracks between towns, waiting for a miracle.

For the lack of anything better to do, Lisbet listened as Karoline read *Struwwelpeter* to her sister. However, when they got to the picture of the naughty boy pulling the tablecloth, tossing all the food on the floor, Arina remembered she was hungry and began to whine. Both girls were famished, of course, Lisbet knew she couldn't stall them any longer, so as much as she wanted to conserve the potatoes, she had no choice but to dig them out before Arina's complaints bothered the sleeping soldiers. Standing up and reaching into the suitcase, she took out the last of the rations, handing a potato to each child. Arina gobbled hers in record time. Karoline nibbled slowly all the while looking at the soldier sitting directly across from her. He was the only one who was still awake and at one point when he caught her eyes on him, he winked.

Buoyed by that friendly gesture, she finished her potato, held out her book and asked if he had read *Struwwelpeter.*

"You bet," he said. "It taught me a lot of good things."

"What?" Karoline looked eagerly at him.

"Well, let me see." He pursed his lips, looked at the ceiling and gave it some thought. "Ah, yes, I remember. *Don't* be cruel to animals. *Don't* play with matches. And *don't* suck your thumb." Again he winked; this time at Arina who was doing precisely that.

The thumb popped out of her mouth. She hid her hand behind her back and turned her face into her mother's shoulder.

"If you were *Struwwelpeter*," Karoline challenged her newfound friend, "and you caught my sister sucking her thumb, would you take out your scissors and cut it off? Would you?"

"Karoline!" Lisbet gave her a severe look. "Such talk! Really!"

"But that's what the book says, Mama."

"I don't care what the book says. And you mustn't bother the..." a quick glance at the stripes on the soldier's uniform established his rank, "the lieutenant with such nonsense. I'm sorry if my children are disturbing you," she said to him. "I'm sure you'd like to sleep."

"No." He flashed a hint of a smile, which smoothed the harsh contours of his face. "I've never gotten the hang of sleeping in an upright position."

"We have!" Karoline said, eager to recapture his attention. "We've been on this train since yesterday. All the way from Berlin. And you know what else?"

"What?" Again he exercised a bit of smile, a little wider this time.

"We were bombed last night!"

"Really?" He looked at Lisbet for confirmation. She nodded.

"Only one car was hit," Karoline was quick to report. "The one at the very end. We had to run and hide in a swamp. That's why my dress is so dirty. My sister is a mess too." She was about to comment on her mother's poor grooming, but stopped herself because something in the man's eyes told her that he thought Mama looked perfectly fine. "And you know what else?" she said instead.

"Tell me." He looked as if he actually wanted to hear what a six-year-old had to say.

"After the bombs stopped and we got back on the train, a man was dead right here in our compartment. He sat in that corner by the door." Karoline pointed to the seat next to the lieutenant, occupied by a man who was sleeping. Suddenly she looked worried as if he, too, might be dead.

The lieutenant gave the fellow a jab with his elbow.

"Hey! Cut it out!" The soldier fended off the attack with a feeble thrust in the air as if swatting a fly, then promptly went back to sleep.

"I guess there's nothing wrong with him." The lieutenant grinned at Karoline.

She covered her mouth with her hands, giggled, and went on to report that the man was already dead when they boarded the train. "He was very old. God wanted him up in heaven."

While Karoline chatted, Lisbet studied the lieutenant. He appeared to be in his thirties, but since the war had its own way of aging people, he might be younger. His uniform, as well as those of his comrades, had seen better days, but he was clean-shaven and his dark blond hair was neatly combed. His well-defined features were hard, but as Karoline rambled on, he smiled more frequently, which softened his mien considerably. Still, his blue eyes remained sharp and alert. He had obviously lived with danger for too long to let his guard down. He kept his rifle between his knees, constantly fingering the cold metal. Lisbet suspected he would react to the slightest provocation with deadly force and speed. She marked him as a trained officer and wondered where he and his men were headed.

Karoline eventually got around to asking him that.

"Denmark," he told her and looked pleased with his itinerary.

"So are we!" she blurted out. "We're going to Copenhagen! To visit our Danish grandparents." Karoline clapped her hands with glee at the coincidence, but in the next instant she remembered that other story, the one about living in Flensborg with a cousin. She also remembered that she was supposed to keep Denmark a secret. She clamped her lips together, lowered her eyes to the floor, and expected to be set off the train.

Seeing the child's fear as well as her mother's sudden pallor, the lieutenant realized a deception was afoot. He leaned forward, extended his hand to Lisbet, and said, "My name's Andreas Voigt."

She shook his hand guardedly. The Nazi insignia on his uniform, albeit the same Fritz wore, glared at her because this man was an officer and had presumably taken his oath seriously.

"I'm Lisbet von Renz," she said tightly, wanting to strangle Karoline. "This," she made Arina face the man, "is my other daughter, Arina."

He smiled at both children before turning back to Lisbet, saying, "I gather your destination is classified."

Lisbet managed a wide-eyed and innocent look, an expression that had worked on the SS officer. "No," she said, retaining a virtuous mien. "We're going to Flensborg. It's no secret. I have the tickets to prove it. My daughter made a mistake. She's tired and disoriented. It's been a long trip."

Lieutenant Voigt shrugged. "Whatever you say. Your itinerary is of no consequence to me. I'm not on border patrol." When Lisbet von Renz still looked uncomfortable, he added, "And I'm not a Nazi informer. No man in this compartment is."

Astounded at his candor, Lisbet's mouth popped open. He was taking an awful chance for suppose *she* was a spy! "Your honesty is refreshing," she said. "So I'll be frank as well. We *are* going to Denmark. I was born there. My parents are meeting us at the border. Hopefully they can help us get across."

"The border is closed to everyone except the military," the lieutenant said. "You might have gotten across a few months ago. Not now."

"I know. But I'm counting on my parents to get a visitor's pass and drive across and meet us in Flensborg. They'll figure something out."

"The border is closed in both directions. Aren't you aware of that?"

"But if there's some sort of family emergency, I should think..."

"Your parents will be not permitted into Germany, no matter what dire emergency they claim. No one from the outside is allowed to see the chaos inside our borders. Foreigners have been banned since the first of the year."

Lisbet sighed heavily. "I know."

"Where's your husband?"

"In Russia."

"Where about?"

"I'm not sure. He was at Stalingrad at the surrender. He has served for sixteen months. For all I know, he might finally have gotten a furlough, in which case I don't care if I get across the border. I'd just as soon go back to Berlin."

"You can forget about a furlough. The War Ministry has suspended all leaves."

"*What?* Since when?"

"About the same time they closed the borders."

"We heard about border closings, but we didn't hear anything about furloughs being canceled." Lisbet was shocked.

"That's because bad news is suppressed rather well. Our Fuehrer is committed to maintaining a level of optimism among the people."

"Optimism? Hah!" Lisbet snorted. "No one in Berlin is optimistic anymore. There's been too much bombing."

"Which is precisely why the War Ministry is no longer granting furloughs. Printed news can be censored, but if soldiers see the destruction of their homes they lose their will to fight. I sure did when I came back from the Soviet Union."

"You were in Russia?" Curiosity made Lisbet's eyes sparkle prettily; it wasn't lost on Andreas Voigt. "Where?" she asked.

"I was in Leningrad with the Fourth Panzer Army under the command of Field Marshal von Leeb. I fought for two years without a scratch. Then bingo! I took a bellyful of shrapnel during a skirmish on the shore of Lake Ladoga. The medics patched me up and sent me home for surgery. In the field they rely on amputations, which in my case wasn't practical."

"Where's your home?"

"Frankfurt. But I was sent to a hospital in Elmshorn. The town we just left. They have a facility that specializes in digging out shell fragments. Now that I'm ambulatory, I've been given command of a replacement unit heading for Denmark, which is the same as being sent out to pasture. There's little action in Denmark except for an occasional brawl with the Danish resistance."

"Where will you be stationed?"

"In and around the town of Odense. If this wreck makes it that far."

Lisbet sat up ramrod straight. "This train doesn't end its run in Flensborg?"

"Not to my knowledge."

"It's continuing right into Denmark?"

"I sure hope so. We don't have any trains left to transfer to. As it is, most of our troops are riding in boxcars. I noticed this one is pulling two, which does nothing to bolster the pristine image the regime likes to convey. I'm sure we'll ditch them before crossing the border."

Lisbet was no longer listening. Her mind was churning. This train was going right into Denmark. Could she stay on board? Could she conceal herself and her children? But where? The train was full of soldiers.

Lieutenant Voigt remained silent; he had lost his audience - part of his audience anyway - for although one of the little girls still looked attentive, her mother's eyes had glazed over. He guessed she was wrestling with her dilemma, that of accomplishing a reunion with her parents on Danish soil. And why not? Why drag around in Flensborg as a refugee if she had family in Denmark able to shelter her?

"Instead of getting off in Flensborg," he said, "why don't you just stay on the train? Unless it breaks down, something that's quite possible of course, it will be the quickest way to cross the border."

"Great idea!" Lisbet quipped, figuring he was joking.

"I'm serious. Why not?"

"Well, for starters, I only have tickets to Flensborg. The conductress knows that and has already told me it's the last stop."

"Last stop for *civilians*."

"Which is what we are. Even if I had the stomach for any adventure there's no place to hide and too many witnesses." Lisbet gestured around the compartment at his sleepy companions.

"Don't dismiss these gentlemen so lightly," Andreas Voigt grinned. "I handpicked them for their sabbatical in Denmark. They owe me."

"What about the conductress and the SS? Do they owe you?"

"The last of the SS left the train at Elmshorn. They were not needed on a military transport. As for the conductress?" He shrugged, "She'll be easy to deal with. Our only problem is the Gestapo. They might search the train at the border."

Lisbet's froze. "The Gestapo," she croaked, "compared with them, the conductress is the tooth fairy."

"Actually, I don't expect they'll bother to check a troop train. It's not the transportation of choice for anyone bent on an illicit border crossing. Good soldiers of the Third Reich don't shelter fugitives."

"So why consider it?"

"For the simple reason that there are very few "good" soldiers on board. Most of us have done some rotten things in this war. Coming to the aid of three lovely ladies..." Lieutenant Voigt's smile included Karoline and Arina, "will be a pleasant change of pace."

"What about them?" Lisbet nodded toward the young soldiers in the corridor. "They don't look old enough to have done anything rotten."

"That's true. But they are schoolboys and won't dare question an order."

Chapter Seventy-two

Having visualized a nobler hiding place, humiliation began pounding in Lisbet's cheeks, jammed as she were in the narrow space under two compartment seats and further concealed by a pile of army knapsacks. Worse than lost pride, the dusty and airless environment tested her lungs; to cough would prove disastrous once the train stopped in Flensborg.

As the locomotive slowed on its approach, a mad drumming began in her chest. She should have shown better judgment. When Andreas Voigt roused his friends from sleep and secured their cooperation, the stunt had sounded so simple when, in fact, it was utter madness. If discovered, this attempt to cross the border would not be looked upon as a prank. Nazi authority was not built on lenience. Blood and vengeance ruled the day. The Gestapo put great store in making public examples of lawbreakers.

Dear God! We'll be hauled off the train and shot!

Clutching her children, the precious coat, and her purse in the cramped darkness, Lisbet fought a rising tide of panic. Of course, there might still be time to avoid a catastrophe. She could emerge and tell Lieutenant Voigt that she had lost her nerve or that the girls couldn't keep quiet.

"Don't forget, lie very still," he'd said, winking at the children before placing the knapsacks on top of them. "Pretend you're tiny mice hiding from a great big scary cat. You'll be safe only if you don't make a sound." Bored with the long tedious trip and happy to play a game, both Karoline and Arina promised to be quiet; especially when Lieutenant Voigt said a prize was involved.

The brakes screeched. Lisbet held her breath and prayed she wouldn't cough. Pressed flat against the floorboards, the sound of metal on metal jangled her frayed nerves. She shivered although it was excruciatingly hot under the seats.

"Flensborg!" The conductress walked along the corridor, her harsh voice echoing in the passageway, while a brisk opening and closing of compartment doors gave proof of a visual check. "Last stop for civilians!"

Lisbet heard the faint voices of women and children disembarking and realized that she and her daughters had not been the last civilians on the train. Suddenly, she envied their freedom to walk off. But, instead of crawling out and joining them as any sane individual would, she shrank further into the space under the seats, drawing her children with her, begging them not to stir.

A moment later when she heard Lieutenant Voigt comment on the weather - the signal that he had not spotted anyone waiting on the platform who fit the description she had given of her parents - she burned her bridges and stayed put, knowing they had not been able to drive across the border. She now began to worry that the young men in the passageway would get cold feet and forget their role in this deadly drama. However, a moment later, the planned argument broke out as one recruit accused another of filching his cigarettes. It came to immediate blows. Others joined in the fight. The men in Lisbet's compartment stood up to watch the scuffle, efficiently blocking the door.

The conductress blew her whistle. "Hey! Save your fights for the enemy!" she shouted above the fracas. "Who's the officer in charge here?"

"At your service, madam." Andreas' voice sounded so close by that Lisbet guessed he was standing right in front of the pile of knapsacks.

"Well, Lieutenant, I'd advise you to keep order and suggest you reprimand these...uh, these men." Uniforms notwithstanding, even the conductress had difficulty calling fifteen-year-old boys men.

"I assure you their conduct will not go unpunished," he said, ingratiatingly polite. "Once we reach our destination, each man will regret his involvement."

"Good." The conductress consulted her spiral notebook. "There are three civilian passengers in this compartment," she said. "Flensborg is their stop."

The men standing in the doorway looked over their shoulders, shrugged, and spread their hands. "No civilians here," one of them said.

"There's got to be." The conductress checked the compartment door to confirm she had the right number. She stretched her neck to see past the men blocking her view. "Hey! Break it up! Let me see!"

"Oh, are you're looking for that blonde with the two kids?" someone asked.

"Yes. Stand aside! They're in this compartment."

"You mean *were* in this compartment," someone else said.

"She and her two girls hopped off when we stopped at Eggebek to ditch the boxcars," another conspirator spoke up.

"Too bad she left," Andreas Voigt added. "She was nice to look at. But as nutty as they come. She kept mumbling about a man who'd gone belly-up in this compartment. Did they actually travel with some poor stiff all the way from Berlin?"

The conductress sighed, exasperated; she had no time to stand around, blowing the breeze with a bunch of wisecracking soldiers. She had to check the train because she didn't for a moment believe that the passengers in question had gotten off without her knowledge. It had been a long shift, she'd been on duty since east of Berlin, had taken a short nap now and again, but had been awake when the boxcars were uncoupled at the Eggebek station. She'd better search the lavatories for the missing civilians, and was about to do just that when the soldiers in the corridor suddenly fell into formation, making way for three Gestapo officers approaching single file along the passageway; one a full colonel.

"Heil Hitler!" the conductress said, and along with everyone else, stood at rapt attention.

Without benefit of vision, Lisbet knew something was amiss. It was suddenly too quiet. The hair rose on her scalp. She strained to listen. What had Andreas Voigt said about a Gestapo search? He had dismissed it, believing it unlikely because this was a military train. Was he about to be proven wrong? Dear God, if only I hadn't agreed to this madness! People were routinely shot for much less than this. The Gestapo didn't differentiate between men and women. All were subject to the same punishment. Perhaps not even her children would be spared.

Clutching her daughters savagely, a paralyzing fear numbed her, communicating itself to Karoline and Arina, making the cat-and-mouse game very real. The children felt their mother's panic and fulfilled their roles as no promise of a reward could have done. Small breathless creatures, they played dead while a truly dangerous predator stalked them. Arina's thumb was in her mouth but she was making no sucking noises.

"Have all civilians disembarked?" a deep, militant voice inquired.

"Yes!" Andreas Voigt answered quickly, saving anyone else from lying to a Gestapo colonel.

The conductress immediately corroborated his claim. "All civilians are off the train, Herr *Oberst*," she said, awed at addressing so illustrious a person and now willing to take the soldiers at their word. She was certainly not about to admit to a Gestapo colonel that she had lost track of three passengers. "All are accounted for."

"Indeed? Not so the luggage." The colonel pointed a black-gloved hand toward an expensive leather valise in the baggage net.

Andreas Voigt drew in his breath sharply. *Christ Almighty, how did I miss that?* His hands began to feel clammy. This maneuver was taking much too long. Delay was dangerous. How long could the children keep still? Up to his neck in quicksand, he grabbed at straws.

"It must belong to the passenger who was in our compartment earlier," he said, sweat forming on his brow. "The lady had her hands full. She was traveling with small children and was in a great hurry to get off the train. I'm sorry I failed to notice the suitcase. I would have drawn her attention to it. My men and I have been taking advantage of the idle time on the train to catch up on our sleep so we can arrive at our new post ready to fulfill our duties to our Fuehrer." The floor near Lisbet shook as Andreas Voigt clicked his heels together and executed a sharp, "Heil Hitler!"

"Sieg Heil!" the colonel replied and ordered the luggage in question be taken off the train and put into the care of the stationmaster until such a time when its owner could reclaim it.

"This is the end of my run, Herr *Oberst*," the conductress spoke up. "It'll be no trouble for me to take charge of it. Tonight when I make the return trip, I can set it off at the lost and found booth in Eggebek where the woman got off."

"Very well!" the colonel snapped, this was a ridiculous waste of his time; he was here to search for stowaways, not sweep up lost belongings. "Hand it down, Lieutenant!"

"*Jawohl!*" Andreas' response was quick, but his feet were slow when he realized he had to step on the knapsacks to reach the suitcase. He had survived the Soviet front. Would Flensborg be his Waterloo?

Alert to the dicey situation, one of the conspirators managed a deep wheezing cough while someone solicitously pounded his back. Taking advantage of the distracting sounds, Andreas Voigt stepped onto the army gear and reached his hand into the luggage net with the speed of a pickpocket.

Moments later when the train pulled away from the station, the conductress could be seen, walking along the platform, carrying Lisbet's valise. The three Gestapo officers stood nearby at a newspaper kiosk, lighting cigarettes, not for a moment suspecting that men wearing the proud insignia of the Third Reich had fooled them.

Chapter Seventy-three

“Mama, can we make noise now?” Karoline whispered as Arina began to wiggle her legs. Both had grown tired of the game.

“Not yet. We have to wait for the signal.”

Compared with the slow pace since leaving Berlin, the train was now going at a rapid clip. Lisbet figured the acceleration was due to the fact that the engineer no longer needed to worry about bomb-damaged tracks. But though she was as anxious as the children to escape their cocoon, she had to be patient until Lieutenant Voigt established that the train was on Danish soil.

At long last the knapsacks were lifted and, squinting against the sudden light, Lisbet found herself staring into Lieutenant Voigt's triumphant face as well as those of his friends who stood in a half circle around him.

Getting to her feet, she impulsively threw her arms around him in profound gratitude. His arms encircled her waist, sending pleasant warmth through her. It had been a long time since she’d felt a man's embrace and it was so exquisitely wonderful that she only broke free when her children began pulling at her skirt.

“You were incredible! All of you!” she said, looking at each soldier in turn and blowing kisses to the grinning boys in the corridor. “If I live to be a hundred, I'll never forget you. Herr Hitler’s soldiers are, indeed, invincible.”

“Naw, this was easy,” the men mumbled.

“Almost too easy,” Andreas agreed. “There wasn’t much sport until the Gestapo showed up. I have to admit the colonel gave us a few tense moments. I'm sorry I didn't think to hide your suitcase. It completely escaped my attention. I hope there’s nothing terribly important in it. It might be a while before you can track it down.”

"I don't care if I ever see it again," Lisbet smiled as she picked up her coat and purse from the floor and hugged her children. "Everything of value is right here," she said, plunking down in her seat, exhausted from the ordeal.

"What's the prize? Did I win?" Karoline eyed Lieutenant Voigt as he and his men also sat down. He had promised a reward and she wasn't about to let him forget it.

He laughed and reached over to tousle her dark hair. "Of course," he said. "You and your sister both win a prize." He dug into the heap of knapsacks on the floor, located his, and produced two wonderful licorice sticks.

Karoline's eyes became as big as her hunger and she greedily accepted the candy. "*Danke schon,*" she uttered reverently, settling down to enjoy it. She loved licorice. It was a far better prize than any she could have imagined.

Arina accepted hers with less enthusiasm. She didn't like licorice and after studying it a moment, decided her thumb was better. Lisbet gave the candy back to Andreas. "You might as well keep it," she said. "She prefers her thumb."

He broke it in half, giving Lisbet the longer end. "You and I will share it," he said. "I wish I had more. I'm afraid this is it."

Lisbet had only eaten one small potato since last night and was ashamed at how quickly she swallowed the treat.

"Licorice is the only candy we get a regular supply of," Andreas explained sheepishly for he, too, had gulped his piece. "It's supposed to be a fatigue reliever. So the army claims. And, of course, it doesn't melt and make a mess in one's gear like chocolate would."

"Chocolate?" Lisbet said dreamily. "When was the last time you had a piece of chocolate?"

"Three years ago."

Lisbet nodded. "Yes, it disappeared in Berlin around that time as well. We were told milk could no longer be used for non-nutritional luxuries."

"Maybe there's chocolate in Denmark," Andreas Voigt mused. "Though I'd gladly settle for some bread with real butter."

Lisbet averted her eyes. During her parents' last visit to Bernau, they had told her that Danes regularly spoiled dairy products rather than let the German soldiers have any.

Chapter Seventy-four

The train was now traveling parallel with a pretty country road and Lisbet spotted several automobiles with Danish license plates. Her face glowed. Never before had she been so happy to see her homeland. Andreas also studied the countryside; everything he saw was tranquil and pleasant. Quaint thatched-roof farmhouses stood intact. There were no ruins. The fields were tended and fat cows were grazing on tuffs of new green grass. It was early afternoon, the cloud cover of this morning was lifting, and streaks of sunlight played on the red tiled roofs of each picturesque village they passed. It was a heady sight.

As the train neared Padborg, Lisbet readied herself and the girls to get off. They were in Denmark and could no longer ride a German troop train. But it didn't matter. In the event her parents had not received her wire, she could use the public telephone at the station, call them, then board a Danish train.

She said a warm goodbye to the soldiers and left the compartment, glancing out the same window where she had waved to Dorrit. How different the scene was. This station was milling with well-dressed people waiting for a local Danish train along with a smattering of German militia expecting to board this one. There were no frightened refugees, no crying children, no starved and anxious faces desperately looking for transportation.

At the end of the passageway, herding Karoline in front of her, Lisbet turned to Lieutenant Voigt carrying Arina. She gave him her prettiest smile. “When the war is over, you must come visit us,” she said. “I want my husband to meet you. We’ll be at my mother-in-law's house in Grunewald. Lindenstrasse number 77. It’s the only address I have in Berlin. If we are not there, my mother-in-law will know where you can find us.”

Andreas promised he would visit.

The troops on the platform stood back to let them climb down the steps.

Shielding her eyes against the sun, Lisbet surveyed the platform. Flower boxes with cheerful yellow and purple pansies hung below the windows of the red brick station house. A kiosk sold magazines, coffee and pastries, while freshly painted wooden benches offered attractive comfort. It was a wonderful and peaceful sight, almost as wonderful as that of her parents standing among other Danes at the far end of the platform. Eying the battered train, Gitte and Harold Lundgren's faces were shadowed with stress. They had left home the minute they received Lisbet's cable, and this was the first train to arrive from Germany. Awash with worry, they were wondering what to do if their daughter and her children were not on it. They had categorically been denied permission to drive across the border and had kept their vigil here in Padborg, praying she was not waiting for them in Flensborg. To make matters worse, they had just heard a rumor on the radio. Train travel inside Germany had ground to a halt! With that terrible news, the Lundgrens had to pin their hopes on this, the last train from Berlin.

"Hello!" Lisbet shouted and, tugging a child in each hand - her purse strapped across her shoulder - ran the length of the platform, her heavy lumpy coat banging against her legs. An instant later, she was in her father's arms while her mother was hugging the children.

Andreas witnessed the happy reunion before making his way back to his compartment, where he dropped heavily into his seat. After a few moments of fighting an odd depression, he made long-term plans for the first time in years. Stationed in Denmark, he could presumably expect to survive the war. Once it was over he would return to Frankfurt and if the Allies had left anything standing, resume his studies and finally become an architect. There would be plenty to design. Entire cities needed to be rebuilt. He had parents, he had a sister, he had lived twenty-nine years; the war had taken four of them and a good deal of his intestines, but he was determined it would take nothing else. In Frankfurt he would find a girl with golden hair, periwinkle eyes, and a musical laugh with a warm smile meant only for him.

The whistle blew. The locomotive began to move. Lisbet turned to watch the train pull away. She raised a hand to wave. Her lips formed his name, but there was no sign of him. Andreas was not standing at any of the soot-stained windows. Still, much to the outrage of her Danish countrymen, she continued waving as the German troop train picked up speed.

"Good luck," she whispered and blew a kiss, oblivious to the murderous stares that particular gesture earned her.

Her parents saw the malice and heard the angry whispers rippling through the crowd on the platform. They quickly hustled their daughter and their German-speaking grandchildren away from the station and across the street to the Padborg Hotel where they had spent the night. The inn was comfortable and had a wonderful restaurant, where they would now enjoy a meal before starting out for Copenhagen.

Chapter Seventy-five

Returning home from Anhalter Bahnhof after seeing Lisbet and the children off, Dorrit was unable to coax Nadia from the basement and she couldn't contact Lillian; telephones weren't working. But, never mind. She was tired; anyway it was probably too late in the day to start out for Bernau. Tomorrow would be soon enough.

The next morning, however, she was still unable to lure Nadia up into daylight, and the telephone lines were still down. Without Lillian and Nadia, Dorrit lost her motivation to go to Bernau. Besides, the cupboards were bare. She had to buy food. Before going out, she called into the basement from the top of the kitchen stairs, "Nadia?"

"Yes..." came a drowsy reply from the depth of the cellar.

"I'm going out to get some food. Would you like to come along?"

"No. I'm tired."

"It's a pleasant morning," Dorrit continued in the hope of enticing Nadia. "The fresh air will do you good and we don't need to go far. Just to Hagen Strasse."

"I...I don't...feel well."

Dorrit sighed philosophically; Nadia had not felt well for quite a while. "All right. I'll be back soon." Dorrit buttoned her trench coat and tied a colorful silk scarf around her neck. "But do come up to the kitchen. There's water in the kettle for tea."

Nadia didn't answer.

Dorrit returned home hours later, exhausted and with nothing to show for her efforts but some carrots and bread, and the shocking news that all civilian travel was shutting down. She surmised that included the *Ring-Bahn* and realized that any decision to leave Berlin had now been made for her, which offered her a certain amount of relief. Because, if she went to Bernau, she would have to confront the burned barony, something she was not ready to do. It could wait until after the war when Max and Fritz were back home. They would give her the strength to face the disaster and take charge of the rebuilding project. Bringing tea and the sparse rations down into the basement to Nadia, Dorrit took heart in the knowledge that Lisbet and the girls had left Berlin in the nick of time.

She went to bed early that evening only to lie awake in sleepless torment. Her chest was heavy, her stomach empty, her mind tired; she longed to sleep, yet couldn't. She missed her family and felt the gloom of the deserted house as never before. Tossing and turning, sleep eluding her, she finally got out of bed shortly before midnight. She stuffed her feet into some slippers, put on a green velvet robe and left her room, feeling the walls like a blind person as she made her way to the pitch-black center hall and along the corridor to the kitchen.

The blackout shades were securely drawn so she lit a candle and, groping through a cupboard, found the tea canister. *It was empty?* Oh, yes, of course. She and Nadia had finished the last of it this afternoon. Shrugging at her growing absentmindedness, Dorrit set some water to boil on the small alcohol burner and found the coffee *ersatz*. It would have to do. While waiting for the kettle to boil, she went over to the basement door and called down to Nadia, asking if she would like something hot to drink. There was no response. Although Dorrit longed for company she was glad the poor dear was sleeping.

The kettle whistled. Dorrit scooped some *ersatz* into a cup, poured boiling water on the black powder, stirred, and took a sip. It tasted better than expected, and the hot liquid also served to loosen the knot of loneliness in her heart. Of course, she reminded herself that her companionless existence meant her family was safe. Their absence from the chaos in Berlin was something to celebrate, not despair over. Only Fritz's absence - his participation in the war - lay heavy on her mind.

Holding the cup in one hand and the candlestick in the other, she left the kitchen for a comfortable chair in the library. Crossing the foyer, the light from the candle brought some envelopes on the parquet by the front door to her attention.

"Letters?" she exclaimed, speaking to the shadowy walls. There must have been a delivery after she went to bed. How extraordinary. A postal delivery - whatever the time of day or night - was surely a good sign. Dorrit put her cup and the candle on the hall table and hurried over to pick up the mail. Maybe the worst was finally over? Perhaps the attack the Allied leaflets had warned about would not materialize.

Much too excited to carry everything into the library in the dark, she pulled up a chair and sat down in the hall to read. The candle gave sufficient light and as she dug into her pocket for some reading glasses, her heart began racing in happy anticipation.

There were four letters. One was from Anna von Steigert. She put it on the table; she'd enjoy Anna's frivolous chitchat later after she had read the others. The next letter was a thick envelope from her solicitors. What on earth did they want? Well, that too could wait, and so could an official-looking piece of mail from a city department she had never heard of. She was fingering the last envelope, turning it over in her hand, only to be terribly disappointed. It was not from Max and Cassandra; nor was it from Fritz. In perplexed surprise, Dorrit saw that it was from Ernst Horstmann. *Ernst? Odd that he should write*, she thought and tried to recall the gist of his previous letter but drew a blank. She tore at the envelope, again berating herself for her forgetfulness.

She pulled out several pages plus a newspaper clipping. Unfolding the clipping, she instantly recognized Cassandra and Max pictured in the article written in Arabic, which she couldn't read, of course. But how wonderful they looked! Max was smiling, his blond hair was windblown and his sleeves were rolled up, the very image of a man at leisure with his work. Cassandra was holding a scroll, pointing at something. There was a pyramid in the background, which meant that this photograph was taken in Egypt, not Turkey. Had Max and Cassandra changed their plans? Were they working in Egypt? Might that account for the lack of letters? Ever since General Rommel's raid into Egypt, mail bound for Germany was presumably impounded and, knowing that, had Ernst taken it upon himself to send this from Turkey so that she might see this wonderful clipping? Yes, that would be just like him. He was a conscientious soul. Dorrit put the newspaper article lovingly on the hall table, took a sip of *ersatz* and began to read Ernst's letter, some of which had suffered a censor's black pen.

My Dear Baroness von Renz:
I am deeply grieved and, with pen in hand, searching for the right words. But of course there are no right words with which to try to explain such a tragedy. Unfortunately, I can add little to what the von

Steigerts have already written you, and the information your solicitors and the authorities in Berlin have supplied you with. Furthermore, I don't wish to add to your bereavement by going into unnecessary details pertaining to the disaster and murder.

Tragedy? Disaster? Murder? Bewildered, Dorrit looked around the foyer; only darkness stared back at her. What was Ernst talking about? Authorities? Wasn't he aware of the utter mayhem in Berlin? Most official agencies had shut down long ago. Only the Gestapo and the SS remained operational and efficient.

In January, when our month-long inquiries regarding Max and his family's whereabouts failed to produce answers, I again contacted Herr Ambassador Enno von Steigert in the hope that he might have learned something. He hadn't. I traveled to Thessaloniki to meet with him and to officially declare Max and his family missing.

Missing? Something twisted inside Dorrit's chest. Her breath came in small gulps as she skipped past the censor's black ink and continued to read.

...the ambassador's contacts had established that Max had crossed into Yugoslavia at Jesenice. The border patrols keep detailed records and since there was no evidence of him having left the country, we concluded that he and his family were somewhere inside Yugoslavia. The ambassador and I traveled to Zagreb, met with ranking members of our German command post, and were given a military escort to help trace Max's route.

We got as far as Bos Dubica where some local officials informed us that a black Mercedes riddled with bullets had been discovered months earlier in a ditch just north of Banja Luka. They explained that the amount of time between the attack and the discovery of the bodies, and the fact that thieves had stripped the car's contents, made identification impossible. Herr Ambassador and I were shocked to learn that no one had thought to trace the license plate. Of course there is no love lost between the locals and our forces, so perhaps this neglect was deliberate.

Sadly, our extensive search for Peter and Sigrid has proven unsuccessful. Our army command in Zagreb believes there is little hope of finding them alive. Of course, as of this writing, their case remains open.

German officials in...

The postal examiners had deleted the following two paragraphs, but skimming past the blotted-out spaces and coming to some fragmented text, Dorrit finished the letter.

...all concur that the untimely deaths are a great loss to the archaeological community worldwide. I am in total shock. Everyone at the dig is grieving...

Chapter Seventy-six

The ground below the huge airborne armada lay veiled in total darkness.

"If I didn't know better, I'd swear we were flying over the Sahara," Major Robert Grantham said, turning to his copilot. "Not a flicker of light anywhere down there," he added with admiration for German discipline

"Yeah, dark as a dungeon," Lieutenant Emerson nodded, looking down from his side of the aircraft.

Robert Grantham checked his watch. Midnight. Excellent. Confirming his position, he was again satisfied. The 9th Bomb Squadron was on schedule, bearing down on tonight's objective without having attracted a single Fieseler Storch buzzing on the fringes of this flying fleet. Major Grantham was not surprised. The Luftwaffe had taken a pounding lately. It was safe to assume that Herr Hitler had precious few flying machines left in which his pilots could commit suicide.

Robert Grantham had flown combat missions alongside the RAF for two years and had participated in countless dogfights over the English Channel, regularly sending German aircraft into the drink. On the base in Cambridgeshire he was rumored to have steel in his veins. His reputation for calm at the controls was such that he'd been handpicked to lead tonight's important assault. Though flattered, he was not particularly delighted because there was little sport in bombing a defenseless civilian target.

Okay, cut the sanctimonious crap, he told himself. Civilians had been warned. Thousands of Leaflets had been dropped on Berlin. Anyone dumb enough not to get the hell out of town had it coming. Besides, if this strike convinced their stubborn Fuehrer to call it quits then leveling Berlin was worth it. Robert made another visual check of his position. Directly below him, the Mecklenburg Chain Lakes reflected the moonlight, serving as a foolproof navigational marker.

"Eighty miles to ground zero," he said to Bill Emerson. "No flack. They haven't spotted us yet"

"Yeah. The krauts got radar. Why the hell don't they use it?" Emerson sounded as if he were being cheated of a fair fight.

"Beats me. We've got enough metal aloft to sound an alarm in two continents."

Indeed, tonight's formation numbered one thousand aircraft, comprised of American-made B-17s and B-24s; long-range workhorses capable of sustaining tremendous flak damage and still remain airborne. Several maneuverable P51 Mustang fighters accompanied this enormous fleet to scout the sky for hostile interceptors. So far they had not encountered a single German reconnaissance plane.

Scanning the horizon, Major Grantham gave a thumbs-up to the British pilots flying wing tip to wing tip on either side of him. He knew them well, they had flown numerous missions in the past, and although he would have enjoyed a bit of conversation to break the monotony, he dared not make radio contact. Some zealous ham operator on the ground might pick it up. Down for the count, batting zero, the Germans were still known to be resourceful.

Grantham looked over his shoulder toward the back of his plane. The men manning the payload were playing cards. The gunners were bored and silent. Grantham figured that, along with the Mustangs, they could have remained on base tonight. Operation *Little Bear* would commence, unimpeded, in a matter of minutes. He made an entry into his log: *23:56. Conditions clear. Forty miles to drop zone. No enemy fire.*

Suddenly he tore off his gloves. His palms were soaking wet. *What the hell?* His upper lip was moist as well! Christ Almighty, what was going on? Why the sudden sweats? An instant later he knew. He had flown sorties before, plenty, but targeting Germany's proud capital was a first for him and this attack would change the city forever.

He called to mind the city's majestic architecture, remembered its monuments, museums, picturesque canals, and glitzy nightclubs. For crying out loud! He and Linda had spent their honeymoon down there. It was sheer lunacy to destroy all that terrific real estate. Christ Almighty, he was about to destroy Fritz's home! How would he ever face him again? This was cockeyed. He swore under his breath and tried to remember when he'd last heard from Fritz. Autumn of '42? Yeah, a helluva long time ago. Fritz had written he expected to be drafted, which meant he could be just about anywhere now. The Nazi army was spread all over the damned globe. Fritz's whereabouts was anyone's guess. He could be in Africa. France? He could even be in Russia. Now there was a sorry assignment. The eastern front was a slaughterhouse. With all due respect, and in view of the fact that the Soviets were on the side of the U.S., Robert had heard their savagery surpassed even that of the Nazis.

"Target in sight!" Lieutenant Emerson said.

Major Robert Grantham brought his aircraft into drop position. Engines droning, the rest of his pilots followed. A thousand aircraft slowed their airspeed and fanned out like a black metal cape behind the lead plane as it dipped below the wispy clouds.

Well, here goes! Sorry pal...

The objective lay a handful of miles directly east. It lay in total darkness, not a single light glimmered to guide the flying fleet. But the inhabitants of Berlin need not have been so diligent tonight. The blackout did not conceal them. The moonlight shimmering on the surfaces of the river Spree and midtown waterways exposed the city to the mercy of fifteen hundred tons of explosives about to rain down.

Robert wondered where Lisbet and the children were. And where was the gracious baroness? In Bernau? Yes, of course. Women and children had been warned to evacuate the city.

Major Grantham replaced his gloves.

His palms were dry.

Chapter Seventy-seven

Sitting immobilized in the hall, Dorrit turned Ernst's letter over in her hand. He had written more but she could no longer read. The words blurred before her eyes and she suddenly dropped the pages into her lap as if they burned her fingers. Several sheets fluttered to the floor and slid from sight into the black periphery around the circle of light the candle provided. Her lips quivering, she put a white-knuckled fist to her mouth while a raw throbbing began somewhere near her temples. A pain, unlike any she'd known, shot through her body. Her eyes, round and hollow, stared straight ahead into the murky void of the unlit hall while an oppressive weight in her chest was suffocating her.

Gasping for air, tears began streaming down her cheeks, fogging her glasses. Mechanically, she removed them, put them in her pocket and, drying her eyes on the sleeves of her robe, looked around the shadowy hall. Earlier on her way to the kitchen, she had vilified the darkness; now it seemed strangely comforting. She sat for a long time without moving. After a while she could begin to draw shallow breaths without effort. The ache in her body began to dull, delivering a pleasant peace.

The candle on the table flickered, its light dancing across the gold-leafed frame of the painting hanging above it. Dorrit pulled a kink from her back and glanced up at the yellow wheat fields where young maidens - flowers woven into their hair - were bringing baskets of fruit to the men laboring in the fields. It was a bright pastoral scene, but its colors were muted for lack of light. She was surprised that the sconce over the picture was not lit; neither was the chandelier hanging from the high rotund ceiling. *Why am I sitting here in the dark hall, daydreaming?* she wondered. *Why are the sconces turned off? Johann insists that fine art must be illuminated. Johann...?*

He was peculiarly late tonight. Had an emergency at the clinic detained him? But if so, wouldn't he have telephoned? Crimping her brow, Dorrit tried to remember if he had called. She saw the sheets of paper in her lap and, gathering them together, studied the handwriting and signature without recognizing either one. She shrugged and put them on the hall table. Reaching for her cup, she took a sip. The coffee tasted awful. She pushed the vile cup aside; one of the servants would clear it away. Grimacing, she got up, leaving the mail for Johann to peruse later. Taking the candle, she crossed the hall and touched a light switch. The foyer remained dark. She walked into the library and tried a switch with the same result. Why was there no electricity? Had a tree limb fallen on a power line? She must send Schmidt out to investigate. She walked over to the fireplace to touch the candle to the wicks of several tapers in the silver holders on the mantelpiece. As she did so, she made a mental note to speak with Frau Schmidt. The maids must be reminded to replace the candles before they burned down into such pathetic little stumps.

Suddenly a strange droning in the night sky disturbed the calm of the library. Holding the candle, Dorrit walked over to the windows, intending to raise the shades and have a look. As she passed Johann's desk, the glow from the flame fell across an assortment of family photographs standing on the fine-grained surface, among them her wedding picture. She lifted it to get a better look. Johann's dark hair was carefully combed and, although he wore a sedate expression befitting the occasion, there was that unmistakable glint of seductive amusement in his gray eyes. For endless moments, Dorrit remained entranced by memories, the noise in the sky forgotten.

"Johann!" she suddenly cried, the picture slipping from her hand and clattering noisily to the floor, her shoulders now shaking with sobs breaking in her chest. The flame of the candle went out, leaving the library in total darkness. "I've had some news…I…I can't bear it. Oh, Johann…" She sank down on the chair by the desk. "Help me! I don't know what to do. Something has happened to Max and Cassandra and the children. Peter and Sigrid are...are lost..."

As the words tumbled from her lips, Dorrit struggled for breath while a black void was again engulfing her. She could no longer put a coherent thought together. She looked around without remembering what had just been on her mind. Her thoughts were slipping away like leaves tossed into a rushing stream. Although lapses in the past had made her forgetful, she was now immersed in a quagmire of total bewilderment. She was crying and didn't know why.

A moment later she was alerted to several earsplitting noises and bright lights flashing in static repetition around the edges of the window shades. She brushed the back of her hand across her wet eyes.

A thunderstorm? Dorrit rose from her chair and walked over to the windows. She raised a shade to peer out. A huge bonfire was burning across the street. A tree must have been hit by lightening. Well, never mind, a fire truck would come along shortly and put it out. She was lowering the shade when a series of new explosions rocked the neighborhood. The windowpanes cracked in front of her. Surprised, she let go of the shade. It rolled up with a snap. She stepped away from the windows just as splintered glass blew into the room. Behind her, she heard the hall chandelier crash to the floor.

"What's happening?" she cried out loud, frightened.

A moment later she lost her fear. Johann was home. She heard the front door groan on its heavy brass hinges and, turning toward the French doors, she saw him stroll into the library, wearing his white surgeon's coat over his pinstriped suit. He must have rushed home from the clinic the minute the storm broke. Coming toward her with long purposeful strides he was smiling and holding out his arms, beckoning her. "Come here," he was saying. "There's nothing to be afraid of. The storm will soon pass."

Dorrit ran toward him and flung herself into his warm embrace. The floor shook violently. There was a thunderous rumble. Books tumbled from the bookcases as the thick stone walls collapsed around her. Flames sprung to life from every corner, greedily devouring everything.

A grim meal.

No sirens were heard. Streets were impassable. The pavements were burning.

An inferno raged across Berlin.

Chapter Seventy-eight

September 1945…

Lisbet was pacing the floor in the hall of her parents' home in Gentofte, an affluent suburb of Copenhagen, where she and the girls had lived for the past seventeen months. It was a Thursday, but it might as well have been any other day of the week because the routine was the same. By nine o'clock each morning she was stationed in the foyer, peering through the window panels on either side of the front door, looking for the mailman. The minute she spotted his bright red jacket near the garden gate, she was out the door and down the path, running with her hand over her heart, her skirts flying.

The mail was late today and so was Harold Lundgren. He had overslept, and as he now hurried downstairs on his way to breakfast, he saw Lisbet in the hall.

"Has the paper come?" he asked, for he couldn't enjoy his breakfast without *Morgen Posten*. His own publication was an afternoon paper and there was always the danger that the morning journal had preempted his headline, in which case he couldn't enjoy his breakfast at all.

"Not yet," Lisbet said, pushing impatiently at the ecru lace on the window panels. "Where's that old slowpoke, Carlsen?" she mumbled under her breath.

"Along with the newspaper, the mail is occasionally late," her father said. "Why don't you come in and eat?"

"In a minute." Lisbet kept her eyes on the garden gate.

"My dear girl. Carlsen won't peddle his bicycle any faster just because you're waiting for him. Besides, with a lion's share of bad news lately, haven't you had enough? Letters don't give you much joy. Why be so eager?" Harold Lundgren was referring to the correspondence from Julianne Niemann, telling Lisbet of Dorrit's entombment in the rubble. The news had swept over Lisbet like a suffocating avalanche and, just when she was beginning to recover; a letter from Ernst Horstmann devastated her anew. Harold Lundgren sighed. Every piece of mail his daughter had received in the months since the war ended contained terrible news. Yet, she never stopped being optimistic that it would change.

Lisbet turned to face her father. "You go ahead," she said. "Go eat. Don't wait for me. The girls need a masculine presence in there." She nodded toward the dining room where Arina and Karoline could be heard squabbling in German, a language they occasionally reverted to although they had long ago learned to speak Danish.

Harold Lundgren touched Lisbet's cheek tenderly; his daughter was the apple of his eye and he hated to see her torture herself. "You jump when the phone rings," he said softly. "You turn pale when a telegram is delivered. And you spend your mornings here in the hall, waiting for the mail. The German War Ministry has asked you to be patient. I believe that's good counsel, though as you know I'm loath to give them any credit."

"How long am I supposed to be patient?" Lisbet said, bitterly. "The war's been over for months and I still don't know where Fritz is. German soldiers are returning from Russia. Last week your own paper reported that a group of eighty POWs from a Soviet camp had made their way back. Suppose Fritz was among them. Suppose he has returned to Berlin."

"If so, he'll call. I'm sure he can figure out that you and the girls are here with us."

"Yes, but..."

"But what?"

"Oh, nothing." Lisbet crimped her brow, turned away and again peered through the window panels.

"What is it, sweetheart?" her father prodded, patting her shoulder.

"Oh, I don't know."

"Come on now, tell me."

"It's only that...uh...I feel so...so guilty about being here."

"Why? This is your home. The only one you have at the moment." Harold Lundgren looked confused. "What on earth is there to feel guilty about?"

"Oh, you know..."

“No, I'm afraid I don't.”

“If…” Lisbet corrected herself. “*When* Fritz calls, how am I going to tell him what happened to his mother? How am I going to explain that I abandoned her?” Lisbet raked a hand through her hair and gave her father a wretched look. “Why did I leave her? I should have stayed. I should have known she and Nadia couldn't make it out to Bernau. Nadia was not herself. Things were so bad in Berlin. It was utter chaos. And knowing it, I left. I left them to die.”

“Look! We've gone through this before. You've got to stop blaming yourself. You could not have saved the baroness or anyone else. Had you stayed, you would only have compounded the disaster by getting yourself and your daughters killed.”

“Not if we'd gone out to Bernau. The Konauers survived. Julianne went to Gransee. She and her boys survived. Even Helmut's parents who remained in Berlin managed to survive.” Lisbet pushed at the lace curtains. *Still no sign of Carlsen.* Turning back to her father, she changed the subject. “Did I tell you that some military records have been discovered in the rubble under the War Ministry's former headquarters on Tirpitz-ufer?”

“No, I don't believe you did.”

“Well, Julianne told me that boxes and boxes have been dug up. The records are surprisingly complete and people have been promised access to them. She thinks they might shed some light on where Fritz's battalion was when the war ended.”

“What good will it do to know that? Clearly, he is no longer there.”

“No, but at least it's something to go on. A point of reference. Maybe I could contact someone inside the Soviet Union. I might try to...”

“Forget it! Not even the International Red Cross has access inside Russia. The Soviets are so damned secretive one can't help wonder what they're up to. As for the Germans, records or no records, it'll take years before they sort out everything. Don't hold your breath, my dear. There are millions missing. Soldiers as well as civilians. People all over the continent are missing. Your niece and nephew are missing. More likely dead somewhere in Yugoslavia. It's a tragic mess. But there's nothing to do but be patient. If Fritz is alive you'll hear from him. If not, you'll eventually be notified through the proper channels.”

“Julianne learned about Helmut on her own,” Lisbet reminded her father.

"That's different. She was lucky to locate someone from Helmut's outfit who came back immediately after the armistice."

"Maybe I could find someone."

"Do you have any names from Fritz's unit?"

"No. But that's why these newly discovered records are so important. Julianne plans to use them to investigate the details surrounding Helmut's death."

"Details!" Harold Lundgren snorted. "Her husband was shot for insubordination. Shot by his commanding officer. And Julianne wants to know *more?*"

"Yes. She believes it was murder. The soldier she interviewed hinted at that."

"Hinted? Couldn't he be more specific?"

"Fear of Nazi reprisal still runs deep. He was afraid to say too much. But he said enough, and Julianne is determined that the officer who shot Helmut be found and questioned. Along with Helmut's parents, she's preparing a full-scale inquiry. The Nazis are no longer in power. No officer can hide behind his uniform. And if a crime was committed..."

"A crime?" Harold Lundgren interrupted with another snort. "More like ten million crimes! The whole damned country ought to be brought up on charges. Just look at those camps that have come to light. Someone should have stopped that sort of atrocity. No one did, and the picture is not helped by the fact that everyone claims oppression, fear, ignorance, and God knows what else."

Lisbet let her father rant. He was a stubborn man. Once his mind was made up, nothing she told him would make any difference. But some of his obstinacy had been passed on to her and she could be equally pigheaded. She was tired of waiting for others to account for the missing. She had been patient for months with nothing to show for it. It was time to take matters in hand. The war had ended five months ago. Traveling to Germany was possible. Difficult, but possible.

During a family dinner the following Sunday, Lisbet slipped her plans for a trip back to Berlin into the general conversation.

Her mother cried at the very suggestion and was so distraught that she had to excuse herself from the table.

Her father made good use of words such as preposterous, absurd, and foolhardy. "Berlin is a wasteland!" he roared. "Divided and ruled by separate nations. For all we know the Soviets are still raping the women. You'll find nothing there. Nothing but mayhem."

Lisbet's sister-in-law, Karin, snickered, unable to conceal her glee with yet another display of Lisbet's impulsive nature.

Torben expressed his brotherly concern with a succinct, "You're nuts!"

Chapter Seventy-nine

Three weeks later, Torben reluctantly accompanied Lisbet to Berlin, arriving at Potsdam Platz Bahnhof early in the afternoon on a brilliant October day. The station had been repaired sufficiently to accommodate a limited number of trains, but there were no taxis waiting at the curb.

Walking along the upended sidewalks of Saarland Strasse toward Belle Vue Allee and the Esplanade - a hotel that had escaped total destruction and was open in a modified capacity - Lisbet recognized street corners by their posted names, not by landmark buildings; there were none. Berlin had been a battlefield during the last desperate days of the war, and remnants of Soviet tanks still littered the streets where rows of blackened shells, remains of the city's classic architecture, stood shoulder to shoulder in utter defeat. Everywhere she looked, she saw mounds of debris and women and children pushing heavy wheelbarrows toward intersections and city squares where older citizens were painstakingly sorting and stacking building materials reclaimed from the rubble. Neighborhoods were being cleared one brick at a time, each stone and tile saved for the rebuilding of the city.

It was three o'clock by the time she and Torben checked into the Esplanade, changed out of their traveling clothes, and went back downstairs to the lobby to hire a car and driver. Torben lost his composure when a rusted wreck peppered with bullet holes and without runners or fenders, pulled up. He turned on the concierge in protest.

"It's the best we can do," the man explained, spreading his hands in a helpless gesture before opening the car door for the well-dressed Danish guests. He admired the woman's red coat and chic black velvet beret, noting that her shoes were spotless patent leather with shiny silver buckles. It had been a long time since he'd seen a fashionable woman in Berlin.

Sitting sad and motionless during the ride to Grunewald, Lisbet stared at each desolate block they passed, her hands inadvertently crushing the stems on a bouquet of chrysanthemums she'd bought from a skinny boy in front of the hotel. When she'd commented on the pretty flowers, the boy had proudly explained that he and his mother grew them in Tiergarten where they lived. As the taxi now drove along this formerly magnificent city forest, Lisbet saw that - sure enough - it had become a truck garden and campground for the homeless.

Reaching Grunewald, the taxi went down Lindenstrasse until stopped by debris. The street had not yet been cleared sufficiently to allow for motorized traffic. Torben and Lisbet would have to proceed on foot. The driver reached for his newspaper and prepared to wait for their return. Stepping around craters and uprooted pipes, they picked their way along until they found a footpath on the park side of the street, which made walking less hazardous. When Lisbet finally spotted number 77, she stopped and gazed in horror. The stately villa was nothing but a cinder cone. She let go of Torben's arm and clawed her way across piles of rubble to some twisted metal all that was left of the tall wrought iron gates. Swallowing convulsively, tears flowing, she stared at the black ruin.

Impatient with any public display of emotion, Torben pushed a hand contemptuously through his blond hair. After some moments of dealing with the appalling sight of his sister crying over a pile of debris, he decided to forgive her this one pathetic scene, if only because no one was around. With the exception of a man riding his bicycle along the narrow path they had just walked, this entire neighborhood seemed deserted. Still, Torben's forgiving nature had a short shelf life.

"For Christ's sake!" he muttered after a few minutes of exercising restraint. He came up to her and reached into his pocket for a handkerchief. "Here, take this!" She ignored him. Engulfed in pain, she was no longer aware of her brother. He shrugged indifferently and put the handkerchief away. "All right, go ahead and soak yourself if that's what's needed to forget all this." He craned his neck and looked around. "It shouldn't be too difficult. There's nothing left. Nothing came of your years here in Berlin. Nothing except Karoline and Arina. Children are a blessing regardless of their parentage." Torben had not endorsed his sister's marriage to a foreigner and had never warmed toward his brother-in-law, barely tolerating Fritz's visits to Copenhagen and, with the exception of the trip to Bernau for the engagement party, had never made another effort to visit. Since the first day of their encounter, he had judged Fritz harshly and without reason, except a bias born of male jealousy. Fritz was too self-assured and far too clever. Torben had struggled with languages throughout his school years, and was thoroughly chastised when Fritz, in a matter of a few trips to Copenhagen, picked up enough Danish to converse quite charmingly. This galling ability had ruffled Torben's self-esteem, which was nurtured in the belief that *he* was the cat's meow. "The Germans got what was coming to them," he muttered. "One would think..."

"Please, stop!" Lisbet begged, tears dripping off her trembling chin. "I know how you feel. Please stop your harping. I don't think I can stand it. Not today. Not here."

"Fine," Torben complied with a weary shrug. He had been opposed to this journey, but his father had pressed him into service because - come hell or high water - Lisbet had been determined to return to Berlin and needed a male escort. "I just hate to see you eat your heart out. You'll find no answers in this wasteland."

"We don't know that yet," Lisbet said. But even as she was saying it something in her heart burst, shattering the optimism she'd clung to for so many months. Here at the scorched site of Fritz's boyhood home, she began to relinquish the cuirass she had worn around her heart against the steady barrage of bad news. Today, for the first time, she began to accept that Fritz was lost to her. Somehow in her silly and romanticized view of life, she had imagined finding him here. Since the day the war ended, she had believed that if only she returned to this spot, she would find him. Of course, that fantasy was nothing but a fool's dream. Fritz was not here. He had died inside the Soviet Union. He would never come back. The War Ministry would eventually send her a letter to that effect. That was her painful reality, the only one.

Her eyes traveled over every inch of the rubble where Fritz's mother, the bravest woman Lisbet had ever known, lay entombed with poor Nadia. And, although not buried here, Cassandra, Max, and their children were part of the total sum of this ruin as well. Looking at the black mound, autumn leaves blowing across the site; Lisbet clamped her lips between her teeth to keep them from trembling. This was Dorrit's final resting place. Bodies were not allowed to be exhumed. It was estimated that over two hundred thousand souls would lie eternally under Berlin's rubble where they had died. Berlin's new structures would rise atop a vast graveyard.

Clinging to the contorted fence, charred wisteria vines crumbling with the slightest movement of her hand, Lisbet let go and made her way up to the marble steps, the only recognizable part of the once sumptuous home. As she climbed to the top landing, she unwound her fingers from around the chrysanthemums. The stems felt like wads of wet grass in her hand, but the pink and yellow blooms remained fresh and glorious.

"For you, Dorrit," she whispered as she bent down to place the flowers where the front door had once been. "Thank you...thank you for the comfort you gave us. Your support. Your generosity. And all those hours. Oh God, those endless hours you spent in food lines so we could eat. I feel so desperately guilty about that. I wish I could make it up to you. I wanted to make it up to you after the war. We made so many plans for after the war. I thought you'd be all right. You saved us. Why didn't you save yourself?"

Lisbet's knees buckled and she sank down on the steps, too distraught to stand, but not too distraught to raise her voice as though Dorrit might hear her if only she spoke loudly enough. "You were so resourceful," she sobbed, giving full throttle to her grief. "Why didn't you leave Berlin while there was still time?" Grappling with Dorrit's tragedy, Lisbet wiped her wet face on her coat sleeve. "But I promise you this!" She clenched her fists. "I will learn what happened to Fritz. I won't give up. Do you hear me? I will never give up!"

Increasingly uncomfortable, Torben glanced up and down the street. If anyone witnessed this scene they might want to confine his sister for observation. Finally, jeopardizing his own dignity, he climbed over the debris-strewn path, scuffing his shoes and getting ash on his trouser cuffs as he approached the steps and pulled her to her feet.

"Come on!" he said. "We've been here long enough. The taxi is waiting. You've seen the ruin and placed the flowers. There's no reason to waste any more time here. It's only making you miserable." Studying his sister, Torben realized she looked a sight. How could he take her back to town like this? Her face was so red and swollen someone might accuse him of having slapped her. "Come on. Let's go," he repeated when she remained motionless. Finally losing his patience, he snapped, "Get hold of yourself! It's late. You're supposed see Julianne today. It's a long drive out to her place and if we don't hurry there won't be time for much of a visit. You and she can commiserate in private. Her husband, too, is dead."

"We don't know for sure that Fritz is d...dead." Lisbet turned on her brother, her eyes brimming. "I still think he could..."

"Could *what?*" Torben bristled. "Walk across Russia on foot? I hear the Soviets still shoot at anything German that slithers through their countryside."

Shocked, Lisbet's mouth dropped open. But she couldn't retaliate. Her tongue lay like lead in her mouth. She wanted to rail at the cruel words but was emotionally spent, depleted of passion, including anger.

Taking advantage of his sister's momentary impotence, Torben took a firm hold on her arm and pulled her none too gently back out toward the street.

Chapter Eighty

Days later, days spent sifting through boxes of old records, crosschecking names against current rosters of survivors, Lisbet and Torben had collected the particulars of some seventy men who had served in Fritz's battalion at Stalingrad and returned to their families in Berlin.

Compiling the names turned out to be the easy part; tracking each one down in a city where old addresses no longer existed and where the Soviet Army discouraged entry into their sector, was quite another. Despite Lisbet's dogged persistence, at week's end she had learned absolutely nothing of her missing husband. Some of the men on her list had left Berlin for other parts of Germany. Others lay at death's door, too ill to be questioned. A number suffered amnesia and many simply refused to talk, the fear of Nazi vengeance too deeply ingrained. Of those she interviewed, all invariably shook their heads, claiming they couldn't remember anyone of the name and description she gave.

Into the second week of blind alleys and dead ends, Lisbet's list was whittled down to a scant six names. Again she and Torben set out early in the morning, riding the same relic of a taxi, the driver waiting at designated corners while they walked streets closed to traffic. Knowing this might be the last day of her quest, Lisbet forged ahead absurdly optimistic while Torben resigned himself to another wasted day. But, he reminded himself, with only a handful of names left, they could finally return to Denmark tomorrow and put an end to this madness.

By noon, now down to three names, Lisbet pushed out her chin, daring her brother to make a wry comment as they drove toward yet another destination. Torben did eventually make a comment, but only to suggest that they do something constructive and have lunch. He pointed to a café on Konigs Platz. It seemed out of place among the ruins, but the chairs and tables on the sidewalk looked scrupulously clean and, being that it was on the sunny side of the square, it was possible to eat out-of-doors; a definite advantage because Torben was not about to venture inside a propped-up structure. He told the driver to pull over, got out of the taxi, and peered through the door to make sure the place was open for business. Along with the wonderful aroma of freshly baked bread, the young waitress inside gave him a decidedly welcoming smile.

He turned and called to Lisbet, "It's open. Come on!"

Getting out of the car, Lisbet consulted her notepad. The next person on her list, Erich Treff, lived only a block away on Herwarthstrasse. "I want to check one more name before we eat," she said. "He lives around the corner. Unless he's infirm, he'll be working and is probably home for lunch. This could be a perfect time catch him." She walked away, leaving Torben to salivate in front of the cafe. He signaled to the waitress, indicating they would return shortly, and caught up with Lisbet; after all, he had promised his father not to let her out of his sight for even a moment.

Rounding the next corner, Lisbet soon found the address she was looking for and quickly climbed down the stairs to a basement dwelling, the only part of the structure that appeared livable. Torben remained standing on the sidewalk until she had established that someone was at home. The two-story building had been damaged, he noted, but not so badly that it needed to be torn down. The sound of a hammer pounding somewhere inside proved the place was being renovated.

"Well, here goes..." Lisbet looked up at Torben, crossed her fingers, and knocked.

The door was opened by a pale dark-haired woman in her mid-thirties, her face a map of past misery. A small tow-headed boy also came to the door but immediately took refuge behind his mother's skirt at the sight of a stranger.

"Frau Treff?" Lisbet asked.

"Yes." Eva Treff's eyes widened with a mixture of fear and curiosity. This well-dressed individual knew her name. Nervously, she tugged at the strings of her soiled apron.

Lisbet took a deep breath, introduced herself, and began her speech, delivering it in a flat monologue born from too many repetitions. "I'm sorry to disturb you," she said. "But I'm searching for veterans from

General Paulus' Sixth Army. The Eighteenth Division. I'm trying to locate someone who might have known my husband. His name is Frederick Alexander von Renz. He served at Stalingrad at the time of the surrender and is still unaccounted for. With the help of records from the War Ministry, I've compiled a list of survivors from his Berlin-based unit. Your husband's name was among them and, if at all possible, I would very much like to speak with him." Ending her pitch, Lisbet fell silent and braced herself for disappointment as routine as her speech.

"I see." The woman nodded and absently removed her apron, but might have done better to keep it on; her faded blue housedress was in a deplorable condition. "You're welcome to speak with my husband," she said, now less fearful, the lines in her face relaxing. "But he's working and I can't call him away from his job. Could you come back later? Maybe this evening? What did you say your husband's name was?"

"Frederick Alexander von Renz. But everyone called him Fritz." As Lisbet was saying this, she felt hopeful because, since Erich Treff was at work, he was obviously not ill or comatose. "Does you husband talk much about the war?" she asked, in order to learn if he was one of those tightlipped men still afraid of the Nazis. If so, she would be wasting her time coming back here.

"Talk? I should say so. He talks to himself if no one else is around. I suppose it's better than keeping things bottled up. I try to be attentive but his stories are so depressing it's difficult to listen."

Lisbet's expectations were suddenly soaring. "Does he ever mention names?" she asked. "Names of those he served with?"

"Sure. All the time."

"Does my husband's name sound familiar? Has he ever mentioned it?"

"Actually..." Frau Treff pursed her lips in concentration, "von Renz does have a familiar ring to it."

"Really?" Lisbet felt lightheaded.

"Yes, but I could be mistaken. I'd hate to get your hopes up."

"Oh, don't worry about that." Lisbet wanted to hug the woman such was her excitement. "My hopes have been on a roller coaster for a long time. The War Ministry and the Red Cross give me such conflicting reports, except in their advice about being patient. But the war's been over for so many months and it's difficult to be patient. My daughters and I are living in Denmark with my parents. I came to Berlin to see if I could learn something on my own."

Sympathy flickered in Frau Treff's eyes. She knew about waiting and not knowing. Her husband had only recently returned home, a shadow of his former self. "How about six o'clock tonight?" she suggested. "Can you come back then? My husband will be finished for the day. He works upstairs, restoring this building, and I can't interrupt him. Every hour of daylight counts. Electricity is not reliable and the work has to be done before the cold weather sets in. We'd like to move upstairs before Christmas. I hope you understand."

"Of course." Lisbet turned and glanced up to the sidewalk where Torben was shuffling his feet. "How is six o'clock tonight?" she called out in Danish.

He shrugged.

"Six o'clock is fine," she told Frau Treff. "My brother and I will be back then."

"Remember, please don't be disappointed if..."

"Don't worry!" In her excitement Lisbet interrupted the woman. "I realize our husbands could have been in the same division and never gotten acquainted. I've been told the units numbered in the thousands."

"Is your husband by any chance a journalist?" Eva Treff asked in the next instant.

"Yes!" Lisbet's heart made somersaults in her chest. If this woman knew that, then Erich Treff must have known Fritz.

"I thought so," Frau Treff smiled. "I remember reading his articles in the Zeitung before the war."

The Zeitung. Lisbet's heart sank. Was that the reason Fritz's name was familiar?

Chapter Eighty-one

At six o'clock sharp, Lisbet climbed back down to the basement dwelling on Herwarthstrasse; Torben followed, carefully planting his feet on the uneven steps.

This time the door was opened by a gaunt man who appeared to be in his fifties although Lisbet knew him to be thirty-nine from the records she had studied. He stood in the doorway, wearing carpenter overalls, a gray threadbare sweater, and looked at her with rueful anticipation. The air escaped her lungs in a sickening gasp. With a paralyzing jolt she knew that she had come to the end of her search. Erich Treff's lugubrious expression spoke volumes. The road ended here and with no happy outcome. She swayed. Seeing her falter, Torben took her by the elbow, forestalling any awkwardness as he introducing himself and his sister.

"Please, come in." Erich Treff kept his eyes on Lisbet. "My wife told me to expect you." He stepped back from the narrow doorway, allowing the visitors to enter a cellar Lisbet immediately identified as a former bomb shelter, complete with the bare bulb dangling from the ceiling, casting an embarrassing wreath of light over the center of the shabby room, leaving its four corners some dignity in their darkness.

Frau Treff, still wearing the same faded blue dress, stepped out from behind a wall partition with her son.

"*Guten Abend*!" she said to Lisbet before turning to Torben and offering her hand.

Torben shook her hand and was about to acknowledge the boy as well but the lad had run off and disappeared into the shadows of the basement.

"Would you like a glass of wine?" Erich Treff asked his guests.

"No, thanks," they both replied. Lisbet didn't want to deprive this family of any more than their time, and Torben wasn't about to accept anything that would prolong the visit.

Since refreshments weren't needed, Eva Treff excused herself to prepare supper. Erich Treff pointed to a sofa, indicating Herr Lundgren and his sister sit down. Lisbet sank into the lumpy couch and when their host pulled up a wooden crate he aimed to sit on, Torben had no choice but to join Lisbet on a sofa. It smelled as if it had been scorched and, trying not to inhale, he lowered himself carefully to the edge of the vile cushions. Noticing Herr Lundgren's uneasiness, Erich Treff felt obliged to explain himself.

"Shortages abound," he said, shrugging. "Housing and furnishings are nonexistent at the present time. We can't be particular. We're lucky to have a roof over our heads."

Torben adjusted his shoulders inside his tweed jacket and settled into the sofa, but gave no indication that he was comfortable.

An awkward lull fell over the small room.

"You're in the construction trade?" Torben finally broke the silence, addressing the host and remembering the hammering he'd heard earlier today along with Frau Treff's reluctance to call her husband away from his work.

"For the time being."

"I'm sure your job is secure. If Berlin expects to be rebuilt, carpenters will be in demand for years to come."

"Carpentry is not my line of work."

"What's your trade?"

"Finance."

Torben's eyes strafed Erich Treff's overalls and calloused hands; it was difficult to visualize him in a suit and tie. "You quit to fight your Fuehrer's battles?"

Lisbet nudged her brother; this was not the time or place to vent his spleen.

Erich Treff eyed the surly Dane whose asperse comments were not unexpected; he figured Germans would have to take a whole lot more before the world forgave them Herr Hitler.

"Actually, Allied bombs put an end to my career," he said. "The Finanz Bank on the Gendarmenmarkt where I worked became an empty lot on a night in November of '42. Two weeks later the army offered me steady work in Russia. My wife was expecting a baby at the time. I applied for a deferment. It was denied. I first saw my son two months ago. Of course back in 1942 no one..."

"Uh, Herr Treff..." Lisbet interrupted gently, recalling his wife's assertion that he talked a blue streak; it was not *his* life story that she had come to hear. "Did your wife tell you why I'm here?"

"She told me you're searching for news of your husband."

"Yes. He was with General Paulus' Sixth Army at Stalingrad. His full name is Frederick Alexander von Renz, but his friends..."

"Knew him as Fritz," Erich Treff finished for her, deliberately using the past tense and avoiding her gaze by looking down at the floor, pushing some loose cement fragments around with his foot. A furious pounding began in Lisbet's chest as she waited for the hammer to fall, which it did with Erich Treff's next words.

"I'm terribly sorry to be the one to tell you that Fritz is dead."

Chapter Eighty-two

Lisbet went limp against the sofa pillows. Although she had expected this and had told herself a hundred times that she could accept it, hearing the words spoken - the cruel finality of them - sent her into a dizzying spiral. She wanted to shake her fist at somebody because it wasn't fair. It simply wasn't fair that Fritz had died when this emaciated person sitting across from her was alive. If this man had survived, why hadn't Fritz? He had gone to war strong and healthy. Struggling with the fairness issue, she heard Torben ask in his halting German, "How well did you know my sister's husband?"

"He and I were inducted at about the same time," Erich Treff said. "We served in the same unit, and were both imprisoned by the Soviets. We were together from December '42 to March of '44. Fritz died that March in a prisoner of war camp near Frolovo. I can't be sure of the exact day. I believe it was toward the end of the month."

March 1944! Lisbet's mind raced back to the very month when she and the girls had fled Berlin.

"Fritz and I ran into each other at Krampnitz during our initial training," Erich Treff went on. "We had enjoyed a passing acquaintance years before at Berlin University and were pleased to rekindle our friendship. There was little else to be cheerful about because within a week we were sent east to help hold the siege at Stalingrad. But as bloody as the siege was, retreat was worse. Trudging through one blizzard after another, we dropped like flies from hunger, frostbite, old wounds, and enemy sniper fire. Divisions became hopelessly separated. The Soviets rounded up some of us stragglers and marched us to a POW camp. They were not known to take prisoners and generally shot captives rather than feed them. I don't know why they made an exception in our case. Of course our officers were killed."

"They resisted capture?" Torben asked.

"With what?" Erich Treff looked at Torben and spread his hands. "We had no weapons after the surrender."

"They shot unarmed officers?"

"No. They nailed them to the side of abandoned farm buildings as human trophies."

Torben had no further questions.

"How did you s...survive?" Lisbet asked in a hoarse whisper, still struggling with the fact that this skeletal individual had returned to Berlin when Fritz hadn't.

"Dumb luck." Erich Treff shrugged shoulders that were like a coat hanger holding up his overalls. "After the armistice, our Soviet captors opened the gates. Those who could simply walked out and headed back toward Germany. Many died along the way, which was a pity after having survived the brutal months in a camp that was nothing but a row of drafty abandoned barns not fit for livestock. Russian political prisoners were housed there as well, along with peasants whose farms had failed to produce the required lots mandated by the Soviet state."

Erich Treff ran a hand through his prematurely thinning hair and went on to tell of torture and straw bedding crawling with vermin. He told of men having their bones crushed as punishment for the slightest infraction; a single bone each day, until they stopped screaming and lost consciousness as blood passed through their skin like sweat.

"How did my sister's husband die?" Torben asked.

"He became ill with pneumonia. Maybe it was tuberculosis. I don't know. He was fine during the initial summer and autumn. He didn't become ill until our first winter in the camp. Our second winter in Russia. None of us had any resistance left. We were thin as rails. Men snapped their ankles, walking, and a cough collapsed a lung. We arrived at the camp malnourished and things got worse. Our daily food ration consisted of a single potato boiled in dirty water which our captors called soup. We barely recognized one another. It was a blessing there were no mirrors because we could all exist in the belief that we didn't look quite as bad as the next fellow. More than half of our original group died during the first months. When Fritz began to decline, he knew his illness was a death sentence in that environment. I think it made him reckless. He condemned himself on a night when the guards walked through our quarters, poking us with rifles. Anyone who didn't move was presumed dead and dragged away. I was in another part of the camp at the time. Inmates were regularly rotated between barracks to discourage fraternization. So I didn't see what happened. I only heard about it later. Apparently, Fritz didn't react quickly enough when jabbed. He just stared at the guard in an aloof sort of way, which must have irritated the fellow because he started to kick him. Fritz got to his feet and, towering over the man, gave him a verbal tongue lashing so lethal the brute blanched. The commotion attracted other guards and while Fritz had their attention he lectured them on international law stipulating humane treatment of POWs. He'd picked up quite a bit of vocabulary from the Russian prisoners and was, unfortunately, able to make himself perfectly clear. His lecture landed him in solitary confinement, a dry well with nothing but slimy stones to sleep on, its top covered so no light could enter. Through the camp's network I heard that the guards took turns banging on the top, depriving him of sleep."

Lisbet's face had turned paper white; she couldn't bear to hear another word. She signaled Torben that they ought to leave. He ignored her, which puzzled her because he hadn't been eager to come here in the first place.

"After about two weeks," Erich Treff continued, "Fritz was returned to the barracks but he was never the same again. And now the guards wouldn't leave him alone. Knowing he understood Russian, they took great pleasure in tormenting him with stories of how German cities were burned to the ground, leaving no survivors. None of us had any idea how the war was going and in our weakened state were susceptible to believing the worst. We lived in a vacuum. We had no newspapers, received no mail, and had no writing materials."

Chapter Eighty-three

Erich Treff paused a moment when his wife came into the room. He got up and pulled out another crate for her to sit on. Cooking chores finished, she sat down, put her son on her lap and rocked him gently. With the absence of dialogue, the room was nestled in a stillness broken only by a simmering pot in the kitchen that gave off a gurgling sound and the sharp aroma of boiling beets.

"Had I known that you had not yet been notified," he said, breaking the silence and looking at Lisbet. "I would have attempted to contact you. It never occurred to me to try to find you because Fritz frequently spoke of a brother who would look after his family. He also talked about his mother."

"She's dead. They are all dead," Lisbet said quietly. Erich Treff had seen too much death to pose a question about the circumstances. "That's why I came to Berlin. I didn't know where else to turn for answers. Corresponding with the Red Cross and the War Ministry was getting me nowhere."

"They will eventually account for every missing soldier, but it might take years. Until you get official notification, I can confirm that Fritz died. I was with him that day."

"How did he die?" Torben asked, with the impartiality of a reporter.

"Happy," Erich Treff said, eying the sullen Dane.

"Happy?" Torben was taken aback. "How's that possible when you've talked of nothing but horror."

"Pleasant weather."

"I beg your pardon?" Torben wondered if this fellow was toying with him.

"After months of snow and ice, followed by driving rains seeping into our quarters, a beautiful day dawned. By afternoon the air was so balmy that the guards became careless. They gathered in little groups to enjoy a smoke in the out-of-doors. In order to catch the full rays of the sun, their backs were turned on our compounds. Curious about how things stood with Fritz, I took advantage of their inattentiveness and slipped past them. Using hand gestures to keep old comrades from calling out and drawing attention to my freedom, I roamed the barracks and learned that Fritz was in the infirmary…a windowless structure the guards called "The Hospital." The rest of us referred to it as the death house because no doctor entered and no one ever left there alive.

"I found Fritz, stretched out on the floor with nothing but his worn army coat between him and the dampness. There were a number of other patients lying about. But, blinded by illness, they paid no attention to me. The minute I spotted Fritz, I knew he wouldn't last long. I bent down and nudged him. He struggled up on his elbows. As soon as he recognized me, he smiled and raised his hand in a mock salute."

"How did you get a visitor's pass?" he wanted to know.

"The weather is warm and sunny today," I told him. "While the guards are getting a tan I'm getting some unauthorized exercise."

"It's sunny? Warm?"

"Yes, it's a remarkable day. I feel it's a good omen. Perhaps we'll be liberated soon."

"Fritz glanced toward the door to verify my harebrained talk of fine weather. But suddenly he coughed so violently that he became too impaired to speak. I thought of helping him outside into the daylight so he could feel the warm sun for himself. I figured it'd be good for his lungs. Of course, unless we were on work detail, we weren't allowed outside, and would only end up in the dreaded dry well. So I kept Fritz entertained with talk of our eventual freedom. While listening, he seemed to gather some strength and began groping the folds of his coat, soon tugging wildly at it. For an agonizing minute I thought he'd lost his mind or that the rats were becoming brazen enough to pester the infirm in broad daylight. I pounded the mud with my fists to frighten the bastards off. Fritz grabbed at my arm and shook his head. His eyes were alert and sharp. He hadn't lost his mind, and if there were rats, he wasn't afraid of them. He was looking for something in his coat, something he must have hidden extremely well because all personal items were confiscated the day we were imprisoned. His eyes implored me to help him while his lips moved in a vain attempt to speak. I pulled him off the worn garment and proceeded to go through the pockets one by one."

"There's nothing in your coat," I told him after searching it thoroughly.

"Gesturing, he kept insisting. Again I looked, feeling every inch of the tattered cloth, until I finally found a photograph in the lining of the sleeve. It was a picture of a pretty blond woman and two little girls. I held it out. He smiled and took it. After studying it for a long time, his eyes closed, his hand tightening around the picture and his arm fell heavily across his chest. He looked happy. He was at peace. I think he died at that moment, but I couldn't be sure because I was distracted by some noise. A new patient was being brought in and the guards discovered me. My punishment was swift. I was beaten bloody and sent out to reinforce a stretch of barbed wire. Feet shackled, I repeatedly tripped into the razor sharp coils, which gave the guards endless amusement. Still, it was better than the well. While working on the fence, I saw two men carry Fritz out to an open flatbed truck parked near the camp's perimeter. He was tossed on top of several other bodies waiting for the trip to a mass burial pit in the nearby woods. The truck left. When it came back a short while later it was empty."

Erich Treff fell silent. His story was finished.

Emotionally mauled, Lisbet looked blindly around the dimly lit cellar. The dark was closing in on her even as she heard the scraping noise of a wooden crate on the cement floor. A moment later she felt someone hold a glass of wine against her lips, telling her to drink. She tried but couldn't swallow; the liquid ran down her chin. Again the glass was pressed to her lips.

Suddenly, a familiar arm tightened around her shoulders with unaccustomed tenderness. On the periphery of her ragged pain she heard Torben whisper.

"I'm sorry, Lisbet," he was saying. "I wish I had let myself know Fritz a little better."

EPILOGUE

One year later...
Lisbet von Renz stood uniquely silent among the throng of boisterous travelers on the deck of the S.S. Gripsholm as it cast off from one of Copenhagen's deepwater piers.

Showers of confetti and colorful paper streamers tossed to those on the dock gave the departure an atmosphere of carnival proportions. Lisbet hoisted Arina up so she could see over the railing and wave to her grandparents, Uncle Torben, Aunt Karin, and her three Danish cousins, all of whom had come to see them off. Caught up in the revelry, Arina squealed and threw as many paper ribbons over the side as the ship's stewards could hand her without neglecting other passengers.

In stark contrast, Karoline stood motionless, blinking back tears. This was almost as bad as leaving *Oma*, and the confetti she'd been given had become a moist clump in her hand. She didn't feel like throwing it and she didn't feel like going to America because she finally felt at home in Denmark.

Horns bellowing, the huge ocean liner slipped away from the dock. Once out in the harbor, the tugboats gradually drew back, and Lisbet could no longer distinguish individual members of her family amid the colorful palette of people bunched up on the quay. Someone unfurled a large white handkerchief, waving it cheerfully. Fluttering in the wind, the sight revived the vision of Dorrit standing on the desolate platform in Berlin. Lisbet swallowed hard and forced herself to concentrate on mundane trivia so as not to be swamped by painful memories. She threw her shoulders back, the sun sparkled on the water's surface, and, gulping the briny sea air, she experiencing the undying conviction that seeking a future in America was the right thing to do.

Linda and Robert Grantham and their two boys would meet the ship in New York, where they'd spend a few days together before Lisbet and her daughters traveled west to California. The Granthams now lived in Washington D.C., where Robert worked at the Pentagon. When they became Lisbet's sponsors, they had tried to convince her to settle there, but her heart was set on California - a place Fritz had talked about in such glowing terms. *Los Angeles...city of palm trees...pink houses...and irrepressible dreams,* he'd often said, promising to take her and the girls there once the war was over. Today, as she embarked on the first step of her long journey, she could almost feel his warm approval smiling down on her.

Lisbet knew that she could never again live in Berlin and had deeded the property on Lindenstrasse to the city with the stipulation that it be turned into a playground for children. The land in Bernau was lost to the Soviet Union. Months ago Lisbet had received a letter from Gerlinde, describing how their estate had also been appropriated by the Soviets. Two grandsons had died in the war, Karl-Heinz was in failing health and, paupered, they were living in rented rooms in Ladeburg with what remained of their family.

Thanks to Dorrit's foresight and generosity, Lisbet had financial security. The von Renz jewels had been appraised in Copenhagen and the value was astounding. The sale of just one necklace could keep Lisbet and her children in clover for years. But she didn't plan to part with a single piece. The jewelry was stored in a vault in Copenhagen; it was Dorrit's legacy to Karoline and Arina. Besides, Lisbet was determined to secure a job. Musicals were being produced in Hollywood and she planned to audition.

The rolling hills of Sjaelland and the industrial coast of Sweden, slowly receded as the channel widened and flowed into the Kattegat Sea, which would eventually merge with the great Atlantic Ocean. The breeze tossed Lisbet's hair playfully and, raising her arm in a final farewell to her birthplace, she took hold of her daughters' hands, turned away from the railing, and strolled along the ship's promenade, nodding to fellow passengers.

Suddenly something vaguely familiar stirred inside her. It began as a small tickle in her heart that sent out ripples of titillating pleasure, flushing her face with warmth. It took a moment before she identified this wonderful feeling that had once upon a time - long ago in Berlin - been part of her life.

It was happiness.

CPSIA information can be obtained at www.ICGtesting.com
Printed in the USA
BVOW010339120911

270949BV00002B/6/P